BURY HER DEEP

Dear Alec,

Remember my engagement yesterday? The annual duty luncheon for the Reverend Mr Tait from which and whom I expected only boredom? I could hardly have been more wrong, Alex dear, and I am this minute packing to follow the Reverend home to his manse in Fife, there to attend a meeting of the Rural Women's Institute. Hardly a house party at which one would usually leap, I grant you, but not only is the man himself a perfect darling—imagine Father Christmas shaved clean and draped in tweed—but his parish, it seems, heaves with more violent passions than a Buenos Aires bordello. A stranger, you see, is roaming the night and pouncing on the ladies of the Rural. At least that's the tale they're telling and the one that Mr Tait told me, but since half the village think he's a figment and he only ever strikes at the full moon, I cannot help but wonder if there's something even odder going on...

Much love and remember me fondly if the dark stranger gets me,

Dandy XX

BURY HER DEEP

Catriona McPherson

WINDSOR
PARAGON

First published 2007
by Hodder & Stoughton
This Large Print edition published 2008
by BBC Audiobooks Ltd
by arrangement with
Hodder & Stoughton

Hardcover ISBN: 978 1 405 68634 1
Softcover   ISBN: 978 1 405 68635 8

British Library Cataloguing in Publication Data available

Printed and bound in Great Britain by
Antony Rowe Ltd., Chippenham, Wiltshire

For my sisters,
Sheila, Audrey and Wendy
with all my love.

CHAPTER ONE

Pallister the butler swept into the dining room with platter aloft and glided to the side of our luncheon guest where he proffered the dish with unimpeachable propriety but with every muscle of his face sending the silent message: 'Don't blame me.' (It is miraculous how, with never a frown nor a smile, Pallister manages to carry a tray of brandies to Hugh's library like a godmother bearing an infant to the altar, and a tray of tea to my sitting room like a maid with a shovel clearing up after a dog.) The Reverend Mr Tait eyed the dish, first through his spectacles and then over the top of them, and his hands twitched a little but he was clearly stumped. I managed to suppress a sigh.

One of the more unforeseen consequences of my recent expansion into the realm of private detecting was the problem of what to do with my fees. I had bought a little motor car with the spoils of my first case two years before but since then I had been reduced to burying parcels of the loot here and there in the household economy and I had developed a new-found regard for the worries of Chicago racketeers. Laundry work, I was fast learning, is no picnic. Grant, my maid, effortlessly absorbed a good chunk of it into my wardrobe and relations between her and me became, as a result, warmer than they had ever been since the days of my trousseau. Grant satisfied, my next thought had been Mrs Tilling, my beloved cook, the only soul under my roof who I could be sure loved and admired me with all of her heart, excepting Bunty

1

of course and even Bunty if given a choice between me and a marrow-bone would, I fear, show her true colours.

Accordingly, I had increased Mrs Tilling's grocery account and reinstated the office of second kitchen maid which had disappeared in the general retrenchment after the war. I had expected these two augmentations to lead Mrs Tilling back to the good old days of plenty, sloshing around lots of cream and Persian cherries and never troubling with rissoles, but I had reckoned without the influence of the cooking columns recently sprung up in even the best newspapers and the endless reams of 'clever' recipes churned out by the new Good Housekeeping magazine, which Mrs Tilling devoured in gulps every month and out of which she had quickly amassed a formidable scrapbook. In short, with an extra girl to help and money to spare, Mrs Tilling's kitchen had taken a reckless leap into the twentieth century and the results were quite something, the current luncheon menu being a case in point.

Mrs Tilling's saddle of mutton had long been a fixture of our table in the colder months; indeed, I think roast saddle of mutton was wheeled out at the very first meal to which Hugh and I ever sat down together in this house, eighteen years before, while Grant unpacked my honeymoon trunks upstairs and the maids peeped curiously at their new mistress and tried not to giggle as they handed the sauces. More than anything else, more than the ring upon my finger, more than the presents heaped in my sitting room demanding thanks, more even than the honeymoon itself, it was that saddle of roast mutton which persuaded me that I really was married and for good. It was, however, delicious and I had come to welcome the sight of it and even the thick, engulfing smell of it on chilly mornings as I came in from my walk.

How I should have welcomed the sight and the smell of it now. Instead, what Pallister proffered with his air of being somewhere else entirely, engaged on quite some other task, was a saddle of mutton only in the sense that a smoked salmon soufflé is eggs and fish. I squinted at it down the table and tried to piece together its history. The fillets had been removed, leaving the backbone and ribcage as a frame for Mrs Tilling's art; the whole had then been covered in a cloud of mousse—one would guess at mutton mousse, although it pained one to imagine those fillets being pounded to paste and mixed with whatever bottled horrors the recipe described—which had been piped back onto the carcass from a bag to resemble a woolly sheepskin coat; a few slivers of fillet, left intact, had been rolled into rosettes to be tucked all around under the thing like flowers in a meadow, or rather like flowers in a florist's.

'It's mutton, Mr Tait,' I supplied, despairing of his ever working this out. 'Just dig in with a spoon.'

Hugh almost always remembers not to scold me when we have guests and he would certainly never lament my management of the household in front of them, even when tried to the extent that this concoction was trying him, but he treated me to a glare which promised me an unenticing conversation when Mr Tait had left.

I felt rather sorry for Hugh, truth be told. Had I come clean to him about my new source of income we could easily have spent the lot long before he

3

had finished appointing the garden boys and under-stewards his beloved estate so desperately required, but then if Hugh knew about it I should not be reduced to laundering it through the household accounts at all and we could put it to better use, making sure that our own two sons did not leave school to become gardeners and under-stewards themselves. Of course, if Hugh knew about it he might well put an instant stop to it, and the question of what to do with the money would disappear, to be replaced by the question—mine alone—of what to do with the days and months and years stretching emptily ahead without it.

So I kept my mouth shut, opening it only to add to the ever taller, ever more rickety edifice of lies necessary to keep the whole thing rolling along. My first two cases, and the only two so far of any length and complexity, had arisen amongst the members of my own set, more or less, and Hugh had been almost insultingly pleased to wave me off on visits and remain at home with his dykers and grooms and visiting fruit-tree-pruning experts, engaged in those mystifying enthusiasms of his, all out of doors and most perfectly filthy, which I think of collectively as 'making mud pies'. As well as those two major cases, murders no less, I had taken on a few lesser problems: a thief at the Overseas League in Edinburgh and a terribly enterprising blackmailer (so enterprising and so nicely judged in her attempts that one almost regretted catching her). For these and other minor engagements which took me briefly from home I had found that Hugh could be persuaded to swallow cover stories of pitiful thinness, so long as I was careful to make my supposed mission appear

4

sufficiently dull. So, I should never tell him that I was off to luncheon at the Overseas League for the third time in a fortnight; that would cause a great deal too much huffing into the moustache and muttering about tying up the chauffeur (as though I did not always drive myself and as though he, Hugh, ever went anywhere anyway), but if I told him I was going to the League to sort clothes donations for some African mission he sent me on my way smiling.

Recently, however, I had wondered whether he was beginning to smell a rat. He had taken to eyeing me very speculatively when he believed I was not watching and he had made more than one rather pointed remark, not quite compliments, about my clothes; my new fur-trimmed evening coat attracting particular attention of a rather sharp kind. I had gone so far as to ask Alec Osborne, dear friend and frequent Watson to my Holmes, whether I should make a clean breast of it. After lengthy consideration, Alec had advised continued secrecy, regular reviews, and a measure of wifely sucking up for, as he had pointed out, if something juicy came along it would be cruel torment to have to wave it by simply to keep on Hugh's right side. Far better, Alec thought and I agreed, to get squarely in his good books in advance and then spend the capital when it was needed. My presence at this luncheon with the Reverend Mr Tait, whose yearly visits I usually avoided, was to be seen as laying down a stiff deposit.

One does, as one's life unfolds, collect acquaintance and connections pretty much willy-nilly and no one can hope for a social circle

5

peopled solely by those individuals so jolly that one invites them to stay for a week and forms parties effortlessly around them simply by sticking pins in one's address book. On the contrary, it is inevitable that there must be at least a few so dull that dinner cannot be borne, let alone an overnight visit, and even although only luncheon is offered, no one else can be invited to dilute the tedium because the only acquaintance who would not be bored into months of sulks are those so cripplingly boring themselves that they would only add to the gloom. Of course, intimates can be taken into one's confidence and begged to help. Alec could have been leaned on today, for instance, but I have never approved of this use of intimates and so I try whenever I can to shoulder the burden myself and not inflict it upon others.

This morning, however, as I had fumbled with the scores of silk-covered buttons on my modish new sailor blouse, fingers clumsy in the October chill, I had begun to think I had bitten off considerably more than I could chew, for a descending scale of guests arranged in order of entertainment and diversion for their hostess runs out long, long before one gets to retired chaplains from one's husband's old school.

'Damn these things,' I said. 'Grant, there are so many buttons there's hardly space between them to get one's fingers in and do them up. And it's freezing in here.'

'Yes, no chance of it gaping,' said Grant. 'Madam. Such a clever idea. Nothing worse than gaping. And you're right. It's wonderfully fresh this morning. You look quite youthful.'

I squeezed the last silk button through its loop

6

at last and looked up to check my reflection in the glass. My cheeks were rosy for once and my eyes clear.

'Hmph,' I said. 'That's not fresh air. That's a muck sweat from wrestling into my clothes.' But I could not help noticing that, for some reason which I admit might have been the weight of the buttons all down the middle, my front was beautifully flat in the new blouse, no billows, no puffs. I did not go so far as to smile at Grant—one cannot prostrate oneself—but I gave her a kind of hard stare and she knows what it means.

Grant duly unbent a little herself.

'I'm sure it will soon go past,' she said. 'And besides, Margaret always says that he's quite a card in his own way. Said that last year Mr Gilver and he were shaking with laughter in the library after luncheon. And Mrs Tilling's got some lovely treats in store too.'

I could quite believe that Hugh and the chaplain would laugh hard and long about the japes and scrapes of schooldays. That was the problem. And I had no doubt either that Mrs Tilling, quite savagely devout in her way and keen to impress a minister of the kirk, would be scouring her *Good Housekeeping* scrapbook, fried fronds of Florence fennel just a dusting of cornflour away.

Even I could not have foreseen the mutton, but I had been quite wrong about Mr Tait too, who turned out to be neither damp nor dour—not like a minister at all—but rather a comfortable figure in country tweeds and with a grey bib to his dog collar. He had a little round nose like a potato and when he smiled, which was often, his eyes were crescent-shaped above his cheeks. The high, bald

7

dome of his forehead lent some gravitas and the slow burr of his Scotch accent, conversing calmly but with great good humour on whatever topic arose, rounded him off to perfection. So, before we had even finished our sherry, I had moved him out of the mental category of duty-inspired bore and entered him onto my list of spare men. Not that I often gave the kind of formal dinner which demanded a balance of the sexes and could be thrown into confusion by a missed train or attack of influenza, but if such a crisis ever did arise I would far rather send to Fife for Mr Tait and park him next to some difficult dowager than trawl round my immediate neighbourhood for the best that it had to offer.

For Mr Tait, I had learned from Hugh, was a widower. He had married rather late in life for a minister, at around forty, and it had been this marriage which had occasioned his giving up the chaplaincy at Kingoldrum Boys' College and taking a parish where his wife would have a manse to call her own. The young Mrs Tait, however, must barely have had time to inter-line her curtains against the east coast haar before she was carried off to the graveyard, leaving Mr Tait with a baby daughter and a pack of attentive female parishioners clambering over one another to take care of him. That is to say, the parishioners were my own conjecture, but I was sure that Mr Tait did not get those cushiony cheeks and that air of great ease from whisking up powdered soup over a gas ring and my theory was only strengthened when after a mouthful of the mutton mousse, he exclaimed: 'Delicious!' and smacked his lips. I considered what a useful talent it was for a minister, and a widowed one especially, to be able to consume this gelatinous filth with such convincing relish. It would never do, after all, if he blanched at the baked offering of one of his less talented parish ladies, a peripheral matter in other sects, perhaps, but the Church of Scotland, make no mistake, gets by on a little doctrine and a lot of scones.

'How kind of you,' I murmured. 'I'm afraid we don't—Hugh and I—always appreciate our kitchen staff's forays into the latest cuisine. I shouldn't have believed how set in my ways I had become, until these odd concoctions from below showed me.'

'Oh, but Mrs Gilver,' exclaimed Mr Tait, 'you must keep up to date, my dear. We must encourage and applaud enterprise wherever we find it. We must not be suspicious of the new, but embrace it in all its forms. This is something I've had cause to think about a great deal just recently at home in the parish.'

I looked at him with expectant interest—clearly there was a story coming—but before he could start, Hugh weighed in.

'Men are suspicious,' he said. 'And prone to discontent.'

I stared at him, speechless. Hugh does not usually go in for that quelling habit of dropping quotations into the conversation and I am glad, since I never know what to do when it happens. Should one simply laugh in appreciative admiration of the other's knowledge of the great writers—but how could one laugh at such a quotation as that?—or should one try to cap it? Or simply agree with what has been said? It must, I concluded, be the presence of Mr Tait and the resulting echo of Hugh's schooldays which prompted his unusual outburst and so I left it to Mr Tait to find an answer. This he managed with aplomb.

'Ha, ha,' he cried in happy recognition. 'Herrick, yes indeed. Robert Herrick. A man of the cloth, like myself, you know. But not . . . my goodness me no, not at all . . . And it goes right to the heart of my recent troubles, as it happens. Men are suspicious. They certainly are prone to discontent at Luckenlaw these days.'

'What's the matter?' I asked.

'Have you ever heard, I wonder, of the SWRI?' said Mr Tait. Hugh and I each frantically tried to assign the initials to something sensible.

'Scottish?' I began. A safe bet.

'Workers' Rights?' ventured Hugh, incredulously. It was a topic he had never thought to have brought to his luncheon table.

Mr Tait threw back his head and laughed.

'Women's Rural Institute,' he said. 'Perhaps it hasn't come to Gilverton yet.' I shrugged. As far as I knew, there was the Women's Guild, exclusively the preserve of the minister's wife and therefore nothing to do with me, the Brownies and Guides and Scouts and Cubs, for which there was never any shortage of hearty volunteers, and that was it. I had heard of the new Women's Institute, of course, but had thought it confined to England and had thankfully embraced the belief that, to quote the wife of our tenant farmer at Gilverton Mains on the topic of Clara Bow's rising hemline, it was all very well down there but it would never do up here with our weather.

10

'Well, the SWRI has landed on the shores of Fife,' said Mr Tait, 'and caused a bit of a stir there. The local men are terribly old-fashioned in some respects—I daresay it's just the same here—and to listen to some of them you'd think their wives were off out to supper and a show.'

'When in fact?' I prompted.

'A perfectly wholesome gathering of respectable married ladies and girls, to discuss matters of domestic interest and learn handicrafts,' he said, sounding like a pamphlet. Hugh said nothing. 'And some of the womenfolk themselves are just as bad,' Mr Tait went on. 'One of my older parishioners, a wonderful old lady, came begging me to stop "thon sufferer-jets" from pestering her. She said she had not been off her farm except to church and market for forty-three years and she was not about to start.'

'Remarkable,' I murmured, although my decades at Gilverton had taught me that it was nothing of the kind.

'So while I daresay there would have been a fair bit of interest in a great many topics, even suffrage itself, the whole thing is having to creep along on tiptoe. Talks on infant nutrition, don't you know, and home-made lampshades. For next month, my daughter tells me they are trying to find a speaker to address "The Household Budget".' He sighed. 'Well, I suppose it's better than nothing. Men are suspicious, right enough. And prone to discontent.'

'Dandy,' said Hugh, and I turned to him. He looked at me out of innocent eyes. 'You could do that.'

'Do what?' I asked, frowning. For a moment I thought it was a clumsy attempt at a joke, implying that I could make a man suspicious and discontented. I soon realised, of course, that it was much worse. He bared his teeth at me and turned back to Mr Tait.

'Dandy here could do a wonderful talk on managing a household budget,' he said. 'She's a whizz at it. Aren't you, my dear?'

'Hugh, I hardly think my languid remarks to cook, butler and maid are quite what Mr Tait's good ladies are looking for.' I laughed a tinkling little laugh, but it turned rather dry towards the end.

'You could scale it down,' persisted Hugh. 'You could extrapolate from a large household to a small, surely. The principle is the same.'

'Indeed it is,' said Mr Tait. 'If you have a flair for it.'

'Oh, she does,' said Hugh. 'She certainly does. You won't be surprised to hear, sir, that things have been tighter and tighter every year since the war, the same as everywhere,'—Mr Tait inclined his head in gentle sympathy—'and yet what Dandy manages to squeeze out of her dwindling housekeeping . . . oh, you wouldn't believe me if I told you: new clothes, a little motor car, extra staff. I don't know,' he finished sternly, 'how she does it.'

I was blushing now to the roots of my hair. So he *did* suspect something. Luckily, Mr Tait took my blushes to be modesty, and he went as far as to lean over the table and pat my hand.

'It's nothing to fear, Mrs Gilver,' he said. 'Just a village gathering, and your name on the list of speakers would help no end in quashing some of the suspicions for good. Can I tell Lorna that you'll come?'

I was trapped, unless luck was on my side with the calendar, so I asked the date.

'Now then, let me see,' said Mr Tait, reaching into an inside pocket and drawing out a slim diary. 'November, November . . . It will be Tuesday the eleventh.'

'Wonderful,' said Hugh. 'There won't be any problem with that. Mid-week, absolutely nothing to hold you back, Dandy.'

He was right. I knew he was.

'I shall have to check my own diary,' I said. 'The eleventh is ringing a distant bell.'

'Very well,' said Hugh. 'Take Mr Tait to your sitting room after luncheon and make quite sure.' I was astonished. Where was Hugh finding these depths of cunning? Of course, I had had no intention of taking the good Reverend with me. I had thought to go to my sitting room, count to ten, and come back with an expression of deep regret and news of an engagement in town, but if Mr Tait were standing right there beside me I could not possibly look at a blank diary page and pretend to find an appointment there.

'I've no idea about this,' I told him again. 'I'm bound to make a fearful mess of things.'

'Come to the October meeting first then,' said Mr Tait. 'It's a hospital sister. You'll pick up some good hints from her.'

Hugh was practically stroking his moustache and saying heh-heh-heh like a pantomime villain by this time.

'When is the October meeting?' I asked, sensing defeat.

Mr Tait once again flicked through the pages of his diary.

'Sunday the—oh, but it won't be Sunday, of course. And I would doubt it would be Saturday. So probably Monday the thirteenth. A week on Monday. I can telephone to you this evening and make sure, of course. But I would imagine it would be on the Monday. They always have it at the full moon.'

Hugh looked rather startled and I am sure I blinked.

'That has some unfortunate associations, does it not?' I said. 'I don't wonder that the men are suspicious of *that*.'

Mr Tait looked confused for a moment and then his face split into a grin, his crescent-shaped eyes dancing.

'For the light, my dear Mrs Gilver,' he said. 'To light their way there and home again. These are simple countrywomen, remember. *They* have no little motor cars, no matter how prudent they are.'

*   *   *

After luncheon, after the caramelised orange pudding which was quite a success with Mr Tait, being hot and sweet and stodgy as many men require their puddings to be, he followed me along the passage and through the breakfast-room to my little sitting room in the south-east corner of the house. By habit, I walked over the thick breakfast-room carpet rather than around it and stepped very gently on the four feet of polished boards between its edge and my door. This is usually a sensible plan, since otherwise Bunty can have whipped herself up into a frenzy of excited whining at my approach and is likely to hurl herself upon

14

me as I enter. On this occasion, looking back, I might have been as well to make a little more noise. Her answering din would have reminded me of her presence and would have prompted me to warn Mr Tait. As it was, I made no sound at all and I can only imagine either that he was unusually light on his feet for such a comfortably proportioned gentleman or that for some reason he was wearing India-rubber-soled shoes. Anyway, I opened the door, telling him over my shoulder that it would not take a minute before we could rejoin Hugh in the library for coffee, and at the sound of my voice Bunty, who had been curled on the blue velvet chair, snapped to attention to stand with her forefeet on its back and her head, as a result, towering above ours and let out a tremendous, welcoming Howwf!

Mr Tait took the name of our Lord squarely in vain and then blushed, rubbed his jaw with a forefinger and apologised, laughing. I had already decided that I liked him, but from that moment I determined that I wanted him as a friend, even if a talk on household budgeting was the price of securing his friendship.

I was disappointed, then, a moment later to see in my engagement diary against Tuesday the eleventh of November two entries, short but unmistakable. *Wreath 11 a.m.*, said one; *Fitting, 2 p.m., Perth*, the other.

Here was the excuse I had been ready to invent, waiting actually in existence for me. Unless . . .

'I'm so sorry, Mr Tait,' I said. 'It seems I'm busy on the eleventh of next month.' He was teasing Bunty, running the toe of his shoe up and down her tummy as she lay wriggling and whining with pleasure on her back on the hearthrug. I have always felt that Bunty is an excellent judge of character and although she is never exactly stand-offish with anyone—Dalmatians never are—this level of instant and total submission only strengthened my own view of Mr Tait as a good egg. 'But I'm wondering,' I went on, 'will they really have the meeting on Armistice Day? Wouldn't it be rather . . . ?'

'Rather what?' said Mr Tait.

'I don't know,' I said, trying to make it sound light. 'Rather disrespectful, I suppose. Rather ungrateful. Would these villager women really want to abandon their husbands and homes on that day of all days and go to a public meeting?'

He stopped teasing Bunty at that and she rolled over onto her side with a sigh and lay looking out of the window at the bird-table on the lawn, her tail thumping the carpet.

'I'm surprised at you, Mrs Gilver,' he said. 'Truly I am. A young woman like you with such old-fashioned notions. I cannot understand where everyone is getting the idea'—he spread his arms wide and looked around the room as though for inspiration—'that the SWRI is a hotbed of socialists and suffragettes. I really cannot.'

'No more can I,' I said. 'I didn't mean to suggest that it was. But I'm afraid if you're sure the eleventh is the day then I shall have to decline your invitation. I'm laying a wreath at the service in the morning.'

'But you'll have plenty time to get down to Fife after that,' said Mr Tait.

I was debating with myself whether to agree, cancel my fitting and face Grant's wrath or make

16

up a more serious appointment to account for my afternoon when his demeanour suddenly changed. He sat down heavily on the blue velvet chair and put one hand on each tweedy knee, leaning slightly forward with the manner of one about to explain something terribly important to a rather backward child.

'I want you to come to the meeting most particularly, Mrs Gilver,' he said. 'I meant to ask you even before Hugh . . . dropped you in it, shall we say?' My eyebrows rose at that and I smiled.

'Why?' I asked. 'I assure you that no matter what Hugh would have you believe, I am no housekeeper.'

'But you have other talents,' said Mr Tait. 'I've been hearing about them from an old friend of mine who recommends you very highly. Very highly indeed.'

I closed my diary firmly. Dresses (and Grant) be damned. I had a case.

CHAPTER TWO

If one considers this kingdom of His Majesty's, stretching from rosy, lazy Somerset and the like all the way to the stark, scoured rocks of Orkney, it is tempting to conclude that harshness and despair rise like the mercury in the glass the further north one goes (with a sharp jump over Hadrian's Wall, of course) and to imagine that a trip to Fife, lying south of Perthshire, would be a little step towards the soft shire of girlhood and home. To think this is to make, however, a fundamental error about

17

the nature of Scotland and of Fife, and to miss the part that the east plays in the scheme of things. Perthshire is snugly in the middle and is on the way to the Highlands, where people drink whisky, wear tartan and kick up their heels. Fife, by contrast, is at the edge, almost all coast, and east coast at that, chilled to its stony heart by the haar and, I have always thought, by its own conviction that chilly is best. I was once at a christening in Fife, and I overheard an old woman, of the type who will haunt christenings if there are no funerals to be had, suck her teeth and say: 'Aye, first breath— beginning of death.' Ever since, that has summed up Fife for me. So, I did not foresee much jollity as I motored down there that Monday afternoon. October afternoons are never very cheerful no matter where one passes them but I fully expected the little village of Luckenlaw, which was my destination, to make Gilverton in October seem like midsummer in Zanzibar.

I had just passed through the Burgh of Falkland, tucked under the north slopes of Falkland Hill, and because of that quite the most gloomy place one could imagine at this time of the year, and I now set my sights on the distant laws. There were three of these laws running west to east, smack in the middle of Fife near its southern shore. (It should perhaps be explained that a law, in these parts, is the name for a cone-shaped hill, isolated and therefore conspicuous like a hill in a child's painting, but I resent having to explain it, or rather I resent being able to explain it. That is, I fiercely resent the many times in my married life when I have been subjected to such outpourings on the topography and nomenclature of Scotland's

18

landscape that I now have the explanation all to hand.)

I thought, as I approached, that Kellie and Largo Laws were not classics of the type, being rather asymmetrical and littered around with little ridges and outcroppings like leftovers that the law-maker had neglected to tidy away. Between them, however, was *the* Lucken Law, in every way the most splendid of the three. It was the highest, almost perfectly conical—looking like a molehill on a putting green the way it rose up from the uncluttered fields around—and then there was its title. All three laws had furnished much of their surroundings with names, of course. Largo Law to the west had three villages, Upper (or Kirkton of) Largo, Lower Largo and Largoward, and a sandy shore named Largo Bay. Kellie Law to the east had no village but, in compensation, boasted the rather grand Kellie Castle. The Lucken Law, however, had not only that impressive definite article—it was always the Lucken Law—but also Luckenlaw village due south of the hill, and a quite breathtaking array of farms, which spoke to the absence of imagination in the Fifish spirit as could nothing else. Over Luckenlaw, Hinter Luckenlaw, Wester Luckenlaw, Easter Luckenlaw and Luckenlaw Mains were nestled in about the law itself like chicks around a mother hen. The big house—and there is always a big house whenever there is an otherwise inexplicable village and a farm called the Mains—lay to the north and was called, inevitably, Luckenlaw House.

The house and park, just like Falkland village, were quite cut off from what daylight was left by the great brute of the hill which rose up before

19

them, and I mused as I drove past that it would be well into spring before the sun shone upon its gardens or into its windows again. I could only hope that the inhabitants were the type to take pleasure from irony, for had I inherited or married into that house—and surely no one would ever have bought the place—I should have called it anything but luck. On these points, as on so many others, I was soon to find out that my assumptions were mistaken and my conclusions quite wrong.

I skirted the hill, passing solid farmhouses squarely built from blocks of pinkish grey stone and attendant cottages made of the same stone in rather rubblier and more heavily mortared pieces, and eventually turned off to take the lane into the village. There were not, here, the crow-stepped gables and red pantiles of the pretty villages on the coast, but it was a pleasant little place; a school and schoolhouse to the left, a row of cottages with a post office on one end to the right, and a handful of houses built in pairs, set around a green with a cenotaph at the far end, last year's faded poppy wreaths still at its base with another month to go.

A gaggle of small girls were busy with a skipping game but they let their rope fall limp and gazed at me as I approached, one or two women as well coming to look out of doors or windows at the sound of the engine. I waved, slowing as the lane narrowed to skirt the green before it led up to the kirk and manse a little way on. One or two further cottages could just be glimpsed straggling upwards, but beyond them the lane ended at a gate into a field. This, then, was Luckenlaw. I swung my motor car into the open gates of the manse just as Mr Tait and a young woman of the same comfortable build and smiling countenance, who must be the daughter Lorna, came out onto the step to greet me.

'No Bunty?' said Mr Tait, as I stepped down. 'I've been telling Lorna here all about her.' I was sure he had, but I have learned from bitter experience that Bunty's absence is the only thing that makes any hearts grow fonder of her and so, while someone who has not seen her for a week can think it a pity that I have left her behind, I am sure that that same someone, faced with Bunty exploding out of the motor car after the constraint of a two-hour journey, would roll his eyes and think: Oh Lord, not that dog again.

I shook hands with Lorna and she made that odd little sideways gesture which is almost a bob, the very last vestige of the curtsey which began to decline in the reign of the last King George but has not quite finished its death throes yet. I do it myself from time to time when faced with someone terribly old or monstrously grand and I hoped that it was some spurious air of grandeur hanging about me which had stirred the impulse in Lorna for, looking at her close up, I could see that she must be around thirty and so was almost certainly less than ten years younger than me. From a distance, one might have said she was older for as well as the comfortable figure she had a mild, wide face which seemed formed for maturity rather than girlhood and which was framed by a lot of dark hair gathered gently into a soft bun at the nape of her neck. Her nose and mouth, sharper than Mr Tait's, must have been inherited from the mother but her eyes and appley cheeks were his and I felt a surge of friendliness mixed with a little relief as I

21

followed her into the house.

The relief does me no credit; it is shallow and self-regarding and absolutely typical, although surely some respect is due me for its admission. The truth is that I had been working myself up into something between a huff and a temper at the prospect of this trip, and not only because a visit to the SWRI meeting and a chance to hear a hospital sister lecture on infant nutrition were so completely without allure. I was disgruntled, too, at the thought of being the guest of a young Miss Tait, with all her life before her, dreading the evidence of my own creeping middle age and the unscalable walls of my chosen path when I compared my lot with hers. One might suppose it foolish fancy for a Miss Leston as was, now Mrs Hugh Gilver, with all that I had and all that I commanded, to feel anything *at all* much less this churlish envy about a girl of Miss Tait's station in life and until very recently one would have been right. My mother would have felt no stab from Lorna's mother, I am sure, but in those days all there was were husbands and all there was to choose between one husband and another were the kinds of things which would see a Mr Gilver of Gilverton trumping a Reverend Tait every time.

Now however, these days, there was the chance that a Miss Tait, beloved child of a reasonable man, would have been to school and perhaps to college too and might be just about to plunge into a life of fun in a flat in the city or about to marry an even more reasonable man and spend her life writing books about Egypt and making frequent trips there with her adoring husband in tow. Such a Miss Tait could easily have made the Mrs Gilver

22

whom I had imperceptibly but now undeniably become feel hopelessly ancient and humdrum by comparison, but such a Miss Tait would have had short hair and smart little pleats to her skirt or at least—Egyptologists not being known for their chic—short hair and corduroy breeches with a penknife at the belt. This Miss Tait, on the other hand, the real Miss Tait, Lorna, wore clothes which were the woven equivalents of her loose-tied bun: pale woollen garments in grey and pink, looped softly around her plump shoulders and hips and decorated only by a heart-shaped brooch pinning to her collar a silk rosebud and black velvet bow which spoke of love and loss.

In fact, by the time I rejoined Lorna and her father in their sitting room for tea, having taken off my hat and washed my hands in the usual chilly expanse of the best spare bedroom, I had quite forgotten my earlier imaginings and just about forgiven myself for them, assembling instead a more seemly collection of emotions towards Lorna; a readiness to like her and a stirring of desire to help her which was almost free of pity. Besides, I was not alone in my reckoning of Lorna as unworldly and slightly to be protected, because as I sat down Mr Tait said to me:

'It is good of you to take your commission as speaker so seriously, Mrs Gilver. Very good of you to make this extra trip just to see the lie of the land. I don't recall any of the other speakers doing so.'

I am not always the most intuitive woman one could imagine—I have dropped hodfuls of bricks in my time—but even I could not mistake the firm way he said 'speaker' and the very direct stare he gave me. His meaning was obvious: Lorna did not know the true nature of my commission and nor was she to find it out. I was pleased enough; the fewer the better is an excellent general rule when deciding who should be privy to an investigation as it unfolds, for not only are the notions and fancies of others a severe distraction from one's own avenues of thought (and very annoying when they turn out more accurate too) but sometimes, in pursuit of the truth, I find myself having to tell such lies—whoppers, my sons would call them—that I could never get through them without blushing if anyone in earshot knew what I was up to. Also—and perhaps, if I am to be scrupulously honest, this is the weightiest consideration—if anyone is told anything, it is all too easy to forget who was told what and it is trouble enough to keep straight the questions of what I know, what I think, and what I have merely conjectured without having to remember what portion of what version I have shared and with whom.

So it suited me perfectly well not to be obliged to sit through Lorna's take on the affair. Instead, we had the usual desultory chat as she fussed with the tea-things, Mr Tait evidently not one of those cosy little ministers who brandish the teapot and toasting fork himself. I do not mean to suggest that he disdained his tea, sitting there blank and superior for as little time as he could decently get away with before escaping back to his study. I have never had any patience with men who do that, for I have found that on days when tea is late, cold, burnt or even—in the event of some household calamity—missed, they complain as loud and long as anyone and thus reveal that they have no business acting so above the proceedings when all goes well.

Mr Tait was the perfect teatime father, quietly appreciative and settled into his chair with no thoughts of moving, and I found time to think what a waste of a man it was, that there was no wife to share in this tableau. Hard on the heels of that came the question of what he would do without Lorna, and whether the day was ever likely to dawn when he would find out. I turned to look at her as this ambled through my head and found her smiling back at me, calmly.

'What a pretty spot you live in, Miss Tait,' I said. 'That is, one can imagine that it's charming in the summertime.'

'Lorna, please,' she said. ' "Miss Tait" sounds like my Aunt Georgia.' She spoke lightly enough, but a quick frown passed across her face, a moment's flickering of her brows and faltering of her smile, like the merest wisp of cloud over the sun. 'Yes, we are lucky to live here,' she went on. 'It's a great good fortune, these days, when so many people seem to lurch about from pillar to post, never settling, or live all cramped up together in bed-sitters. I count myself a very fortunate girl.'

Oh dear, I thought. How sad and, if I am honest, how rather dreary too. Lorna then, like so many others, was fighting a desperate battle under that limpid façade. She was still mourning whoever it was whose death had put that rose and ribbon at her neck and half of her wanted no more than to call herself blessed to have loved at all, while the other half was beginning to panic at the passing years, to make sure and call herself a girl but wince each time she was reminded that she was fast becoming a Miss Tait like her Aunt Georgia before her.

There were many in the same boat and by now, six years after the end of the war which put them there, one was beginning to see distinct patterns in how these poor girls responded to their fates. Some simply married the first male creature to come into view and so joined the rest of us in the great lottery of life. Others dedicated themselves to the memory of their lost loves and let the rest of the world grow indistinct. Yet others railed at their misfortune, turned bitter and sneered at anyone who had what they lacked, pretending not to care, not to grieve, hardly to feel, and I usually thought these the saddest of all. Lorna was threatening to make me change my mind, however, for her path it seemed to me now was even more painful to witness. She was one who would hope and hope and fade, quite out in the open for all to see, causing friends and kind strangers to plot matches for her and crueller types to pity and, in the end, despise her for her sadness and her helpless longing. Oh dear, I thought again, and I smiled at her father who smiled back and might well have been thinking 'Oh dear' himself.

Then I told myself sternly that I was not here to comfort and befriend poor Lorna, and that, although I should certainly ask Hugh if there were any young men of good prospect lurking around Gilverton who seemed not to be finding our own collection of poor Lornas to their liking, this evening I had to harden my heart and not allow myself to be sidetracked, for there was still much to be learned.

My introduction to the case, after all, that day in

my sitting room at Gilverton had necessarily been rather short what with Hugh and the coffee tray waiting.

'There is an unfortunate state of affairs developing at Luckenlaw, my dear Mrs Gilver,' Mr Tait had begun, 'and although it is too far advanced for it to be nipped in the bud exactly, I think we could still weed out the pest before it sets seed.' Long years with Hugh had equipped me ably to handle any horticultural metaphor and I nodded, encouraging him to go on. 'It started in the spring,' he said, 'and at first it was rather worrying. A dairy maid from a local farm arrived home one evening with a tale of being set upon in the lane. She wasn't hurt, but she was very badly shaken. Naturally the police were summoned and they, along with the men of the village and the neighbouring farms, searched high and low for the rascal but found nothing. As the days and weeks passed, the girl put the nasty experience behind her like a good sensible lass and no more was thought of it until it happened again. A different girl, the same story, another search and no one to be found. The third time it happened the police went through the motions, as they must, but with no great hopes of catching him, and that's when people started wondering aloud whether there was really anything in it. Some of the details of these attacks were extremely fanciful, you see, and the sergeant told me that it wasn't the first time they had wasted a lot of effort on girls' silly nonsense, nor would it be the last. I preached a good stiff sermon on as near a topic to wasting police time as I could find in scripture'—here I could not help a chirp of laughter and I longed to ask Mr Tait for

27

chapter and verse—'and that seemed to do the trick, for a while. But now it's started again. And it's not silly girls any more, Mrs Gilver, anything but. Farmers' wives, sensible married types with children of their own, women I've known for years to be steady and down-to-earth, women who would no more make mischief with a lot of silly tattle than they would . . .' He took a deep breath before starting again. 'Now, as you can imagine there are all sorts of rumours and fantastical stories flying around and I'm afraid that it's beginning to be spoken of outside the village. Lorna, my daughter, told me that it came back to her from a friend she has down in Earlsferry, five miles away. No details and Luckenlaw was not mentioned by name thankfully—that's the last thing we need—just a tale that there was a "dark stranger" roaming the hills in Fife and grabbing girls who were out alone at night.'

'Grabbing them?' I asked.

'You see!' cried Mr Tait. 'Already it's getting worse in the telling. The girls—if there's any truth to the tale at all—are certainly not being "grabbed". They're not really being harmed at all. Just waylaid. And frightened.'

'I can imagine,' I said.

'And while it's bad enough to think that a Luckenlaw man could be doing it,' said Mr Tait, 'someone I see from the pulpit every Sunday, someone perhaps that I've christened and married myself, at least *that* could happen anywhere. The alternative—that the women are making it up—is much worse.'

'And so you would like me to speak to them?' I said.

28

'My dear, if you would,' said Mr Tait. 'I would hate to see Luckenlaw get a name for this kind of thing.'

'You've grown fond of the place then?' I said. 'It always seems rather brutal to me the way a minister is just landed in a parish and must make a home there come what may. I'm glad you've been "lucky" at Luckenlaw.'

'Oh no, Mrs Gilver,' said Mr Tait. 'You are quite wrong on both counts. At least, my dear late wife was a Luckenlaw girl—she grew up on a farm there—and the village took me quite to its heart because of that. And the name of the place has nothing to do with luck. But there, you're English. You'd hardly know.'

I tried to look interested in the history lesson I felt sure was on its way.

'It's a common mistake,' he continued, 'but actually the Lucken Law gets its name the same way as the old luckenbooths did.'

'Luckenbooths?' I echoed.

'Silversmiths' shops,' said Mr Tait. 'Literally locked booths. Locked up because of their precious contents. Likewise the Lucken Law: the locked hill. That is to say, containing a sealed chamber. You find them throughout Scotland. Hard to know what they were originally used for: hiding places; ancient ceremonies, perhaps. Certainly, there were burials for a time in the Luckenlaw chamber.' And then, amazingly, he stopped as though the subject were at an end. It was the shortest lesson on the thrilling history of ancient Scotland I had ever encountered and surprised gratitude spurred me on to speak.

'Very well then,' I said to him, 'I'll do my best.'

'And I hear that your best is very good indeed.'

I should not say I was an excessively modest woman, and certainly not one who cannot bear to be complimented when compliments are due—I have always felt that to rebuff perfectly reasonable praise is churlish and, in its way, more demanding than simple thanks would be: one forces the giver into much greater efforts at subtlety and evidence than most casual admirers would care to take, for one thing. At the current moment, however, I felt I really had to speak. It would be better to set matters straight from the outset than to waft along on undeserved praise and disappoint him in the end.

'I have to say, Mr Tait,' I began, 'that I have no great expectations about solving this for you. If it's a mare's nest I doubt whether anyone knows who started it, much less why. These things do tend to take on a life of their own. Look at the Loch Ness Monster, for instance. Whose fault is that? And even if the dark stranger exists, if no one knows what he looks like then catching him at it seems the only hope, and unless we can discover some kind of a pattern to the thing, we won't know where to look. So, please, be sure that I will do my best but do not, I beg you, get your hopes up.'

Mr Tait nodded and appeared to take my protestations to heart.

'Like you,' he said, 'I don't know whether to hope that he exists or not for each possibility is as unappealing as the other. But as to a pattern, that's very clear. Didn't I tell you? It's the SWRI that's the pattern, my dear. It always happens after one of their meetings. That's half the trouble. It always happens on a night when just about every man in the place is on his own and no wife to say where he's been. It always happens on a night where almost every woman is out walking in the dark, when the very best of them might fall prey to fancy.'

'Except they're not out walking in the dark, are they?' I said, recalling what he had told me. 'It's the full moon.' Mr Tait put his head in his hands and groaned.

'Yes,' he said, straightening up again at last and heaving a mighty sigh. 'There is that. A man out prowling the lanes or a woman making up silly stories would be bad enough, but it has to be said: there is that too.'

CHAPTER THREE

There was hardly a moment between tea by the fire and the early dinner which was to allow Lorna and me to get to the meeting on time, but Mr Tait just managed to show me the few points of interest in his church—a stone pulpit carved all over with representations of twining branches which made it look rather varicosed and a gargoyle grimacing from the top of a pillar—while I snatched the chance to run through my plan for the evening.

Such as it was. Mr Tait had sent me the names of the women who had reported encountering the dark stranger and I had committed them to memory but my intention was to accompany home another of the ladies, someone who lived a fair walk from the village, in the hope that tonight she might be the one and I might be a witness—a very faint hope since all the previous victims had been alone.

'Are the women organised into parties now?' I asked. 'Surely none of them is brave enough still to walk home without a companion? Come to that, I find it odd that the meetings are rolling on at all. If this has been going on since the spring, I mean. I wonder the husbands and fathers haven't put their feet down and ordered their womenfolk to stay away.'

'I rather think most of them go along with the police sergeant's view of things,' said Mr Tait. 'And in a couple of cases I know that the wives have encouraged them in it, precisely *because* they would otherwise put their feet down and the women would never get off the farm again. As to banding together . . . I did suggest that Lorna might get my old Napier out and ferry them—she can handle it although it's a bit of an antique now—but they seem to relish the fresh air and the extra measure of freedom that their moonlit walks afford them.'

We had come out of the church again and were threading along the gravel path between the gravestones towards the gate. Out on the green, the skipping game was still going strong, two volunteers keeping the rope whipping round as a chain of girls wove in and out of it, concentrating fiercely and singing as they went:

> 'Here she comes, there she goes,
> Here she comes, there she goes,
> Here she comes, there she goes . . .'

It was rather mesmerising and Mr Tait and I

paused to watch them. On and on it went and I was beginning to wonder if they would simply keep going until called into bed, when at last one stumbled in the rope and all the others yelled: 'Caught you!'

The unfortunate one untangled her ankles and with a fairly gracious shrug took over one end of the rope, letting the girl who had been holding it join the rest. Slowly the two girls began to work up a rhythm again and when the rope was whirring round faster than ever, one of them shouted 'Not last night' and the others began singing.

> 'Not last night but the night before
> Thirteen grave robbers came to my door.
> Dig her up and rattle her bones.
> Bury her deep, she's all alone.
> Dark night, moonlight,
> Haunt me till my hair's white.
> Moonlight, dark night,
> Shut the coffin lid tight.
> Knock knock, who's there?
> Knock knock, who's there?
> Knock knock, who's there?'

Their voices followed us as we crossed towards the manse and we were just passing through the gate when the chanting stopped and a chorus of voices yelled: 'Maggie.'

'It's very democratic, skipping, isn't it?' I said. 'I only have sons, as you know, and none of their games are anything like as fair as that.'

'Only it doesn't do to listen too closely to the words of the songs,' said Mr Tait. 'Just like nursery rhymes. If you were told the meanings of the sweetest little nursery rhymes, it would make your toes curl.'

'So I believe,' I said. 'Especially the eighteenth-century ones—the three men in a tub, for instance, are best left well alone.'

*   *   *

After dinner, Lorna and I set out well wrapped against the raw evening to make the short journey across the green and down to the school where the SWRI meetings were held. All around us, cottage doors slammed as we passed and soon we were heading a small caravan of village women. I wondered briefly whether it was fear of the dark stranger making them move en masse like this, but I soon concluded that it was just their natural politeness and sense of what was due to Lorna as the minister's daughter which led them to watch out for her and fall into step.

We could see the faint outline of another group coming up the lane towards us and there was a light bobbing in the darkness further away across the field, someone with a lantern taking a short cut from one of the farms.

'A beautiful night,' said Lorna, turning her face up to the sky. 'There should be a good turn-out on a clear, dry night like this.'

'I hope so,' I said. 'Your father hinted at some disapproval. In fact, he seemed to be worried that the venture might fold altogether.'

'Oh, it's not as bad as all that,' said Lorna. 'There was a bit of opposition at first, and we're treading carefully but—' She was interrupted by the sound of a motor car coming up the lane from

34

the main road. It overtook the foot party in the distance and swept ahead of us at the corner, everyone drawing in to the hedge to let it pass, whereupon Lorna said under her breath: 'Or at least we're trying to.'

'This is most unfortunate, Miss Tait,' said a voice from behind me, and a squat little person, fair of skin and pale of lash, with all her hair tucked into a crocheted tammy, drew abreast of us and stared after the motor car, shaking her head and frowning.

'Now, Miss McCallum,' said Lorna. 'We welcome all comers, don't we?'

'Hmph,' said Miss McCallum. 'The women don't come to sit and be laughed at.'

There was no time to follow up this intriguing exchange; we had arrived at the school and we trooped into the porch to wriggle out of our coats and unwind our scarves and mufflers, although Miss McCallum, I noticed, kept on the crocheted tammy which, being an inspid shade of pale peach, did nothing at all to enliven her shrimp-like colouring. Indeed, I noticed that there were an inordinate number of crocheted garments amongst the gathering: a few cardigan jerseys, one ambitious if rather droopy tabard, and a smattering of shawls. Lorna had restricted herself, very sensibly I thought, to carrying a crocheted work-bag.

Through in the schoolroom a ring of chairs had been set, and a fire was burning cheerfully in the grate. A young woman, unmistakably a schoolmistress with her long black skirt bagged about the knees from sitting on low chairs and with chalk smears across the back of her black crocheted jersey, clapped her hands and cried out a rather strained welcome.

'Here we are, here we are,' she said, and I thought I recognised the note in her voice. It was just the note which used to creep into mine when Nanny finally returned to the nursery after a long absence to relieve me of an infant who had, of course, begun to snivel as soon as she left and was now boiling hot, soaked in angry tears and shrieking like a train. The reason for the present panic stood before the hearth: two ladies, surely the occupants of the motor car which had swept past us in the lane, warming themselves and lighting cigarettes in long holders with a taper from the fire. They turned and waved.

'Lorna, darling,' said what I decided must be the elder of the two, a fine high-breasted figure, who was standing four-square in front of the chimneypiece. 'Look at us. Aren't you proud?' She jabbed the end of her cigarette holder first at her own chest and then at that of her companion, who struck an angular pose beside her. Two excrescences in brown wool were attached to their clothes.

'We've crocheted ourselves a brooch each,' said the younger one. 'Supposed to be heart-shaped—with a crown on top, naturally—but they've come out looking like mincemeat pies.'

Miss McCallum in her tammy turned a deep and painful shade of pink and flumped down onto the nearest of the ring of seats, her breast heaving with affront under her own heart-shaped brooch which was only just managing to hold her cardigan closed.

'Ahem, yes,' said the schoolmistress. 'Perhaps I

should explain. It's Mrs Gilver, isn't it?' At this, the two ladies felt they had been given permission to notice me without seeming forward, and they both smiled. 'When we have a suitable demonstration one month we try to bring along—or even wear— our efforts the next month and Miss McCallum, our postmistress, gave us a splendid practical demonstration of crochet in September so—' At this point she was interrupted.

'And what brings you to this forgotten corner of Christendom?' asked the younger lady, giving up on her cigarette and stubbing it out against the chimneypiece before tossing it into the flames.

'Mrs Gilver is giving the talk next month,' said Lorna. 'And she's come along tonight to learn the ropes.'

'But my darling Lorna, what a triumph for you.' She grinned at Lorna who smiled uncertainly back, and then she turned her attention to me. 'I'm Nicolette Howie of Luckenlaw House,' she said, 'and this is my sister Vashti. Come over to the fire. It's dismal in this place if you venture an inch from the hearth. Come and get warm.'

I could hardly refuse, but this development was entirely counter to my hopes and plans for the evening. I wanted to be unobtrusively ensconced amongst the villagers, listening to their talk and trying to guide them towards the topic that interested me above all, not making a trio with these two fish out of water, and missing everything. Worse even, I noticed that their presence seemed to be subduing the rest of the women to the extent that there would be nothing to miss, for the other members of the institute took their seats in near silence, despite the schoolmistress's continued attempts to jolly everyone up. Presently a deputation of very lowly women—I should have guessed at labourers' wives—arrived and their faces sank when they saw the party at the fireplace. I could sympathise; what rotten luck to tramp across the fields hoping to let one's hair down only to find that one's betters, with whom one's hair must stay firmly up, have beaten one to it.

I suppose it could be argued that there was nothing to choose between my presence and theirs when it came to fitting in except that, while I had been all set to keep my head down, everything about *them* set them apart, from the casual cigarettes to the clothes they wore, startling get-ups for any setting, but quite ludicrous here in the schoolroom this evening. The one who had been introduced as Vashti—a name, incidentally, which I only knew because I had had a Dartmoor pony called that when I was seven (it was supposed to be a carriage pony, but I do not remember it ever being persuaded into harness, although I do remember it nipping me hard on the arm once when I stroked it)—had kept her long hair and wore it wound up in a thin silk scarf making a kind of turban shape. With this she wore an evening dress of a vaguely Eastern style, a long square tunic and an even longer skirt underneath it, very wide sleeves and an indistinct pattern of peacock feathers and lotus flowers in a lozenge shape over the middle part, which had surely been introduced onto the garment by the application of some kind of craftwork rather than by dressmaking proper. It looked like a potato print to me. This peculiar costume was in several shades of pea-green and murky purple and did nothing at all to enhance its wearer's dark complexion, making her look, in fact, rather dirty.

The other woman, Nicolette, did not appear to have changed, causing one to wonder at the running of their presumably shared home, but wore a little wool suit, very tight and short and electric blue in colour. She had high heels to her shoes and a tiny hat of red wool rather low over one eye. As well as the crochet-work brooch on her lapel, she wore at least four strings of pearls and coloured beads, and around her wrists she had several enormous art-jewellery bangles in pewter, enamel and what might be rather nasty bright gold. Her fingers too were jammed with garish rings, large, cheap stones such as amber and amethyst, set about not by diamonds which can make an amethyst ring rather pretty, but with more of the same bright gold. They looked the kind of trinket found in a Moroccan market, the kind of trinket I had considered bringing home from my honeymoon as presents for my bridesmaids until I thought sensibly about how they would look under the cold, grey, English skies and reached instead for cushions.

Neither lady seemed to mind, or even to notice, me staring at them. They were fussing over Lorna, with great affection.

'Darling,' said Vashti. 'It's been an age since we saw you.'

'And I've won a bet,' added Nicolette. 'I told Vash you wouldn't be *adorned*.' She jabbed Lorna's work-bag with a crimson fingertip. 'She insisted you would. Ten shillings you owe me, Vashti.'

Lorna laughed uncomfortably and glanced over her shoulder to where Miss McCallum sat, ostentatiously not listening to this traducing of her art.

'You sweep, Niccy,' said Vashti. 'How dare you. She's adorned with a bag. She's adorned to the nines. That counts, doesn't it, Mrs Gilver?'

'Dandy,' I said, glad to be able to respond without actually answering. Before she could press me, there came a loud clapping from behind me in the room. The schoolmistress, perhaps unable to help herself, was summoning the attention of the gathering in the way that schoolmistresses do. I spied an empty chair at the other side of the room and made for it purposefully, leaving Lorna and the two interlopers behind me.

'Can anyone just sit anywhere?' I whispered to the woman next to me—a ruddy-faced type I took to be a farmer's wife. She nodded and gave a tight smile.

'Now then, ladies,' began the schoolmistress, 'we have a packed programme tonight. Mrs Hemingborough has kindly offered to provide a demonstration of plucking a bird, with suggestions of what to do with the feathers. As well as that we have Sister MacAllister from the children's ward at the Victoria here to lecture us on infant nutrition—I'm sure we're all looking forward to that. Our competition is "A Pot of Bramble Jelly" and we'll be voting for the winner with a silver shower as usual. Now, before I hand you over to Miss McCallum for tonight's motto and roll-call, I just want to welcome Mrs Gilver here.' Thirty pairs of eyes swivelled in my direction and I gave a faint simper in recognition. 'Mrs Gilver is speaking next month on "The Household Budget" and she has come along tonight to have a recce, since there is

40

no Rural in her own village in Perthshire. Who knows? Maybe tonight will light the spark, Mrs Gilver.' There was a general titter at this and I joined in, while thinking my quiet thoughts. 'In a spirit of welcome,' she finished, 'I would like to invite Mrs Gilver to decide on tonight's social half-hour. It can be anything at all, Mrs Gilver: dancing, singing, games, stories. Or even just a chat.' She beamed at me, unaware of the cold stone she had just settled on my chest. Of course! How could I not have known? How could I doubt that to be a guest at any gathering with a committee is to be instantly handed the most unwelcome task. Why only the summer before I had gone along to a fair, all innocence, and found myself judging bonny babies so of course I was going to lead the ladies of the village in song tonight. Of course I was.

The blood thundering in my ears had drowned out all external affairs for a moment, and when I returned to the room Miss McCallum had taken the floor.

'Thank you, Miss Lindsay,' she said, nodding to the schoolmistress. 'I'm glad to see so many of you wearing the results of your forays into crochet tonight.' There was a little smothered laughter from the corner where Vashti and Nicolette Howie had settled and two spots of pink bloomed high up on Miss McCallum's pale cheeks, but she raised her plump chin and carried on. 'I propose that the motto of this evening's meeting should be: If you are wrong, regret it; if you are wronged, forget it.' There was a round of fierce applause from the audience at that, and I found myself murmuring: 'Hear, hear!'

'Absolutely,' said Vashti from her corner. 'Very

well said.' Although her tone was as superior as ever, the general mood of the room took on a conciliatory tinge and we moved on to the fowl-plucking demonstration in a spirit of comradeship; much the best spirit with which to face dead poultry out of the blue.

Mrs Hemingborough, another amply proportioned matron as tightly trussed in her good calico blouse and worsted skirt as any chicken could ever hope to be, calmly slid a basket from under her chair and drew out a sheet of sacking which she spread upon the floor at her feet, a crisp apron which she put on and tied firmly under her bust and, finally, two dead hens. These provoked a variety of reactions amongst the assembly. Nicolette and Vashti Howie shrieked. Lorna Tait looked as though she might have liked to shriek but instead she took a deep breath and beamed. Others, those who were most unmistakably farmers' wives, looked on with either politely concealed boredom or gimlet-eyed readiness to find Mrs Hemingborough's technique sadly wanting. Miss Lindsay and Miss McCallum, who I was beginning to suspect were the instigators and chief defenders of the SWRI in Luckenlaw, sat forward looking eager if rather pale and several others of the village women also stirred themselves into greater alertness: here, they seemed to say, was something worth coming out for on a cold, dark night, no matter the mixed company one had to endure to get it. And to be fair, it was more interesting than one might have imagined, as it always is to watch someone do something he is very good at. (I spent hours hanging over the estate carpenter's workshop door as a girl, goggling, with my mouth hanging open and my brain absolutely empty and I would do so still if I thought I could get away with it.) The noise of the ripping out was a tiny bit sickening, especially with the old boiling fowl—Mrs Hemingborough had brought one of these as well as a plump young hen to show the different techniques demanded by each—and some of the suggestions for the use of the feathers were beyond arresting—I could not foresee myself making a poultice of boiled feathers and bran should I ever come down with a blister— but the time passed and soon the sacking was tied around the mound of feathers, the apron and newly naked fowl were back in Mrs Hemingborough's basket and it was time for tea.

'Which I'm sure we're all ready for,' said Miss Lindsay, bravely, through lips still blue-ish from disgust. 'There's nothing like . . .' but she gave up. The tea, which she took with lots of sugar and no milk, soon revived her however and we sturdier souls dug into the accompanying scones with gusto. I had imagined that such a forum as an SWRI meeting—all of one's female neighbours gathered together and paying attention and no men (always so easy to please and therefore quite irrelevant)— would bring forth some fiercely excellent scones and I was right. We promenaded the room scooping spoonfuls of bramble jelly from competing pots as Lorna explained to me the working of the 'silver shower'; one put a sixpence down beside one's favoured pot of jelly and thus the winner was chosen and the picnic funds swollen too, and it seemed such a neat and decorous sort of competition that, added to the warmth and chumminess, I was almost ready to go home and start agitating for a Rural of my own. I settled back into my seat again feeling full, cosy, and suffused with sisterly bonhomie.

Sister MacAllister of the Victoria soon damped that flame. She took a scientific view of infant nutrition, all calorie values and protein metabolism with not so much as a mashed banana to bring it down to earth. I listened until I heard her say that 'the coagulation of human milk in gastric juice is much more loose and flocculent than that of cows' milk and therefore . . .' and then I tried very hard not to hear any more. Clearly, Sister MacAllister was going to furnish me neither with recipes to take home to my nursery nor with a template for a successful talk on the Household Budget in a month's time, and I felt that anyone who used the words 'gastric' and 'flocculent' (whatever it meant) in the same sentence and straight after tea did not deserve my attention. I peeped at Miss Lindsay just to check that she was not about to faint and then closed my ears and tried to think about the case.

That there were thirty-odd women here tonight in spite of everything was a sign, I thought, that no one really believed the tales. Only of Vashti and Nicolette could I think the prospect of being mauled by a dark stranger might be an enticement to come along; they were possibly young enough to have caught the current fashion for greeting almost anything in life as a 'scream'. One heard oftener and oftener that a friend of a friend had been arrested, drunk in charge of a motor car or swimming in a public pond, and always there came with the story an unspoken demand for one to find the whole thing a 'scream'; my inability to do so

44

made me feel elderly sometimes.

The other women of the Luckenlaw Rural would certainly take a very different view, I was sure. If any of their number actually encountered the stranger, she would scream holy murder, retell the tale with sundry embellishments at every opportunity for months and pester the doctor for tablets and tonics to help with her nerves for the rest of her life. In short, she would turn a nasty moment into something Wagnerian and utterly without end. I could safely assume, then, that none of them really believed in a dark stranger, out there right now waiting to catch them.

So, perhaps the task before me was the equally ticklish one of trying to find out who had started the story and why and why she had been joined by others backing it up. But who to ask? I had not been introduced to any of the women and none of the names I heard in passing had chimed with those on Mr Tait's list; neither Miss McCallum, Miss Lindsay nor Mrs Hemingborough had reported an encounter with the stranger. I let my gaze drift around the room, wondering which of these women it was who had. They all looked so very stolid sitting there, some nodding in the warmth as Sister MacAllister's lullaby washed over them, some grimly upright, some gaping with boredom. Nicolette and Vashti were sprawled in their seats like delinquent schoolgirls, making no effort at all to hide their feelings as the voice droned on and on, and looking at them I found my own legs begin to twitch as they had not done since the days of German dictation, so that I longed to slide from my seat and roll about on the floor. I caught the eye of a young woman sitting beside

Vashti and looked quickly away. The next face I noticed was looking at me too and as I darted glances all around the room I began to perceive that all eyes were upon me and that Sister MacAllister was in her seat, shuffling her papers and with a look of satisfaction at a good job well done shining upon her face.

'Mrs Gilver?' said Miss McCallum, and her tone told me it was not the first time she had said it.

'Ah yes, of course,' I said. 'Sorry, I didn't catch the last thing you said, I'm afraid. Stupidly, I didn't bring a notebook and I was, um, trying to commit Sister MacAllister's vitamin list to memory while it was still fresh in my mind.' A tremendous snort from the corner convinced me that one of the Howie ladies at least had seen through me, but Miss McCallum only beamed.

'I was saying it's time for our social half-hour. What would you like to propose? Songs around the piano, perhaps?'

Nothing would have persuaded me to plump for songs around the piano in the present company; I should have given no odds at all that the Luckenlaw women knew a great many woeful ballads all with twelve verses and I should not put it past the Howies to dredge up something from a revue just out of sheer mischief. General chat would be ideal if it could go on long enough to let me get around the room and give me time to work the conversation up to the point each time, but half an hour was pitifully short for that. Only one sensible possibility presented itself to me.

'I'd like stories,' I said. 'Good old-fashioned stories. What could be more fun?'

There were a few groans from the younger girls

46

but most of their elders were clearly equal to the challenge.

'And on what topic?' said Miss McCallum.

'It can be anything at all?' I asked.

'Except party politics and sectarian religion,' chorused Nicolette and Vashti as though they had said it many times before. There was a slight embarrassed titter.

'Well, yes,' said Miss Lindsay, 'although I'm sure Mrs Gilver would not have dreamed of that.'

Actually, Mrs Gilver had dreamed of something much worse. My heart was knocking at the thought of my temerity, but it was irresistible.

'Since it's almost Hallowe'en,' I said, 'let's have ghost stories. We must all tell a story—a true story, mind—that begins "One dark night, I was all alone and . . .".'

There was a blank silence and a few of the polite smiles around the room began to falter.

'When I was a girl we always used to love to tell ghost stories,' I said. 'Just for fun, you understand.'

'Aye well,' said a voice, calmly. I did not look to see who it was who spoke. 'That's down there for you.'

As though things were not bad enough, in the silence which followed this leaden pronouncement, a girl who had been coughing quietly throughout the evening and had blown her nose repeatedly, suddenly let out an explosive sneeze and instead of the usual bless you, her neighbour said loud and clear: 'Sneeze on a Monday.' She bit it off short, but everyone in the room carried on in thought: kiss a stranger.

'Or poems,' I said, trying very hard not to sound frantic. 'Everyone must know a poem.'

And so it came to pass that I let myself in for listening politely to half an hour's worth of the most torrid Scotch poems imaginable: drowned maidens, duelling swains, doomed soldiers and even, I was irritated to note, a fair sprinkling of ghosts.

CHAPTER FOUR

Lorna, the soul of diplomacy, would never have mentioned my faux pas, but as we made our way back up the lane to the green the Howies' motor car slowed beside us and Vashti stuck her head out of the window and hailed me.

'Such a hoot, your ghost story idea,' she said. 'Just the breath of fresh air this place needs. In fact, if you're staying overnight at the manse, do come round in the morning. You too of course, Lorna darling.' She withdrew her head as Nicolette 'revved' the engine and they roared off, leaving Lorna and me in awkward silence.

'I must apologise,' I said at last. 'One forgets, even after all these years, what might cause offence up here in Calvin's stamping ground.' I remembered, too late, that Lorna's father was a minister of the very church that was Mr Calvin's legacy. 'Not that I've anything against . . .' but I could not continue. How could one not have at least *something* against some of it?

'Oh, it's not that,' said Lorna. 'Gosh, no. Luckenlaw is just as in thrall to a good spooky story as anywhere. You'll have heard about the locked chamber?'

'A little,' I admitted.

'Well, you wouldn't believe the superstitious stories about it. Except that it's rather mean to call it superstition, my father always says. Folklore, he says, is just history without the books. Or is it history that's just folklore written down? Well, anyway,' she concluded and in the cold glare of the moonlight I could see her beaming smile.

The women had come up the lane in a clump but were now splitting into small groups and pairs and setting off in their various directions, up to the green, down the lane to the road, through gates into the fields. No one seemed to be striking out alone, as I was relieved to see since I had not managed to attach myself to a likely victim, and no one seemed exactly what one would call anxious. There were no high spirits to be sure, but the cold air and the prospect of a long walk home might have been enough to account for that and I suspected too that the drawing to a close of this interval of camaraderie and a resumption of duties towards husband and home might be responsible for the downward droop of some of the shoulders and for the hefty sighs I heard being heaved on all sides.

Mrs Hemingborough, lugging her basket and accompanied by a young woman in a rather threadbare coat, walked with Lorna and me as far as the manse gate and carried on.

'Have they far to go?' I asked Lorna, gesturing after the pair. 'I could always get my motor car.'

'Oh no,' said Lorna. 'Only a step. Mrs Hemingborough is at Hinter Luckenlaw Farm and Jessie—she's married to their cowman—has a cottage on the way.'

I was satisfied. Young Jessie was safe and the doughty Mrs Hemingborough with her strong hands was as likely to come off best in a tussle with the stranger as she was *un*likely to be the object of his peculiar affections.

Anyone who has followed my short career, or indeed spent an afternoon with me I am afraid, will not be surprised to learn what happened next. Mr Tait and I were sitting before the fire minutes later, sipping our cocoa and already beginning to think of bed—Lorna had disappeared into the kitchen quarters with an apology and a muttered word about the next day's menu—when we heard a hammering at the front door. Mr Tait put down his cup and rose to his feet and I was just thinking that he was taking this late-night rumpus suspiciously calmly, when he said to me:

'Please excuse me, Mrs Gilver. It sounds as though some poor soul is in extremis tonight.'

At that moment, Lorna appeared through the connecting door into the dining room—a short cut from the kitchen, I guessed—and her father nodded at her. 'Lorna will take care of you,' he said. 'Sleep well and I will see you in the morning.'

'Poor Father,' said Lorna once he had gone.

'Yes indeed,' I said. 'I should have thought that being summoned to deathbeds in the night might make him regret those naughty little boys at Kingoldrum even if nothing else did.'

'He does miss them sometimes,' she answered, 'but Luckenlaw called and my mother was very happy to come home again, I think.' She looked as though she were about to say more, but at that moment Mr Tait hurried back into the room.

'Mrs Gilver,' he said. 'I wonder if I could trouble

50

you for a minute of your time.'

'Father?' said Lorna, half rising from her chair.

'More unpleasantness, I'm afraid, Lorna,' he said. 'More of the same.'

She made as though to follow us out—I, of course, had leapt to my feet as soon as he spoke—but he raised his hand to stop her.

'No, my dear,' he said. 'I don't want you mixed up in this.'

'But Father, our guest?' she protested.

'Was a nurse in the war,' said Mr Tait. 'You don't mind, Mrs Gilver, do you?'

Between remembering that Lorna did not know that I knew what more of the same unpleasantness would be, and making sure to look suitably puzzled as a result, and also trying not to think about what I might be just about to witness, as well as trying to contain my eagerness to get at it, whatever it was (within reason), I could neither assemble a sensible expression nor summon a sensible response, and so I simply squeezed Lorna's hand and left the room after her father, at a trot.

In the sitting room across the hall, horribly cold now hours after the teatime fire had begun to die down, Jessie the cowman's wife was perched on the edge of a chair hugging her arms and trembling slightly either from fright or from chill.

'Oh, my goodness,' I said, guilt washing over me. 'Oh my poor dear girl.'

Mr Tait was at that moment taking possession of a blanket and a steaming cup of something which a maid had brought to the room. He handed the cup to Jessie and wrapped the blanket around her shoulders with the tender dexterity the father of an orphaned daughter might be expected to show.

51

She lifted the cup to her chin, breathing in the steam, and slowly her shivering began to ease. She was no more than twenty-five, at a guess, getting careworn—the wife of a farm worker has no easy time of it—but still young enough for the sweet steam from a teacup to turn her face instantly bonny and pink.

'Now, my dear,' said Mr Tait, with infinite patience in his tone. 'You must tell Mrs Gilver everything. She's here to help.'

'It was jist like they said,' said Jessie after another stiff swig of her drink. 'A dark stranger.'

'Start from the beginning,' I told her. 'You and Mrs Hemingborough left Lorna and me at the gate, and then what?'

'We kept on up tae the corner,' said Jessie, 'and turnt into the farm road. My wee hoose is halfway along and the farmhoose is at the end, so I got hame first and Mrs Hemingborough carried on. I should have gone straicht in, but . . . I dinna ken, maybe because it was such a lovely nicht with the moon and a' that . . . anyway I jist stood at my gate a while.'

'You weren't frightened?' I said.

'I was not,' said Jessie. 'I didna believe in this stranger, to be honest. Pardon me, Mr Tait, but it's the truth.' Mr Tait inclined his head graciously. 'I always thocht that believin' in all-what-have-you was for them as had a big wage and a wee family and no' the other way on. I've been that proud and that sure o' myself.' She began to look white again and gently I tried to urge her back to the story.

'What happened then? While you were standing at your gate.'

'I saw somethin' in the field,' Jessie said. 'It was

52

movin' richt fast, running across towards the lane, and before I got a chance to shout oot, I saw it lowp over the dyke and I heard Mrs Hemingborough.'

'Mrs Hemingborough?' I echoed. 'It wasn't coming for you?'

'Oh no,' said Jessie. 'Thank the Dear. It made a beeline for Mrs Hemingborough and I ran to see could I help.'

'Terribly brave of you,' I said, thinking that there was a lot more iron in the soul of this girl than I could be sure of having in mine.

'No' really, madam,' said Jessie. 'More like I jist didna think. I never even thocht to go in and get John. I jist took off along the lane towards them. He had gone for her jist in the shade o' a wee bush but I could still see them, quite clear I could see them in the moon we've got the nicht. They were strugglin'. Mrs Hemingborough and a man all in black. And Mrs Hemingborough was shoutin' at him so I shouted too: "Get away fae her. Get away, you filthy so-and-so." And when he heard me, he let go of Mrs Hemingborough and he was back over that dyke and away across the fields afore you could snap your fingers at him. And Mrs Hemingborough was standin' there, wi' her hat torn off and her hair all hingin' doon and those blessed feathers burst oot o' her sack and swirlin' aboot.' Jessie, finally, gave a sob and then took another draught from her cup.

'And where is she now?' I said. 'At home? Have your husbands gone after him?'

'Well, this is the thing,' said Jessie, and her face puckered with concern. 'Mr Tait, I jist don't know what to think. I got to her side and I asked her if

53

she was a'richt and she telt me of course she was, she jist tripped and drapped her bundle and look at the feathers! And she was laughin'—tryin' to anyway.'

'Laughing?' said Mr Tait, sounding more severe than I had ever heard him.

'I hardly kent what to say,' said Jessie. 'What aboot *him*? I asked her. Did he hurt you? And she drew hersel' up and said she didna know what I was talkin' aboot and she didna want to hear any nonsense fae me. Well, I know my place and nobody can tell me I don't but my dander come up at that. I saw him, I telt her. I jist saw the whole thing plain with my own two eyes, and then I telt her that I was goin' to get her husband and mine and send them away after him. But there was no shiftin' her. She said she didna know what I was talkin' aboot and she was "disappointit". She said she had never thocht I was the kind o' lassie who would start up wi' a load o' silly nonsense. She said that her husband needed a good cowman and a good cowman needed a good steady wife and I should think on that afore I started tattlin'.'

'Whatever did she mean?' I said.

'A threat,' said Mr Tait. 'Quite obviously a threat to give John Holland the sack.'

'And we're in a tied hoose, madam, with three bairns,' said Jessie, growing visibly upset again. 'If I lost John his place, and the lot o' us ended up putten out on the road I would jist never forgive myself. So I never went and telt Mr Hemingborough and I willna tell John either or anyone else. Only I had tae tell somebody, so I came roond to Mr Tait.'

'And you're absolutely sure of what you saw?' I

asked her, looking very closely into her face. She nodded vigorously.

'As sure as I'm sittin' here,' she said. 'And I ken it's no' richt to let him get away wi' it, no matter whit Mrs Hemingborough says. I dinna ken what's wrong wi' her.'

'No more do I,' I said, 'but I'm going to try to find out.'

'No, madam, please,' said Jessie, looking quite stricken with anguish. 'Oh Mr Tait,' she wailed. 'Please. If Mrs Hemingborough finds oot I've telt—'

'I'll keep your name out of it, Jessie, I assure you,' I told her. I had no clear idea how I should manage this, but I trusted to think of something. 'Now,' I went on, 'this is very important. Tell me everything you can remember about this fellow. Tell me everything you could see.'

Jessie shuddered but spoke up gamely. 'He was a' dressed in black, I ken that for sure.'

'Tall, short? Thin, fat?' I said. 'Could you tell if he was a young man or was he stiff and elderly in the way he moved?'

'Oh no,' said Jessie. 'He was anythin' but that. No' very tall, I dinna think. He wasna loomin' over Mrs Hemingborough and she's no' much taller than me. And no' fat. He was . . . snaky.' She seemed almost as startled to have said this as Mr Tait and I were to have heard it, but after blinking she nodded. 'Aye, that's it. He was snaky. The way he moved, you ken? He wasna like a man in heavy boots moves, he was jist snaky. The way he come over the dyke and the way he was all over Mrs Hemingborough.' She shuddered again. 'It was horrible.'

'It sounds it,' I said. 'Now come along. I'm going to run you home.'

*   *   *

When I stopped the motor car at the Hollands' cottage gate and stepped down to let Jessie out, she pointed to the great mess of feathers lying on the lane and caught in the bare branches of a hawthorn bush a little way along. In the moonlight, they were as plain as day and I could see no possibility for Jessie to have imagined the scene she had described to me. The sound of the engine brought a young man to the cottage door—John, I guessed—and since he frowned in puzzlement, I called to him.

'We ran on late at the Rural, Mr Holland. I'm delivering Jessie home.'

He nodded, although still frowning slightly, and Jessie scurried past him into the house. Perhaps my presence and the lift in a motor car would, in John's eyes, tip the Rural firmly over into the realms of gadding about and young Jessie's monthly excursions would be over. I hoped not, but then one had to question whether after the experience this evening she would ever cross her door in the dark again. I drove on a little way—I had to turn in a field entrance—and stepped down to look at the scene in the light of my headlamps. There were a great many trodden and over-trodden footprints in the muddy lane just by the hawthorn bush with feathers pressed into them here and there, but much as I should have liked to point to two distinct sets of vastly different sizes, nothing so clear presented itself to me. Anyway, the 'snakiness' of the dark stranger had to have its origin somewhere in his physique or deportment even if Jessie could not put her finger on its source and I imagined that anyone light enough in his movements to earn the description must have rather neat little feet. Full of questions and utterly empty of answers I got back into the motor car and drove home.

*   *   *

In the morning, I had a rare brainwave. I was at the washstand in my bedroom, shivering in my petticoat despite the fire which had been relit at seven by a cheerful little maid, and admiring the scene outside the window; the spare bedroom of the manse was at the back and looked out over fields towards the law. It was the hill, naturally, which held my attention at first but then movement in the foreground caught my eye and I saw a farmer on a cart, precariously laden with turnips, making his careful way along between the hedgerows one field's distance from the house. After gazing at him until he was out of sight again in the usual witless fashion of the early morning, I suddenly realised several things: that this lane must be the one which led to Hinter Luckenlaw Farm; that since I could see the lane from my bedroom window I could perhaps—had I been looking out at the right moment last night—have seen the scuffle with the stranger; and that the wiry little man on the cart whom I had just watched lumbering along this lane was more than likely Mr Hemingborough—for he was too well turned out to be a labourer and who else would be

57

heading away from his farm in the morning with a cartload of turnips—which probably meant that Mrs Hemingborough was at home alone.

I dressed rapidly and waved my hairbrush around my head in a token gesture at a toilette—in fact, whenever Grant sends me off on an overnight stop without her, she sets my hair so very firmly the day before that it would take far more robust a tool than a mere hairbrush to make a dent in it—and skipped downstairs hoping that breakfast in the manse was a brisk affair and I could soon escape.

The sight of Lorna beaming behind two enormous teapots and Mr Tait in a cardigan jersey and with a napkin tucked in at his neck soon did away with any thoughts of a hasty exit from the morning gathering of the little household however. Not wishing to be rude, I settled myself for the duration.

'I really should apologise for my father, Mrs Gilver,' said Lorna, once the fuss of setting me up with my desired breakfast dishes was behind us. 'He's always so very keen to protect me from nasty things, I swear he must still believe me to be a child.' Her smile faded for a moment then reblossomed as she carried on in a rather too hearty voice: 'When in fact, of course, I'm comfortably old enough to take all manner of things on the chin.'

'And are you old enough to talk about your father in thon disrespectful way?' said Mr Tait, twinkling at her. 'I told you, my dear. Mrs Gilver was a nurse in the war and last night young Jessie Holland was in such a state of shock I thought a nurse was called for. Mrs Gilver did not mind.'

He turned to me, inviting me to agree with him,

58

and I nodded, although I was tackling some ferociously thick porridge and could not, at the moment, answer. I never do remember when away from home but still in Scotland, how long it took me to coax my own cook back from the excesses of Scotch habits, so that my winter days could begin with the soothing, creamy treat I expected and not the vile, salty lump which passes for a good plate of porridge around these parts. Once, I witnessed Hugh dig his spoon into the edge of his porridge only to have the whole thing shoot away up the far side of the dish and land, all of a piece, on the tablecloth. Yet still he has the cheek to prefer his to mine.

'Of course I didn't mind,' I said at last. In fact, had young Jessie really needed a nurse I should have minded like anything, and I should have been quite useless, my nursing duties at Moncrieffe House having been confined to playing cards, lighting cigarettes and muttering the occasional 'there, there'.

'Such a shocking thing to have happened, though,' I went on. I knew that Mr Tait did not want Lorna in the thick of it, but it would have been beyond peculiar not to discuss the matter at all.

'It is,' said Lorna. 'A very nasty affair. We had hoped, hadn't we, Father, that it was all behind us. I know Miss McCallum and Miss Lindsay will be very sorry to hear of last night's trouble. They've worked so hard to get the Rural off the ground.'

'And truly no one has any idea who might be behind it?' I said. 'There's no one around the village who's known to be a little odd? It must be a local chap, don't you think, if the trouble's confined to Luckenlaw again and again.'

Mr Tait and Lorna looked as uncomfortable as might be expected to have a guest in their house thus impugn the neighbourhood, and Mr Tait in addition began to frown at me. I had, I realised, begun to betray a little more knowledge of the facts than Lorna could suppose me to have come by and I swept on with a change of subject before she could begin to wonder.

'I can't help admiring your lovely brooch, Lorna,' was the best I could come up with. She was wearing the same rose, ribbon and love-heart as the day before and I realised just too late that it was hardly sensitive to draw attention to her mourning.

Mr Tait dropped his spoon into his porridge, but Lorna only smiled gently and fingered the little brooch before answering.

'Yes, it was my mother's,' she said, and I winced slightly in case I had caused Mr Tait pain too.

'You must have been flattered to see the Howie ladies attempting to imitate it,' I said. Lorna looked momentarily puzzled by this.

'Well, that was by the by,' she said. 'The Rural badge is a very similar design, based on it indeed, except the Rural one has just four points to the crown. For S. W. R. I., you know. But the older ones like this always had five. Why would that be, Father? Why was it always five?'

'A lucky number, I daresay,' said Mr Tait, looking uninterested.

'But it's seven that's lucky, isn't it?' I asked.

'That's right,' said Lorna. 'I remember from the skipping song.'

'I'm not familiar with that,' I said. 'The girls on

60

the green didn't include it in their repertoire yesterday. How does it go?'

Lorna hummed a few notes and then shrugged. 'I can't remember it,' she said. 'It must be a skipping song, though, mustn't it? One and one make two and two makes true love. Then, how does it go, Father? Three is mighty, five is good. Seven is certainly luck.'

'I can't bring it to mind at all,' said Mr Tait, sounding rather strangled and looking a little pale. Perhaps it was not a skipping rhyme after all; perhaps it was a lullaby or even a love song and it reminded him more painfully of his wife than even the brooch itself.

'I wonder what happened to four and six?' I said, trying to lighten the mood.

Lorna giggled.

'They're both terribly unlucky,' she said. 'I mean to say, six is the number of the devil himself, Mrs Gilver.'

Mr Tait, if anything, looked more troubled than ever although whether it was the minister or the man who was suffering was hard to say. Lorna did not seem to notice, at any rate.

'Well, be thankful the Rural doesn't have six initials, then,' I said, and Lorna laughed again.

'But why is four so unlucky, I wonder?' she said. 'Father, do you know?'

'Do I know why four is an unlucky number?' Mr Tait echoed. 'It'll be lost in the mists of time. And anyway, you might as well ask why the sky is blue, Lorna dear. Luck and sense have no connection.'

'Hear, hear,' I replied. 'I have never had much patience with luck, good or ill. I always find it impossible to remember what I should and shouldn't do in the cottages I visit. I must give tremendous offence.'

'You'd be better off at Luckenlaw,' said Lorna, 'with just one big source of luck that everyone agrees on.' I raised my eyebrows. 'I'm sorry,' she said. 'I thought my father had told you. About the sealed chamber in the Lucken Law.'

'I told Mrs Gilver the facts, Lorna dear,' said Mr Tait. 'I did not trouble her with the rest of it. It's the usual thing, Mrs Gilver. Any secret chamber you care to mention has engendered some tale or other about all the good fortune depending on the sealed door and trouble raining down if it is broken. Thankfully, though, not *everyone* gives it credence, no matter what Lorna says.'

'You are not usually so scornful,' said Lorna.

'I'm not scornful at all,' her father protested.

I was feeling scornful enough for all three of us, being firmly with young Jessie Holland in believing that such fancies were for those with too much time and nothing better to fill it.

'I promised Jessie I would visit this morning,' I said, using her name since it had come unbidden into my thoughts. 'I'd like to see how she's bearing up, of course, but also I thought I might sound her out about household matters. In advance of my talk, you know. In fact, I might pay a few visits around the district to get some ideas about what might be useful.'

Mr Tait looked tremendously impressed, as well he might, at my effortless subterfuge and even Lorna nodded with approval.

'Only please do be careful,' she said. 'The

62

villagers are terribly proud, terribly private about anything to do with money.' She chuckled. 'Now later this morning will be quite another matter. You can say whatever you like about money and budgets then. Vashti and Niccy talk of nothing else.'

'Ah yes,' I said. 'Our visit to Luckenlaw House. I had forgotten.'

'Great favourites of Lorna, that pair,' said Mr Tait, with an edge to his voice. 'And she of them too.'

*　　　*　　　*

Which, I mused to myself as I trundled out of the drive and up towards Hinter Luckenlaw Lane shortly afterwards, was rather a mystery. Lorna was a sweet girl but Vashti and Nicolette Howie, on our short acquaintance, had seemed rather too sophisticated to choose a sweet girl—and especially a sweet girl from the village manse—for their companion. Perhaps the paucity of other options might explain it. At Gilverton years ago, had it not been for Bunty, I might easily have thrown myself on the doctor's wife and the minister's daughter had I been the type; as it was, I had always felt that the few minutes of my day not hounded and harried by Grant, Nanny, Hugh and the rest of them were delicious islands of peace and not to be disturbed lightly. Now, of course, there was occupation and diversion to spare what with my trickle of commissions—or could it now be called a flow? a steady trickle anyway—and with Alec ensconced at Dunelgar and gratifyingly in need of all manner of advice on his household, although I admitted to myself with a quick frown that these days, his staff in place and his furniture arranged, it was Hugh he turned to more often than not, the pair of them, over trout stocks and deer fences, growing as thick as two thieves and as dull as two Hughs at times.

I was well advanced along the lane to the farm before I dragged my concentration back to the matter of the moment and, shaming as that is to admit, it is not the worst of it. Much worse is the fact that I was distracted enough by my musings almost to miss an important point of physical evidence or rather, in true Holmesian fashion, the absence of one—which amounts to the same thing. The barkless dog in this instance was the lane itself, stretching from road to farm gate quite bare and featureless; someone had been out and gathered up every single feather from the night before.

I threw the car into the reversing gear and rolled back along the lane to the hawthorn bush. Even this was picked clean, not a single feather left in its branches, which must have taken quite some time even though the job had clearly been hurried, with numerous little twigs being snapped off here and there. Chastened—imagine almost missing this!—but more than ever a-quiver to get to the bottom of it I started up again and shot along the lane to the farm, sweeping round into the yard, sure of finding Mrs Hemingborough in her kitchen.

There indeed she was. She came to the kitchen door in her pinny to meet me and I took a huge bolstering breath and launched into my performance.

'My dear,' I said, taking both of her hands in

mine. 'My poor dear Mrs Hemingborough. What a relief to find you up and about. You look marvellous! I do hope you don't mind my coming round—I know we've barely met, but I couldn't help myself. Mr Tait is going to pop in later too.'

When I had got to the end of this Mrs Hemingborough, surprisingly to me, was looking just as calm, but decidedly colder. She flapped a hand which I took to be an invitation to enter and I swept into the kitchen and plonked myself into a chair at the end of the table furthest from the range, the other end being spread with a padded cloth for the ironing which waited in a basket on the floor.

'Mrs Gilver,' began Mrs Hemingborough, disapproval and natural politeness fighting each other in her voice, 'please don't think me inhospitable, I beg you, but I'm not following you. Did someone tell you I was ill?'

For just a fraction of a second, she and I eyed one another. She knew that I knew, I knew that she knew and we both knew that no one was going to give in. Her look to me seemed to say 'Let battle commence' and I hoped that mine to her said the same.

'Mrs Hemingborough, dear,' I said. 'I understand absolutely if you want to keep it quiet and I've told no one except Mr Tait, but no matter what he did to you you have nothing to be ashamed of and you must not bottle it up. Now, Mr Tait told me that your dreadful experience was not the first and he told me too—quite shocking!—that the police are dragging their feet, which almost beggars belief.'

'I don't want to be rude,' said Mrs

Hemingborough, and still she spoke quite gamely but was betrayed by a tiny tremor in the hand which lay on the table top as she sat down and faced me, 'but I have no idea what you're talking about.'

'Why, the attack,' I said, all innocence. 'The dark stranger. Last night.'

At this Mrs Hemingborough drew herself up magnificently, so magnificently in fact that I began quail. What if Jessie had been imagining things? I remembered the feathers and, with that thought, rallied again.

'I see someone has been telling tales,' said Mrs Hemingborough, 'but I can assure you, Mrs Gilver, there is no such person as this "dark stranger" and even if there is he made no attack on me last night.'

'But Mrs Hemingborough,' I said, gearing up for my masterstroke, 'my dear, I saw it. I was looking out of my bedroom window at the back of the manse, you know, and in the moonlight, I saw the whole thing. Now, Mr Tait asked me to make his apologies to you for not immediately coming round to help, but the truth is that I didn't tell him until this morning. I could hardly believe my eyes, you see, and I put it out of my mind, or tried to. And then when I did mention it, at breakfast, of course Mr Tait assured me that it was not a trick of the moonlight at all. It was just the latest instalment in this horrid affair. Well, you can imagine how I felt then. But I daresay, since Mr Tait is not a young man he would more likely have been hindrance than help to any search party and he assured me that you have a good handful of men about the place better suited to it, and your

66

own telephone to summon the police. I suppose it's too much to hope that they found him?'

At last I stopped talking and I watched her intently to see what the effect of this outpouring might be. She licked her lips with a quick darting gesture and clasped her hands together on the scrubbed table top, but remained silent for so long that my attention began to wander. Around me, the farmhouse kitchen spoke of an ordered, capable life; the life of the woman who could pluck a chicken on her lap, no less. The kettle was on the back of the burnished range, an array of irons sitting on the hotplate before it, and above the range the dolly groaned with the rest of the wash, jerseys and men's overalls turning the air soft as they dried. In the sink, however, an unwashed porridge pot balancing on top of a frying pan told the tale of a morning rushed and upset by the need to go out in the lane and pick feathers as soon as the sun had come up.

Mrs Hemingborough cleared her throat; she had gathered her wits about her once more.

'I don't know how to account for it,' she said, 'but I'm afraid you're mistaken. I know the story you're referring to—a lot of silly nonsense—and I can assure you nothing happened to me on the way home last night.'

'But I saw it,' I said again. 'I can't for the life of me imagine why you would deny it. Oh!' The exclamation escaped me before I could bite my lip, for all of a sudden I *could* see. I *did* see. 'Oh dear.'

Mrs Hemingborough raised an eyebrow at me with an admirable attempt at detachment, but for the first time I had really rattled her.

'I understand,' I said. 'But I can't say I approve.

67

After all, even if you are able to take it so unaccountably in your stride, who's to say who's next?'

'Well, I'm glad to have your understanding, Mrs Gilver,' she said. 'I only wish it was mutual. And though I'm sorry to have your disapproval, there I think I can say we're more in step.' And with that she rose and went towards her irons, leaving me gasping at her rudeness. 'Forgive me, Mrs Gilver. I know you're a friend of Mr Tait's and he's a good man, been a good friend to Luckenlaw since he came here, and his wife was a lovely girl we had all known from her cradle, but . . .' She tested the temperature of one of the largest irons—and although I know that spitting on it is just the way it is done, I could not help but feel there was a bit of a message for me there too—and selected a garment from the top of the crumpled pile in the basket on the floor.

'It's perfectly plain to me,' I said, liberated from any call on my own politeness by her extraordinary behaviour, 'that the only reason for you to deny it, in the face of a witness'—here I did that little thought-dance which is the mental equivalent of crossing one's fingers behind one's back; after all there was a witness—'is that you know who it was and you are protecting him.'

'And why would I be doing that then?' she said, scathing enough to sound quite insolent.

'I can't imagine,' I retorted. 'If it were me, no matter whether it were my husband, son or brother, I should not shield him.'

'I don't have any sons,' said Mrs Hemingborough. 'Nor any brothers.'

The unspoken thought hung between us, but it

was ludicrous enough to make me blush and she give a short, sneering laugh; for why would her husband bother to rush around in the night just to catch his own wife who was on her way home to him anyway.

'I do not accuse your . . . anyone in particular, Mrs Hemingborough,' I said, trying to sound haughty. 'I only say I think you know who it was and are refusing to name him.'

Mrs Hemingborough had got the shirt stretched out flat to her satisfaction on the padded table and she looked at me, her meaning plain: she wanted me to leave and let her get on with her busy day.

'Is that what you think, then?' she said. 'Aye well, you play bonny.'

This was a little saying I knew well and one which had always irritated me, cutting one off at the knees as it does and rendering any further protestations quite useless. It has no equivalent in the King's English, the nearest thing being when Nanny Palmer would say, 'Heavens, we *are* in a temper' in that maddening, cosy way of hers when one's entire world had collapsed and one had ceased to practise any restraint in the face of it. I remember this happening once in my nursery over the matter of whether a poached egg could be eaten off a slice of toast with a knife and fork or must be mashed up in a cup with bread squares and fed to one with a spoon. 'Heavens,' Nanny Palmer had said over the din of my howls, 'we *are* in a temper' and feeling foolish, I had shut up.

It is a peculiarly British response to distress, I think. At least, I remember holidaying in Florence once, watching a fat bambina of three or so work herself up into just the same state, although one

69

doubts it was over poached eggs and bread squares, and all of the grown-ups around her cooed and consoled, sent for cool cloths to lay on her cross little face, and generally commiserated with her over the tragedy that is this our life, some of them even wiping away a tear or two of their own as they did so.

'That child should be smacked on the bottom and sent to bed with no supper,' Hugh had hissed through his teeth, as though expecting me to step in and effect this for him.

'Oh, I don't know,' I said. 'It must be rather nice to have a tantrum met with ice cloths and kisses.'

'Yes, and end up with half your officers in retreat and facing the firing squad,' said Hugh, which put paid to the conversation at a stroke.

Now, in Mrs Hemingborough's kitchen, this jumble of memories only served to spur me on and quite wiped out the quelling effect of her scorn.

'I intend to,' I said. 'Play bonny, that is. I intend to get to the bottom of this nonsense before anyone else—anyone perhaps more sensitive—is hurt.'

'Aye well,' said Mrs Hemingborough, 'you're harming no one. Do what you will.'

'Indeed,' I agreed, still rather nonplussed at her equanimity. 'I'm harming no one at all. I certainly feel quite unencumbered by the demands of compassion with respect to you, Mrs Hemingborough, since you seem so utterly and bewilderingly unaffected by your ordeal.'

'I am that,' she told me. 'What's for you won't go by you. Not,' she added, 'that anything happened.'

'What's for you won't go by you?' I echoed as I let myself out and climbed back into my motor car.

'What's for you won't go by you?' What in heaven's name did she mean by that?

CHAPTER FIVE

Lorna and I walked to Luckenlaw House in the end. I had reported back to Mr Tait upon my return to the manse, and he seemed no more able than I was to account for Mrs Hemingborough's peculiar reaction, confirming that she had no male relations and so no one obvious to protect in the face of his having leapt over a wall in the dead of night and made mischief with her.

'If it weren't for the feathers,' I concluded, 'I should say that young Jessie was mistaken. If it weren't for the feathers.'

'And she said "What's for you won't go by you"?' said Mr Tait.

'Which is most odd, I think you'll agree,' I answered. Mr Tait said nothing. 'Don't you think?' I prompted.

'Oh yes, yes, indeed. Very strange,' said Mr Tait.

So, feeling I needed fresh air and thinking time, I agreed readily to Lorna's suggestion that we leave the motor car and walk around the law to visit the Howies.

'It's a bit further if we go down past the school instead of cutting around the farm lanes,' she said, 'but much drier underfoot and there are lovely views.' I assured her that a long walk on ash was far preferable to a short slither through the mud and worse of a couple of farms, and we set off, practically arm-in-arm, for there was something about Lorna which took one straight back to one's schooldays. I half expected her to produce a liquorice stick from a knicker pocket, bite it in two and offer half to me.

It was morning playtime at the school and Miss Lindsay was standing in the doorway, wrapped up in a thick coat and sipping a cup of tea as she watched her young charges.

'Such a conscientious schoolmistress,' said Lorna, waving at her.

In the playground, blithely ignoring the several balls which the little boys were scuffling around, a coterie of girls were once again busy with their skipping rope.

'Spring a lock o' bonny maidie,' they sang, weaving in and out of the swooping rope.

> 'Summer lock o' wedded lady.
> Harvest lock o' baby's mammy.
> Who will be my true love?
> Three times twist me,
> All that I wish me.
> First time he kissed me
> He will be my true love.'

And then once again with the same air of knuckling down to it, they began to chant the alphabet, looping in and out and round behind the girls swinging the rope. As the chant wore on, one became aware that some of the boys were paying a measure of sideways attention to the game, and when one of the girls stumbled and got her feet caught in the ropes on the letter 'P' a volley of laughter and whistles went up all around.

'Ella loves Peter,' the children chanted, in that

familiar infuriating sing-song. 'Ella luh-huves Pee-heeter.'

Ella, looking thunderous, shouted, 'Forfeit, forfeit!' and the girls swinging the rope were joined by another two, the four together beginning to whip it round faster and faster until it was almost a blur, whereupon Ella capered fearlessly into its path on the upswing and began to skip while the rest of the girls clapped and whether the clapping grew faster and the rope matched it or vice versa, certainly before long the rope was flashing round, zinging off the ground with sharp cracks, and the claps were thrumming. Then the singing began.

'My mother is a queen and my father is a king.
I'm a little princess and you're a dirty thing.
Not because you're clarty and not because you're clean,
But 'cos you've got the chicken pox and measles in between.'

Poor Ella was purple in the face and blowing hard when it was over but looked satisfied to have paid the price and detached her name from Peter's. Peter himself—whichever one of the small boys he was—kept his own counsel.

It was all new to me. I had only sons and even the farms and cottages on the estate had been going through a very boyish era in recent years, with blue ribbons threaded through all the christening robes and dollies packed away in paper against the day when the tide would turn. Here in Luckenlaw, I noticed, doing a quick tally of the playground, the balance was currently on the other

73

side.

'What a lot of girls there are,' I said to Lorna. 'I was just thinking how in my village we run to boys these days and I couldn't help but notice.'

'Oh yes,' said Lorna. 'Luckenlaw is famed for it. We say there must be something in the water, you know.' We had moved on from watching the children and were now descending the lane towards a small burn with a ford and footbridge.

'Have you ever heard the theory—goodness knows where I came across it—that in times of war women begin to have more boy babies? I always thought it quite horrid if it's true. Much too obliging of the mothers docilely to provide cannon fodder. I'm with Luckenlaw on that score.' I glanced at Lorna as I spoke and noticed that her face had turned quite solemn. Of course! How tactless of me to witter on about cannon fodder and even about there not being enough boys to go around if what I had surmised about her on the strength of the rosebud and velvet ribbon were true. 'Much better have girls and keep them safe and sound,' I went on, willing myself to shut up. I managed it at last. Briefly. 'I think I must have said something to upset you, Lorna dear,' was how I filled the silence. 'I do apologise.'

'Not at all, don't be silly,' said Lorna, the beaming smile in place as ever but her eyes shining rather than twinkling for a change. 'I'm far too sensitive, I know. Morag—Miss Lindsay—is never done telling me I need to toughen up, and I'm sure she's right.'

'Oh well, as to that,' I said vaguely, thinking of the Italian bambina and Hugh's instant diagnosis of military downfall, 'who wants to be tough, really,

74

when you get right down to it? Talk to me, if you like, dear. I shan't tell you to toughen up, I assure you.'

Odd, the way one twitters oneself into a hole single-handed. Somehow Mrs Hemingborough's coarse unconcern over her assault and my automatic impulse to take the other side to Hugh on any point of debate had ended up with me begging this rather droopy girl to share her tale of woe and promising to be all sympathy while she did so, when in fact nothing in the world could be more designed to embarrass and bore me. Unfortunately, Lorna did not need to be told twice.

'There's nothing much to say,' she began, which is never, I have found, an indication that there will not be a great deal to hear. 'I was engaged to be married,' she went on haltingly. 'His name was Walter. He went to war and didn't come back. Like so many others. And the worst thing is that in his heart, he was a conscientious objector. Only he dared not take a stand. He simply dared not. And I didn't stand behind him. I was afraid of what everyone would think. So he signed up when his papers came. He only lasted a month, then he died of dysentery. He always had a very delicate constitution.'

One hardly knew whether to laugh or cry. Lorna herself was hardly swashbuckling, but to think of her pining and berating herself for a decade over a conshie without the nerve even to be a conshie was, in my present mood, simply tiresome and it was hard to resist the thought that this Walter had died of his tummy upset just to show the rough boys what a sensitive soul he was. (I can surprise

75

myself with my own unpleasantness sometimes.)

'Do I detect a trace of guilt in your voice, Lorna?' I said. 'I promised not to tell you to toughen up, and I shan't, but you must at least stop that. You're a lovely young woman'—I stopped on the footbridge and faced her to hammer my point home—'with a whole life ahead of you.'

'I know,' sighed Lorna, and I was sure that she had been told just this many times before. She gazed over my shoulder. 'We were going to live there,' she said. I turned around and followed her gaze towards a cottage on the far side of the burn. It was a long, low and rather mossy-looking affair, apparently empty as far as I could tell from its dusty windows, and standing hardly higher than the burn which chuckled along in front, darkened by the overhanging trees of the lane.

'Oh my dear,' I said, kicking myself for choosing just this spot as a setting for my pep-talk, although surely she could not really regret the cottage; it was bound to be damp. 'What did your Walter do?' I asked, doubting that a country solicitor, the local doctor or a businessman from town would ever be drawn to settle in such a place, and unable to think of a single other suitor for the minister's daughter who would. I rather suspected a curate, if truth be told.

'He was a poet,' said Lorna.

Ah, I thought, but I said nothing and with a last sighing glance at the cottage, she turned and walked away.

'Good girl,' I said firmly, myself turning away from the blank windows and tussocky garden and following her. 'You really should put the past behind you, you know.'

76

'I know,' said Lorna again. 'And at least I *have* the past. No one can take it away.' Whereas, I thought, there might be no future of which to speak. There was no guarantee, at any rate, that anyone would roll up to bring her one. That much was inarguable, and in the end Lorna's mood prevailed: we plodded on in gloomy silence, and since it was far too cold for plodding—only a day for a walk if that walk were a brisk stride out with the head up and the shoulders back—by the time we arrived at Luckenlaw House we were both chilled to the bone.

The Howies, it immediately became clear, were taking the other route from the Gilvers through their even more desperate financial straits. Hugh and I had hung on to the old routine through the lean years, me in my sitting room and he in his library, with smaller fires and thicker jerseys. Here at Luckenlaw House, we were shown into a long room which might once have been a dining hall. It was wonderfully warm and cosy with two fires burning and a paraffin heater belching away besides, but the entire household seemed to be corralled there, two men sprawled in armchairs with newspapers and the women sharing a sofa, smoking, chatting, and stroking what I first took to be an elderly muff but which soon showed itself to be, in fact, an elderly cat. What is more, a dining table set up by a sideboard near the windows suggested that the Howies took their meals in this room, and a card table by one of the fires, set around with four chairs and having a trolley of decanters drawn up handily beside it, was a sign that they spent their evenings here too.

'Lorna, my pet,' cried Vashti as we were shown

in by a girl. I hesitate to call her a maid, for she was wearing a brown woollen skirt and a yellow jersey and she did no more than fling the door open for us before turning on her heel and disappearing back from whence she came. Vashti sat up and stubbed out her cigarette in a rather full ashtray balanced on top of a pile of magazines on the sofa beside her. The cat rose and yawned luxuriously, showing us a pink tongue and rather few, randomly scattered, yellow teeth.

'And Dandy dear,' said Nicolette. 'Johnny, this is Dandy Gilver. From Perthshire. I told you last night.' Johnny, who had not been prompted to rise by Lorna's and my entrance, stirred himself at the sound of his wife's voice and came to shake hands.

'Delighted to make your acquaintance,' he mumbled. With this, social obligations evidently discharged, he returned to his armchair and fell into it with a sound somewhere between a groan and a sigh, like a slumbering dog. From the other—unmistakably his brother with the same high, bony nose and crinkled hair—there was not even as much as that. He only folded his newspaper across one middle finger and waved it at us. Vashti looked over at him, rolled her eyes, and looked away.

'Ignore my lump of a husband, won't you,' she said.

'Your husband?' I said, glancing around the four of them, trying to sort out the family tree. 'I thought . . .'

Nicolette giggled and explained.

'They are brothers and we are sisters,' she said.

'How . . . neat,' I replied. Really, I was wondering which match was made first and whether the one who threw her sister in the way of the spare brother was now suffering pangs of remorse, for neither of the Howie men looked like much of a catch and there was nothing I could see in this grim, dank house which might serve as a sugar-coating for being landed with him.

Coffee was ordered, the girl who had answered the door just pert enough to heave a sigh at the extra work we had brought her but not pert enough actually to demur, and we four ladies settled ourselves to wait for it. The Mrs Howies were no less startlingly dressed this morning; indeed their costumes were rather more disconcerting in the light of day, Vashti's particularly. Her floating panels of the evening before had been replaced by a swathe of fine but mud-coloured wool, ornamented with scarves in vivid orange and scarlet, which pooled around her feet as she sprawled on the sofa and billowed out like flags in a breeze as she rose and strode to the fire to heap it with more coals. Had it not been for these scarves and a long chain of beads I might have taken her still to be in her dressing gown for it was hard to cast her garment as any kind of day-dress. It was positively medieval, as though Vashti were dressed up for a play. Next to her, Nicolette appeared almost unexceptional although, in another short, tight suit—of bright tweed this time—and another pair of very narrow shoes with high heels and pointed toes, she too was rather out of place in the setting. Once again, she clanked with bracelets and bangles and once again her fingers were rendered all but useless with rings (I should have given a sovereign to see her try to play a piano). What entertaining creatures they were,

79

but what decidedly odd chums for Lorna. I wondered again who, out of the three of them, had first promoted their obvious intimacy, and why.

'Have you always lived here?' I asked, thinking that perhaps they and Lorna had been girls together. It was difficult to hazard a guess at their ages—Vashti had that rather thick, grubby-looking skin which ages hardly at all (and I have always thought it a rare case of fairness on the part of Mother Nature that it should be so. Why should not the Vashtis of this world, sallow and plain in their youth, suddenly find themselves looking rather better as the bloom faded from the milkmaid cheeks of their rivals?). Nicolette was a more ordinary English rose, but so lathered in make-up that she could have been anywhere between twenty and forty, at least when seen against the light.

'Long enough shading into too long,' drawled Vashti unhelpfully. 'Five years, Nic?'

'Is it really only five?' said Nicolette and sighed. Lorna smiled mildly, as though she was used to hearing the like.

'Five years since we abandoned all hope and entered,' said Vashti in an archly sorrowful voice. This time Lorna giggled, and I bit my lip, while shooting a look at the two brothers, faintly concerned on their behalf to hear their wives give way to such open regret at the lives they had chosen. For while a man railing at his fate might be thinking of a dozen different aspects of it, a woman at the same game must always be understood, essentially, to be despising her husband. In this case, though, I was wrong.

'Johnny and Irvine are from Ross-shire, of

course,' said Nicolette and waited. 'They're really Rosses on their mother's side,' she added and waited again.

'Ah,' I said, catching up at last. 'The Invergordon Rosses?'

'Exactly,' said Vashti. 'We had hoped we could all settle at Balnagowan, but the cousin who got her paws on it sold up and we were banished to walk the byways like a band of gypsies looking for a hedge to huddle under.'

'There was never the faintest hope of keeping the old pile,' said Johnny Howie suddenly, making the rest of us jump. 'I said that all along.'

'. . . as well have saved your breath,' said Irvine, saving as much of his as he could while still getting the words out at all. 'Women . . .' He did not trouble to finish the thought.

'We met our dear husbands while on a tour—a pilgrimage, almost—in the Highlands,' said Nicolette. 'Vash and I have always been simply fascinated by . . . history, I suppose you would call it.'

I nodded my understanding. In other words, they met their mates while on a shameless husband-hunt in a part of the world known for its old families and enormous castles. For 'history', I surmised, one could read 'pedigree' and it must have been a shock to the sisters to realise that they had attached themselves to a side-shoot of the illustrious Ross clan and one which could so easily be snapped off and sent packing.

'So we ended up here,' said Vashti flatly. 'We persuaded Irvine and Johnny to buy the place and we moved lock, stock and barrel.'

'Turfed out the dozier tenants and got the place

shipshape again,' said Johnny. 'Do you know there was no one at all managing the home farm? The neighbours had simply helped themselves to our fields and had their hay stacked up in our barns.'

'. . . nerve of them,' mumbled Irvine.

'Then we offloaded the creaking servants and sat back to enjoy the rest of our lives,' said Vashti. 'We must have been mad.'

I managed not to look around, not to glance at the windows where on this wintry morning no sunlight whatsoever penetrated the rather dusty, rippled old glass, but I could only agree.

'I can tire of country life at times too,' I said sympathetically, feeling myself warm to these kindred spirits a little.

'Hindsight is one of the cruellest curses,' said Vashti. 'How were we to know?'

'To know . . . ?' I prompted. Vashti gazed blankly at me for a while and then sniffed.

'Oh, just how much everything was going to change,' she said. 'Money, chiefly.'

'But it's not just money,' said Nicolette. 'You must know what we mean, Dandy. Nothing's the same as it was.' I did, of course, know exactly what they meant and while it was refreshing to hear it talked about in this way, for proud shabbiness is far more of a social minefield than plain old shabbiness any day, I felt a little impatience with them too, with the paraffin heaters, and the ennui. They should really . . . I caught myself short. My thoughts had just been turning towards a brisk walk in the fresh air and an order to the girl to wash the windows. Hugh has a great deal for which to answer.

'Now Lorna darling,' said Vashti, rousing herself

far enough to light another cigarette, 'tell us the news.' She waved her cigarettes in my direction and when I nodded lobbed her case to me over the low table.

'None of it is good news, I'm afraid,' said Lorna. 'I'm sorry to say that last night there was another attack. Mrs Gilver and Father were called in to help.'

'Blood-curdling scream,' said Nicolette with great relish. 'Tell all.'

'And then,' said Vashti, 'we'll tell you.'

'Tell *us*?' said Lorna. 'Tell us what?'

'No, no, no,' said Vashti. 'You first.'

'Well,' said Lorna, 'it's much the same tale as before. He did no real harm and she didn't recognise him. Just the same as always.'

'And was there a search?' said Nicolette. I was aware that some of the conversation had penetrated the newspapers again and the Howie men were listening in.

'She didn't want one,' I said. 'She didn't want anyone to know. In fact, she seemed very reluctant even to admit that it had taken place.'

'Who was it?' said Johnny Howie.

'Oh, yes of course,' Vashti chimed in. 'You must tell us who it was. Don't be bores and say it's a secret.'

'It was Mrs Hemingborough,' I said, then I caught my lip. I should have kept that to myself and not blurted it out to avoid being called a bore.

'And she's one who wants it kept quiet?' said Nicolette. 'Well, well, well. She never seemed an imaginative sort to me.'

'Before you think we've all gone mad, Dandy,' said Vashti, 'perhaps I should explain. There are

83

quite a few souls in the village and surrounding farms who don't quite believe in this dark stranger.'

'So I gather,' I said. 'But I wouldn't have said that Mrs Hemingborough didn't believe in him. Not exactly.'

'Let me put it another way,' said Vashti. 'There are those who believe that our dark stranger is not the sort of stranger who can be caught by the police and clapped in irons.'

'Vashti, really,' said Lorna. 'I'm surprised at you. Miss Lindsay and Miss McCallum are sure . . .'

'Oh yes,' said Nicolette. 'Miss Lindsay and Miss McCallum are perfectly sure. No nonsense about them. But, Lorna darling, we're not saying we think that. We're just passing it on.'

Lorna smiled uncertainly.

'You're such teases,' she said. 'I never know *what* you think.'

'Well,' said Vashti, 'our minds are made up now, Lorna, I can tell you that. Because . . .' She paused dramatically. '. . . last night, we saw him.'

The effect she produced was surely exactly what she was expecting: a stunned silence which lasted until Nicolette broke it.

'Speak for yourself, darling. I saw nothing. I was concentrating on the road.'

'All right then, I saw him,' said Vashti. 'Running across the field that goes around behind the manse. Just as we were driving down the lane. I was sure it was him. And now that you've told me about Mrs Hemingborough, I know I'm right. He was headed straight for her farm.'

*   *   *

I considered the story for a moment and I could see that it made sense. The timing was a little odd, mind you—Vashti and Nicolette had swept past us practically at the schoolyard gate, so if they had seen the stranger crossing the field a moment later and yet he had not set upon Mrs Hemingborough until she was almost home, he must have lain in wait for quite some time.

'Can you describe him?' I said, eager for more to add to young Jessie's rather sparse description.

Vashti hummed a little tune under her breath, clearly enjoying herself. Nicolette was still looking rather annoyed. One presumed that her sister had been attempting to convince her of this sighting since the moment it had happened, that Nicolette had been standing firm and saying 'Tush!', and that she was none too pleased to be proved wrong at last.

'Very hard to say,' said Vashti. 'He was extremely fast across the ground and he was in shadow most of the time, but my overall impression was one of . . . Oh Niccy, I do wish you had seen him too. I can't think how to describe it. He was . . .'

I could not help myself.

'Snaky?'

Lorna flinched and Nicolette and Vashti turned round eyes upon me.

'Now why on earth would you say that?' Vashti said.

I was thinking furiously. I could not claim that Mrs Hemingborough both denied his existence and described his appearance, and I could not in all conscience tell tales on Jessie Holland to this pair.

I did not doubt for a moment that Mrs Hemingborough would put the young family out of their cottage if it got back to her ears and the Howie ladies were quite clearly gossips of the first order.

'I was at my window,' I said. 'Upstairs in the manse.'

'You saw him?' said Vashti, looking thunderstruck. 'You actually saw him?'

I was aware of Lorna's troubled look at my side; she knew very well that I had been downstairs in the library when the knock came at the door.

'Why shouldn't Dandy see him too?' said Nicolette.

'And he struck you as snaky?' said Vashti, looking highly diverted. She repeated the word again softly to herself. 'Yes, you're right,' she said at last. 'That's exactly what he was. That's exactly the word I was looking for.'

*　　　*　　　*

'You must think me quite appalling,' I said to Lorna as we made our way back to the manse a little later. 'Cheerfully telling whopping fibs like that. Only I didn't want to drop poor Jessie Holland in it.' Lorna still looked far from happy. 'I know the Howies are friends of yours,' I went on, 'and so *you* might be sure that they wouldn't breathe a word, but I promised Jessie and there was no other way to explain how I hit on just the right way to describe him.'

'*Jessie* said he was snaky?' Lorna asked.

'She did.'

Lorna shuddered briefly. Then with a smile she

squeezed my arm.

'Please don't worry,' she said. 'I'm sure you did the right thing. After all, a promise is a promise and I'm not entirely blinded by affection. I do see that Nicolette and Vashti are . . .' She stopped; I waited and then we burst into peals of laughter.

'Oh, I shouldn't,' said Lorna eventually. 'They're so kind to me and such fun. And they've as much right to be at the Rural as anyone, even though Miss Lindsay and Miss McCallum would love to find a way to amend the constitution and keep them out. Miss McCallum has been in a terrible sulk since they started coming.'

'I rather wondered at that,' I said. 'They are hardly at home there.'

'They were drawn in by our American Night,' said Lorna. Seeing my look, she hastened to explain. 'It was Independence Day, you know, and we happened to have a clergyman from Wisconsin staying at the manse with his wife. It seemed like such a good idea . . .' She trailed off rather mournfully.

'What happened?' I asked her.

'Nothing!' declared Lorna. 'Absolutely nothing. And besides,' she added, rather detracting from the vehemence of her denial, 'Vashti and Nicolette are my dear friends. They're even giving a birthday party for me next month. Did my father tell you? Isn't that kind?'

'It is indeed,' I said. 'I can see why you're fond of them. They are very . . . open.'

In fact, of course, I was grateful to their openness since it had given me an interesting question to ponder: why in heaven's name should the neighbourhood split down the middle, as

Vashti Howie had suggested, on the question of whether the stranger was real?

'I must say,' I ventured at last, 'it's a monstrous piece of good fortune for this scoundrel, whoever he is, to pick out a playground for himself where so many people seem so peculiarly willing to turn a blind eye. You believe in him, don't you?'

Lorna hesitated.

'I don't quite know,' she said. 'I certainly don't believe that he's . . . I think either he's real or it's an absolute figment of everyone's imagination. I don't believe the other thing.' She was growing quite agitated as she spoke and I could guess why. She did not want to keep me in ignorance but she just simply could not spit it out. It was up to me to say it and then she would agree.

'You don't believe,' I said gently, 'that it's real but he's not? Is that what you mean?'

'Exactly,' said Lorna with enormous relief. 'I don't believe that for a second.'

'But why does anyone?' I said. 'I'm sure that if the same thing happened at Gilverton no one would even dream of such a thing. Why should Luckenlaw be any different? Why?'

Lorna was silent for a long time and we were almost back at the village before she spoke again.

'You'd better ask my father, Mrs Gilver. I'm sorry this has come up to spoil your visit and I hope, if you find out, that it won't stop you from coming back to the meeting next time but if you really do want to know, you had better ask my father. He can explain it all so much better than me.'

CHAPTER SIX

Accordingly, Lorna withdrew herself from the luncheon table as soon as she politely could, with talk of jelly-making and a young kitchen maid who could not be trusted to scald the jars.

'The crab-apple from last week is cloudy already,' she said, 'and we're starting this afternoon on the damsons.'

'Ah,' I said. 'Well, you must certainly hurry along then. Crab apples are one thing . . .' Actually I cared not a hoot for either the lowly crab apples or the precious damsons—one visit to the SWRI had not made quite so much of a mark as all that—but I recognised my cue.

'Dear Lorna,' said Mr Tait once the door had shut behind her. 'This is far from the life she thought would be hers but never a word of complaint.'

'She did mention something,' I murmured. 'But,' I went on heartily, 'she seems very happy as you say. Good friends all around her. I hear the Howies are giving a birthday party for her soon.' Mr Tait threatened to frown but managed not to.

'Indeed,' he said. 'You must make sure and come along.'

'Now, Mr Tait,' I said and I may even have sounded a little stern. I certainly felt a little stern. 'I have had a number of rather peculiar conversations this morning. The meeting with Mrs Hemingborough you know about already, but also at Luckenlaw House and again talking to Lorna I get the distinct feeling that there is rather more going on here than you told me.'

'My dear Mrs Gilver,' said Mr Tait. 'I assure you that I've told you all I know.' And yet there was a teasing quality in his voice which invited me to keep trying even as his words told me there was nothing to learn.

'Can you explain then,' I persisted, 'why it should be that everyone—no, not everyone; but some—are so ready to believe what seems to me quite unbelievable? That this dark stranger is not real.'

'But you knew that from the outset,' Mr Tait insisted. 'I told you.'

This was true but when we had discussed the matter in my sitting room that day, we had entertained two solutions to the trouble at Luckenlaw. Now, as Lorna had struggled to relate, there seemed to be a troubling third.

'It's more than that,' I said. 'I don't mean that the women are imagining a man, or making a man up out of mischief. I'm referring to the idea—and the Howies talked about it quite matter-of-factly; even Lorna concedes it—that this dark stranger is . . . very much of the darkness and rather more than strange?'

'Is that what they're saying?' said Mr Tait. 'I see.'

'Yes, but why?' I demanded, my voice rising. '*Why* do you see? I don't. And *what* do you see?'

'It's all nonsense of course,' he said, 'but it's the kind of nonsense that can easily take root even in the most ordinary of places. I assure you, Mrs Gilver, that Gilverton would succumb just as easily under similar trials.' I must have looked sceptical. 'We were speaking of much the same

90

thing this morning—the chamber of the Lucken Law.' He folded his napkin, patted his mouth firmly with it and sat back in his chair. 'You would scarcely credit the panic when it was opened.'

'It was opened?' I said, my eyes wide.

'Yes, just after the war,' he said. 'With all the interest in archaeology and all those eager pilots looking for excuses to stay in their cockpits, anywhere with an interesting name and a whiff of a past got used to the sight of a rickety little contraption overhead and someone hanging out of the side with a camera, and as soon as someone had taken a look at the place from up there they found the entrance. That much was to be expected.

'Now, however, we move into the realms of pure fantasy—a mixture of pharaoh's curse, an understandable confusion about the name of the place, and . . . human nature, I daresay.' He had the air of regret one might expect in a minister who sees so much of it. 'When the news broke that the archaeologists were coming, decent God-fearing folk started barring their doors and demanding blessings and goodness knows what else. I had to preach on it more than once, and even in the kirk pews I saw a few stubborn looks thrown back at me.'

I could imagine. I have long thought that Hindustanis with their endless gods would feel quite at home in Scotland with the blasphemous jumble of saints, fairies, charms and omens which seemed to trouble neither priest nor congregation ever a jot.

'You see then, Mrs Gilver,' he said, 'it is not really a surprise to find that a faction of my parishioners is willing to whip up a ghoulish

91

fantasy about the next thing to come along. Willing to believe, that is, that our dark stranger is not of this world.'

'I still think it's very odd,' I insisted, 'but it might play into our hands. You see, if everyone half believes the dark stranger is some kind of phantom they might well ignore any clue that doesn't fit. They will have been very interested in his snakiness and his ability to fly over walls and not at all concerned, for instance, with such mundane facts as where he flew from or what kind of boots he had on. Do you see?'

Mr Tait nodded.

'That makes a good deal of sense, Mrs Gilver,' he said. 'A rationalist, I see.'

'In this instance, I better had be, don't you think?' I countered, although one would not care to be accused of anything quite so cold as rationalism in the general way of things 'So,' I concluded, 'leaving aside the exasperating Mrs Hemingborough, I have the three girls from the spring to talk to and then the farmer's wife from the summer.'

Mr Tait screwed up his eyes in concentration and began to count them off on his fingers.

'Elspeth McConechie, the Palmers' dairy maid, was the first,' he said. 'You'll find her at work this afternoon at the Palmers' place: Easter Luckenlaw Farm. Then Annie Pellow. A Largo lass. She works in the kitchen at the Auld Inn in Colinsburgh but she lodges here with Mrs Kinnaird. The house on the green nearest the pillar-box. And the third one was Molly . . . I forget her surname . . . but she's up at Luck House. Maid of all work, near enough.'

'Luckenlaw House, do you mean?' I said. 'In

that case I think I saw her this morning.'

'You would have,' said Mr Tait. 'There's just her most days now. Heaven knows how they run the place. There were a dozen indoor servants before the war.'

'And then nobody for two months and then the farmer's wife?' I prompted. 'Mrs . . . ?'

'Young Mrs Fraser,' said Mr Tait. 'From Balniel Farm down to the main road. She came straight to me, frightened out of her wits. I don't think you'll have any trouble getting her to tell you all about it.'

'And then just one month of peace before Mrs Hemingborough,' I finished up. 'Bafflingly *not* frightened out of her wits by it and very unlikely ever to give me the time of day again, I'm afraid.' Mr Tait said nothing. 'I even wondered if she knew who it was and didn't want to drop him in it.' Mr Tait was silent once more. 'Or perhaps Jessie Holland was not telling the truth after all. Perhaps Mrs Hemingborough stumbled and dropped her bundle and Jessie's imagination supplied the rest. Except, of course, Vashti Howie's sighting certainly does back Jessie up. Oh, bother it,' I said, rising from the table and smacking down my napkin. 'I refuse to be fuddled by this. I shall put Mrs Hemingborough and her mysteries out of my mind in hopes that when I get to the answer it will shed light on her extraordinary behaviour too.' Mr Tait did not look at all convinced by my sudden optimism and I could hardly fault him for that but in truth I really was buoyed up by the prospect before me. If only I could keep my thoughts firmly on the facts and put aside all the nonsense I should surely prevail. I would start at Easter Luckenlaw Farm, where Elspeth would be in the dairy; I would take in the refreshingly normal Mrs Fraser and then hope to catch Mrs Kinnaird's lodger in the pub kitchen at Colinsburgh. I did not see quite how I might organise a trip to Luckenlaw House to talk to the Howies' maid but I had more than enough for one afternoon already and I had promised Hugh to be home for a late dinner, so she would have to keep.

I opened the front door of the manse moments later to let myself out—all hands appeared to be on deck in the kitchen safeguarding the clarity of the jelly—and was confronted by a face. I stepped back sharply and then stayed back, for this face was not only unexpected but, even after a second and a third look at it, extremely unnerving. It was a thin, white face, indifferently shaved, and boasting a pair of narrow eyes and a lantern jaw, grimly set under pursed lips. It sat above a high-buttoned and rather rusty black suit and below an equally rusty black bowler hat worn so far down on the bony skull beneath it that it must surely have been crammed on in a moment of violent rage, in lieu, perhaps, of throwing something through a window.

The jaw unclenched.

'I'm here tae see the meenister,' said an accusing voice. 'I've something to say.'

With that the man stalked past me, rather insultingly careful to make sure his garments brushed against none of mine, and made for the study. He clearly knew Mr Tait's habits, and was sure where to find him.

I hesitated before following; after all, parishioners must visit all the time—that must be amongst the heaviest of a priest's burdens—and so this individual could be here about anything at all, but surely such an air of offended outrage could not spring from an everyday matter and it was not too fanciful to imagine that *his* business with Mr Tait might also be mine. Perhaps, although he did not look like a farmer in his black suit, this was Mr Hemingborough come with information. Perhaps—as I had the thought I broke into a trot— he had come with a confession. I sidled into the study just in time to see Mr Tait lay down his book and fold away his spectacles with a patient air, although with his customary sunny expression somewhat dimmed.

'And whae's this?' said the man, turning to look at me from the perch he had taken up in a chair opposite the desk.

'This is Mr Black, Mrs Gilver,' said Mr Tait, very properly ignoring the query and presenting the man to me. 'One of my parishioners. This is Mrs Gilver, from Gilverton in Perthshire, Dick, she's my guest here.' He did not carry on and say that he would thank Dick Black to keep a civil tongue in his head, but I understood it and gave him a grateful smile.

'Aye, I ken all about you,' said Mr Black. 'You'd be as well to hear this too.'

Thus given permission to stay, I subsided meekly into a chair and waited.

'I tried again last nicht, Mr Tait,' said Mr Black. 'While those Jezebels were carousing and cavorting in that schoolhouse, I tried again and again I failed. You have to take a stand, now, before the very pit opens under our feet and swallows us all.'

'Mr Black is no fan of the Rural, Mrs Gilver,' said Mr Tait with breathtaking understatement.

95

'He always drops in the day after the meetings. It's getting to be quite a tradition.'

'I can assure you, Mr Black,' I said, 'there was no cavorting and carousing last evening. I was there myself.'

'I ken you were,' he said. 'I heard you. The lot of you . . . chanting!'

'We did recite a little poetry,' I said. 'Did we disturb you? I shouldn't have thought it was loud enough to carry to another house.' Mr Tait was sitting back, enormously entertained it appeared to me.

'I was ootside in the lane,' said Mr Black. 'I heard it as plain as day. Chanting.'

'You were outside?' I said, my interest aroused.

'On my mission,' he announced, startlingly. 'As how I wouldna have to if them as should *would*.' With that he turned away from me and addressed Mr Tait once more. 'I went as far as the Frasers' last nicht. I thocht he'd be sure to give me his ear what with his wife seein' the licht, and him stayin' at his own fireside since she did, even if he was as bad as the rest for wanderin' beforetimes. And he should ken to listen to his elders and betters, but do you know what he said to me?'

'I cannot imagine,' said Mr Tait.

'He said, "He that is without sin among you, let him first cast a stone."'

'Well, Dick,' said Mr Tait, 'you can hardly expect me to disagree with that.'

'Not one sorry soul did I bring back to the richt way o' thinkin' last nicht,' Mr Black went on. 'For most o' them were nowhere to be found, Mr Tait. The men as bad as their wives, everybody oot in the nicht, givin' the devil an easy job tae find

96

them.' Mr Tait was trying to interrupt the flow, but Mr Black spoke all the louder and drowned him out. 'Right roond the lanes and not a soul could I raise,' he said. 'Logan McAdam, Drew Torrance, Jim Hemingborough, Bob—'

'It's no crime, Dick,' said Mr Tait. 'When the cat's away, you know.'

'All the husbands were out?' I said.

'Aye, a corpse rots fae the heid doon,' said Mr Black. 'What can we expect o' a pack o' women if their men are lost to sin?'

'Come now,' said Mr Tait, hoisting a smile out of his seemingly bottomless store of goodwill. 'Lost to sin? Lost, perhaps, to a quiet game of cards or a glass of ale but no more.'

This, I concluded, was pure mischief and right enough Mr Black's white face began to change to a mottled purple and he struggled with himself in silence for quite some time before he spoke again.

'And what can we expect fae the common fowk when their meenister and their masters see Satan comin' and jist wink at him?'

'What masters are these?' said Mr Tait.

'They feckless eejits up by Luck Hoose,' said Mr Black. 'Sodom and Gomorrah on our very doorstep, Mr Tait. I saw it with my ain eyes last nicht.'

'You went up to Luck House?' said Mr Tait. 'You should know better than that, Dick. You've overstepped yourself there.'

'Steeped in it,' said Mr Black. 'Soaked in whisky, the pair o' them. I wasted my time even tryin'. And I see I'm wastin' more of it here today.' He stood up and glared down at Mr Tait.

'You are that, Dick,' said the Reverend. 'That

you are.'

Cramming his bowler back onto his head as tightly as before, Dick Black stalked from the room without a goodbye and without so much as a glance in my direction.

'I'm sorry you had to witness that, Mrs Gilver,' said Mr Tait, when he had gone. 'Our Bible tells us that "whom the Lord loveth He correcteth" but He hasn't worked His way round to Dick Black yet as far as I can see.'

'Oh, I don't know,' I said. 'It was rather useful. I've learned—if Mr Black can be believed—that the Howie brothers are in the clear, as is Mr Fraser, although I suppose we knew that, since Mrs Fraser has "seen the licht" and given up the meetings and her husband could hardly be out without her knowing. But, it seems, other husbands have no alibis for yesterday evening and countless other evenings too. And of course, I've learned that Mr Black himself is wont to prowl around on Rural nights.'

'Oh come! Mrs Gilver!' said Mr Tait.

'Well, I'm sorry,' I said, 'I know he's one of your flock but you can't deny that he's . . . peculiar enough.'

'He's not peculiar at all,' said Mr Tait. 'He's all too common, him and the likes of him. And anyway, Dick Black was born in Luckenlaw and lived here all his days. If he was the stranger, he wouldn't *be* a stranger, would he?'

I had to admit that there was a great deal of sense in this, but still I determined to mention his name to the victims.

*　　　*　　　*

98

To the victims, I now turned my thoughts once more. I said goodbye and, with no more encounters on my way, I left the village and strode out along the farm lane, a pad of writing paper and a pencil clutched in my hand, all practicality and purpose, all thoughts of secret chambers and snaky strangers far from my mind. The going was not nearly as dirty as Lorna had feared and the view was, if anything, better: a long sweep of flat fields all the way to the coast where the Forth lay glinting like a bolt of grey silk held in place by the great stud of the Bass Rock. Or was that the Isle of May I could see? Before I had decided I found myself past the Hemingboroughs' place and turning away from the sea, around the bottom of the hill, to Easter Luckenlaw Farm beyond.

It was an agreeable spot. The square, grey farmhouse faced to the south with its long garden laid out before it and the yard and buildings, as was usual, tucked away behind out of sight. In the sunshine this afternoon, the drying green and vegetable patch inside the garden wall were a feast of cheerful ordinariness to my eyes and I thought I recognised from the Rural meeting of the evening before the woman who was busy at the washing-line, pressing the clothes against her lips to see if they were drying. I stopped and watched her for a while, hoping for her to notice me and let me strike up conversation in an unobtrusive way, but she was intent on her task, working her way along, smoothing, stretching and repegging the succession of petticoats, winter camisoles and knickers, woollen stockings and jerseys, all in strict order on the line. When she was finished, she turned to seize a stretching pole and spotted me at last. She nodded politely.

'I hope the wind picks up for you,' I said.

'I doubt it will,' she called back. 'And the sun'll be ahint the law soon enough.' She gestured and following her pointing finger I could see she was right. The outline of the hill was already dazzling a little and it would not be long before the afternoon, here at least, was over.

'I was at Mrs Hemingborough's this morning,' I called to her. 'She has a contraption in her kitchen and she was ironing already.'

'Aye well, she's the lucky one,' Mrs Palmer said, coming down the garden. She was a red-complexioned woman in her thirties, plain and rather severe in her dark dress and apron with her hair pinned tightly off her face, but there was a sturdy charm about the way she strode towards me and her face was frank and friendly-seeming. 'Jimmy cannot stand wet cloots about his ears in his kitchen,' she said. 'I've seen it Thursday before it's all pressed and away again wintertimes. But there, it's best out here getting a blow about, isn't it?' We both looked at the washing, hanging straight down with not a wisp of a breeze to move it, and laughed.

'It's Mrs Gilver, is it not?' Mrs Palmer said. 'You're a friend of the Howies?'

'No!' I blurted out, far too decisively for politeness. 'A friend of the Taits.' Mrs Palmer smiled broadly at me.

'And so what can I do for you?' she said, suggesting that any friend of the Taits was a friend of hers.

'Well, yes, you can help me actually, as a matter

100

of fact,' I said, and cleared my throat. I was rather proud of my little plan and had further refined it while walking here, but as always when the moment came my heart was in my mouth. 'As you know, I'm talking at the Rural next month on household budgets and rather than just spout on I thought it would be a splendid idea to find out what would be most useful to you. I mean, not just to you, you understand, but to everyone.'

Mrs Palmer was blinking at me, her mind clearly an absolute blank as I am sure mine would have been if someone had asked the same of me.

'I don't mean to put you on the spot,' I assured her. 'The idea was to come back in a few days perhaps and see what you've come up with. If anything. If you care to.' I began, as I so often do, to babble. 'I mean to say, things have been very different recently for all of us. Why even the ladies at Luckenlaw House were saying as much this morning. And farming, gosh. Farming is never the most . . . My husband farms and so I know.'

'Well, as to the farm,' said Mrs Palmer, 'we've been lucky. I tell Jimmy that, time and again. There's no need to go fussing and fretting. We're fine as we are.' I thought I could discern a kindred spirit here, for clearly 'Jimmy' was another Hugh and how I wished I could prevail upon *him* to stop 'fussing and fretting' about *his* farms.

'And we should count wur blessings,' Mrs Palmer went on. 'The Hemingboroughs have had a terrible time with the blight down at Hinter Luck these last few years and I cannot begin to tell you the troubles over at the McAdams'. Some long fancy name for it, but fifty good cows dead and gone for dog meat was the upshot. And then there's the kind of troubles, there's just no name for.' On that cryptic note she stopped at last, with a shudder.

'It was more the household side of things really,' I said hastily. That was bad enough, but I could not have worked sick cattle and blight into my address if my life depended on doing so.

'If anything,' Mrs Palmer said, 'off the top of my head . . .'

'Yes?' I prompted, with real eagerness. For not only was this exercise in reconnaissance my cover story but also there was, actually, the talk. I had a month, it was true, but already every time I let my imagination stray towards it my mouth went dry.

'I mean to say if it was my man you were asking . . .' said Mrs Palmer, 'but I'm not sure if that's the kind of thing you mean . . .'

'I'm open to any ideas at all,' I assured her.

'Well, what I really wish I knew more about,' she said, 'is insurance.'

'Insurance?'

'Jimmy's forever pestering me about it. I say to him we should trust to Providence, but then I see folk all about struggling away, like you said, Mrs Gilver, and I just wonder. Our well went dry, you know. A few years ago now but it was a terrible thing when it happened. It was summertime and there was beasts in the fields to be watered and crops in the ground and we'd to give a fortune over to the spaeman to find us another one, not to mention Jimmy and the men taking so much time off to howk it we had to hire an extra man to do the farm work. Then blow me if the same thing didn't happen again with the new well that winter. Or at least, it went sour. If we couldn't have

102

collected the rainwater we'd never have got through. So what I would really like to know is if there's insurance for that? Water insurance. Would you know anything about that? For trouble aye comes in threes and the next time could break us.'

'Water insurance?' I echoed limply.

'All insurance really, I suppose,' said Mrs Palmer. 'Jimmy's just as keen on life insurance, if you would credit it, but there I have put my foot down, for it's just not right. Mind you, goodness only knows how we would manage if anything happened to him, with all my girls still at the school. And I do worry about the house after that fire over by Wester Luck. You won't have heard about that, Mrs Gilver, not belonging Luckenlaw, but it was a dreadful thing. The house was left a shell and half the buildings too, and I worry, even though I know it's wicked of me.' She stopped at long, long last and gave me a brave smile that I managed to meet with some sort of sickly stretching of my own lips.

'That's my Jimmy's question for you,' she said. 'Does it make sense to spend the money every month or not? And my question would be'—she broke off and looked searchingly at me for a moment—'is it right? Should we even try to outwit our fate thon way?'

'I'll—I'll do my very best to answer you,' I said, and I think she believed me. In truth, I was reeling. 'What I can say right now, is that it's not wicked of you to worry about it. Far from it—it's natural.'

'I'm not so sure,' she said. 'We should maybe just take trouble when it comes and let it run its course. What's for us will never go by us, especially if we've brought it upon ourselves, mind.'

103

Suddenly, I was sure I knew what she meant but I hesitated about how to broach it. 'Mr Tait told me about the troubles,' I started gently. 'But I have to admit to feeling a little sceptical. I don't quite see how unlocking a chamber could cause blight. Or start a fire either.'

'Well, of course it couldn't,' said Mrs Palmer, looking at me as if I had sprouted feathers. 'Did Mr Tait tell you that?'

I shook my head and, chastened, tried to marshal some of my departed dignity.

'Now Mrs Palmer, is there anyone else about the place I should speak to? In the spirit of the Rural I want to be sure and talk to everyone, not just the lady of the house.'

'No, just me,' she said. 'My daughters are still girls, a long way from a woman's cares, I'm glad to say.'

'Really?' I persisted. 'I'm sure Lorna Tait mentioned a dairy maid when I said I was coming round here. Elspeth, was it?'

At this, Mrs Palmer's expression grew rather fixed and she put her head back and looked at me from under her lids.

'Elspeth is our dairy maid,' she said, 'but she's not in the Rural. She went a couple of times but she didn't stick at it.'

'How strange,' I said, affecting innocence and wondering whether Mrs Palmer would tell me the reason for Elspeth's departure. She did not. 'It was all tremendous fun last night. I think,' I went on, 'I think I'll just pop in and have a word with her anyway, Mrs Palmer. One never knows, perhaps if I ask her what she would like to hear included in my talk next month, I might be able to entice her back.' I began to make my way to the mouth of the drive which ran up the side of the garden and disappeared around to the yard. I was pretty sure I should be able to find the dairy without much trouble: farmyards are much the same throughout the land.

'But Elspeth doesn't run a household,' Mrs Palmer persisted, trotting up the garden on the other side of the wall from me. 'She doesn't need to know about budgets.'

'She'll have to learn one day,' I said, still marching very purposefully onwards, 'if she marries and gets a house of her own, and I think it will be most interesting to hear what concerns her most about the prospect, don't you?' At that moment we reached the spot where the garden wall turned the corner and joined to the side of the house, the usual fierce separation of the agricultural from the domestic realm which was designed, I suppose, to keep the sheep out of the flowerbeds but which served an equally useful purpose to me now. Short of clambering over to join me in the lane, Mrs Palmer had no choice but to rush into the house at the front and out again at the back in an attempt to meet me.

I was too quick for her. I sped around the corner into the yard, hopping and leaping over the inevitable deposits underfoot, and made a beeline for the whitewashed building with fly-mesh over the windows and ventilation flaps high up in the walls, which I surmised must be the dairy house. I was right and, slipping inside, I found myself in a dim, cool room where a girl in a capacious apron and with a cap pinned over her hair stood on a slatted board bending intently over an enormous bowl. She glanced over her shoulder on hearing me then, slightly surprised I expect to find me a stranger, she put down the ladle she was holding and turned around wiping her hands.

'Elspeth?'

'Madam?'

She was a pretty little thing, very much in the style of storybook dairy maids, with her pink cheeks and her yellow curls peeping out from under her cap, and although she must work hard here at her butter churn and her cheese moulds there was as yet nothing of Mrs Palmer's brawny competence about her arms and her soft little hands. A spike of anger stabbed me to think of some beastly lout frightening her in the dark and my resolve was strengthened. Before I could even begin to tiptoe my way towards the questions I must ask her, however, I heard Mrs Palmer's boots clattering over the cobbles of the yard towards us.

'I'm not going to take up much of your time,' I managed to get out before she reached us. 'I know you're a busy girl.'

'And dairy work cannot be kept waiting,' said Mrs Palmer behind me, panting rather. 'You've still the butter to finish, mind, Elspeth.'

'Of course,' I said. 'Elspeth, do carry on. I shan't mind talking to your back under the circumstances. Not at all.' Elspeth glanced uncertainly between her employer and me and then turned her back and plied her ladle once more. I repeated my spiel in as unconcerned a voice as I could muster, while Mrs Palmer hovered at my elbow, saying nothing.

'I dinna go to the Rural, madam,' said Elspeth when I was finished. 'Not any more.' She was holding the ladle over a dish, letting the skimmed cream drop from it in soft dollops.

'So I hear,' I said. 'But I'd hoped you might come back if I promised to address your questions in my talk, you know.'

'No, thank you, madam,' Elspeth replied. 'I canna see me goin' back again.' She scraped the last of the cream off her ladle with a wooden spoon and turned back to the bowl.

'Don't upset yourself,' said Mrs Palmer. Then to me: 'I'll not have her vexed.' It is, I suppose, very commendable in any employer to be concerned with her servant's peace of mind and, if I could have been sure that was all that lay behind Mrs Palmer's sprint up the garden and her anxious hovering now, I should have been absolutely on her side. But had young Elspeth been in need of such solicitousness—had she still been, after all these months, quite as fragile as all that—she would surely not have held such a steady hand above the cream dish, nor looked around so calmly at the sound of my approach. I knew from my nursing days that anyone still wobbly from shock would have jumped a foot in the air at my sudden entrance into their quiet room.

'I can't imagine what you're referring to, Mrs Palmer,' I said. 'I don't intend to ask anything that could possibly cause upset. What on earth do you mean?'

'I stopped goin' to the Rural,' said Elspeth.

'You don't have to say anything,' said Mrs Palmer. 'You don't have to speak to anyone about it ever again.'

'I seem to have stumbled into something I shouldn't have,' I said. 'I do apologise, Elspeth.'

'That's all right, madam,' she said. 'I dinna mind

107

tellin' you.'

'Least said, soonest mended,' said Mrs Palmer, a philosophy for which I have never had much time, unless by 'mended' one means 'well-hidden but causing a nasty atmosphere for evermore', but one which they go in for in quite a big way in Perthshire, and I imagined here in Fife too.

'I was . . . I was . . .' said Elspeth, turning round to face us again and folding her arms firmly across her chest. 'Common assault, the policeman ca'ed it. And they nivver caught the man, if it was a man, and half the folk in the village think I made it up.'

'Why would anyone think that?' I said. 'How horrid for you.'

'It was,' said Elspeth. 'It is.' She was far too well-trained a servant and I daresay too sweet a girl actually to glare at Mrs Palmer, but in her studious refusal even to look at the woman she got her point across.

'Oh . . . do what you will,' said Mrs Palmer, sounding as though she meant anything but, and she took herself back across the yard, leaving us. I heard the kitchen door slam shut.

'Well,' I said, in the camaraderie which always ensues when one of a trio sweeps off in a huff and leaves two calmer souls behind. 'I take it Mrs Palmer is one of the ones who thinks you're telling stories, Elspeth.'

'I do not ken, madam,' said Elspeth. 'And that's a fact. I sometimes canna make head nor tail of *what* she thinks.' I took the chance to sit myself down unobtrusively on a wooden chair just beside the door, hoping that the girl would speak unbidden if I wore a sympathetic look and said nothing.

Perhaps, though, loquacity is not essential to the dairy maid's art; Elspeth merely turned her back with a sigh and left me with all the work to do.

'When you say assaulted . . .' I began.

'He rushed up ahint me, madam,' she said. 'Pushed me over—I put the knees oot o' my good stockings and it was the first time I had had them on—pulled my hair so hard that some of it came oot. I thocht—I thocht—'

'Well, you would,' I said. 'I should if it were me. They never caught him?'

'They nivver did.'

'And you have no idea yourself?'

'None,' she said firmly, unrolling a straw mat over the big bowl of milk and pushing it to the back of the table. It hit the stone wall with a clunk. 'I didna recognise him and I couldna tell you now who he was or what he was, for I've thocht it all roond and roond until I'm birlin' with it.'

'But your first instinct—that night, I mean—was that he was just an ordinary man?' I was determined to keep the facts firmly in hand. She nodded. 'And if you didn't recognise him you must have got a good look at him?' I said, my heart leaping at this cheering thought.

'No,' she said slowly. She had put the dish of cream away on a dim shelf at the back of the room and now she turned and spoke to me directly, wiping her hands and appearing to be casting her mind back. 'He come up ahint me and then like I said he flitted off again afore I had richted myself. But he was nobody I kent. I've never met anybody anything like that, not roond here, nor anywhere else.'

'It couldn't have been . . .' My nerve crumbled. I

109

could not name blameless men I had never even met, not on Mr Black's say-so. I could not even, as it turned out, name Mr Black. 'There's no one you even suspect?'

'I kept a sharp eye oot, at the kirk, and roond the village, and I would have kent right away if he had appeart again,' she said. 'There was . . .'

'Yes?'

'Folk kept sayin' . . .'

'What?'

'Well, John Christie up by there has no' been around that very long and he's no' that well kent, but it wasna him, no matter whae whispers his name.'

'You sound very certain,' I said.

She had finished wiping her hands and now she laid them flat on the table, leaning towards me, remembering. 'He was the richt height and all that. And John Christie's a young laddie, fit for scaling' dykes, to be sure. But the one that come at me that nicht was different. He was . . . how wid you say it?' I bit my lip to keep from prompting her. 'He was . . . sort of . . .' She gave up. 'It's no' even like he was big,' she said. 'If I'd seen him first I could mebbes have pushed him off me or ducked and run. I'm wee, but I'm strong and I'm fast on my feet when I have to be.'

'When someone jumps out at you, he always has the advantage, Elspeth,' I said. 'You cannot berate yourself for being surprised.'

'It wasna like that, though,' she said. 'He didna jump oot. He came doon the lane, I'm sure o' it. Doon to meet me. At first I thocht it was maybe an owl's wings I could hear, and then I thocht a deer was runnin' in the field and I stopped to look for it.

110

So I was keekin' over the dyke when he landed on me.'

'An owl?' I said. 'A deer? He must be remarkably light on his feet for you to think that.'

'I suppose so,' said Elspeth. 'I never thocht before but I suppose he must be.'

'Did you mention it to the police?' I ventured, but at that Elspeth seemed to come out of the trance of memory which had engulfed her. She sniffed decisively and seized a large jar which had been upended over the sink, dripping, then she shook it until a heap of new butter fell out onto the table with a flat slap.

'I did, madam,' she said. 'And they jist laughed. I wouldna send for the police again to save my life or theirs.'

'And once again, I have to agree with you,' I told her. 'It must have been absolutely infuriating.'

'Aye well,' said Elspeth. 'Let them as got knocked over and their hair pulled oot by the roots say it's all tattle, that's all.'

I believed her, but just to make sure, I thought I would try a little experiment. I thought I would ask her a question she could not possibly be expecting and see if she blurted something out—always a mark of honesty—or if she took time and made something up, the way that honest people never need to do.

'If you fell over and didn't manage to push him off you,' I said, 'he must have been pretty close.' I paused, then spoke sharply. 'What did he smell of, Elspeth?' The answer came back without a moment's pause.

'Eggs,' she said. We both blinked.

'On his breath?' I asked her. 'As though he had

been eating them?'

'No,' said Elspeth, looking so startled at what had come out of her mouth that I was convinced she was telling me the plain unvarnished truth. 'I mean, yes. I mean, it must have been, must it no'? How else could someone smell o' eggs, after all?'

CHAPTER SEVEN

On my way to Mrs Fraser at Balniel, I was aware of a lessening of enthusiasm for the encounter, a dread of hearing about any more horridness. Mrs Fraser, however, proved to be just what I needed. Working on the principles of those German doctors who treat like, rather perversely I have aways considered, with like (while watering down their ingredients like an unscrupulous butler eking out the gin) Mrs Fraser's whole-hearted embrace of the most fanciful elements of the dark stranger had me retreating determinedly into a conviction that he was no more than a farm labourer with an unfortunate kink. We went through the preliminaries: what aspect of household budgeting would interest her most? She had joined the Rural at first, with her husband's blessing, almost at her husband's urging, but she did not go now. Heavy emphasis on the 'now' and a significant look practically commanded me to ask why not and the floodgates opened.

'Well, Mrs Gilver,' she said, glancing over first one shoulder and then the other, although we were quite alone in her kitchen and all the doors were firmly closed, 'I'll just have time to tell you before the men get in for their piece. I had a verra Distressing Experience'—the capital letters were clearly audible—'after the August meeting. On my road home, out there in my own lane that I've walked up and down, morning, noon and night, woman, girl and bairn, for I was born in Luckenlaw and lived there all my life until Eck brought me here last year. Aye, right there on that lane where I have walked in rain, hail, sleet and snow'—this last was Fifish for 'come rain or come shine'; I had heard the expression before—'I was visited by evil.'

'Golly,' I murmured, since she had left a pause to be filled.

'Black as the night he was, fleet as the wind. I saw him coming for me over the field—'

'Which field was that?' I interjected, sensing that Mrs Fraser would not be thrown off her course by any number of interrupting questions.

'The lang howe,' she said. 'West of the village road.' I made a mental note and as I had expected, she took a deep breath and plunged on. 'Saw him coming, flying over the ground, but could I move? Could I never. I was Transfixed'—she drew nearer and dropped her voice—'and Ravaged.' She drew back again the better to view the effect she caused in me.

'Heavens,' I supplied and she nodded gravely.

'Ravaged,' she said. 'He streamed over the dyke and just *lunged* at me. Knocked me clean off my feet, pinching at me, plucking at me, all the time breathing his hot breath on me.'

'Did you scream?' I asked. She looked as though she could put up a pretty fair bellow if she tried.

'He had his hand over my mouth,' she told me. 'A grip like iron it was too.'

113

'So what did you do?'

'I prayed,' she said. 'And he heard me.'

'He heard you praying?' I echoed. 'What did he do then?'

'No,' said Mrs Fraser. 'I mean, He heard me and He answered my prayers.' I must have looked sceptical, for she hurried to assure me. 'I cannot explain it any other way,' she said. 'For as soon as it had started it stopped again. Up he got and off he swooped, back over the dyke into the field. I just thank the Lord I have always lived a good life and asked for nothing until that moment. Aye, He heard my prayers.'

I should have been happier to have some other, rather more mundane, way to account for the abrupt end to the ravagement, but I thought it most politic to say nothing. Instead I decided to attack on another flank.

'I don't suppose that you recognised him, did you?' I began. 'I mean, I know that had you recognised him at the time you would have said something, but thinking it over since, have you ever thought of who it might be?'

'Certainly, I recognised him,' said Mrs Fraser.

'John Christie?' I said, before I could help it.

'Oh, yes,' said Mrs Fraser. 'His name's been all around the place. He's an incomer. Lives up there on his own and by all accounts he's a bit of a queer one, although his notions are no more daft than many I've heard from old enough to know better. He's a tenant of those Howies, you know, and they're not liked. Oh yes, it would have suited some folk down to the ground to blame Jockie Christie.'

'But it wasn't him?' I guessed.

114

'It was not,' she said stoutly. 'I knew right away who it was and I went straight to Mr Tait at the manse to tell him. I'm surprised, if ye're staying there, that Mr Tait hasn't told you.' As was I.

'And?' I prompted. 'Who was the man? Who was this dark stranger?'

'Oh, it was no stranger,' said Mrs Fraser. 'It was Himself.'

I ran quickly through the possibilities that this extraordinary statement seemed to offer. She could not mean that it was Mr Tait himself; anyone less snaky could hardly be imagined. Nor could she possibly be hinting that it was a visitation from God or one of His angels. For one thing, He would hardly swoop over dykes and knock people down, and for another, visions of God were far too theatrical for the likes of Mrs Fraser. No, there was only one being by whom a self-respecting Fife housewife would submit to being bothered on a dark night.

'Ah,' I said.

'Aye,' said Mrs Fraser. 'He doesn't ayeways come on cloven hooves.'

'Indeed,' I said. 'Well, I'm not surprised that you opted for Mr Tait then, in preference to the police.'

'You'd think,' said Mrs Fraser with some asperity. 'Him being a minister o' the kirk. But he's all for it.'

Again, I forced myself to stay within the bounds of reason. She could not possibly mean what her words implied. I took a guess.

'All for the Rural?' I said. 'All for the gallivanting which opened the door to . . . it?'

'Aye, there's that for sure,' said Mrs Fraser. 'The

115

devil watches, waits and picks his time, right enough. But it's not that I was meaning. Mr Tait does not believe in keeping out of evil's way. He invites evil in. Mr Tait has unleashed the beast.'

'He's done wh . . .' I began.

'And given it succour,' said Mrs Fraser.

I took my leave rather hurriedly after that, as might well be imagined, but on my way out of the door I did steel myself enough to ask one question.

'Please don't think me prurient, Mrs Fraser,' I said, 'but is it true what they always say? What did this beast with his hot breath and his hand clamped over your mouth . . . What did he smell of? Can you remember?'

Mrs Fraser lifted her chin in the air as though sniffing at the memory.

'Beer?' she ventured, but she shook her head and tried again. 'No, not beer. But definitely yeast.'

'Yeast?' I had been ready for eggs, of course.

'Yeast,' she said again.

*   *   *

What did she mean? I asked myself as I retraced my path back to the village. Mr Tait unleashed the beast? What *could* she possibly mean? I marched straight back to the manse to ask him.

'Yes,' said Mr Tait, removing his spectacles and rubbing the bridge of his nose. I was perched on the hard chair in front of his desk where Mr Black had been but, unlike Mr Black, I was beginning to feel my self-righteous indignation seeping away. 'Mrs Fraser no longer believes that I am a right-thinking man, you see. And so she imagines I am quite happy to see my parishioners being ravaged

116

by evil spirits in the night.'

I was speechless.

'It was most unfortunate,' Mr Tait went on. 'Nothing to do with our current troubles of course. This was years ago. When the archaeologists came.'

'To open the chamber?' I said. 'This chamber certainly does keep popping up, doesn't it?'

'Nice chaps,' Mr Tait said, ignoring me. 'Two of them lodged here with us. Well anyway, they found a body.'

'In a burial chamber?' I asked drily, expecting another of Mr Tait's teases.

'Oh certainly,' he said. 'There were numerous cists in there and a sort of sarcophagus in pride of place too. But as well as those there was a body. Unembalmed and unsheltered, just lying on the floor.'

'Heavens,' I said. 'Who was it?'

'All that they could say was that it was the body of a young girl who had died by violent means.'

'A murder victim?'

'Just so.'

'But how long had she been there?' I said. 'I thought you said the chamber was sealed.'

'Oh it was, it was,' said Mr Tait. 'I've misled you, I think. When I say body I should more properly say skeleton. The skeleton of a girl. And as to how long she had been there, there was no telling. Hundreds of years anyway. That much the scientists could say at a glance, for her poor bones were as light as a bird's and as soft as biscuits.' I shuddered. 'Their phrase, Mrs Gilver, not mine. And it's only a small part of their . . . callousness, will we call it? Detachment is kinder, perhaps.

117

Because of course they wanted to take her away to their laboratories and try to find out more about her, but I put my foot down.'

'You did?'

'They called on me when they found her, and after that I felt I had a say in the matter, as minister of the parish. I felt it was my duty to the poor child to see that she had a decent burial at last.'

'I don't suppose there was any thought of trying to find out what happened?' I said. 'The police?'

'They came along,' said Mr Tait. 'They wrote in their notebooks. But seventy years is the rule for starting up with a murder inquiry, you know, and this body was hundreds of years old, maybe even a thousand—nobody really knew.'

'Couldn't you tell from the style of her clothes?' I said. 'Or had they rotted away?'

'I try to hope that they had rotted away,' said Mr Tait. 'Certainly there were no clothes to be seen.'

'Oh dear,' I said feebly.

'And they say she was only a child. Perhaps twelve or thirteen.'

'Oh dear, oh dear,' I said. 'Even if it *was* a thousand years ago, one doesn't like to think of a child of thirteen . . .'

'Indeed not,' said Mr Tait. 'I suppose that's partly why I was so determined to get the poor girl buried. I thought it would be the final indignity to have her taken away to some laboratory and . . .'

'I agree,' I said, grimacing at the thought of it. 'And so she's buried here? At Luckenlaw?'

'She is,' said Mr Tait, with a hard edge to his voice. 'And so we come to the crux of the matter.

She was buried in the face of some opposition.' I wondered at that for a moment.

'You mean there was a worry that she might be much older than a thousand years. Too old for a Christian graveyard?'

'That's rather a sophisticated line of argument for those who were doing the arguing, I'm afraid,' he said. 'It was more a feeling that if she had been killed and denied burial in the first place it must have been for good reason.'

'Surely not,' I said. 'That's horrid.'

'Roots run deep in a place like this,' said Mr Tait. 'Some of those making the most noise about it were no doubt thinking that if their own ancestors had decided she was to be dishonoured then who were they to gainsay it now.'

'But if she were a thief or a murderess or something dreadful like that, she would still have been buried. Somewhere, surely.'

'Ah, but that's not what they were imagining at all,' said Mr Tait. 'This is what I'm trying to tell you. There were those—and this was only a few years ago, remember—who thought the bones should be burned at the stake, who wondered why she hadn't been dealt with that way in the first place. They thought my giving her rest was a sign that I had been taken in by the devil himself. Yes, my stock fell sharply over that business. And it has stayed rather depressed in some folk's estimations ever since. So, when Mrs Fraser came to tell me about her recent ordeal and I tried to reason with her—tried to get something as trifling as a description from her—I'm afraid she took it as more evidence that I had lost my way.'

My head was reeling. The only time in my life

119

before I had felt so dizzy was when I had been persuaded to dance the Viennese Waltz after drinking two glasses of champagne at a hunt ball and had had to go and stand on the terrace for fear I might disgrace myself, and, while young men in high spirits can be expected to whirl their partners around without a care, I had never dreamed that a minister of the kirk sitting in his study in a manse in Fife could make my head swirl in just that way again. Witches, lucky chambers, ghostly strangers? I needed some fresh air.

*   *   *

Miss Lindsay was in the school playground again, waving off the last of her charges for the day, and when she saw me she raised her arm higher to include me in the salute. Here was quite another kettle of fish. Here was respite and a return to cool sanity after the unexpectedly torrid session in the kitchen at Balniel and the staggering interview with the good Reverend, so I turned my steps into the school lane passing the last of the stragglers and presented myself just as Miss Lindsay was drawing the gates closed. Hospitably—for who could blame her if she had wanted nothing but peace and quiet after a long day with a roomful of children; I should have been lying down with vinegar paper had it been me—she threw the gates wide again and invited me in.

'Still among us, Mrs Gilver,' she said. 'Come away in and have a cup of tea.'

Minutes later we were ensconced in her sitting room, where a kettle was already beginning to pipe and a tray of biscuits, which I can only assume

120

she had thrown together with schoolmistressly competence either before breakfast or over luncheon, was scenting the air and making my mouth water. Not that Miss Lindsay seemed the domestic type overall. The sitting room was well provided with books and dust and rather sparse when it came to the lacy covers, china rabbits and framed studio portraits of loved ones which I had always imagined the home of a woman who lived alone might boast, extrapolating from the knick-knacks which had cluttered up the tops of our dressing tables at school. She did not strike me as the sentimental type either. She might wear a heart-shaped brooch on her black cardigan jersey, as Lorna did too, but there was no rose nor ribbon here.

'I've had the most extraordinary afternoon,' I said, dropping into a sofa, rather lumpy and needing a cushion but a far more comfortable perch than Mrs Fraser's kitchen chair or the seat in Mr Tait's study, since it seemed unlikely that the devil and his minions would be joining us here for tea—china tea too, I noticed, as Miss Lindsay spooned it into the pot. 'It began as an attempt to ensure satisfaction for my audience next month. I meant to ask around and form an idea for the content of my talk.' As usual at the mention of the talk, even from out of my own mouth, my insides made their presence felt. I ignored them and went on. 'But my choice of informants conspired against me. I went to Mrs Palmer at Easter Luck and then to Mrs Fraser at Balniel and I'm afraid that poor old household budgets didn't stand a chance.'

Miss Lindsay, proffering a cup and a biscuit, gave a slight sigh and rolled her eyes wearily.

121

'I can imagine,' she said. 'At least I can imagine what Mrs Fraser had to say. She's a pillar of the kirk and she's one of those who to use the local parlance "wid dae little for God if the devil wiz deid."'

'What do you make of it?' I asked her.

'The "dark stranger"?' she said with emphasis almost so heavy as to be ironic. I thought this was a bit much since she was the only one of the entire Rural Institute who was not required to walk home after the meetings and so have to face him. 'I can't say I'm surprised, but it's rotten luck just the same and if I got my hands on the scoundrel, I wouldn't be responsible for what happened to him.' Her annoyance, dismissal of the man as a scoundrel and desire to give him a good punch on the nose were just about the first normal reaction to the entire affair I had come across since I got here.

'Who do you think is behind it?' I asked her. 'Have you any idea?'

'Oh, a husband, I'm sure,' said Miss Lindsay. 'Or a father. Even a little band of them perhaps. Who knows how organised they might get to win the day.' And as quickly as that, I discovered that Miss Lindsay had just as many peculiar ideas, albeit of quite a different stripe, as anyone else. 'They want to stamp us out, you see,' she went on. 'You've no idea the trouble we had to get the Rural up and running, Mrs Gilver. Just to secure one evening a month—one a month!—away from the children and chickens and mending.'

'Well, Mr Tait hinted at it,' I said.

'Mr Tait didn't have to bear the brunt,' said Miss Lindsay stiffly. 'Mr Tait is treated with respect wherever he goes.' This was far from being

122

true but I did not correct her. 'No one would call names after *him*,' she finished with a sniff.

'Who called names after you?' I asked, thinking that here was the first whiff of a suspect, for surely Miss Lindsay must have recognised at least the voice of the caller.

'Mr McAdam,' she said. 'Although he denies it. I saw him quite clearly at my gate. And Mr Hemingborough.'

'Mr *Hemingborough*?' I blinked at her in surprise. 'But his wife is a member.'

'Now she is,' said Miss Lindsay. 'She joined in the summer with Mrs Palmer—I've heard that she wears the watch-chain in that house, so I daresay he couldn't prevent her. But last winter he stopped his cart on my lane and called me some very unpleasant names.'

'Such as?' I asked her, but she only shook her head, flushed slightly, and concentrated on nibbling away furiously at her biscuit. 'Mr Tait said there were political concerns,' I hinted.

'Oh, that too,' Miss Lindsay admitted. 'They found out that Miss McCallum and I had gone on the Women's March and decided we were planning to lead Luckenlaw into revolution, beginning with their wives.'

'But you saw them off,' I said, suppressing the thought that two spinsters from the Women's March would have sent exactly those same tremors through Gilverton and, I admit, through me.

'And now, since the *men*,' this was spoken in very withering tones, 'can't bully us into giving up they—or at least one of them—are trying to sabotage our efforts by frightening the women away. And succeeding. We'll never see Mrs Fraser

123

or young Elspeth again.'

'But Mrs Hemingborough and Mrs Palmer started coming along after the trouble began,' I reminded her. 'And didn't the Howie ladies join rather recently too?'

At the mention of the Howie ladies, Miss Lindsay pursed her lips.

'The meetings were never meant for the likes of them,' she said. 'And I am sure that the unfortunate event in July could have been handled perfectly discreetly if only they hadn't picked that very meeting to roll up to.'

'This was the Wisconsin preacher?' I prompted, as agog to hear the details as I was unable to imagine them.

'And his wife,' breathed Miss Lindsay with such a look of anguish that I could not bring myself to ask any more. Her thoughts, however, soon returned to the Howies and anger rallied her. 'Of course, they've been there every month since, hoping for sport,' she said. 'And I don't deny, Mrs Gilver, that if I could see a way of getting them out and keeping them out, I would not hesitate to use it.'

I thought quietly to myself that Miss Lindsay was not a socialist in the classic mould, being rather keen on getting precisely her own way.

'So, apart from Mr Hemingborough and Mr McAdam,' I said, getting back to the central issue, 'is there anyone else you can think of who might be behind it?' She shook her head apparently without giving the question much thought. 'Or looking at it from another angle—opportunity instead of motive for a change—is there any newcomer, any loner, any odd type? Anyone at all who wasn't born here and doesn't have ten generations of ancestors and a web of relations to vouch for his good standing?' I wanted to see if the same name would pop up again, unbidden.

'I suppose you mean Jock Christie,' said Miss Lindsay. 'I'm not sure who first started bandying his name around, as if a Luckenlaw man who'd lived here all his life couldn't be behind it. They're all the same. It could be any of them.'

I took my leave shortly after, finding Miss Lindsay's jaded view of the male sex as unhelpful, in the end, as Mrs Fraser's peculiar fixation and Mrs Hemingborough's even more peculiar dismissal of the stranger altogether. At least there was an explan-ation of sorts for it, however, even if her spinsterhood and her view of men were a chicken and an egg of cause and outcome. As to the others, I still did not find Mr Tait's explanation satisfactory. It was one thing surely for spooky discoveries in the dark hillside to bring with them a few legends, but quite another for spooky stories to be the first choice if ever an explanation were needed for anything at all.

As I skirted the green, I heard the children's voices raised, as usual, for a skipping game. They carried easily in the still afternoon and I recognised the rhyme.

'*Not last night but the night before,*' they sang, '*Thirteen grave robbers came to my door.*'

I shivered and then, smiling as I remembered Mr Tait telling me not to listen too closely, I turned away and almost missed the rest of it.

'Dig her up and rattle her bones.
Bury her deep, she's all alone.

Dark night, moonlight,
Haunt me till my hair's white.
Moonlight, dark night,
Shut the coffin lid tight.'

I stopped with a gasp, mouthing the words over to myself, and then shook my head in disbelief at my own stupidity, at my wide-eyed trust of my charming employer. Mr Tait, I now saw, while making a great show of answering my every question, had been far from candid with me. He had fed me the story drip by drip—of the sealed chamber, its opening and the discovery there—all the time stressing that here were more examples of the kind of nonsense that credulous villagers might believe. Here were further instances of nastiness, nothing more. But that girl in the hillside was not just another story. She was at the heart of *this* story. She was the key.

Before I could help it my steps had turned for the gate into the churchyard and I was walking amongst the headstones, searching, noting the names—the Palmers and Frasers, Gows and McAdams—reading the verses inscribed near the ground as though intended to be as much a message for the grave's occupant as for those walking above. *Suffer the little children to come unto me*, I read and *Even so in Christ shall all be made alive*, listening to the teasing, lilting sing-song: 'Knock, knock, who's there? Knock, knock, who's there?' The girls were evidently in fine step today, the chant going on and on, fainter as I passed behind the church to the shadowy side where the ground of the graveyard began to slope up with the rise of the law. Here the earth was soft and the

126

gravestones mossy and lichened. Here was Mrs Tait, beloved wife and devoted mother, *Father into thy hands I commend my spirit.* Here too under an enormous monument, bristling with curlicues, was the grave of the Reverend Empson, Mr Tait's forerunner, and the rather more confident: *Well done thou good and faithful servant. Enter thou into the joy of thy Lord.* I came back around the side of the church. My feet, cold and clumsy, were slipping on the soggy tussocks, and the girls' voices were beginning to sound weary, slowing a little. 'Knock, knock. Who's there? Knock, knock. Who's there?' I was almost back where I had started. 'Knock, knock. Who's there? Caught you!'

There it was. This must be it. A stone cross with no name, no date of birth or death but only the words: *Buried here 21st June 1919 AD* and along the bottom *In my father's house are many mansions* and *Her sins, which are many, are forgiven.*

'A hard-won compromise,' said a voice behind me and I jumped, pressing my hand to my chest.

'I didn't hear you, Mr Tait,' I said.

'I saw you come in the gate and guessed what you'd be looking for,' he said. 'I came to guide you to it, but of course, you with your detective's nose . . .' He smiled at me and tucked my hand under his arm.

'What did you mean by a compromise?' I said. Mr Tait gave a laugh that was three parts sorrow.

'It was not our finest hour at Luckenlaw,' he said. 'I told you there were those who would have denied her burial altogether. They certainly wouldn't have stood for what I suggested first: "To be with Christ", which is far better.'

'Very apt, I should have said, considering.'

127

'They would rather have had: "Strait is the gate and narrow the way."' He laughed again and I almost joined him.

'I saw that on a headstone once,' I said. 'I could hardly believe it. Imagine choosing such words for one's dear departed. It's almost like saying, "Good luck, but I don't fancy your chances." How did you prevail?'

'Oh, quite easily in the end,' said Mr Tait. 'It's my church and what I say goes.'

This, I reflected, was hardly very lamb of God (which is what vicars are usually aiming for), but I can imagine that it was effective and, remembering I should be suffused with just this spirit of getting the job done, I decided to talk plainly to him.

'You misled me,' I began. 'I have been mystified about why no one fully believes in this dark stranger and you have let me be so, knowing all along what a starring role this poor child has in the current drama.'

'Indeed,' said Mr Tait.

'Even though everyone agrees that the dark stranger is a "he" and the archaeologists were sure that that skeleton was a "she".'

'True,' he acknowledged.

'So,' I went on, 'shall we say that by putting her into hallowed ground you have awakened the devil himself?'

'That's certainly one version,' said Mr Tait. 'Not by any means the only one, but I've heard it.'

'It's what Mrs Fraser thinks. How did she put it? That you unleashed the beast and gave it succour.'

'Shelter anyway,' agreed Mr Tait. 'Other versions would have it not only that the luck has left Luckenlaw since she was released but that now her spirit walks abroad, bringing calamity.'

'There has certainly been a run of poor luck around the farms anyway,' I said, but Mr Tait cut me off.

'Oh no,' he said. 'My farmers' wives are far too canny to blame dry wells and beef prices on this tortured soul.'

'But I've heard hints of troubles too dreadful to name,' I said, trying to remember where and what exactly. Mr Tait only shook his head, his eyes closed patiently. 'Well,' I said at last, stuck for any other conclusion, 'why on earth did you spoon it out in such tiny spoonfuls instead of just telling me everything right from the start?' Mr Tait opened his eyes again and had the grace to look sheepish.

'Shall I answer honestly?' he began, leading me away at last. 'Foolish as it seems now, since it's all come out in under a day, I hoped that you would not need to know. Also, I thought if I told you before you had been here you might decide you wanted no part of it, whereas if you got the scent . . .'

I was forced to concede both points: I might well have felt this hotbed of phantoms and curses was no place for me, but now I was here in the thick of it, a dozen sealed chambers concealing a hundred skeletons could not drive me away. I admitted as much to him with a rueful smile.

We were back in his library before I spoke again. Mr Tait, displaying another of his armoury of priestly skills, waited quite contentedly with his arms folded across his ample frontage to see what I had to say.

'Might I ask one more thing?' I began. 'I've been mildly wondering why Lorna was not told of my true mission here. Was it because you thought she would pour it all out and sway my judgement?'

'No, no,' said Mr Tait, shifting uncomfortably as he often did when Lorna's name came up. 'Lorna and I do not discuss the matter daily over tea, but no, it wasn't that. More that Lorna has a very trusting nature, almost to the point where we could call her suggestible. Certainly, she is easily led. And although she is no gossip, she is inclined to be rather warm and open with her many friends. Miss McCallum and Miss Lindsay, for instance.'

'Not to mention the Luckenlaw House contingent,' I added.

'Indeed,' said Mr Tait. 'It seemed best.'

I agreed, although I did not entirely go along with the idea of Lorna being easily led. She had none of the chameleon-like quality of the truly suggestible, picking up neither the arch amusement of the Howies nor Miss McCallum's cheery vigour, but remaining her own mild, calm, kindly self whatever was going on around her. It was a quality I much admired, since I was forced to be much more like an egg with a truffle these days, fitting in anywhere, all things to all men. (The thought that it was chiefly in the immediate pursuit of confidences and the ultimate pursuit of truth was not much comfort. To be a sucker-up and a flatterer when ulterior motives prompt one into it is hardly a characteristic one would wish included in one's eulogy.)

A clock chimed five as we sat there and the sound of it, doleful and muffled as it was, jolted me back to life.

'I must go,' I said. 'I still need to pop in to see Annie Pellow and Hugh is expecting me home.'

'Ah, Hugh,' said Mr Tait. 'He was a fine boy and he's grown into a fine man.'

I am not entirely sure why I heard this as a rebuke; perhaps because with all the names and dates, the farms and lanes, the lurid tales of the dark stranger, and the whisper of sabotage whirling around my head like dust motes in winter sunshine, I needed Alec Osborne as I had never needed him before.

'One thing,' I said, rising. 'Miss Lindsay is stuck on the notion of an irate husband with a grudge against the Rural, Mrs Fraser is determined that the stranger is not of woman born at all, and Elspeth no longer knows what to think, but is there any hard evidence against this Christie fellow? Did the police question him?'

'Not a shred,' said Mr Tait. 'There is nothing more than parochial insularity at work there. He's a newcomer and he was given a farm to run that was running just fine without him, that's all. The Howies were perfectly within their rights of course, but changes are always unwelcome in a backward-looking place like Luckenlaw.'

CHAPTER EIGHT

'I'm pleased you got along so well with the Reverend,' said Hugh the next morning. 'He's a fine chap, and his daughter seems a very good sort too. Exactly the kind of people one wants to encourage.' Touching, I suppose, the way that Hugh begins each day fresh-faced and eager, believing that today will be the day he wins the battles against weather, vermin, prices and, in the case of his current tribulations with the low water pressure in his stock-feeding system, gravity itself and that it will also be the day when his wife, out of the blue, becomes the woman he wishes she would be and takes up with kindly clergy and their wholesome daughters for a change.

'So you've met Lorna, have you?' I said, rather surprised. I had thought the yearly luncheons at Gilverton were Hugh's only connection with Mr Tait these days.

'I've stopped off now and then, yes,' said Hugh. 'I'm sure I told you I was there a few years back to watch the excavation. In fact, I asked you to come along.'

'This would be the archaeologists opening the chamber?' I had no memory of the episode, but I could believe that Hugh, hearing of scientists moving earth and digging holes in hillsides, would have been right there with his tail wagging. Neither did I have any trouble believing that he would have asked me to join him as though suggesting a picnic, nor that he would actually have believed I might come, nor that I would have heard the word 'dig' and refused, without listening to any of the details. I did think, however, that it might have registered when he told me what they had found.

'I don't remember you regaling me with the thrilling outcome,' I said. Hugh cleared his throat and became intensely interested in sawing the top off his boiled egg.

'Well, no,' he said at last. 'Beastly business. It gave me nightmares and I thought it best not to trouble you.' I smiled at that. I suppose it is far too late now for Hugh ever to change from being the absolute Victorian which, let us face it, he is.

'Did you actually see her?' I said, knowing that I would be shocking him but agog for details.

'No, thank heavens,' he said, shuddering. 'There wasn't room for Mr Tait and me inside what with all the university chaps and their equipment; we were supposed to get in for a poke around once they had finished. But after the discovery it wouldn't have seemed right, somehow.'

'I don't see why not,' I said. Sometimes Hugh's chivalry brought out an answering indelicacy in me that was far beyond my real measure of it. In fact, sometimes Hugh and I seemed as bad as the boys: Donald gorging himself sick on oysters just because Teddy was scared to try them; Teddy half drowning himself swimming underwater simply because Donald had never learned. 'I mean to say, we tramp around cathedrals and chapels eagerly enough, don't we? People sprawl on tombs and take rubbings.'

'People,' said Hugh witheringly, 'sprawl in public parks in their bathing dresses playing gramophones, but that doesn't mean people like us have to ape them,' and he gave me the look, a quizzical frown with lips pushed forwards making his moustache bristle, which he has started giving me with depressing regularity this last short while.

This look had puzzled me at first, I must own, but recently I have come to understand it. My life, quite simply, has changed. I have looked upon evil and battled it for one thing but, more to the point, I have sat at cottagers' doors and shared cool drinks of water with them; I have watched a wise woman at her herbs; I have clambered out of a shale mine in the dead of night and walked into a public bar in the light of day; I have interviewed laundry maids, kitchen maids, barmaids and coalmen and run about woods, along beaches and through empty houses as I have never run in my life since I was a girl. Why, only the day before this breakfast, I had raced up a drive and beaten a farmer's wife to the dairy.

My life then, as I say, has changed and inevitably that is beginning to show, even to one as unobservant and uninterested as Hugh. It would be far odder if all of my experiences had rolled off me like water from a duck and I had remained exactly the same creature as before, languidly proper, decently shocked by nasty stories and primly disdainful of anything which smacked too much of pulsing reality. Of course, from Hugh's point of view, lacking the knowledge which would serve as explanation, the new heartiness and vulgarity have no cause at all, hence his frequent recourse to these little reminders about people like us and my just as frequent attempts not to giggle at them.

'What did you make of it?' I asked him. 'Who did you think she was? Did the archaeologists have any ideas? Did Mr Tait?'

'What on earth do you mean, Dandy? "Who she was"?'

'Or why she was in there, rather. The Luckenlaw villagers have whipped up no end of lurid stories, I can tell you. But what did you think?'

'I think: "We should not make imaginary evils, when you know we have so many real ones to encounter",' said Hugh. I blinked at him. 'Goldsmith,' he added. I blinked again. The habit of quotation appeared to be taking root. 'Sound

134

thinking, if you ask me,' he concluded stoutly and retired behind his newspaper taking his piece of toast with him.

'I'm motoring over to Dunelgar,' I said to the newspaper presently, 'if you had any message for Alec.' Silence greeted this. 'I shall bring back news of Minnie for you.' Hugh had recently given Alec one of the latest litter from his favourite spaniel bitch.

'Milly,' said Hugh, unable to resist correcting me although he rustled the newspaper into a tighter and more impenetrable shield as he did so.

*　　　*　　　*

'And how is Hugh?' said Alec, as soon as I had stepped down onto the drive an hour later and taken a minute to make sure that Bunty and Milly were going to play sensibly and not need to be chaperoned. Bunty, having subjected Alec to her usual besotted greeting, pranced about, whining with excitement, twisting herself around and whipping her tail as the fat little bundle that was Milly darted in and out of her legs, squeaking and nipping at her, with her tail going round like a suckling lamb's.

'Stern, grumpy and quoting Oliver Goldsmith,' I answered. 'I cannot imagine what the matter is and I cannot be bothered trying.'

' "All his faults are such that one loves him still the better for them",' said Alec, although whether he was talking about Hugh or Goldsmith was not quite clear.

'Don't you start,' I answered. 'Now give me some coffee and get ready to listen and have

135

brilliant ideas, because I am absolutely stumped.'

We went through the passages to the conservatory at the back, partly so we could keep an eye on the dogs, now tumbling together on the lawns which stretched away behind the house. Alec, living here, was used to the place by now but I still had to stop in doorways sometimes and gather myself, willing away the memories of the first time I had come, the first time I had seen a case through to its grisly end. Thankfully, Dunelgar was close enough to Gilverton for me to avoid ever spending the night and so I was never forced to climb the stairs and recreate the nastiest memory of all. Besides, the conservatory was an easy place in which to ignore the ghosts: lush with ferns and glossy palms, the air a shingle-wrecking fug from the steam pipes, the floor tiles and window panes sparkling, it was hard to recall the dusty emptiness which used to reign here.

'I do hope Bunty doesn't squash her,' I said, watching the dogs rolling together down a slope towards the obligatory bird table at the bottom, disturbing the collection of sparrows busy with their morning titbits. (When Hugh gets a bee in his bonnet he can become quite peculiar and he had been pressing these little bird tables on all our friends.)

'Fat chance,' said Alec. 'She's as unsquashable as a beach ball. I simply cannot get Barrow not to feed her treats and if she gets into the kitchens . . .' Barrow was Alec's new valet cum butler. He was a terribly smart young man, born in London but trained at Chatsworth no less and, while heaven only knew why he had chosen to incarcerate himself in a bachelor establishment in Perthshire which did not even run to a housekeeper, the resulting power was beginning to turn his head and he was already shaping up to be the kind of dictator who would make Pallister look like a mother's help.

'He's quite a find, nevertheless, your Barrow,' I said. 'You look positively svelte.' Alec shrugged the compliment off, but it was true. His hair shone, his nails gleamed, and although he was wearing tweeds and brogues he exuded the air of a man in a silk dressing gown with his feet in a basin of water and scented oils.

'It's the tweeds,' he said. 'Feel that.' He shot a leg out and I rubbed a piece of the cloth between thumb and forefinger.

'Heavenly,' I said. 'Wasted on you.'

'That's what I keep telling Barrow,' said Alec, 'but he's very determined. Now,' he went on, leaning down to scoop up Milly, who had tired as quickly as puppies do and had come waddling in from the garden to find him, 'tell me all about the case.'

'It's a nasty one,' I said. 'A man, no one knows who, jumping out at girls and women at night, assaulting them and running away.'

'Every night?'

'No, far from it. Not exactly frequently, but not quite irregularly—when he does show up it's on the night of the full moon, or'—I held up my hand for him to let me finish, for his face had fallen and he had started to protest at the thought of the full moon—'or rather after the SWRI meetings which happen to be held on the night of the full moon. Scottish Women's Rural Institute,' I added, guessing that I would need to explain.

'Sounds like a job for the local police,' said Alec. 'Where do you come in?'

'That is one of the many peculiarities of the case,' I said. 'The local police were called in, and they concluded that the girls who reported the attacks were making it up. Refused to have any more to do with it.'

'A very strange thing to conclude,' said Alec. 'Did these girls have a history of telling tall tales?'

I thought back to Elspeth and to Annie Pellow, whom I had interviewed at the Colinsburgh pub on my way home. She had told me what was fast becoming a very familiar tale: a swift approach, a swift attack—ripping her hat as he wrenched it off her head regardless of the stoutly stitched elastic— and a swift retreat whence he had come.

'Not the girls, no,' I said, 'although Luckenlaw itself has a fair talent for horrors. The first was a perfectly ordinary sort—a dairy maid from one of the local farms—and nothing I saw when I interviewed her makes me think she was the type for silliness. The second girl seemed just as sensible. I haven't yet spoken to the third,' I said, 'although I've seen her and she didn't appear the flighty sort.'

'And when you say they were assaulted,' said Alec, 'assaulted how?'

I flicked through the little notebook where I had been jotting down the details of my investigations.

'What have they been saying?' I mused. 'Ah, here we are. Pinching, plucking, nipping, tearing, pulling hair, ripping off clothes—well, a hat—that kind of thing. Anyway, those three happened all in a row. Then after a break, Mrs Fraser, a farmer's wife, was attacked in August. She has a different

138

view of the matter. She firmly believes that the stranger was . . . don't laugh, Alec, promise me . . . the devil.'

Alec did not laugh, but I could tell it was a struggle.

'Then two nights ago, Mrs Hemingborough, another farmer's wife, and quite the most practical woman one could imagine—she had just finished giving a demonstration of chicken-plucking—was attacked. Her reaction is the strangest of all.'

Alec waited for me to explain.

'She denied that it happened,' I said. 'Even though the attack was witnessed by one person—Jessie Holland, a farm worker's wife—and the fellow was seen approaching by another—Vashti Howie, who saw him from her motor car—Mrs Hemingborough just tidied up all the chicken feathers, told no one and denied it until she was blue in the face when I challenged her.'

'Chicken feathers?' said Alec.

'From the plucking. Now, no one has been able to put a name to this chap, but let me read you some of the descriptions.' I flipped through my little notebook again, tracing the scribbles with the tip of my pencil. 'Swooping, flitting, flying over walls, fleet as the wind, sounding like owls' wings, running like a deer and above all . . . snaky.' I paused to see what effect this description would have. Alec merely raised his eyebrows and stared at me, all the while continuing to stroke Milly's silky ears back over her head. 'Everyone also agrees that he has a distinctive smell,' I said. 'Although no one can agree what it is. Elspeth said eggs, Mrs Fraser said yeast, possibly beer, and Annie Pellow said flowers—bluebells, cowslips and something else, something spicy but definitely still floral, she was sure.' Alec's eyebrows were still raised.

'Eggs?' he said. 'Sulphur, do you think she means? Sulphur, also sometimes known as brimstone?'

'Yes, it gave me pause too, for a moment,' I said. 'But then what of the yeast and flowers? Would it be possible to mistake sulphur for either of them? Could anyone imagine that a flower would smell eggy?'

'And what about the woman with the feathers? Did she get a sniff?'

'She's denying it, remember,' I said. 'And the witness was too far away.'

'So what's the feeling around the rest of the village?' said Alec. 'Amongst the non-victims, I mean.'

'There are various schools of thought,' I said. 'The redoubtable Miss Lindsay and Miss McCallum, spinsters both and respectively the schoolmistress and the postmistress, suspect a reactionary saboteur intent on stopping the SWRI movement before it takes hold—they've had names shouted at them in the street. I rather go along with this and so does the Reverend Mr Tait, who called me in—he'd *heard* about me, if you can believe it—but at least one of the two cat-calling husbands in question is middle-aged, although wiry with it, and anyway, both their wives have since joined. The other sane and sensible possibility is that it's just some unfortunate with a monomania, who needs to be pitied and locked up.'

'And is there anyone around the neighbourhood who seems to fit the bill?'

140

'There is one,' I said. 'A newcomer who has aroused suspicions, but nothing more. Mr Tait and the farmers' wives seem equally adamant that it can't be him. As far as the locals go, there's no one with a history of anything that would point the way. It's possible of course that someone who has always lived there has suddenly developed this nasty twist and, because of the SWRI meetings, there are a lot of men on their own on just the evening in question. In fact, they rather take the Rural night as giving them carte blanche to go out on the town. Or down to the pub at Colinsborough, I suppose.'

'So all in all no one seems likely.'

'No, which brings us to the third option: the girls are indeed making it up; there's a kind of hysterical fad taking hold and they're all joining in.'

'This fad being . . . ?'

'That the devil has been conjured or whatever it is one does with the devil and is walking the night.'

'And how likely is that?' said Alec. 'I must say, Dandy, I do prefer a good solid murder with a corpse and no question whether or not the damn thing happened at all.'

'Well,' I began, 'there is *some* kind of basis for it—if one half shuts one's eyes. And there is actually a murder at the bottom of it all, but I doubt very much whether it's a murder we can solve.' Now I had his attention, and I went on to tell him about the chamber, the girl, the burial, the disapproval of the burial, and the fantastical imaginings—of Mrs Fraser at least—that this unquiet soul had summoned Satan himself.

'I never thought I'd say it,' said Alec, when I was

141

done, 'but I do believe the counter-revolutionary band in league to stop the bolshie schoolmarm might be the less unlikely theory here.'

'You haven't, I gather, spent much time in Fife.'

'Have you?'

'Thankfully, no, but the housekeeper at Gilverton when Hugh was a little boy hailed from a fishing village there and her sayings entered family lore. "Keep yer heid doon lest ye meet the devil's stare" was a favourite but they're much of a muchness, all employing the same small cast.'

'I suppose,' said Alec slowly, 'that it makes sense of the chicken woman's behaviour at least.'

'Mrs Hemingborough?' I said. 'Does it?'

'Doesn't it? Don't you think that she might want to keep it quiet if she has attracted the attention of Old Nick? I'm not sure I would put a notice in *The Times* if it were me.' I laughed, but his words had reminded me of something. Once again, I riffled through the pages of my little book.

'There!' I said, when I had found it. 'Alec, I think you're right. She said to me when I bearded her in her kitchen the next day, "what's for you won't go by you". It struck me at the time as rather odd.'

'What does it mean?' said Alec.

'Oh, more east coast wisdom,' I said. 'It means that whatever is meant to be will be and there's no avoiding it. At least, one more often hears it being wheeled out to express the opposite view: that whatever is being withheld from you is *not* meant to be, so you should shut up and stop pining. They are not really words of comfort, to my way of thinking.'

'But very revealing here,' said Alec, 'if you can

credit anyone with such stoicism that she would accept being roughed up by the devil, given a guilty enough conscience.'

'If there is anyone anywhere with as much stoicism as that,' I said, 'Luckenlaw would be just the place to find her. I wonder what she thinks she's done?'

'Unimportant,' said Alec, rather imperiously. 'A red herring. We must stick to the facts. *Are* there any other facts? Anything practical and possible that we should take note of?'

'I did try to piece together a picture of where the fellow might be coming from,' I said. 'All the witnesses and victims so far are agreed that he takes a good run at things, so I thought it worth paying attention to the direction he ran.'

'Possibly,' said Alec. 'Although he could hide under any hedge he liked when you think about it. Still, in the absence of anything better . . . I'll ring for some paper and you can sketch me a map.' Carefully, he worked his fingers in under the slumbering Milly and lifted her onto my lap. She rolled over, as floppy as a rag doll, dead to the world. Bunty, asleep on my feet, opened one eye to remind me that a puppy on the lap was tolerated out of the goodness of her heart and that the arrangement could be terminated at any time.

Barrow himself responded to Alec's ring and rose to the occasion with a luxurious pad of snowy white sketching paper and a pair of new pencils in a silver card tray. I noticed that he had the quelling effect on conversations that one finds in Parisian waiters—Alec and I fell silent as he entered and didn't speak again until he had left.

'You're going to have to watch him,' I said, when

143

he had drawn the doors closed behind him with a respectful backward sweep and a slight bow. 'He's another Pallister in the making.'

'Nonsense,' said Alec. 'Pallister is a prig and a bully. Barrow is a treasure. There's no comparison at all.'

'Hmm,' I said but left it there, and bent to the task of sketching out the village of Luckenlaw. 'Now,' I said, when I had got as close an approximation down on paper as we needed or I was capable of producing, 'where does the dark stranger come from? In March he came down the lane towards Easter Luck Farm from the north. All the farm names are shortened to Luck, you know, isn't it charming? In April he came crashing through the woods behind Mrs Kinnaird's house, where Annie Pellow lodges. That is, he came from the west, and could have come round the law, meaning that once again he came from the north. I have no idea about the attack on Molly in May; that is one of the many things I need to ask her. In August, he came across the fields from the west towards the lane that leads from Luckenlaw to Balniel Farm.'

'A completely different direction then,' said Alec.

'Quite so,' I agreed. 'And then the other night, he once again came from the Balniel road direction up around the manse to the Hinter Luck Farm lane. Both Jessie and Vashti agree about that.'

'So he's not coming from the same place every time,' said Alec. 'There are at least two patterns to it, and for all we know Molly could tell us something that destroys even those two patterns

144

completely.'

I regarded my little map in sorrow for a moment and then, reluctantly agreeing, I screwed it up and dropped it on the floor for Bunty and Milly to play with when they awoke.

'And he's not doing it regularly,' Alec went on, 'at least not since his three monthly outings in the spring, and he's not even going for any particular type, so it's not as though we can warn the likely next victim.'

'No,' I said. 'And that makes the gaps between his appearances rather odd, doesn't it? I mean, he plumped for three young girls first which, horrid as it is to say so, at least makes some kind of sense. The next time he felt moved to go prowling he set his sights on a married lady of no great appeal and then on Monday past, he ignored the rather lovely Jessie Holland and took on the much more considerable task of trying to topple Mrs Hemingborough.'

'As you say,' said Alec, 'it doesn't make sense. If he was choosy, that would explain the gaps but if his tastes are as catholic as it appears he should really have been able to find a victim every month. That might be to our advantage, mind you.'

'How so?'

'Because if we find someone who was away or otherwise engaged in June, July and September but free to do his worst in March, April and May, in August, and again the other night we'll know that's our man.'

'I see,' I said. 'Thank heavens for Jessie Holland, then. If we had been relying on the victim, we'd have October down as another month he missed.'

Not for the first time, the same thought occurred to both of us in unison, and in unison too we blushed in shame that it had taken us so long.

'Of course,' said Alec at last. 'Oh, I'm so glad there isn't a Dr Watson writing this up for the scoffing public, aren't you?'

'There are no gaps,' I said. 'He attacks every full moon and somewhere in Luckenlaw there are more women who, just like Mrs Hemingborough, have borne it and not said a word.'

'And possibly others who have witnessed his approach or his flight and also kept quiet,' said Alec. 'After all, if Mrs Hemingborough had seen him swoop down on Jessie instead of the other way around she would have suppressed that too.'

'Excellent,' I said. 'I did so want to make a go of this for Mr Tait. Surely if I can find the missing victims I'll be able to make some headway.'

'And I'll help,' said Alec. 'I'll come down with you.' I quite understood his enthusiasm, but I could not let it pass.

'Absolutely impossible, darling,' I said. 'You can't go knocking on doors and interviewing women in their kitchens. I have a legitimate reason to be there and a place to stay, even a handy story to trot out should anyone ask what I'm up to. You certainly can't come galumphing down, bereft of any disguise and ruining mine.'

'I don't galumph,' said Alec. 'And besides, as those revolting children of yours would say: same to you with knobs on. If I can't haunt the kitchens you can hardly mount a proper attack on alibis amongst the local men.'

'But it's not a local man who's doing it,' I insisted. 'Everyone at Luckenlaw knows everyone else and no one recognises this stranger.' Alec shook his head looking mutinous.

'Context, Dandy, context,' he said. 'Haven't you ever passed your barber in the street—well, milliner or something in your case, obviously—and been absolutely unable to place him, out from behind his shop front, stripped of his apron?'

'I think if my milliner bore down on me and tried to claw my eyes out it would spark some recognition,' I said. 'Anyway, where would you stay?'

'Don't you have any friends in the area where I could be absorbed into a house party and make no ripple?'

'Only the Taits,' I told him. 'And they're out of the question. House parties of bright young things are not Lorna Tait's milieu. There are the Howies, who are rather fun and wouldn't turn a hair, but it's as far a leap from their drawing room to a cottage kitchen as it is from here. Really, Alec, you're going to have to leave this one to me.'

'I'm not a bright young thing,' said Alec, rather humourlessly. 'I'm thirty-three, I'm running two houses and I'm keeping on top of a very difficult new butler as you said yourself.'

'I'll send frequent dispatches,' I assured him. 'And I'll telephone to you if I need to mull things over. You've been no end of help today.'

CHAPTER NINE

It has never with any truth been said of me that I am the methodical type. It is my great good fortune to have been born when I was and not any later, for if I had been forced to sit at a desk in an office somewhere threading a typing machine with inky ribbon and shuffling carbons into order, some blameless man of business who had employed me would surely have been driven to distraction and bankruptcy. (Likewise, I count myself very fortunate to have been gently born; never to have grappled with a loom in a dark mill, a gutting knife on a harbourside, or a mangle and irons in a fragrant laundry, for I should certainly have garrotted, disembowelled or strangled myself if I had tried.)

So it was a considerable strain to force myself, upon my return to Luckenlaw the following week, into a visit to Molly of Luck House (as I now thought of it, feeling quite the local) to complete my interviews with the known victims, instead of immediately plunging into the delicious task of sniffing out the others. It had been challenge enough to wait this tantalising week, even though I knew that there was a full month before another attack would happen and I would be far better to stay quietly at home, making notes and getting rosettes for wifely attentiveness, than to charge off again on the instant, putting Hugh's back up and missing half the clues I was finding for the lack of thoughtful preparation which would help me see them for what they were.

Lorna accompanied me to the Howies' once more, but in the motor car this time owing to the filthy weather, and so we avoided any more dawdling on the footbridge over the ford and sighing at the abandoned cottage where she and her poet were to have settled to their married bliss. She was, as a matter of fact, in more cheerful spirits than I had ever seen her, much taken with Bunty, who had come back with me, although thrown into a domestic twitter by the arrival of Grant besides (for Grant would not hear of being left behind again, not now that the new items ordered for my winter wardrobe had arrived; it would have been intolerable to her to wait at Gilverton with the boxes and bags while I mucked along at Luckenlaw in my autumn frocks and coats with an extra vest for warmth and last year's shoes). The Taits had never had a house guest bring a lady's maid before, and Lorna was concerned that Grant might find the servants' quarters beneath her or baulk at sharing a bedroom with another maid, but I knew Grant better than that; to get out from under Pallister's eye would be as good as a week at Eastbourne and the chance to let a poor little maid of all work see her, Grant's, hand-embroidered underclothes and the tissue-layered packing of them—for she was just as fussy about her own belongings as she was about mine—would be meat and drink to her.

I had made a feeble remark or two about leaving some of the more startling purchases behind, but my mind was taken up with the case and I did not have enough spare attention to win the day. Accordingly, I was headed for tea with the Howies decked out in an ankle-length coat of Persian lamb, with a sable collar like a surgical neck-brace and silver clasps worked in the pattern of Celtic knots holding shut the belt. A hat somewhere between a Beefeater's pancake and a paper sailing ship in its construction had been firmly jammed onto my head in the spare bedroom before I left the manse.

'And don't take it off,' said Grant. 'Madam. I'll look into getting some rainwater for tomorrow morning'—Grant never trusted the water for hair-washing purposes if we were anywhere near the sea—'but for today, please don't take it off. I've packed a turban for this evening.'

I rolled my eyes at her in the mirror. A turban, I knew, meant evening clothes to match it, and there was no way I was sweeping downstairs to dinner with Mr Tait and Lorna in beaded chiffon lounging pyjamas, Ali Baba pantaloons or whatever Turkey-inspired excesses Grant had come up with now. I heartily wished the whole Ottoman adventure in couture would blow over some season very soon.

'My, my,' said Vashti Howie as we were shown in, 'don't you look splendid.' She was dressed as usual in a collection of what would have been trailing wisps had they been silk but, since they appeared to be made out of hand-dyed sacking, could be more accurately described as flapping hanks. The hand-dyeing was no more successful than the cut either, with the purple and mustard fighting both each other and Vashti's sallow skin. I wished Grant were there; if she could have witnessed a sight like Vashti commending me for my style, she might have taken fright and ordered me something more becoming. Nicolette, as ever, was in stiflingly tight, bright tweed and high heels, and I thought that if she were not careful she would end up with those tennis ball calf muscles like a country dancing mistress I once had as a child, whom I admired terrifically for soldiering on with her profession despite the nameless and surely painful condition afflicting her poor bulging legs and her pitiful feet, which arched like leaping salmon when she pointed them.

The Howies, as before, were corralled in their ground-floor drawing room, littered about on sofas and armchairs, and all the signs were that they had spent the day there: there was a barely shifting cloud of cigarette smoke hanging just above the level of the lampshades and the fires were pulsing heaps of orange, having been lit first thing and fed repeatedly as the day wore on. The menfolk remained sunk in torpor despite our entrance, but the ladies sprang very flatteringly to life.

'Darling Lorna,' cried Nicolette, throwing down the paper she had been reading. 'We haven't seen you in an age and we have so much to talk about.'

'We're throwing a little party next month, for Lorna's birthday,' Vashti explained to me.

'I had heard,' I said. 'It's very kind of you.' Nicolette and Vashti giggled gently.

'Not at all,' Vashti said. 'We're simply dying to. It's the culmin-ation of our entire year.'

'Long time since we had a party,' said Johnny Howie, with his chin on his chest. 'Changed days.'

'Ah, the parties we had at Balnagowan in the old days,' said Nicolette. 'Bonfires on every hilltop, pipers on every headland—'

'I could have done without the pipers, to be brutally honest,' said Vashti. 'Oh but remember that midsummer!'

151

'We had such swags of flowers hanging from the chandelier chains, Dandy—monstrous great things; it took all the garden staff to lift them—that they brought the house down. Well, a good lot of the plaster anyway.'

'. . . said they were too heavy,' muttered Irvine Howie. '. . . never listen.'

'And that was the end of that,' said Vashti. 'Cousin Sourpuss wouldn't let us back.'

'No more parties at Balnagowan,' sighed Nicolette, in an amused sing-song, sounding like Nanny telling Baby that its bowl of pudding was 'all-gone'.

'So you didn't actually live in the house?' I asked, pitying the cousin a little.

'No, more's the tragedy,' said Vashti. She was blunter than I had ever heard any woman being about exactly what her unprepossessing husband had to recommend him and had either of the Howie men looked conscious of the insult I should have blushed for all of them, but Irvine was staring straight ahead, at the glowing tip of his cigarette, as though in some kind of Eastern trance, and Johnny had shut his eyes again.

'. . . comes of handing it over to the female line,' said Irvine, after a long silence. 'And now even that's withered and died.'

'Don't be so disparaging about female lines!' said Vashti. 'Remember it was your illustrious ancestress that brought you Vash and me. Have you ever heard of Lady Fowlis, Dandy? Katherine Ross by birth and—'

'We need to think about the decorations,' said Nicolette, cutting across her. I supposed there were excesses of snobbery that even the most

152

unashamed social climber could not bear to hear and dropping mentions of one's grandest forebear really was beyond the pale. I began to wonder about Vashti and Nicolette's beginnings and then, feeling like Lady Bracknell to be doing so, I put it out of my mind.

'Of course,' said Vashti, changing tack smoothly. 'What are you wearing, Lorna darling? Do you know yet? We need to make sure the whole room is a setting for the jewel that is you.'

'Like an altar with a bride,' said Nicolette. 'Please give us some clues.'

'Are you holding the party in here?' I asked, wondering how any decorations could be squeezed in amongst all the furnishings and realising a little too late that I should not have drawn attention to the way they lived, all in one room together like travelling tinkers in their caravan.

'No, no, no,' said Vashti. 'We're opening up the ballroom for the night. And it's rather a barn without some frillies. So please tell us what palette we're working on, Lorna darling, so we can get stuck in.'

'I don't want you to go to a lot of'—I am sure that Lorna was about to say 'expense' but she managed to bite her lip on it—'bother.' The subtlety was wasted, however.

'Don't worry, darling,' Nicolette cried. 'We're in funds for once in our miserable lives.'

'Oh?' said Lorna, trying not to sound too surprised.

'We've let the cottage,' Vashti said. 'Can you believe it?'

'Ford Cottage?' said Lorna, faltering slightly over the name.

153

'Vash, you are a bull in a china shop sometimes,' said Nicolette. 'I'm sorry, my darling, but yes. We've found a new tenant at last. At least for a while.'

'Fella needs his head looking at,' said Johnny Howie. Having seen Ford Cottage, I had to agree.

'He's a painter,' said Nicolette. 'An artist. He's taken it for the light, you oaf, not the fixtures and fittings.'

'Good luck to him,' said Johnny, unabashed. 'Precious little light down there in July, never mind the depths of winter.'

'The quality of light, you double oaf,' said his wife. Then she began to talk in a throaty voice, waving a hand in languid circles. 'The soft light through the bare winter trees, the gentle milky light of a foggy afternoon. Anyway,' she said, her voice changing back to normal, 'he's paid up two months in advance and says he might stay until springtime. So don't worry about a few vases and tassels to make your party a feast to the eyes, darling Lorna. We can afford it.' She linked arms with Lorna and shook her gently. Vashti beamed at them and I smiled too. Generosity is always attractive, even such reckless generosity as this was.

'Oh but what a shame it's such an awkward time of year for flowers,' Nicolette went on. 'We have the most beautiful spring flowers here, Dandy. All the usuals, of course, and a sea of those divine white narcissi with the pheasants' eyes. It's utterly drunk-making to walk up the drive in April, isn't it, Vash?'

'Yes, I'm afraid the decor can't be predominantly floral, darling, rent or no rent. Not if we're to have something to drink too. I declare, the twentieth of November must be the most impossible day of the year to try to dream up a theme for a party. Too late for Hallowe'en—no matter what you say, Niccy.'

'We could always hearken forward to Yuletide and go all out for evergreens,' said Nicolette. 'Oh Vash, don't look so sneering. It's close enough. We've fudged like this who knows how many times.'

'Only when we've had to,' said Vashti. 'And it's an entire month out.' Lorna too was shaking her head at the idea.

'Absolutely not,' I said. 'It's unforgivable to lump someone's birthday in with Christmas even if the poor thing is born on Christmas Day. Out of the question in November.'

'Pink,' said Lorna at last. 'I'm wearing pink. So if you insist, I suppose some pink ribbons would be a pretty touch.'

Nicolette and Vashti looked so aghast at the idea of all their flamboyant plans coming down to a few pink ribbons that it was all I could do not to laugh.

'Anyway,' I said, trying to sound natural and probably failing, 'talking of good fortune and windfalls, if you'll excuse me, I'm going to go and have a word with your maid.'

All four Howies swivelled their eyes to gape at me.

'For the household budget talk,' I supplied. 'Actually, it's beginning to look as though it might make a pamphlet. So I thought I'd start by gathering the thoughts of as wide a social sweep as possible. You, obviously, being the first family of the neighbourhood,' I guessed that a little flattery would do me no harm, 'and your maid right down at the other end of things.' That, of course, ruined the flattery completely. It might be true that a girl trying to run this place single-handed was necessarily at the bottom of the heap—and make no mistake, the serving classes have easily as many gradations and nuanced shadings as do we—but it was hardly diplomatic to make such plain reference to it.

'I won't, of course, be asking her about her housekeeping budget,' I said. 'Nor about her personal wages.'

'What does that leave?' said Johnny, frowning at me, and I could see that he had a point. Feeling myself flushing and hoping that the overhang of my silly Beefeater's hat would hide it, I rose with as much dignity as I could muster and walked away.

'Ring from the hall for her,' Vashti advised me. 'It's a rabbit warren behind the door. You'll never get out alive.' And then her attention was given back to Lorna.

'Pink ribbons are certainly a start,' she said.

'But when you say pink,' said Nicolette, 'you surely don't mean pale rosebud, do you? A good rich fuchsia would be much more propitious.'

'Let's start at the top and work down,' Vashti was saying as I closed the door. 'The headdress is really the thing.'

*   *   *

It took an unconscionably long time for Molly to answer my ring, with the result that I had just rung again when the door under the stairs swung open.

156

She scowled at me in that way that little boys and sulky girls do when they are caught falling short of the ideal.

'Molly, isn't it?' I said, and she bobbed vaguely in reply, no more than a clenching at the knees and a downward look. 'I'd like to talk to you, if you please. I'm gathering snippets for an article I'm writing, on household affairs, and Mrs Howie invited me to interview you.' This sentence contained a number of little greyish lies, not least, I was interested to note, that the talk which had become a pamphlet was now a full-blown article. I wondered in passing if it would end up in three bound volumes with an index.

Molly looked rather cheered at the prospect of an interview, as those with dull daily rounds usually are at anything which promises a break in the routine. This, I am sure, is at the bottom of the taste for excitement which infects the serving classes, and at which their employers are wont to scoff; I am sure I might greet a fire in the attics with gleeful welcome, as did the Gilverton maids a year or two ago, if I thought it might get me out of my five o'clock start and another day of dustpans.

'I can come back through to the kitchens with you, if you are busy,' I said, thinking that I should get more from her if she were in her own little kingdom than if she remained standing here, shifting from foot to foot in the hallway. She bobbed again and went back to the door, passing through it first rather rudely but at least holding it open as I followed her.

'I should have unravelled the hem of my jersey and tied it to the door,' I joked as she led me through a series of passages, round corners, up and

157

down little flights of steps.

'Aye, it's a mess o' a place,' said Molly, an original and none too flattering turn of phrase, although spot-on as it happened. There were bundles of laundry, baskets of kindling and flour sacks littered around the corridors, all of which surely should have homes in definite and separate corners of the household quarters and not be lying around jumbled up together on the floor to be tripped over.

'But aren't you ever frightened here on your own?' I asked as we reached the kitchen at last. The kitchen at Gilverton is no bower, with its monstrous black range and those shiny, brick-shaped tiles from soaring ceiling to stone floor, and I have seen other kitchens in my time just as cheerless, with their requisite north-facing windows and their biblical verses adorning the walls, but the kitchen of Luckenlaw House was unsurpassed. The solitary high window was choked up with cobwebs on the inside and moss on the outside, giving a subterranean feel to the place. The tiles were a nasty shade of orange-brown which clashed with the red tiles on the floor and the work table, dressers and cupboards had all been painted a uniform dull black, even their brass handles slopped over with it. The range was lit but seemed unequal to the task of heating so much as the hearthrug in front of it never mind the room beyond, and the one skimpy armchair drawn up close to the fender was pitiful enough to make one weep. In the seat of this chair the elderly cat I remembered from my first visit was huddled in a tight ball, tail over its paws for warmth.

'Frightened?' said Molly. 'Naw. Fed up

158

sometimes, but what's to be feart of?'

'Well, there's this strange man I keep hearing about,' I said, thrilled to be given such an opening so early on, but trying to hide it.

'Aw, him,' said Molly, and pulled her cardigan tightly around her, holding it in place with crossed arms. The gesture was not self-comforting but rather belligerent, a kind of squaring up. 'Well, as tae him, madam, he's been and gone.'

'I'm sorry?' I said, thinking it best to profess ignorance.

'He's already hud a go at me and I sent him packin'.' I looked suitably shocked and impressed and Molly went on, warming to her tale as she did so. 'Away back in May it was,' she said. 'The nicht o' the full moon. I hud been a walk.'

'To the Rural?' I prompted. She gave me a very pert look and only just managed not to follow it up with a snort of laughter.

'Eh no, madam,' she said. 'Marriage stones o' ancient times and babies' bootees? No. I wish I'd been there in the summer, mind you, when thon meenister's wife did *her* wee turn.' Molly sniggered and peeped at me out of the corner of her eye. 'In May, I was just away out a walk mysel', seein' it was sich a lovely nicht. He got me on my road back. Jumped oot at me from ahint one o' they outhouses just in the yard there, whipped the feet oot fae under me, hit me such a skelp over my face I couldna breathe and then well . . . you can imagine, can you no'?'

'He pinched you?'

Again Molly gave me a look of pity.

'It was a bit more than pinchin',' she said. 'He was a' over me, the dirty beast, stinkin' o' whisky

159

and pinnin' me doon.'

'Whisky?' I interjected.

'Whisky, aye,' said Molly looking at me rather oddly. 'I mean, that's to say, I think it was whisky. I'm no' a drinker mysel' and my faither nivver touched a drop in his life, but I've worked to the Howies long enough to learn what whisky smells like.'

Such insolence could not be tolerated and so I decided to pretend that I had not heard her (and thus escaped having to wonder how, if Molly were typical, the good name of Gilver might be dragged around like a floor-rag in my own kitchen at home).

'Pinning you down, eh?' I said, returning to the narrative where I wished I had never left it. 'What did you do?'

'I kicked him,' she said. 'Hard. And I caught him a guid smack on the back o' the heid. Then I kicked him again, richt in the belly. The stomach, madam, excuse me. And that saw him off. Up he got and away he went.'

'I take it you didn't recognise him?' She shook her head. 'I've been hearing a name,' I went on, casually.

'Aye, I'll just bet ye have,' said Molly. 'But I've seen Jockie Christie three an' fower times a week for the last five years and I'd ken if it was him. And it wasnae because he's a fine, well-set-up laddie wi' his own big hoose and he'd nivver dae suchlike and anyway it wisnae a man at all everybody says and I believe them.'

Overwhelmed by the ferocity of this, I struggled in vain to frame an answer. What was there to say? Clearly there was a campaign to climb the social scale going on below stairs at Luckenlaw House which was equal to anything the ladies in the drawing room had ever attempted and Molly was not willing to harbour nasty suspicions of a fine, well-set-up young man with the tenancy of a big house, in whose path she had been throwing herself week in and week out for years. I told myself that she must really know it was not him. For even if Nicolette and Vashti had overlooked the dullness of their fiancés in their quest for Highland castles and pipers on headlands, no woman alive could turn a blind eye to such vile habits as the dark stranger displayed. Not for a farmhouse, anyway.

'So,' I said. 'What happened next?'

Molly was only too ready to take up the thrilling tale once more.

'As soon as he got off me I lowped up and bolted for the back scullery door and I went straicht to thon telephone to get the police. I didna ask "permission" either. And I'd dae the same again tomorrow; I dinna care what anyone says.'

I surmised from this that poor Molly had been given a ticking off for taking matters and the telephone into her own hands.

'You're a good brave girl,' I said, thinking that if a little pertness came along with the courage to kick and slap one's way out of trouble, then it was a price worth paying. Much better that than milky docility which lay helpless and suffered the worst.

I thought about it again though, on the way home in the motor car. Luckily Lorna too seemed preoccupied, dreaming of her party probably, and so did not seem to resent my silence. Perhaps, I thought, Alec and I were wrong; perhaps Molly's robust defence of her honour gave the stranger such a fright that he really did take three months to pluck up the courage and venture out again. I tried not to dwell upon a further thought which Molly's story had started rolling: that the stranger was not content with pinching and frightening after all and had been about to do much worse to Molly until she fought him off. I wondered if Mrs Fraser had kept some of the most upsetting details of her attack to herself, and wondered too just how bad things might have got for Mrs Hemingborough had not young Jessie seen the start of it and charged along the lane shouting.

In the end, though, I decided to press ahead with my search for the three missing victims, and so after luncheon I set off up the lane beyond the manse, meaning to sweep through the village from the foot of the law to the Colinsburgh road and flush out whatever was hiding behind these brightly painted doors. Miss Lindsay had not yet rung her bell for afternoon school and the voices of the girls were, as ever, raised in song. This one I recognised and as I tramped along I sang it myself softly.

'The wind, the wind, the wind blows high,
The snow comes scattering from the sky,
Dandy Gilver says she'll die
If she doesn't get the boy with the roving eye.
He is handsome, she is pretty.
They are the couple from the golden city.
Come and say you'll marry me . . .'

I was singing quite loudly now and I even began to skip for the finale.

'With a one'—I gave a little hop—'with a two'—another little hop and a glance out of the corner of my eye—'with a one, two, three,' I finished awkwardly as I realised that, from the gateway of the nearest cottage, a woman was watching. 'A very good afternoon,' I called to her. 'I'm afraid you caught me reliving my youth.'

'Whit ye dae alane is seen by ane,' came the reply.

'Indeed,' I acknowledged, although I rather thought my immortal soul would survive a little skipping being witnessed by my Maker. 'I am enjoying watching the girls at play as I come and go. I'm staying at the manse, you know.' I had not seen this one at the Rural meeting the week before; I should have remembered the face for, even in a land renowned for those complexions upon which harsh weather and harsher living had etched their history, hers stood out and yet her hair was scraped mercilessly back from it as though to promote its clear display. The hands clasping the gate were dried to scaliness and had deep red fissures running between the fingers. She could have been any age between thirty and sixty.

'Are any of them yours?' I said.

'Any o' whit?' said the woman.

'Those delightful little girls,' I said, hoping not for their sake.

'Aye, twae,' she answered. 'The bonniest flooer oft wilts the quickest, mind.'

'Well, I'll tell you why I'm asking. I'm planning a little something for the next Rural meeting . . .'

'That's nithin' tae dae wi' me,' she said. 'They swim in sin, they'll drown in sorrow.'

'You've never been?' I said, wondering if I could

163

cross her off my list. Molly, granted, had not been en route from the Rural when she had met the stranger but something told me this woman would not take many moonlight walks by herself just for the joy of it.

'Cross the step a bride and leave a corp,' said the woman. 'I've all I'm needin'.' Of course she did not mean it literally. She would leave her house every Sunday to go to church, but I am sure that what she said was otherwise true.

'Well,' I said, 'I don't want to keep you back. Lovely to have met you.' And I scuttled away up the lane heading for the last house. When I knocked and a sweet-faced young woman with a flowered apron tied over her protruding middle answered the door, I could not help blurting out:

'I've just come from your neighbour. My dear, rather you than me.' Of course, this was very silly. The woman might have been her relation or even her dearest friend, but my outburst was greeted with a sorrowful little laugh.

'My mammy ayeways telt me to see the good in everyone,' she said, 'and Mrs Black keeps hersel' to hersel . . . mostly.'

'Mrs Black?' I said. 'I believe I've met her husband. Well, your charity does you credit, dear.' The girl stood aside to let me in.

'It's Mrs Gilver, is it no'?' she said when we had gone along the passageway beside the staircase and come out into the kitchen, where a rather patched and ragged sheet of pastry dough showed that she had been engaged unsuccessfully in trying to make a pie. The air was redolent with the beef she was boiling up to fill it. 'Miss Tait told me about you.'

'Did she say what I was doing?' I said. 'Mrs . . . ?'

164

'Muirhead,' said the woman. 'She did and if it's household hints ye're givin' oot then here's one for you. How can I get this bloomin' dough to hang thegither long enough to line the dish wi' it? I'm about at my wits' end and I promised Archie.'

'Um,' I said, racking my brain. 'An egg, perhaps?'

'An egg!' she exclaimed as though I had handed her the key to all mysteries and waddled away to fetch one.

'It's just an idea,' I called after her, loath to be responsible for the ruination of Archie's supper. 'It's not really my bag, baking.' Saying that, though, reminded of what *was* my bag and I planned a subtle approach to my area of concern.

'On the subject of your delightful neighbour again,' I called gaily, while she was still out of sight, 'she can at least be sure never to meet this dreadful "stranger" character I keep hearing about, keeping herself to herself as she does. One would almost forswear a social life to stay out of *his* way.' Silence greeted this. 'Mrs Muirhead?' I cocked my head and listened, but there was not a sound. Eventually I rose and, calling her name again, went out of the kitchen door, across a tiny back hallway and through the half-open pantry door beyond. Amongst the shelves, thinly arrayed with pots of jam and a few strings of onions, she stood with one hand clutched over her mouth, the other pressed against her straining waist, her eyes showing white in the false twilight of the windowless room.

'Mrs Muirhead, dear!' I cried. 'What is it? Come back to the kitchen and sit down.' Gently, and praying that whatever was the matter it was not the imminent arrival of a baby, I drew her back across the little hallway and installed her at the kitchen table.

'Now,' I said, shrugging off the Persian lamb and folding it over the back of a chair, 'I'm going to make you a nice cup of tea and you're going to tell me what's wrong.'

By the time I had got the kettle hot and assembled a pot, some sugar and a jug of milk, however, young Mrs Muirhead had rallied a little and was trying to brush my solicitousness off with a smile.

'You must forgive me, Mrs Gilver,' she said. 'I'm awfy subjec' to these funny turns just noo.' Her hand, however, shook a little as she took her cup from me and she looked up to see if I had noticed just as I looked down. Our eyes met and some of the nervous lift went out of her shoulders as though conceding defeat.

'Tell me,' I said, sitting opposite her and scraping my chair forward. 'I'm so sorry I spoke of it as lightly as I did. Please tell me what you know.'

'I cannot,' she said, rocking back and forward so that some of her tea slopped into the saucer. 'Dinna ask me, madam. I dare not. God help me. What am I goin' to do?' With that, she put her teacup down, put her head into her hands and began to weep sustainedly. Oh good work, I said to myself. A subtle approach, indeed.

'Hush now,' I said, smoothing back her hair. 'Sh-sh. Try to calm down, my dear. It isn't good for the baby.' At that, the sobs only strengthened in volume and I settled back to wait out the storm, only hoping that 'Archie' would not appear before it was over and box my ears for me. Eventually, sobs were replaced with sighs and she sank into her chair a little, although still holding her hands to her face.

'When was it?' I asked. There was only snuffling for a while but at last she answered.

'June,' she said and I am sorry to relate that in a small, shabby corner of my detective's soul I cheered, just for a second, before humanity prevailed.

'Monstrous,' I muttered. 'Monstrous devil.' Mrs Muirhead raised her head at last and looked at me out of sodden eyes.

'You believe?' she said.

'Of course,' I told her.

'What am I goin' to do?' she said. 'What am I goin' to tell Archie?'

I had no idea what she meant, but I had no intention of saying the wrong thing again and provoking another bout of weeping. It has never felt so cruelly wrong to do so, but I am afraid that I employed the inestimable trick of saying absolutely nothing and waiting for her to fill the silence for me. She soon did so.

'I wish ye had come sooner,' she said. 'I ken there are things you can dae. But who could I ask? Who could I turn to? Ma mammy's gone and the only one I could even imagine tellin' just wouldna listen to me.'

'Who was that?' I asked. 'Who wouldn't listen?'

'Auntie Bessie,' she said. 'Mrs McAdam. She came tae see me—I think she had guessed, when I stopped goin' to the Rural—but she took no heed, jist telt me to keep quiet and no' to be so daft.'

'I'm not sure I follow you,' I said. 'If this Mrs McAdam guessed at your ordeal, what is it that she wouldn't listen to?' Mrs Muirhead stared

167

at me, breathing fast and shallow, her eyes flickering in fright.

'Promise me,' she said. 'You must promise me on your life, you'll no' tell a soul.'

'I cross my heart and hope to die,' I told her.

'It's the baby,' she said. 'What am I goin' to do?'

CHAPTER TEN

We sat in silence for a long, empty moment, listening to the clock ticking and the soft patter of rainfall beginning outside. Then I took a mustering breath and began to speak, looking just over her left shoulder as I did so.

'You do nothing,' I said. 'When the baby comes you will love it just the same. We must catch this beast, my dear, make no mistake about it, but you do nothing. Knit and sew and get ready and, you'll see, it will all be fine in the end.'

'But what if the baby . . .' she began. She was looking at me strangely. 'What if it's no'. . . a baby?' I was speechless. 'Mrs Black next door telt me,' she went on. 'It happened to a woman fae Dundee and it wasna a baby she had, nothin' like.'

'Mrs Muirhead,' I said. 'I'm going to speak very plainly and I hope you forgive me. This creature is a man. He is not a demon or a devil, just a very bad, evil, nasty man. Of course, your baby is going to be a baby. Put that nonsense right out of your mind.'

'But then where did it come fae?' said Mrs Muirhead. 'He swooped down on me and hung over me. He pulled at me, but he didna . . . I mean,

168

no man could o' made this happen just by his evil touch. It's no' possible. Oh, what am I goin' to do?'

'Well, of course it's not possible,' I exclaimed. 'Are you saying that this creature didn't force himself upon you?' She shook her head. 'And your husband?'

'He thinks it's his,' wailed Mrs Muirhead.

'Then why, I beseech you, do you think otherwise? What in the name of sanity are you frightened of?'

'It started that nicht,' she said. 'I ken it did, for the next mornin' I was as sick as sick could be and every mornin' since too.'

'But my dear,' I said, 'that means nothing at all.' I was not about to launch into a lecture on biology, but I had to say something; she had told me her mother was dead and Auntie Bessie McAdam was obviously of little practical help if 'keep quiet and don't be daft' was typical advice from her lips. 'The sickness doesn't start the very next day, you know,' I told her, trying to sound both fierce and gentle. 'The . . . night in question'—at this point we both blushed—'might have been weeks before that. Simply weeks.'

'But Mrs Black,' she whimpered. 'Mrs Black next door telt me I had opened my soul to the devil and asked him in. And then Auntie Bessie asked me if I had been visited, but she disna believe in the devil, none o' them do, and so she jist said that whit's for me would never go past me and no' to worry.'

I was rubbing the bridge of my nose between finger and thumb, trying to see a thread of sense in this tangle.

'Why did Mrs Black accuse you of such a thing?'

169

I said. 'Did she see him? If she did, then she's a sweep for not backing you up.'

'She saw nothin',' said Mrs Muirhead. 'She said I had invited him in wi' a' my traipsin' about at nicht. When she saw me start to show she said a bairn takes in sin wi' its mither's milk and that this one would be a foot sojer for Satan. That's what she said. And then she telt me aboot the woman fae Dundee who had met the devil on the road and nine months later . . . it was terrible, she said.'

'My dear girl,' I said, trying to speak briskly although I was shaking with anger. 'Mrs Black would have us all in the fires every day, just for breathing. Don't ever *ever* pay any attention to anything she tells you and you won't go far wrong.' I sat back and passed a hand wearily over my face, trying to restore myself to something more everyday. 'Now,' I said, 'let's get this completely straight and clear. Most unfortunately, at just the moment when you should have been overjoyed by your happy news, *purely* by coincidence . . .'

'Coincidence?' she echoed.

'Truly,' I said. 'I promise you. I give you my word of honour. I'm a mother myself twice over and was a nurse in the war.' Ludicrously, since maternity wards hardly dominated in military convalescent homes, it was the nursing that appeared to clinch it and at last, she let her shoulders drop and gave me a watery smile.

'So now that we agree what didn't happen,' I went on, 'perhaps you would tell me what did. You were walking home from the Rural meeting in June and . . .?'

'He come doon the lane fae the law, as fast as fast, fairly flyin' over the ground he was and then . . .' She stopped, trembling again.

'He pounced on you, knocked you over, held a hand over your mouth so you couldn't scream, and pinched you.'

'Just so,' said Mrs Muirhead, with enormous relief that I had taken the worst part of the memory out of her hands. 'He was trying to jab at my face, but I kept my head doon and so he just plucked away at it with his claws—'

'Nails,' I said sternly.

'His nails, aye,' she said. 'Then he disappeart again.'

'Back where he had come from? Back towards the law?' She nodded. I took another deep breath, resisted the urge to cross my fingers and asked the question that was burning in me.

'Cast your mind back,' I said, 'and tell me this: was there a smell of any kind when he was close to you? Can you remember anything like that?' Mrs Muirhead's eyes flared, fear beginning to grow on her face again. 'Don't worry if it seems odd,' I assured her. 'Just tell me.'

'It disna,' she said. 'It's just what you'd think.'

'Whisky?' I ventured. It would not be the first time in my experience that the demon drink had been interpreted as literally as that. She shook her head, still holding her bottom lip in her teeth and with eyes still widening. 'Sulphur? Yeast?' Young Mrs Muirhead looked more and more horrified with each outlandish suggestion. 'Flowers, perhaps?' I suggested.

'Flowers?' she echoed. 'No, nane o' that. He smelt o' the fire itself. He smelt as though he'd come straicht fae . . . there.' She looked down as she spoke.

171

'Brimstone?' I said.

'I dinna ken what that smells like,' she said. 'He just reeked o' smoke.'

*   *   *

'Whisky, smoke, eggs, flowers and yeast,' I repeated to myself as I left the cottage a moment later. Mrs Muirhead was restored to something approaching serenity and the pastry dough had come together at last, so I made my escape while the going was good and during a break in the rain. I did take the time, however, to stop off next door.

Mrs Black answered my peremptory rap looking more than ready for me; I was sure she had heard the Muirheads' cottage door close and had been watching me.

'You ought to be ashamed of yourself,' I said, before she had a chance to talk. 'Mischief-making, salacious creature that you are. I've a good mind to tell Mr Tait what you said to that poor girl.'

'Him!' spat Mrs Black. 'I'm no feart fur him. A fine state my immortal sowel wid be in if *he* wis mindin' it.'

'It's a great sin,' I told her firmly—I thought I might as well address her in her own tongue—'a very great sin to cause the kind of trouble and unhappiness you have caused.' Mrs Black drew herself up.

'Nae whip cuts sae deep as—'

'Spare me,' I said, talking over her. 'Mischievous, salacious and a crippling bore to boot. Goodbye, Mrs Black.'

With that, I stamped back to the manse, far too cross to attempt further interviews and needing a

172

good long stint of hurling sticks for Bunty from the shelter of the porch before I was ready for tea.

Mr Tait was installed as before in front of the sitting-room fire when I entered, looking even more cosy than ever; he evidently felt that after a total of three days in his household I was no longer to be treated as an outsider and he was wearing carpet slippers now as well as the cardigan jersey and had an embroidered tea-napkin tucked over his dog collar. Lorna, however, was nowhere to be seen.

'Pancakes, my dear,' he sang out to me, 'or you'll know them as drop scones, I daresay. Come, come, while they're hot. And before Lorna gets here from wherever she's lost herself, tell me: how does it go on today?'

'Tremendously well, as a matter of fact,' I said. 'I've unearthed another victim.'

Mr Tait made a creditable job of registering concern, admiration and interest all at once with just one expression and then he circled his butter knife in the air as though whisking something, telling me to carry on.

'Well,' he said. 'Who was it? What poor soul has been suffering in silence?'

'I don't think,' I said slowly, 'that I'm at liberty to say.' I could not remember whether young Mrs Muirhead had sworn me to secrecy or not—the whole conversation had been rather fervid and the details were blurred—but if she had not, I was sure it was because she had taken my discretion as a given.

'Oh, come,' said Mr Tait, looking rather startled. 'I'm sure there's not one of my parishioners who wouldn't give me her troubles to share.' I forbore from pointing out that there was at least one of his flock—Mrs Black—who would scarcely give him the steam off her porridge to share.

'But she didn't, did she?' I pointed out. 'And so I rather think I shall keep my own counsel too.'

'Very proper,' said Mr Tait, almost managing to sound as though he meant it. 'But you can surely tell me this much: has it filled in another piece of the puzzle for you? Has it moved things along?'

The honest answer to this was, no. I had gained confirmation that the stranger often came around the law from the north, but I had known that anyway. I suppose I had gathered another note to add to his signature scent, but all I had really achieved was confirmation that there really were missing victims and that it was worth pursuing the rest of them, in the hopes that one of the others might provide a more vital clue.

'Ish,' I said, and Mr Tait smiled at me ruefully. 'There's always a great deal of "ish" before one finally breaks through.'

'Can you at least assure me that she is quite well after the ordeal? That she has rallied and put it behind her?'

Again, I could not easily think how to answer. Up until this afternoon she had done anything but and had been set fair for a complete blue funk, but now I flattered myself that if she took my words to heart she would begin to recover.

'She's fine,' I said in the end, crossing my fingers and trusting that it was true.

'Splendid,' said Mr Tait. 'They are a stalwart band, these farmers' wives of mine, are they not?'

I was about to agree with him—they certainly

174

were—and then I checked myself.

'What gives you the idea that she is a farmer's wife?' I asked.

Mr Tait grew very still at that and did not answer for a moment or two.

'I can't honestly imagine,' he said at last, sounding interested. 'How peculiar of me. Unless . . . perhaps the strange case of Mrs Hemingborough made me assume that this latest doughty lady must be another like her. Or perhaps,' he chuckled, 'it's just that my dear late wife was a farmer's daughter, as I've told you. In the ordinary way of things she might have married a farmer and been a farmer's wife too, but she married a clergyman who kept her from her home . . .' His normally cheery face had clouded, his cushiony cheeks falling.

'But brought her back again,' I said, trying to comfort him.

'All too briefly,' said Mr Tait. 'And now her home, where generations of her family tilled the good soil, has passed into other hands.' He gathered himself with a brave sigh. 'But you are quite right, my dear. Even although there are so many farmers' wives and they're all so very good to the kirk I should not forget the others.' This, I was sure, was closer to the truth, and might even account for why the likes of Mrs Black felt so disapproving of him. A minister should not have favourites, but even that first day at Gilverton when Mr Tait had told me the tale he had mentioned farmers' wives and, in reality, Mrs Fraser of Balniel was the only wife of any sort who had come forward with a story about the stranger by then. That had always niggled me in some way I

175

could not put my finger on, but I set it aside as the unmistakable sounds of Lorna arriving home, late and flurried, came to us from the front hall.

She appeared to have been out tramping around in a very different October afternoon from the one I had endured for, although her hair was frizzed with rain and a dark patch on each shoulder showed where her mackintosh seams had let in water, her eyes were alight and her smile as sparkling as any I have ever seen on a sunny picnic.

'Do forgive me, Mrs Gilver,' she said, beaming as she sat and ignoring her father's mild remonstrances about the wet hair and shoulders. 'I've been visiting, Father. Welcoming our new addition to the parish.' Mr Tait looked understandably put out at that; it was his job to welcome incomers, not to mention his job to know they were coming. 'Ford Cottage is let at last,' she went on. 'To an *artist*.' She was almost breathless as she said this, and I very briefly caught her father's eye.

'He's been walking in the area and he passed through the village only last week,' said Lorna, accepting a plate absent-mindedly, 'looking for inspiration, he said, for "a piece". When he saw Ford Cottage he immediately sent a telegram to the Howies begging them to let him rent it, and moved in the very next day.'

'What kind of artist?' said Mr Tait. 'A painter?'

'Yes,' said Lorna. 'He's got great big canvases stacked everywhere all over the living room.'

'And what's his name?' said her father.

'Captain Watson,' said Lorna, rather reverently it seemed to me. 'He's just resigned his commission and he's looking for somewhere to

176

settle down.' Her father looked slightly comforted at that. A Captain Watson with such a respectable excuse for finding himself rootless was much to be preferred to the impulsive wastrel he had at first understood this stranger to be.

'We've never had an artist at Luckenlaw before,' said Lorna, cheerfully, and she took a hearty bite out of her buttered pancake. 'I must tell Miss Lindsay and Miss McCallum. He could do a painting demonstration at the Rural, or at least give a talk.' She gave what I thought was a little shiver of anticipation. Her father, however, thought otherwise and took her cup and tea plate out of her hands, setting them down firmly on the table again.

'I insist you go and wrap your hair in a towel,' he said. 'You're chilled, Lorna dear. Wrap your hair and change your blouse like a good girl and I'll pour you a fresh cup when you come down again.' Lorna beamed at him and felt her damp hair as though noticing it for the first time, then obediently rose and left the room.

We were silent for a while once she had gone. I was thinking hard about this artist; he did not seem quite plausible to me. Mr Tait too was troubled at the thought of him.

'Odd for this chap to want to settle here, don't you think?' he said. 'Just after the war, of course, there were plenty of officers who wanted to escape the world, but a career soldier, as this Watson must be . . .'

'. . . might be expected to look for something a bit more lively,' I agreed.

'Different story with the poet, of course,' Mr Tait went on. 'Have you heard about him?'

177

I nodded. 'I was wondering about what Lorna said; that this artist had been walking in the area. Moonlight walks, do you suppose? Might his recent passage through the village have been on the night in question?'

'Surely not.'

'It's certainly worth making sure that Elspeth McConechie, say, or Annie Pellow, gets a look at him to see if he seems familiar.'

'On the quiet, mind,' said Mr Tait softly as we heard Lorna returning, and we shared a smile.

After tea the rain began to fall more determinedly than ever and the two Taits and I settled in by the sitting-room fireside for a long evening of respectively mending, snoozing over a book of essays and making notes on the case under cover of planning my talk. My beginner's luck that afternoon had been considerable, but I could not hope to meet such good fortune every time I ventured forth and I quailed when I looked in the Post Office Directory and saw just how many dwellings there were scattered about the lanes where my other missing victims might be waiting. There must, I thought desperately, be some way of doing this more efficiently, of avoiding the time I might waste knocking on doors where no one had ever been to the Rural or was not there on the night in question. July and September were the months which were missing a name to enter against them, so if I could find out who had stopped going by then—scared off by the stranger or forbidden by a protective husband, perhaps—I could save myself the kitchen visit, the household budget subterfuge of which I was already growing weary, and the chastening haughty put-downs

178

which were bound to ensue if I accused some blameless woman of being implicated in the trouble that beset Luckenlaw. If Miss Lindsay kept a record, it could be just what I needed. But what excuse could I give her for wanting to see it?

'Can I help you?' said Lorna, and I realised that I was staring at her as I tried to think.

'I do apologise,' I said. 'I was miles away.'

'Only . . . you haven't asked me yet,' she went on. I stared at her. 'About my household budget, I mean.'

'Of course!' I said. 'Well, I'd be very grateful for anything you can tell me.'

'I may not have much to tax me just now,' she said. She glanced over at the drowsing head opposite and went on softly. 'My father has a very generous stipend and a pension from Kingoldrum as well and my mother had money of her own, so I don't really need to worry as long as it's the manse we're considering. But'—another glance at her father—'I was all set to run my little household once before using my own small inheritance, and I would have been equal to it, would have delighted in it.'

'Of course you would, my dear,' I murmured, trying to ignore the echo of Professor Higgins in my head, sneering at anyone who essayed happiness on a pittance and called it fun.

'And I haven't changed my mind or grown too set in my ways,' she went on. 'A daughter of the manse I might be but I could be happy with a much less . . . a much more . . . I mean, a *bohemian* life can be managed on a shoestring, don't you think?'

I refrained from hazarding a guess about how big a hole daily servings of opium and absinthe

179

would make in her mother's money, and anyway I am sure that the mild, smiling Lorna meant something quite different when she spoke of a bohemian life. I supposed too that it was inevitable for her to harbour some wistful thoughts upon hearing that another artistic soul had come to rest, and in such romantic circumstances, in her poet's cottage, and perhaps he had seen in her his heart's desire when she hove through the rain towards him and she was only responding in kind, but I doubted it and I hoped for her sake that she was a little less transparent in this Captain Watson's hearing and in the Howie ladies' too; they were bound to laugh at her, friends or no friends, for Lorna was just the kind of girl to tease little spikes of cruelty from the best of hearts and the Howies, although kind, were always on the look-out for diversion too.

Once again Lorna looked over at her father and when she spoke again it was almost in a whisper.

'Do you believe in fate, Mrs Gilver?' she said. 'I do.'

'Um,' I said.

'This afternoon,' she went on, 'when I went to Ford Cottage, I could almost have sworn . . . Well, what I mean is, I'm glad I knew already that Captain Watson was there. If I had just caught sight of him I would have sworn Walter had come back to me. It took quite ten minutes for the feeling to disperse, and I think it's a sign.'

'Really?' I said. One would have imagined that a pacifist poet and a retired soldier with enormous canvases strewn about would be at either end of the spectrum of artists, nothing much in common at all. But perhaps it was just red hair or something. 'Is there a very strong likeness, then?'

'Oh no,' said Lorna. 'None at all, really. It was just seeing him there, I daresay, in Walter's cottage. In Walter's setting.'

Or, as Alec would say, in Walter's context. Was he right after all? If Lorna could be persuaded that she recognised someone just because of where she saw him, was it possible that frightened women would not recognise a neighbour just because they saw him where they could hardly believe he would be? Was I wasting time with the women when I should have been sleuthing away after the men? I had a small, sneaking feeling down inside that I had blundered.

*   *   *

It was long after dinner, almost bedtime, just the moment when one is deciding whether to ring for more coal or bank the embers and begin to turn down the lamps, that all the commotion began. There was a banging at the manse door and Mr Tait heaved himself to his slippered feet with a weary sigh and padded out to see what was the matter. Lorna and I followed him, for surely this hammering was something beyond the usual supplicating call for the minister.

In the hallway, lit by a housemaid's raised candle, stood a large man of early middle-age, who was twisting his cap and breathing heavily, although whether from some turmoil or just from the exertion it must take to move his bulk around—he really was quite enormous when one got close—was hard to guess at immediately.

'Logan?' said Mr Tait. 'What is it? Is something the matter?'

181

The man flicked a glance at Lorna and me, but clearly was in no mood to observe niceties and demand that the womenfolk be protected from whatever he had to say.

'They've arrested Jockie Christie,' he announced. Lorna, standing beside me, breathed in with a harsh gasp.

'Arrested him for what, Mr McAdam?' she said.

'Prowling,' came the answer. 'Constable Whatsisname spied him at it and went down to the police station to get Sergeant Doolan, then the two of them came up and nabbed him and took him away to the jail and if Ella Doolan hadn't sent her lad up on his bicycle to tell Bessie we'd never have known a thing about it. It looks bad for him with this "dark stranger" starting up again.'

'But that's ridiculous,' said Mr Tait.

'Will you help? The lad's done no wrong, not really, and you don't like to think of him in a jail cell, Mr Tait. Will you go down and speak to Mike Doolan in the morning?'

'I'll do better than that,' Mr Tait answered stoutly. 'I'll go down there now. There's no reason for the poor lad to spend a night in a cell. Prowling, indeed! Prowling where?'

'I'll be getting back then,' said the messenger, lumbering round awkwardly on the mat and preparing to take his leave. 'Thank you, Mr Tait. It's much appreciated.'

'The least I could do,' said Mr Tait, sounding rather gruff, as though embarrassed, as we watched the door close on the visitor's departing back. Logan McAdam, I thought. Husband of Auntie Bessie McAdam of Over Luckenlaw Farm and one of Miss Lindsay's erstwhile name-callers.

The very floor shook as he descended the porch steps and I thought that at least he could be crossed off my list of potential snaky strangers. No one in the world could fail to recognise *him*.

Lorna, with a little twittering about making up a parcel of biscuits and a hot flask, disappeared along with the kitchen maid. Mr Tait went into the little cloakroom by the front door and sat down on the bench there to pull on his boots. I followed him, casually.

'Why would the sergeant's wife tell Mrs McAdam that John Christie was arrested?' I said.

'Ella Doolan is Bessie McAdam's cousin,' said Mr Tait.

'I see, but what's the connection at the other end? Why are the McAdams bound up in Christie's concerns?'

Mr Tait looked puzzled for a moment before he answered and then he shrugged.

'They're neighbours,' he said simply. 'They're at the next farm round.'

'Would that we all had such neighbours,' I replied. 'Would that we all had such ministers too, Mr Tait. I'm afraid the incumbent at Gilverton Manse would be as likely to let the boy cool his heels as to set out into the night to secure his instant release.'

'I am very glad to hear that you approve, Mrs Gilver,' he said, his voice straining as he bent over his bootlaces, 'because I am going to have to enlist you.' He sat up and puffed out the rest of his breath. 'As a chaperone. The best way of getting Sergeant Doolan to see sense, as far as I can think, is to take a handful of the stranger's victims to the police station and have them tell him that he's got the wrong man.'

'I suppose,' I said, suddenly feeling very doubtful. Perhaps if the victims saw him huddled in a prison cell—in the setting, that is, where such fellows belonged—they would be convinced that he was the stranger after all. Could 'context' manage all of that? Mr Tait was looking at me expectantly. 'I mean, of course,' I said hastily, 'I'll certainly come along. I mean, everyone I've spoken to is quite sure it couldn't be him, so the police are surely in error—although there's still the prowling.' Mr Tait waved a dismissive hand at me.

'Taking a walk after supper is not a crime,' he said. 'Now, who should we ask to go with us?'

This was not a straightforward matter, I thought, as I went upstairs to dress for the unexpected outing. Clearly, Mrs Muirhead was out of the running in her condition and I was not keen to include Mrs Fraser in the party. Annie Pellow had seemed a level-headed girl, but she lodged on the green and it would be terribly public for her to be dragged out in her curl-papers at ten o'clock at night in front of her neighbours. Molly Tweed was a far better bet: she had had a good look at her assailant that night in the spring. She was favourably disposed to young Mr Christie, but I still believed that her preference for him would only guarantee her making no mischief if he was not the one, and could not possibly lead her as far as covering for him if indeed he were guilty. And then Elspeth McConechie could perhaps be persuaded to come along too, for she was a sensible soul.

It took some doing to winkle Elspeth out of her employers' protective grasp in the end; I had

184

forgotten just how solicitous Mrs Palmer had been when I had tracked Elspeth down to her dairy.

'Come now, Mrs Palmer,' Mr Tait had said with a stern look over the tops of his spectacles, as we stood on the kitchen doorstep at Over Luck, 'Elspeth has no objection and Mrs Gilver is here to take care of her. You surely don't want our young friend languishing in that nasty jail, do you?'

At which, Mrs Palmer had—very reluctantly—nodded to Elspeth that she was free to go and had left us to it, with a 'Do what you will then, you're harming no one' thrown over her departing shoulder.

Our reception at Luckenlaw House could hardly have been more different. Vashti and Nicolette were summoned by the noise of Mr Tait's motor-car engine—he had unearthed the fabled Napier for the expedition and it made a racket like twenty aeroplanes running out of fuel together in a hailstorm—and were only just persuaded not to come along, as though the trip were laid on for their fun, but settled in the end for giving Molly an archly solemn pep talk each.

'Remember,' said Vashti, 'take a very good look and make sure you are quite certain before you say yea or nay.'

'And only go in if you are you sure it won't be too upsetting,' said Nicolette. 'I should hate to think you're going to relive that shocking ordeal.'

'Well, we had better be off,' said Mr Tait, 'and let you ladies get back to your refreshment.' He glared at the cocktail glass in Nicolette's hand.

It was only a few miles down to Colinsburgh, where the blue light above the police station shone out alone into the darkness. There were no streetlamps on the long stretch of terraced cottages which made up the bulk of the little town and with the public bar shut up and shuttered and lamps already out behind almost every pair of drawn curtains, it was a picture of slumbering respectability. Mr Tait's ancient motor car shuddered to a halt and he climbed down.

'Wait here, won't you please, ladies,' he said. 'I have high hopes of Sergeant Doolan. You might not have to go through with it at all if he can be brought to his senses.' With that he left us.

'I dinna ken why everybody's so set on Jock Christie,' said Molly once we were alone. Mr Tait had subdued her on the journey, but she was clearly quite unbowed by my presence alone. 'It's no' him, eh it's no', Elspeth?' Elspeth shook her head. She was in less ebullient spirits than the irrepressible Molly, shivering slightly beside me and looking ghastly pale in the faint blue light. Before she had plucked up the nerve to speak, Mr Tait was back again. He opened the door and climbed in, shutting it behind him with what amounted to a resounding slam at this hour of the night in a quiet village.

'Confound the man,' he said, treating the three of us to a scowl which was surely Sergeant Doolan's by rights. 'He's adamant. Said Christie was behaving suspiciously, creeping around in the edge of a field at Balniel with no excuse for being there, and now he's in his office there stamping pieces of paper and tying up files with pink tape left, right and centre. I'm afraid, my dears, that you are going to have to steel yourselves for a rather unpleasant ten minutes or so. Now who wants to go first? Or shall you both go together?'

186

'I canna,' blurted out Elspeth. 'I'm sorry, Mr Tait. I canna thole goin' in there.'

'But it's John Christie, my dear,' Mr Tait said gently. 'You are not about to face your attacker again. It's Jockie Christie and you know it wasn't him.'

'I canna,' said Elspeth again, her voice rising. 'My mother would drop deid if she kent I had walked into a police station and looked at a man in a jail cell. She wis afrontit enough that I didna keep ma mooth shut aboot the stranger. She would dee and she would kill me first, and I *canna*.' She stopped talking but continued to shake her head over and over again. Mr Tait looked for a moment as though he were planning to attack this stout resolve, but in the end he turned to Molly, with a sigh.

'So, it falls to you, my dear,' he said. 'You must come in and tell Sergeant Doolan—once again, as though you didn't tell him until you were blue in the face in the springtime—that you had no idea who attacked you and John Christie is not the man. Come along.'

'No!' wailed Elspeth. 'Don't leave me, Mr Tait.' Her nerve, which I had thought so firm, had quite deserted her and so, since she could not be left howling alone at the roadside and Molly could not be sent alone into the jail, I took a deep breath and stepped down into the street.

If truth be told, I was rather wobbly about the knees at the prospect of entering the place. I had been inside a police station once before, but it had been in the daytime and I had been taken in a side door to be interviewed as a witness in a room with an ordinary window; I had never before heard

187

clanking keys and looked through bars at a prisoner. I told myself not to be a ninny and strode through the door sweeping Molly before me.

The front desk was hardly alarming, looking with its worn, polished surface, gleaming brass bell and backdrop of shallow shelves full of wire baskets where papers were neatly filed, just like any other slightly shabby office one might encounter. Sergeant Doolan awaited us behind the counter, hatless of course and with the collar of his tunic unbuttoned in a concession to the lateness of the hour and, no doubt, his sense that he was being highly accommodating to Mr Tait and indeed to Mr Christie.

'Madam,' he said, nodding politely at me, before turning to Molly. 'Now, Miss . . . Tweed, isn't it? I ken you said away back when we spoke before that you did not know the man who assaulted yer person, but I want you to keep an open mind and look right close at this fellow we've got here. We've put a low light on in the cell so you'll be seeing him much as you would have seen him yon night he attacked you.'

'Um, Sergeant?' I said, unwilling to let this pass.

'Oh quite so,' said Sergeant Doolan. 'I mean, you'll be seeing him in the same light as whoever it was you saw that night. Now, let's go through.' He produced a satisfyingly huge bunch of keys from under the skirts of his tunic and picked through them as he strode unhurriedly along a passage leading towards the back of the building. We filed through the gap in the desk made by a lifted flap and scurried after him.

'Now,' he said, when he had fitted a key into a door at the end. 'Just take a good look at him,

188

Molly, and tell us the truth. You can do a tremendous good deed by all your friends and neighbours if you help us—'

'Sergeant, really!' I remonstrated again. Molly was beginning to breathe rather fast and, as the sergeant turned the key, she put her hand into mine. Even through my glove I could feel that her fingers were icy and I squeezed them as we stepped through the door and into the dimness on the other side.

CHAPTER ELEVEN

'Molly?' said a voice in the dark.

'Miss Tweed to you, if you don't mind, son,' said Sergeant Doolan.

Slowly, my eyes were adjusting. The room we stood in was no more than ten feet square and was divided into two halves by a set of stout bars running all the way from floor to ceiling. On our side of the bars was a kitchen chair with a newspaper, open at the racing pages, lying on it. On the far side was a small camp bed with a thin blanket folded neatly on top of the equally thin pillow, and a young man sitting bolt upright facing us and staring.

'Stand up, son,' said Sergeant Doolan. His voice was far from friendly; I expect the epithet was habitual more than anything, since most of those who passed through his hands must be young men and he had to call them something. 'Now, Miss Tweed. Tell me, is this the man who knocked you over in the yard that moonlit night in May?'

189

Molly, letting my hand fall away from hers, took a step forward and peered through the bars at Jock Christie. He was a striking figure, even in his present humbled state, standing there in his laceless boots, clutching at the waist of his beltless, braceless trousers. He was perhaps twenty-five, perhaps not as much as that, with fair hair brushed forward in a shock, and those jug-handle ears which I have always found rather endearing in a young man, perhaps because they remind me of my sons, newly shorn for their return to school which is when I love them best. He had the look of a farmer, hands swollen and roughened, arms and legs slightly bent while at rest as though braced against the weight of a hay bale or the pull of the plough horse, but he was far from bulky, even in his heavy clothes. Would anyone say he was snaky? Molly was hesitating, saying nothing at all.

'Miss Tweed?' said Sergeant Doolan, and his voice betrayed a little of the hopeful excitement her hesitation must have been affording him.

'Molly?' I said, wonderingly. She turned to face me and her eyes were wide and dark in her stricken face.

'I dinna ken what to say,' she whispered. 'Oh, why did I ever come here?'

'You mean, you've changed your mind?' I breathed. She stared hard over my shoulder for a minute or two, remembering I daresay, although there was a calculating look on her face rather than the expression of effortful concentration which might be expected. At last, her brows unknitted and she turned back to face the sergeant and the prisoner.

'It wasna him,' she said in a clear voice.

'You're sure?' said Sergeant Doolan.

'As sure as I'm standin' here,' said Molly. 'It wasna John Christie that jumped oot at me that nicht.'

The young man in the cell sat down heavily on the camp bed again with his shoulders slumped forwards and his hands hanging down between his knees. He looked up at the sergeant from under his shock of hair.

Sergeant Doolan glanced between him and Molly once or twice and then cleared his throat importantly.

'Aye, well,' he said. 'There's still the matter of what you were up to tonight, though, isn't there?'

'I was out a walk,' said John Christie. 'I told you that.'

'Out a walk in a field in the dead of night with no lantern?' said Sergeant Doolan.

'It was nine o'clock,' said Christie. 'And I like walking in the fields. I like to feel the earth under my boots. I'm a farmer.'

I could see that Sergeant Doolan had trouble swallowing this and it did not ring quite true to me either, for every farmer I have ever met—and that is many—has been only too desperate to put the horse in its stall at the end of the weary day and shut the door against the crops and the beasts and the endless troubles they bring. Even Hugh, who charges around the fields and woods from dawn until dusk in all weathers, is ready to turn his back on them after dinner and settle into an armchair.

'So you're admitting you often do this, are you?' said Sergeant Doolan. 'Tramp about in the cold and dark when every other buddy wi' any sense is by his own fireside?'

'My own fireside is gey lonely,' said Christie. 'I'm happier out under the sky, day or night the same.'

And troubled as he was, certain as he was that something here did not add up, Sergeant Doolan had no choice but to let him go.

*　　　*　　　*

We delivered Elspeth back to Easter Luck Farm, making no mention of the sudden attack of dainty disinclination which had beset her—there was no harm done after all—and then rumbled around the back lanes to Luckenlaw House to return Molly to her kitchens. Once again, a party from above stairs turned out to greet us, the Howie men this time accompanying their wives to the door, and much to Mr Tait's disgust and my slight exasperation all four of them were now rather drunk. Still, it was the first time I had ever seen Irvine Howie on his feet and he had even left his newspaper behind, bringing with him only a brandy glass and a half-smoked cigarette.

'Hurrah for Molly!' Nicolette chirped as Mr Tait opened the side door of the motor car and she stepped down. 'Well, was it him?'

Molly shook her head and, giving a kind of flying curtsey as she passed, scuttled round the side of the house to the back door.

'No, it wasn't him,' said Mr Tait sternly. 'You'll be very pleased to hear, Mr Howie, that your tenant will soon be back at the farm.'

Johnny Howie had the grace to look sheepish at this; after all, one might have expected a little more solicitousness from the menfolk at least

192

when a young man in their bailiwick was clapped in irons.

'Yes, steady on there,' he said to his wife. 'It's a serious matter, you know.'

'Oh, don't be so utterly dreary,' said Nicolette. 'Come on, Vash, let's go and ask her about it. Such a scream!' With that, the sisters disappeared giggling into the house.

'. . . excuse our wives,' said Irvine, taking a last lazy draw on his cigarette and flicking it onto the gravel. '. . . more sense than a pair of geese, sometimes.' And he too strolled unsteadily away into the lamplit hall without so much as a farewell, much less a thank you.

Mr Tait was beginning to look thunderous, his jaw stuck out and his eyes for once without the merest hint of a twinkle.

'Yes, I must apologise for them,' said Johnny, who was unfocused around the eyes but otherwise seemed in a rather better state than the rest of them. 'They are beyond any pale, but there's no harm in them really, you know.' His words sparked a memory in me, but I could not catch at it. 'Just high spirits.'

'It's hardly a matter to raise the spirits!' said Mr Tait.

'No, no, you misunderstand me, sir,' said Johnny. 'Their spirits were high anyway, and simply failed to come down to a seemly level for this nasty business.'

'Well, there are worse crimes than being too cheerful, aren't there?' I offered, thinking that anyone who managed to hoist their spirits off the ground at all when incarcerated in this spot with these husbands deserved some credit for it.

'Poor things,' Johnny Howie went on and he leaned against the doorframe as though settling in for a lengthy chat. Perhaps he was just as intoxicated as the others after all, but rather better at hiding it. 'When we married, you know, they thought life was going to be one long round of parties. No wonder they're so excited about putting this bash on for Lorna.' It was perhaps an innocent remark, but still it served to remind Mr Tait that he could not afford to be absolutely disapproving and superior, and he grunted in a conciliatory kind of way.

'Aye well,' he said. 'A quiet life in the country is not for everyone, right enough.'

'How true, how true,' said Johnny Howie. 'When I think of those two girls who arrived at Balnagowan all those years ago, stuffed to the brim with the thrilling history of the Rosses—they weren't joking, you know, when they said it was our ancestress who was the chief attraction—when I think of them reduced to finding diversion at village meetings and an artistic new tenant in a damp little cottage . . . my heart aches for them, really it does. I could refuse them nothing it's in my power to give.'

Neither Mr Tait nor I could think of an answer to any of this and so urging him to go inside and showering him with goodbyes we hurried back to the motor car and left.

'I'm not at all sure I'm happy to see Lorna get any closer to that lot, if I'm honest,' said Mr Tait, speaking loudly over the thump and screech of the engine as we trundled down the drive.

'Oh, I don't know,' I said. 'They have very fashionable manners—that is to say no manners at all—but they're terribly fond of Lorna. She might even be a good influence on them in the end.'

'What did you make of young Jock Christie?' said Mr Tait, and it is quite something when giving one's impression of a prisoner and possible prowler can be seen as moving on to safer topics.

'He seemed rather dejected to find himself behind bars, as might be expected,' I said. 'And while I am sure he wasn't "prowling" really—what good would prowling round a field be, anyway? Unless to poach rabbits—he wasn't absolutely convincing with his tale of a blameless stroll either, gave the rather feeble excuse of finding it lonely at home and being happier out. But it's hardy *less* lonely, is it? And that makes me think, Mr Tait. Why is his fireside lonely? I should have thought that a fine young man like that, with a farm to boot, would be married. There's certainly no shortage of single girls for him to choose from.'

'Who's to say?' said Mr Tait. 'I was forty myself before I married.'

'Yes but . . .' I began and then stopped, unable to think of a way to phrase my meaning that was not blunt to the point of coarseness. I decided just to say it anyway. 'But it was different then. Before the war, I mean. There were . . . well, enough men to go round, weren't there? Now, at Luckenlaw the same as everywhere else, there are scores of young women—Miss McCallum, Miss Lindsay, Annie Pellow, Elspeth, Molly—and those are just the ones I've met in a day or two.'

'Not to mention . . .' said Mr Tait, thinking of Lorna, I am sure.

'Not to mention all the others whom I haven't,' I supplied, thinking of Lorna too. 'So I simply don't see how Jock Christie has managed to live here for five years and stay single. And I'm sure there's something behind it. Something Johnny Howie said just now reminded me. Aha!'

Mr Tait turned to look at me, making the motor car swerve. We were back in the village by now, headed for the manse drive.

'Aha?' he said.

'Yes. Mr McAdam said a very strange thing earlier this evening. When he was entreating you to help, he said of Jock Christie that he "had done no wrong, not really" and so he didn't deserve to be in jail. Johnny Howie just said something very similar about his wife and sister-in-law: that there was not really any harm in them. Now in the case of the Howie ladies, I can see what he meant. No harm in them although they are rude and silly. But what did Mr McAdam mean about Christie? If he has not *really* done any wrong, what is it that he *has* done? Do you see what I mean?'

'I do, I do indeed,' said Mr Tait, letting the motor car roll to a stop in front of the old stable in the side yard of the manse. 'But you are being carried away by your detective's nose, my dear Mrs Gilver. I am afraid that Logan McAdam was merely thinking of the farm. As I mentioned before, what the lad did was take over a farm that he had no business taking over, not at his age and with his college learning and no farming in his blood.'

'Ah yes,' I said, remembering. 'I've heard a bit more about that now. Hadn't all the neighbouring farmers more or less moved in and helped themselves? It seemed like fearful cheek to me, but I can understand why they hoped it might go

196

on for ever. Whoever it was who sold the estate to the Howies sold it not a moment too soon if a good farm was lying empty, don't you think?'

'That's not how it was seen at Luckenlaw,' said Mr Tait, and his voice was rather cold, to my surprise. 'Farmland cannot lie useless and it was a lot of hard work for the neighbours to keep the place in good heart, and as for old Lady Muirie—well, she had a lot of respect for the old ways and no taste for change.'

'I apologise, Mr Tait,' I said. 'I seem to have said something that's upset you.' At this, he softened again and the twinkle came back into his eye. I could see it quite clearly in the light of the lamp the manse servants had left burning for us above the door.

'Not at all, my dear,' he said, patting my knee through the travelling rug folded there. 'I am being too sensitive by far. Only, it was my wife's family's farm, you see. They had been the tenants there as long as anyone could remember, connections of the Muiries away way back. And since she had no brothers or sisters, when her father died and she was all the way up in Perthshire, there was no one to run the place.'

'I am sorry,' I said again, but it still sounded most peculiar to me. Why, it must have been empty for decades, and no matter how fond of tradition this Lady Muirie might have been, I was on the side of the Howies (and of Hugh, I would wager) in thinking that a farm needed a farmer, even if he was a slip of a lad whom no one knew and for whom no one much cared. It was shocking, somehow, to think that nothing more than parochial gossip and sour grapes lay behind all the mutterings of Jock Christie's name in the case of the dark stranger.

*   *   *

The next morning, putting all thoughts of the farming dynasties of Luckenlaw out of my head, I turned back to the question of the missing victims and set off resolutely after an early breakfast to beard Miss Lindsay when her den was about to be overrun by cubs. (I had decided that she probably kept her SWRI records all together somewhere and that if I landed on her unannounced just before school began she would have no choice but to leave me with them and tend to her charges.) The skies had cleared before the ground had dried last night and now there was a crackling glaze of frost underfoot, the fallen leaves picked out in white along their veins and stuck fast to the ground. Bunty pranced ahead, as skittish as always when she felt the earth unaccountably tingle and splinter under her paws, and I huddled inside my Persian lamb coat and Beefeater's hat hoping that I would not slip as I picked my way down the drive and across the green to the school lane.

'Here she comes, there she goes,' sang the girls, at play inside the railings waiting for the bell.

'Torn stockings and hairy toes,
A broom in her hand and a wart on her nose,
Here she comes, there she goes.'

I decided not to take it personally and gave them a benign smile as I passed them. Bunty made a few feinting darts towards the skipping rope but

198

thought the better of it and followed me to the schoolhouse door.

Miss Lindsay was too polite to do other than greet me and usher me in, but she glanced not all that surreptitiously at her fob watch as she did so, and I made haste to explain that I was on a quest to view her Rural register the better to pin down those farms and cottages where I should look to find my audience for the talk.

'What a good idea,' she said. 'You certainly do seem to have a talent for organisation, Mrs Gilver.' With that staggering remark—one I had never heard directed my way before—she slapped a stout cardboard file on the table before me, took up her hand bell and left. The summoning clangs had sounded and faded away before I recovered myself and bent to the file, unwinding the ribbon tape holding it shut and feeling a thrill of anticipation for what I would find there.

I was in luck. The list of members was practically the first document in the—not inconsiderable—pile and, Miss Lindsay being Miss Lindsay, not only were the departing members scored off and the newcomers added in at the end but the dates for these comings and goings were included in her clear, round, schoolteacher's hand. I opened my notebook and began to copy it down, fearing that when the morning prayers which I could hear droning away in the schoolroom were finished she might leave her class at work and return to me. Bunty, having padded around the sitting room and subjected everything in reach to a thorough sniffing, had decided that although there were no biscuits in the immediate offing this place was otherwise acceptable and had curled herself in front of the fire and gone to sleep.

Elspeth the dairy maid, Mrs Fraser from Balniel, and Mrs Muirhead had resigned their memberships exactly when one would have expected they might—immediately after the meetings which had ended so horribly for each of them—but I noted as I was copying this down that although there were other fallings away—a Mrs Gow, two Misses Morton and a Mrs and Miss Martineau—none of these had left after the July or September gatherings and so did not seem likely to be the missing victims. Besides, surely a Mrs and Miss Martineau must be mother and daughter, must live at the same address and must therefore have walked home together and kept one another safe. The same had to be true of the Miss Mortons, or at least it would be easy enough to find out. Mrs Gow was certainly worth a visit, even though it was the August meeting which had seen her off, after which it had been Mrs Fraser of Balniel who had succumbed to the stranger and sent him packing with her deserving goodness and her prayers.

So much for the droppers-off. As for the joiners-in, a Mrs Torrance had come along for the first time in June; the Howies—famously—had turned up in July to witness whatever cataclysm the preacher's wife had unleashed on the gathering and how I wished I knew! Mrs Hemingborough had finally fallen into step only in time for the meeting in September, which was rather hard luck when one considered that it was after the very next get-together, in October, that she was ravaged in the lane. September, in fact, showed rather a flurry

200

as Mrs McAdam also had her first experience of the Rural meeting and Mrs Palmer, Elspeth McConechie's mistress, too.

A very fruitful exercise, I concluded rather smugly to myself, tucking my notebook into my pocket, and now I should tidy the papers back into their box and be on my way. Instead, however, I continued to leaf through the pages in the file, mostly rather dreary official communications from the grandly titled Federation Headquarters or else carbon copies of earlier talks, which made my heart sink: I was no more able to pound out my talk in triplicate upon a type-writing machine, than I was able to dream up anything to say. Towards the bottom, things got marginally more interesting again, with photographed displays of handicrafts and recipes copied out in handwriting upon decorated cards. One of these, I noted, was for a concoction called Boiled Dressing (to be used in place of salad oil) and its long list of ingredients began with flour, vinegar and hot sour milk. I shuddered, praying that Mrs Tilling would never come across such a thing, and quickly turned it face down.

I was nearly at the bottom now, just a page or two to go and then something lumpy underneath. The very last sheet of paper bore some sketches in watercolour, rather nicely done, and since the notes which accompanied them were in Miss Lindsay's writing I surmised that the painting was her handiwork too. I stared at the sheet and my heart began to bang so hard in my chest that I was sure I could hear it and glanced down at Bunty to see if she could hear it too. All of the pictures were of a heart shape or a pair of hearts entwined, some with a banner across them, some with crowns above them: in short they were sketches of the jewel that Lorna Tait, Miss McCallum and Miss Lindsay herself wore as brooches, that Nicolette and Vashti Howie—to Miss McCallum's disapproval—had rendered in crochet-work for themselves. What was causing my heart to bang so painfully under my ribs, however, was not the sketches but the title, emblazoned across the top of the page in an extravagant copperplate with illuminated capitals and curlicued underlining. *The Witch's Heart*, it said.

I lifted the sheet out of the box and reached for the final item—the heavy, irregular shape I had felt—sure that I knew what I should find. It was a roll of stiff leatherette tied with a strap, something like a needle case, which creaked and crackled impossibly loudly as I opened it. I looked warily at the door and then again at Bunty, knowing that if footsteps were approaching even from a distance she would have an ear cocked by now.

When the last fold of squeaking leatherette was released, I gazed down at what lay before me. It was set out like a travelling salesman's display case, which was fairly close to the truth, and the sales had been going rather well. Quite half of the little loops were empty with only a couple of pinpricks on each to show where the pins had been pushed through when the roll was full. There were still plenty left though, done in blue enamel, with some white and some gold; row after row of witch's hearts waiting for takers.

My fingers steady, although my heart continued to imitate a carpet beater, I folded the roll up again, tied the strap, and carefully replaced the pile of photographs, recipes, and documents on top. Then I closed the lid, wound the tape tightly around the fastening and pushed the file to the middle of the table. I was still regarding it, trying to digest what I had just seen, when the handle of the sitting-room door turned and the door itself swung towards me. I shrieked and shot out of my chair, joined by Bunty, who sprang up half in response to my shriek and half just in the normal way of things whenever a door was opened. Miss Lindsay, for of course it was she, gave a small squeak of her own and leapt backwards before we both laughed, apologised, flushed a little and busied ourselves with the hair-patting and hem-straightening which always ensues when one has made a chump of oneself or, in Miss Lindsay's case, witnessed a near stranger doing so.

I thanked her profusely for letting me see the register, apologised for making so free with her sitting room as to drowse by the fire long after I had finished and, grabbing Bunty, made an undignified exit. My head, owing to holding onto a dog collar and to a desire for invisibility, was down and so I could not help but see a glint of sunshine off the enamelled hearts and crown points on the brooch pinned to Miss Lindsay's black serge lapel.

Outside, before I had even passed beyond the schoolyard railings, certainly before I had begun to think calmly about what any of this might mean, I was hailed in hearty tones and I turned to see Miss McCallum stumping up the lane from the ford in stout walking shoes and a capacious hairy coat, like an Afghan.

'Beautiful morning, Mrs Gilver,' she cried. Bunty waggled her entire rear end and whined. She adores people who speak very loudly.

'Oh, quite. Indeed. Where have you been? Is the post office not open today?' I gabbled. I have noticed more than once a tendency in myself to turn waspish when flustered.

'It's not quite time yet,' said Miss McCallum. 'I always try to get out for a good long tramp on dry days before opening time.'

'Jolly good for you,' I said, trying to sound a bit friendlier and succeeding only in patronising her, I fear. 'Rather cold this morning though, wasn't it?'

Miss McCallum put her hands on her hips and straddled her legs, looking like a little round principal boy. 'Not once you get your pace up,' she said. 'I'm as warm as anything under here now.' And to prove it she undid the bone toggles on her coat and threw it open to reveal her grey flannel postmistress's dress underneath. There it was, on the breast pocket, glittering in the sun. I am afraid I did not manage to stop my eyes flashing when I saw it and Miss McCallum looked down, squashing her many chins against her chest as she peered at it.

'Admiring my brooch?' she said. I nodded, dumbly.

'It's your SWRI badge, isn't it?' I said.

'Now it is,' said Miss McCallum, 'but it's been around a fair bit longer than the Rural, believe you me.' She gave me a broad smile and with a look towards the church clock, she scuttled off, her boots thumping.

Could this be real? Three of the leading lights of the Luckenlaw Rural emblazoned with the secret symbol of a witch's heart. But had not Lorna Tait said that her brooch came from her mother? A minister's wife? What did any of it mean? I headed down the lane, meaning to walk on just long enough to give Miss McCallum time to get to the post office before I retraced my steps, but when I stopped and turned, Bunty refused to follow.

'Come on, darling,' I cajoled, in that way that turns Hugh purple with rage. Bunty ignored me. She was standing stock still in the middle of the lane, with her ears pricked and her tail wagging.

'Come on,' I said rather more sharply. 'I don't care how many R-A-B-B-I-Ts you smell.' She wagged her tail even harder at me; Bunty knows how to spell 'rabbit' very well. 'Heel,' I said. 'Now.' She paid no heed and, looking closely at her, I began to think it could not be rabbits after all. Her nose was not twitching; she was listening to something. I put my head on one side and listened too. Very faintly, from down by the ford, the sound of whistling could be heard, but Bunty is not usually so very interested in whistling. I listened again. It grew slightly louder as though the whistler had come closer—come outside, perhaps—and then it broke off as he coughed a luxurious and rather disgusting morning cough.

Bunty yelped and before I could stop her she raced off down the hill into the trees, her paws thundering, more like a greyhound at a track than a carriage dog of impeccable breeding.

'Stop this instant!' I bellowed. 'Bunty! Bad dog! Come to heel now!' but I sprinted off after her, knowing that the commands alone would achieve nothing. Down here the frost was as thick as midnight, since no sun ever shone to melt it, and it was frost over moss which is a uniquely treacherous combination down which to sprint in polite shoes, so it was no surprise to find myself skidding, bumping down onto my behind and finishing the journey to the ford in a long, graceful slide.

Bunty had jumped the stream and was in Ford Cottage garden, wriggling with delight, and threatening to knock over an easel and some water pots set up there, as she submitted to having her ears tickled by a young man in a pink canvas smock and a silk neck scarf, wearing a soft grey hat stuck with a peacock feather. This feather waved flamboyantly as he crouched over Bunty, kissing her head and letting her lick his face joyously. I shuddered. Much as I adore Bunty, I should never let her lick my face. Hardly anyone would; in fact only one person in her acquaintance ever did. I exclaimed and he looked up at last.

'Dr Watson, I presume,' I said drily. 'Or—sorry—it was Captain Watson, wasn't it?'

'My dear Holmes,' said Alec, wiping his face with a handkerchief and walking towards the little footbridge. 'What an entrance, Dan. Let me help you up.'

CHAPTER TWELVE

'And actually, I'm very glad to see you,' I told Alec, when we were ensconced in the damp little kitchen-living room of Ford Cottage, watching my coat steam gently over a rack in front of the stove. 'I hope that coat doesn't pucker or Grant will go into mourning until Christmas. And thank goodness my shoes escaped unscathed.'

'It's coming to something when you're thankful your shoes survived, given that your legs didn't,' said Alec. He was rummaging in a wooden box with a red cross on the top which he had found under the sink. 'Usual useless rubbish,' he said. 'An eye bath and a sling, but no sticking plaster or aspirin.'

'I don't need any,' I told him. 'Grant's view is that cuts heal and bones mend, but when shoes and clothes are wounded they never get better again.'

'Grant's view has been warped by repeated inhalation of benzene, I think,' said Alec. 'And of course you're glad to see me. I knew you would have come to your senses and realised I was right.'

I forbore from telling him that this realisation had dawned as recently as the evening before and had come to me by way of a chance remark of Lorna's rather than springing from any native intelligence of my own. 'So, you're going to track down suspects and check alibis?' I said.

'Beginning with this queer young farmer,' Alec said. I was shaking my head before he had finished.

'I think I might have cleared up that angle,' I said. 'Well, nearly.' And quickly I related the events of the evening before. 'So you see,' I concluded, 'it's probably no more than prejudice and envy that's been arousing suspicions. Even Sergeant Doolan can see that walking around in the evenings is no crime.'

'Fishy, though,' said Alec. 'And you say there was something troubling Molly? More than the natural feelings of a respectable girl upon finding herself mixed up with the police?'

'Yes,' I said, trying once again, and failing, to put my finger on it. 'And although I wouldn't like to say

207

Molly is not respectable, I'd be surprised if she went in for quite those sorts of feelings as a rule. It can't have been that that was bothering her.'

'Well, I think I'll definitely have a good close look at Jock Christie, then,' said Alec. 'Set up my easel somewhere on his land and hope to distract him from his ploughing as he passes. If he really does walk about at night it shouldn't be hard to get him talking about landscape and moonlight and . . .' Alec waved his hand with expressive vagueness.

'If that's your angle, the best of luck to you,' I said. 'It might work on young Christie but I can't see it going down well with the more established farmers. And can you even paint?' I asked. I had never heard of it, if he could.

'I'm very modern,' said Alec austerely. 'In other words: no.'

'You don't look modern,' I said, eyeing the smock and scarf. The hat with its feather lay on the table, but I could now see more clearly the rest of Alec's get-up and it was astounding. 'You look like Toulouse Lautrec. Where on earth did you get the boots and the britches?'

'The cavalry boots are mine,' said Alec. 'But I concede to you on the britches. They came from a dressing-up box I found in the attics at Dunelgar. Quite something when combined with a smock, eh?'

'But since you are here,' I said, still half convinced that his entire disguise, not to mention the expense of the cottage rent, was a waste of effort, 'at least you can listen and help me straighten some of it out, because my head is absolutely spinning, even without the trip to the jail cell last night.' Quickly, I told him Molly's tale, the woes of the expectant Mrs Muirhead, and all about the Miss Mortons, the Martineaus and Mrs Gow, still to be tracked down. 'But that,' I concluded, 'pales into transparency beside what I found this morning. Or what I might have found anyway, although it's so preposterous and so unlikely . . .'

'Save the preposterous and unlikely for now, Dan,' said Alec. 'I want to hear about things properly. Go back to the start and take your time. First, Molly. Any smell reported? Any other clues?'

'Well, horribly enough what she told me seemed rather to suggest that you were right,' I said generously. 'About things turning nastier, I mean. The stranger made a very determined effort at Molly's virtue, far beyond the nipping and pinching I've heard about from elsewhere, and he smelled, on that particular evening, of whisky.'

'Rather run of the mill, smelling of whisky, compared with his other chosen colognes,' said Alec.

'Indeed. Beyond that, Molly added nothing, except to say that for once, that night, the stranger was behind . . . what was it, now? Oh, some kind of coal shed or something, rather than flitting across the fields.'

'Curiouser and curiouser,' said Alec. 'Why would he hide and jump out that one month in particular? I'll bet he was back to his usual routine in June.'

'He was,' I said. 'He flitted down the lane to Mrs Muirhead and smelled, she told me, of smoke.'

'And I'll bet he didn't do anything more than his signature "pinching" either.'

'True.'

'Well, there you are then,' said Alec. 'Molly's embellishing, I'd say. I've never seen the girl, but does she strike you as the type who might embellish for dramatic ends?'

'Possibly,' I said, 'but why, if she wasn't going to be strictly truthful, would she make up something so nasty?'

'Nasty?' said Alec. 'Read your notes again.'

' "He was pinning me down," ' I read. ' "I kicked him, hard. And gave him a good smack on the head. Then I kicked him again, in the stomach and he got up and ran away." How you can call that anything but nasty beats me.'

'Quite simply because, my dear Dandy, it's a tale of immense heroism on the part of Molly, intended to put her in the best possible light. Or it would be but for the fact that it didn't happen. Modesty prevents us from actually trying it out, but just think: if someone is lying on top of you, you might be able to smack his head, but could you kick him? Could you kick him in the stomach? And I bet that explains the whisky too. He wasn't actually close enough for long enough for her to smell anything, so when you asked her she made up the answer— said he smelled the way she imagined he would.' He shook his head at me pityingly. 'And you told me you didn't need me here,' he said. 'You've quite clearly got hopelessly tangled in all the gossip and horrors at that Rural meeting and—'

'Well, just listen to the latest—horrors, that is; not gossip—and then tell me if you wouldn't have got tangled in it too.'

'What is it?' Alec said.

'It's what I was going to tell you; what I was bursting to tell you before you bullied me into giving a report, like a sergeant-major. And it's *about* the SWRI as it happens. The Rural is absolutely germane to all of these goings-on, for a reason that explains far better than any disapproval of "gadding about" why some upstanding member of the parish might want to scare them.'

'Oh, get on with it,' said Alec.

'I think they—the Rural ladies—are dabbling.'

'In what?' he asked, not having been brought up on Nanny Palmer's euphemisms as I had.

'In the occult. I think they are dabbling, my dear Alec, in witchcraft.'

There was a long silence; long enough for Bunty to wrinkle up her brows and look at each of us to see what was going on.

'Dandy, my darling, from where I stood it looked as though you fell on your bottom, but perhaps you should check for bumps on the head.'

'They have a badge with coded symbols,' I told him, 'and its name is the witch's heart. I just found a stock of them at Miss Lindsay's, along with the key to its meaning. She wears one, as does Miss McCallum and countless others. There are four points to the crown and four—as everyone knows—is a terribly unlucky number.'

'The SWRI ladies are witches?' Alec said, regarding me with something beyond pity now.

'Of course not,' I said. 'But perhaps they're nodding as they pass. I mean, look what they believe about the girl in the cave. Or perhaps the instigators—the schoolteacher and the

211

postmistress, I'm sure—are leading the others towards it unbeknown. I had thought their socialism was the worst of it, but perhaps when they spoke of men calling out dreadful names . . .'

'All under the eye of their many guest speakers?'

'The point is, Alec, that if one of the God-fearing majority caught a whiff of it, they might decide to teach the women a lesson, do you see? The husbands and fathers might very well band together, as Mr Black's evidence suggest they have. Perhaps, while their wives are at the meetings, they're at meetings of their own planning sabotage.'

'Why wouldn't they just forbid their wives to go?'

'Because then other wives and spinsters would still be in thrall to it. And believe me, Luckenlaw is well served for spinsters.'

'It seems rather a brutal thing to subject the women to, even to teach them the lesson that they should leave witchcraft alone.'

'I suppose the men might just tell themselves that if women want to poke their fingers into such things they should jolly well take whatever dark strangers flit their way.'

He merely shook his head again.

'I'm not saying I believe in witchcraft,' I carried on and even to me it sounded sulky. 'Just that if someone else does and someone else *again* has found out about it . . .' I gave up. 'I think it would at least be interesting to see who wears the witch's heart and who doesn't.' Once again, Alec said nothing, but just waited patiently for me to return to my senses. 'So,' I went on, in quite a different voice, 'the Martineau ladies, the Miss Mortons and

Mrs Gow need to be tracked down.'

'Oh, I'll take care of the Miss Mortons for you,' Alec said airily. 'I already know where to find them.' He smiled. 'That nice Miss Tait told me when she came to see me yesterday. She suggested I drop in on them, in fact.'

I tried and failed to hide my astonishment.

'They dabble too, you see,' said Alec. 'In watercolours. Miss Tait reckoned they'd be enchanted to see some of my work. But maybe she's luring me into a trap, eh? Maybe she's a witch?'

'We can agree to differ,' I said haughtily, 'without any need for sarcasm, surely.'

*   *   *

After luncheon, I set out purposefully across the green—Mrs Martineau rented the house in front of the kirk wall and shared it with her grown-up daughter who worked in Colinsburgh—planning to take her in first and then cut round the farm lanes to Wester Luck Cottage, where the wife of Mr Gow the ploughman could be found.

Mrs Martineau, for all that she had given up the Rural in the spring, was clearly still within sound of the drums as far as life in general was concerned, for she knew who I was, where I hailed from and what I was (ostensibly) up to, as soon as she opened the door. She was a well-turned-out widow upwards of fifty, but still with a fine line to her jaw, roses in her cheeks and a high shine on her greying curls, who lived very comfortably on her army pension, her late husband having been a quartermaster-sergeant all his days.

'And are you Luckenlaw born and bred?' I asked her, thinking I could hear something rather more exotic in the lilt of her voice, but knowing that an army life can do strange things to anyone's tongue.

'Not me,' she said. 'I'm a Glasgow lass. Give me lights and shops and music halls any time.'

'So what brings you here?' I asked her, mystified. Anywhere less like Glasgow than the village of Luckenlaw was a stretch to imagine.

'Oh, we used to have our holidays here whenever Wallace was on leave,' she told me, 'and my daughter—we only had the one—was always great chums with the wee Fraser boy, played together on the farm and wrote each other letters when we went away again. Then, as soon as she had left school, she announced that she was coming back here to work. Well!' Mrs Martineau drew herself up and folded her arms, in the gesture that makes a bosomy woman look like a bridling little pigeon but gives more svelte individuals such as she the outline of a *Vogue* fashion plate, all shoulders and angles. 'I know very well that Mrs Kinnaird takes in girls as lodgers, but they are barmaids and shop workers, and my Annette is in an office. You can see the problem, can't you?' I could indeed; the problem was that young Miss Martineau had been determined to come to Luckenlaw and land the wee Fraser boy, without a thought to decorum or her mother's affront.

'So here we are!' said Mrs Martineau, staring blankly out of her window at the empty square of green and the solitary telephone kiosk on its far side.

'And the wee Fraser boy?' I asked gently.

'Married last year to a local girl with a face like

214

the back of a bus,' she said. 'Said he knew Annette would never settle to a farming life after a job in an office and her own pay-packet.'

'Farming life?' I said. 'You don't mean Mrs Fraser of Balniel, do you?'

'A friend of yours?' said Mrs Martineau warily, regretting the bus comment I supposed.

'Not at all,' I said. 'And I should say Mr Fraser had more to worry about than her face.' I hazarded a guess that I was safe to say it. 'I mean, of course it's wonderful to behold such godliness in these shocking times, but to be married to it . . .?' Mrs Martineau gave a comfortable chuckle, and nodded understandingly.

'He's certainly repenting at his leisure now,' she said. 'But it's too late to unmake the bed and he needs to learn that he can't have his cake and eat it for ever.'

After which impressive string of clichés, she closed her mouth firmly and nodded just once as though that was the matter put to rest for good and all.

'Just so,' I said, not quite following. 'Now, Mrs Martineau—'

'Oh, call me Moyra, do,' she said, plaintively. I drew back, not shocked really although somewhat more than surprised. She saw my look and sighed heavily. 'Forgive me,' she said. 'That would never do in Luckenlaw. What was I ever thinking?' and I recognised in her amused despair a faint echo of the slump Gilverton can settle on my shoulders. Still, one cannot throw all of civilisa-tion to the four winds.

'My dear Mrs Martineau,' I began again, as a compromise, 'I wonder if I can ask you one or two

215

questions to help me prepare my little talk.'

'I'm not in the Rural any more,' she said. 'I stopped going when . . . Well, I stopped going.'

'When what?' I asked carefully.

'Och, it was never really my cup of tea anyway,' she said.

'They do have some very odd ideas,' I murmured, 'about—um—folklore and ancient traditions and so on . . .' but far from Mrs Martineau falling on my neck and pouring out a store of suspicions she merely looked puzzled.

'And of course: Votes For All,' I said, guessing again.

'I'm not a fan of that caper right enough,' said Mrs Martineau, 'and there's only so much fun to be had from knitting and baking. I only went because Annette was so keen on it.'

'Then she tired of it?' I said, hoping that my questions were not beginning to sound too pointed.

'Her?' cried Mrs Martineau indignantly. 'She was never there. Oh yes, she joined up and she pushed me out the door keen enough every month, but she was always "too tired after her work, Mother" or "needing to wash her hair, Mother" and off I went as though I'd come up the Clyde on a biscuit.' The arms, I noticed, were folded even tighter now, threatening to nip her slim figure quite in half.

At that moment, I had one of my very rare flashes of inspiration. All at once, I understood the source of Mrs Martineau's affront, why Mr Fraser might have been said to be having his cake and eating it too, why Annette Martineau was so keen to have her mother out of the way on evenings

216

when Mrs Fraser was also occupied, why Mr Black could not find Mr Fraser when he went looking earlier in the year, and the reason for the Martineaus giving up the Rural meetings, although . . .

'Was it August you stopped going?' I asked her. 'I rather thought it was May.'

Mrs Martineau stared at me, as well she might. Why on earth should I know or care when it was, after all?

'My dear,' I said again, 'please don't be concerned—I'm a woman of the world and I know that girls will be girls. I just assumed that it would be Mrs Fraser stopping at home that foiled your daughter's . . . moonlight interludes.'

'Moonlight interludes!' she cried. 'That's a new name for it.'

'I shan't tell a soul,' I assured her. 'And really—childhood sweethearts and all that—it's rather romantic.'

I could see her trying to maintain her disapproval although her eyes were twinkling and her lips beginning to twitch.

'Oh, well, at least it's over,' she said, sighing. 'And no little mementoes on the way, thank the Lord. Now, as soon as Annette's finished her training and worked out her notice we'll be off back to Glasgow and I'm going to dance up and down Sauchiehall Street in a red dress.'

'Good for you,' I said, imagining that not only might Annette snag herself a beau once they got there, but her mother was sure to attract a follower or two as well, what with the curls, the cheeks and the army pension, red dress or no. 'So if it wasn't Mrs Fraser spoiling the party, do you know what it was? What went wrong in May?'

'They quarrelled,' said Mrs Martineau. 'Because he wouldn't walk her home. I came in from the Rural that night, gasping for a . . . well, a gin if you must know . . . and she was sitting here in her dressing gown by the fire, crying her eyes out, and saying she never wanted to see him again. "See who again?" I asked, thinking: first I've heard that you're seeing anyone. She wasn't going traipsing around in the dark after him any more, she said. If he didn't even have the courtesy to see her home to the edge of the village—too scared of being spotted—then he didn't deserve her and he could go and raffle.'

'Good for her too,' I said stoutly, although quietly to myself I rather thought that it was the marrying someone else and meeting Annette once a month on the sly that showed the discourtesy, not the leaving her to make her own way home.

Back outside on the village green, I made the mistake of pausing to gather my thoughts before heading off for the path around the law which would take me to Wester Luck and Mrs Gow and while I stood there, playing choo-choo with my breath in the cold and crunching patterns into the frosty grass with the toe of my boot, I heard the sound of a familiar puttering engine and the Howies' motor car trundled into view, circled the cenotaph and drew up beside me, with a blast of its horn. Vashti Howie leaned out and grinned at me.

'What are you doing?' she asked but luckily did not wait for a sensible answer. 'Hop in,' she said. 'I've been at the post, sending off orders for Lorna's party whatnots, and spending precious moments with dear, dear Miss McCallum, of course. Always such a treat, any day when one gets the chance to refresh one's spirits with that marvellous creature.' She rolled her eyes. 'Come on, this thing'll flood if I leave it idling.'

'Where are you going?' I asked her.

'Speaking of marvellous creatures,' she said, 'I'm going to pick up Niccy. She popped in at our new tenant's while I did the boring bits, as usual. Dandy, I tell you, you must see this. You won't believe your eyes, but you must see it anyway.'

'See what?' I said, knowing quite well but remembering that I should not.

'Captain Watson,' said Vashti as I climbed into the motor car and she swung around the green for the school lane. 'Luckenlaw has never seen anything like it, and even in Soho he would cause a bit of a stir.'

'He's an artist, isn't he?' I said cautiously. 'I rather thought there was an artist or two scattered about here already. The Miss Mortons?'

'Scream!' said Vashti. 'The Miss Mortons are nieces of a bishop who paint kittens in baskets, darling. Our Captain Watson is exploring the outer edges of expressionism in lavender trousers and riding boots. I left Niccy trying to pretend she'd heard of Kandinsky.' Which was rather a relief, I thought, for if she *had* heard of Kandinsky and knew anything at all about him, she would surely have seen through Alec straight away.

'Lorna Tait seemed to like him,' I said.

'Oh, that's the cripplingest of all,' said Vashti. 'Lorna—poor sweet innocent soul—is smitten!' She waited for my guffaw and when it did not come she explained. 'Captain Watson, I would stake my life upon it, never dreamed of smiting her. Captain

Watson is . . . how shall I put it? . . . shriekingly Not the Marrying Kind.'

'Oh,' I said. 'I see.' I did; the feather, the pink smock, the theatrical boots might say 'artist' to Luckenlaw, Lorna and me but not to Vashti Howie, who had clearly met artists before. She had sought another explanation for Alec's fantastic appearance and, apparently, had found one.

* * *

How doubly uncomfortable then, when we splashed through the ford to the cottage a minute later and Vashti swept in with a rap on the door and an air—justified, admittedly—of owning the place, to find Alec squirming in a kitchen chair, Nicolette Howie perched on the arm of a sofa with her cigarette holder at an elegant angle and Lorna stationed opposite, clutching a glass of something she did not appear to be enjoying, but smiling pinkly nevertheless. I could feel giggles beginning to form deep down inside me.

'I'm not stopping,' I said firmly, before Alec could fluff things with a reference to my earlier visit. 'Please don't concern yourself, Captain . . . Watson, is it? I just wanted to come along and say hello.'

'Mrs Gilver is visiting from Perthshire,' said Lorna. 'Do you know Perthshire at all?' Alec looked as though he was trying to think if he had ever heard of the place and then shook his head. Lorna turned to Vashti.

'Captain Watson has agreed,' she said. 'We've never had a real artist, doing a real demonstration of his art before, have we?'

'I take it we're not counting Miss McCallum and her crochet?' said Vashti. Lorna looked troubled and Alec, I considered, did a perfect imitation of one whose mind was on higher things. Lorna cleared her throat.

'Shall you do a sketch, do you think, Captain? Or work on the painting of the moment? I am very ignorant about artistic things.'

'I'm surprised you haven't asked the Miss Mortons,' said Alec. 'They work in watercolours and it lends itself so much better to sketches. I shouldn't like to cause a stir, by seeming to sweep in and take over.'

'You're always so attuned to the emotional plane, aren't you? You . . . um . . . artists,' said Vashti, causing Nicolette to snort and Lorna and Alec to frown in puzzlement.

'The Miss Mortons left, Captain Watson,' said Nicolette, when she had cleared her throat. 'When was it now? They weathered that thrilling night in July, all right. What was it that drove them off in the end?'

'Mrs Gilver is planning to address the Rural too, you know, Captain,' said Lorna, cutting into Vashti's speech in a rather quavering voice.

'A fellow artist?' said Alec.

'Not at all,' said Nicolette. 'Don't let the hat fool you, Captain Watson. She is doing some sociological research.'

'Well, hardly that,' I said.

'Darling, if you went as far as the charmless Molly at our place, I'd call it sociology, wouldn't you?'

'Anthropology, even,' said Vashti and they both tittered.

'Did you get any joy from Molly?' Nicolette asked me, blithely unconcerned by any thoughts of her servant's indiscretion.

'Not anything very useful,' I assured her anyway. 'She tends rather to the melodramatic.'

'Ah yes, her famous ordeal in the privy yard,' said Vashti.

'Don't you use watercolours then?' said Lorna in a loud voice.

'It paid off handsomely for her with the adventure last night,' said Nicolette, before Alec could answer. He was looking rather wildly from right to left, like a spectator at a tennis match, trying to follow all the conversational threads at once.

'You seem very unsympathetic to poor Molly,' I said to Vashti.

'So would you be if you had to eat her cooking,' said Vashti, making me laugh in spite of myself. 'And besides,' she went on, 'a moonlight walk! I ask you!'

'We thought a visit to a prison cell might shake the nonsense out of her once and for all,' said Nicolette, even less sympathetically.

'Prison cell?' said Alec, as Captain Watson would have, I was sure.

'Our tenant farmer got himself arrested and locked up last night,' said Nicolette. 'The most excitement there's been at Luck House since Irvine sat on the cat.'

'Yes, it was odd, the Miss Mortons going off in high dudgeon like that,' said Lorna frantically.

'But they let him go again,' said Nicolette, just as though Lorna had not spoken.

I took pity at last. Saving Lorna from

mortification and Alec from the challenge of remembering what Captain Watson should know and what should puzzle him, I turned the conversation adroitly to the coming party (thinking regretfully, as I did so, that the adroit turning of difficult conversations was an unmistakable sign of creeping age).

'It's going to be very romantic,' Vashti said. '*Love* is the theme.'

'Because you are beloved, darling Lorna,' said Nicolette.

'And very loving to us too. So what else could the theme be?' said Vashti. 'We adore themed parties, Captain Watson. Life, don't you think, should be full of celebration. Hallowe'en, St Valentine's, Easter, Beltane. If you add some well-spaced birthdays the year can be full to the brim.'

'Beltane?' said Alec.

'May day,' Nicolette explained. 'An old Scots word. You'll get used to them, if you settle here, and I do hope you will.'

'But don't mislead the Captain, Vashti,' said Lorna, sounding mild but determined. 'You make Luckenlaw sound like an endless whirl. We don't actually have parties all that often.' Vashti, who had been looking almost transported, now slumped down again.

'True,' she said. 'Money is such a bore. Still, we do our best, don't we, Niccy?'

'We always have and we always will,' said Nicolette, making it sound like a motto, her valiant tone quite at odds with the long cigarette holder and the clattering bangles.

'You must excuse me, Captain Watson,' I said,

although I was loath to drag myself away. 'As Lorna said, I am busy with my research, and I have a full complement of interviews to conduct this afternoon.'

'On what particular topic?' said Alec.

'Managing the household budget,' I replied. I looked around the cottage living room at the fully stocked drinks tray and the meagre packet of bread and pot of jam on the table. Alec followed my eyes and smiled.

'I should serve better as a recipient of your advice than a provider of handy hints,' he said, and I could see, out of the corner of my eye, Lorna regarding him with determined pity, and dreaming I am sure of just how many home comforts she could bring his way. 'As long as I have my art,' he went on, 'I am happy. And something tells me that my art is going to flourish here at Luckenlaw. I'd like to speak to some of the farmers. Starting with that tenant of yours, Mrs Howie. Something about the clash of the two worlds, you know. The rolling empty fields and the closed prison cell. If I could capture that, I'd have something worth having. Do you think he would let me sketch him? Do you think I might sketch all the farmers? Such faces they have—etched with toil, landscapes in themselves, don't you see?'

Vashti and Nicolette just managed to keep their countenances at this sudden outburst of artistic nonsense while Lorna, predictably, looked transfixed. I could only marvel and envy; how much easier and more fun to stride about with a sketchpad and spout gibberish that no one had to be convinced by than to drone on about budgets and have to make sense while one did so.

CHAPTER THIRTEEN

The trim grey cottage had smoke curling prettily out of its chimney and beads of moisture in its lighted kitchen window, hinting that someone was already busy inside 'getting the tea'. I knocked diffidently and prepared my little speech once more.

Mrs Gow could easily have written the talk, pamphlet, article or indexed volumes for me, that much was clear from the outset; her kitchen was sparkling, her larder pantry—which she took care to let me see as she went to fetch potatoes to peel—was stocked as though for a siege and the pastry she was rolling out was flat, smooth-edged and perfectly oval. I imagined that only tremendous prudence and skill could produce such snug plenty on a cattleman's pay packet.

'I manage my budget jist fine,' she said, confirming this impression. 'Mind you, there's many a lass tryin' tae run a hoose wi' no more sense than a day-old chookie, and doubtless they'd be in sore need o' some help, madam.'

'I rather wonder that you don't come along to the meetings,' I said. 'You could pass on your wisdom there, for I believe that some quite young girls have joined, looking, as you say, for a bit of advice from their elders.'

'Aye well,' said Mrs Gow, turning a potato round and round under her scraper as a coil of peel grew and fell onto the paper. 'It micht o' been guidance they were looking for, madam, but that's no' what they got. Those poor lasses, and then everybody up and sayin' they didna believe them.' She tossed the potato into a pot, wiped her hands on her apron front and selected another one.

'You believe them, at least,' I said.

'I do that,' she told me. 'For I saw him mysel'.'

'No!' I said, thankful that I had managed not to say yippee. 'Did you tell anyone? If one of the girls had had you backing her up . . .'

'It wisna then,' she said. I knew what she would say next. 'It was the nicht o' the meetin' in July I saw him. I stopped goin' after that.'

'You stopped going right then?' I said. I was sure it was August.

'Well, I went once more. I felt sorry for that nice schoolteacher, if I'm honest. I was feart that after what happened in July she'd be there all on her own the next time and so I went back just the once, to be polite like. Gowie dropped me doon there in the cart and came back at the end to pick me up again.'

'But the August meeting was as busy as ever,' I said.

'It was,' said Mrs Gow shaking her head and sucking her teeth. 'And so I said to myself they could carry on without me.'

'Do you mind if I ask . . .?' I said, then forced myself away from the tantalising question of the Wisconsin preacher's wife. 'Did the stranger actually get you, Mrs Gow?'

'No fear. He didna even see me, madam. I had come straicht roond the back to my wee patch here, thinkin' to catch some of they blessed snails that were eatin' up my lettuces as quick as I could get a row in. It was that bricht with the moon that nicht, you know. And I seen him, jist *ripplin'* across

226

thon field as if the devil was after him. Well, there's only one farm up there and so I kent exactly what he was up to. I'd left Mary—young Mrs Torrance—no' a minute afore to carry on to the farm, and so I come in the back door and took doon a pot and ladle, then back out I went and skelped that pot bottom like it was a cheeky bairn. I reckoned that would fricht him.'

'It would certainly fright me, if I wasn't expecting it. I take it he didn't catch Mrs Torrance then?'

'Your guess is as guid as mine,' she said. 'Gowie and me—Mr Gow that is, my husband—took aff along the lane and here but did we no' meet Mary comin' back, askin' what all the noise was.'

'Well, bravo,' I said. 'You seem to have sent the fellow packing with your pot and spoon brainwave. Well done you, Mrs Gow.'

'I'm no' so sure,' she said. 'Mary's hair was all hingin' doon and there was a streak o' dirt across her face, but she said she'd never seen a thing, nor heard nothin' either, exceptin' my racket.'

Just like Mrs Hemingborough, I thought to myself. Almost exactly the same.

'I canna get used to it, I suppose,' said Mrs Gow. 'I've kent Mary a' her life, for Gowie worked to her faither since we were first wed, and I still think of her as a bairn—I never had my own, madam—so when it comes to bein' stared doon like that and as good as told you're haverin', not to mention bein' warned to keep your mooth shut aboot it! To think o' her standin' there, sayin' how she'd hate to have to make changes aboot the place, when there had been enough loss and leavin' already, since the happy days of childhood. Oh, she has a silver

227

tongue on her, like all o' them, richt enough.'

'I'm not sure I follow you,' I said. 'Mrs Torrance said all this? About the halcyon days of yore and all that. Do you mean that the farm belonged to Mary's family?'

'Aye, Drew Torrance is from over Ladybank way. A cousin o' some kind, come to work to his uncle since he had four brothers at home and there was only Mary here. And it's just as well he did come too. You'll no' have heard about the fire, will you?'

'Someone did say something about a bad fire,' I said, vaguely remembering. 'I can't remember if I knew it was Wester Luck.'

'The house went up like a lum,' said Mrs Gow, 'and it spread to the byres too. Beasts screamin' like bairns, the horses breakin' their legs in their stalls, and jist us wi' a poor few buckets tryin' to stop it. What a nicht that was. Like hell on earth, madam, if you'll excuse me puttin' it that way. Just like hell on earth. Mary's mother was ill wi' it after, the smoke and all, for her chest was ayeways bad in the winter at the best o' times. She went richt doonhill and old Gil—Mary's faither—was no time ahint her. So thank the Dear for Drew Torrance, is all I can say, even if he is turnin' oot to be a sicht harder to keep in check than Mary bargained for.'

Here, perhaps, was a trace of what Alec was set to sniff out. I went after it like a bloodhound.

'Hard to manage?' I said. 'Does he go out drinking and gambling then?'

'Och, no,' said Mrs Gow. 'Nothin' like that and to give Mary her dues, she's no' one of they soor-plooms who'd have us all damned for a game o' whist. No' like some I could mention.' At the

228

thought of—I guessed—the Blacks and Frasers, Mrs Gow seemed to regret even saying what she had. 'No, Mary's had a hard time of it and Drew was a godsend.'

'Hear, hear,' I said. 'And if you've helped them through all you have, I can see why your palm might itch if you thought Mary was telling fibs to you and making you appear foolish in front of your husband. But, Mrs Gow, perhaps she *didn't* see the stranger. Why would she lie about it, after all?'

'Och, she was ayeways her mither's daughter,' said Mrs Gow. 'Gil was a fine man but Mary's mother—she was Mary too—was a gey queer buddy. Ask anyone and they'd say the same, madam; it's no' just me.'

'So you fell out and stopped going to the Rural together?' I guessed, smarting on Mrs Gow's behalf, for why should it be the elder who withdrew from the field if their quarrel meant they could not rub along together?

'No, no, nothin' like that,' said Mrs Gow. 'I jist got scared, plain and simple. I had thocht this stranger fellow—if he was real—was goin' after girls wi' nobody to look out for them—Annie, and Elspeth and thon funny one up at Luck Hoose; they're a' girls alone, but if he was startin' in on the likes o' Mary Torrance wi' her man there beside her, I wasna for takin' a chance that he micht come after me.'

I must have failed, as is quite usual, to keep a poker face and I fear Mrs Gow saw the quick look of incredulity I could not hide.

'Oh, I ken what you're thinkin',' she said. 'Why would anyone come oot on a dark nicht and run across fields tae pinch me where he shouldna?' I grinned at her. 'Aye, well,' she said, but she refused to expand any further.

Her meaning became clear however when I drew level with a young woman who turned out to be Mrs Torrance while I was trudging home. She was bound for Hinter Luck, she said, taking a fat duck to Mrs Hemingborough in exchange for some bacon. I remembered her vaguely from the meeting and, although she had merged into the crowd somewhat that night, as I subjected her now to a brief spell of close study out of the side of my eye, I am sorry to say that I thought the dark stranger must have had some compelling reason of his own for setting his sights on this good lady on a night when so many other females were tramping home across the countryside besides her. I had already wondered at his taste in regard to the Mistresses Hemingborough and Fraser but Mary Torrance was the biggest mystery of all and I agreed with Mrs Gow that if *she* was tempting then no woman alive was safe from him.

She was, I should guess, in her thirties, thick and sturdy, with a face far from hinting at faded beauty like the faces of most farmwomen I have seen—a country girlhood being as conducive to pretty looks as a country life is certain to wear them out in the end. Mary Torrance's countenance, in contrast, must have seen her through a plain babyhood, childhood and girlhood and must, if anything, be less of a burden now when, husband secured, all thoughts of fascination were past her. Her hair grew low on her brow which itself jutted out like an overhanging cliff above dark eyes and was balanced although not by any means softened by a boulder of a chin supporting a short, no-nonsense mouth whose lower lip covered its upper, lending her whole face an expression of pugnacity which, although I am sure it was quite accidental, would have seen off most ravagers from a field away.

'I've been visiting your Mrs Gow,' I said, when greetings had been exchanged.

'Auntie Dot, I've ayeways called her,' said Mary Torrance. 'She was like another mammy to me when I was growing up.'

'And what a comfort to you now,' I said. 'I heard about the dreadful fire and about your parents, Mrs Torrance. How awful for you.'

'Aye, I've no' had my troubles to seek,' she said stoically. 'But I keep my mouth shut and my head up.' She suited the action to the word, clamping her lips tightly and hoisting her chin skyward.

'Indeed,' I said, feeling quite unequal to this stout rebuff, for it was impossible to view it in any other light. 'Well, I hope happier times are on their way.'

'They're here,' said Mary. 'I tell Drew that till I'm sick of telling him. We're doing just grand now and he's no need to worry.'

'It's in the nature of farmers to worry,' I said. 'I mean, a fire must have been the final straw, but the last few years have been wretched everywhere.'

'Don't I know it,' said Mary Torrance, almost at a bellow. 'Drew reads those blessed market lists out every day, as if he was saying his prayers, and I could tell you the beef prices at Kirkcaldy market in my sleep. I keep telling him, a fire would have swallowed up a milk herd the same as it did the beasts.'

I was beginning to see what Mrs Gow might have meant by Drew Torrance being a handful, for

231

it seemed that Mary felt she had inherited the say-so along with the acres and was affronted to find that her husband disagreed.

'And forby,' she went on, after tramping along in silence for a while, 'the way I look at it is: a fire comes and then it goes. What about the Palmers over there, with their well drying up on them time and again? You cannot farm without water, can you? Or the McAdams at Over Luck, fluke in their meadows and clubroot right through their turnip fields, as if the very earth was turning against them. And as for what's happened at Luckenheart . . .' She stopped and a shiver ran through her. 'I'm not complaining, Mrs Gilver.' I knew what she was about to say before she said it. 'The fire was terrible, but what's for you won't go by you, no point in hoping it will.'

'Oh, quite, quite,' I said.

*   *   *

At times in my short detecting past I have felt that there were hidden patterns tantalising me but I had no such ticklish sense of answers just out of reach now; my poor head was a maelstrom of Torrances, Gows and Martineaus, lovers and husbands, farms and houses, fires and deaths, witches and spirits, demons and strangers and clanging saucepans to boot and I wished that I had the nerve to affect a headache and ask for eggs on a tray. The spare bedroom was icy, but cool, clear air was exactly what I needed because if I gathered even another day's worth of names and interviews without tidying what I had so far, I was likely to do as our cook used to when I was a child, whenever unexpected guests, kitchen maids' afternoons out and the cooling off, inexplicable and unstoppable, of the temperamental kitchen range all fell together, which was to shriek, throw her apron over her head and rush out to hide in the stables, sobbing.

Guessing that Lorna and Mr Tait would fuss, however, I endured breaded cutlets in the dining room and sat afterwards listening to the fire crackle and watching Lorna at her embroidery for as little time as I thought I could politely get away with, then retired with cocoa, a hot bottle and a fierce determination to get on top of things while I still had a chance of it.

March, April, May, I wrote on a fresh sheet of paper. *Elspeth, Annie, Molly. Eggs, flowers, whisky.*

June, July, August, were next. *Mrs Muirhead, Mrs Torrance, Mrs Fraser. Smoke,???, yeast.*

September and October.??? and Mrs Hemingborough.??? and??? as far as smells were concerned.

And then what? What chance that Mrs Hemingborough's tussle in the Hinter Luck lane was the end of it? Also, this possibility just occurring to me, had there been attacks before the one on Elspeth McConechie? Were there more who, like the mistresses Muirhead, Torrance and Hemingborough (and??? in September too), had kept it quiet? If this band of four had been silent, why not?

Except, when I really thought about it, or rather when I forced myself *not* to think about it but just to let the feel of the thing take charge for a moment, the four I had just clumped together did not make . . . not *sense,* for *sense* was not what was

233

at issue here, I should say it did not make . . . I knew not what word to use for it.

As a girl, when I swung on the estate carpenter's door and watched him planing and sawing, my unfocused mind was most receptive and I remember a good bit of what I heard—him talking perhaps to me, perhaps to himself, in that slow, easy way of his, or perhaps to the wood itself, praising it and cajoling it, making it meet him halfway, offer up the prettiest grain and split obligingly in crisp sharp angles when his chisel commanded it. One particular thing he often said, which has stayed with me ever since, was that unlike making a piece of cabinetry which was to stand on its own legs, when one was constructing a cupboard to hang in a room, or putting a window into a wall, or even just nailing up a shelf in an outhouse, one could measure as much as one liked, with rules and tapes and plumb lines; one could take a spirit level and work from the floor, the ceiling, or the distant horizon, and it would make no odds if the thing was not 'eye-sweet'. 'That's what you mun remember, Miss Dandelion,' he would say. 'Never mind your straight edge and your square angle, you leave them in the schoolroom. Never mind your plumb or your level: it mun be eye-sweet and when it is you'll look upon it and you'll know it, same as you know anything.'

And right now, all these years later, it just was not eye-sweet to say that terrified Mrs Muirhead and the two farmers' wives, the cold Torrance and the tough Hemingborough, made a set, even though they had all kept quiet about the attacks upon them. Far sweeter, it seemed to me, to say that Mrs Muirhead kept quiet out of a sense of shame, her ear full of poison from her ghastly neighbour but Mrs Hemingborough on the other hand, and Mrs Torrance too from what Mrs Gow had just told me, felt no shame much less any terror and kept quiet from a sense of . . . once again I could not complete this train of thought. I could not imagine what might make a woman accept such beastliness without even a hint of umbrage. When it was Mrs Hemingborough alone I imagined she knew who it was and was protecting him, but who could it be for whom both she and young Mrs Torrance would seal their lips? And if I could stretch some loyalty across both of them, I could not easily account for September's victim. Would she be another stoic or would she be a second terrified girl? No, I thought, she couldn't be; it wouldn't be eye-sweet.

As soon as I had this thought, lazily to myself, I tried to catch it and see what was behind it. I thought hard; I let my mind drift. I asked questions; I made bold statements to see if a bit of my brain would reject them. I drew a map and marked it with farm names, victims' names, months and even arrows to show where the stranger had sprung from each night. In short, I did every kind of thinking I knew how to do, but it got me nowhere.

Still, cheered even by a vague hint that there was a pattern there somewhere, I turned to what *could* be thought out here in my room: first, were there any before the spring? Secondly, was there any way to work out who November's victim was going to be? Or even to narrow it down to a set from which the stranger might choose?

In answer to the first of these questions I felt an

enormous pull, like an undertow, towards something my eye would find simply delicious. I longed to say that of course Elspeth was first and I wanted to go even further: to say that there would be exactly one more. Three in the spring, three in the summer and three in the autumn sounded just right, but I should be no kind of detective at all if I could not resist this pull, for it is as spurious as it is ingrained—the feeling we have that all things for good and especially for ill must come in threes, like Goldilocks's bears and the wolf's little pigs. Pure superstition, I always told Grant, when she regaled me in sepulchral tones of the third calamity to befall someone.

'First it was her leg,' she would say. 'All over ulcers like the doctors had never seen. Then the very next month her poor old dog that she had had from a pup died in the night, and now, three years to the day after she buried her mother, if she hasn't gone and lost her grandmother's locket. And'—she would pause here to let the thrilling moment reverberate around us—'the locket had her grandmother's and her mother's hair plaited together with a few little hairs from her doggie's tail that she took while he lay dying, and that makes . . . three. Madam.'

'But if she goes blind tomorrow, you won't count it as number four, will you?' I would protest. 'You'll just start counting again on a new set of three and wait like the ghoul you are for the next instalment.'

'You can scoff all you like. I've seen it too often to doubt it.'

'And the leg ulcers?' I would say. 'What connection to the locket there?'

'Now,' Grant would say, drawing herself up and twisting her nose as though she was mixing a dish of waving lotion, 'you are being disgusting.' And there would be no 'madam' at all because I did not deserve one.

So there might well be more to come after November and there might well have been a few before March. As to predicting who might be next, I could not say. I stared glumly at the paper in front of me for a while, but it was well after eleven, the fire was dying down, my hot bottle had cooled and, I was sorry to notice, I had forgotten to drink a good third of my cocoa. *Find Miss September*, I printed in thick black letters underneath the map, then I stood, stretched and walked over to warm myself at what remained of the fire before undressing for bed.

Approaching the fireplace, however, meant that I also approached two windows, terribly draughty despite the heavy curtains which the maid had drawn. (I have often thought it an unmistakable expression of the Calvinist soul of Scotland how often a fireplace is set between two windows in a long wall, as though the architect defied us to find any cosiness in his designs. Far preferable is the habit of setting the fires into the inner walls, so that high sofa backs can protect one against icy blasts and the chimneys are clustered prettily about the roofs like birthday-cake candles rather than rearing up looking like battlements around the edges.)

Eventually, I stopped rubbing my hands and turned around to warm my other side, shivering, then stepped over to the bed and debated with myself whether to ring for Grant or just shuffle off my clothes as quickly as possible and hop in. I looked at my watch: almost midnight, rather late for Grant, and besides I should be much warmer with the shuffle and hop. A moment later I climbed into bed, hugging the last warmth in the bottle.

I was getting drowsy despite the temperature when I realised that, in the light from the embers, I could see the curtains trembling. The window must have been left open after the room was aired that morning—I should have known it could not really be that cold, even in a manse—and so I slithered out of bed again trying to leave all the warmth I had managed to muster undisturbed for my return, crossed the floor, parted the curtains and felt along the bottom of the window for a gap. I certainly could not tell by looking, for it was as black a night as any I have ever seen. Right enough, there was a slice of colder air where the window had not been properly fastened and with both hands on the transom I gave it a good downward shove to see if I could close it all the way.

Just then, while my face was pressed almost flat against the glass, I thought I saw something.

I stopped, holding my breath and staring out into the blackness, feeling—as one always does when looking hard into the impenetrable dark—as though my eyes were slightly bulging. Again, very obliquely, I thought I saw it: a flicker to the left somewhere. I latched the window and let the curtains fall shut again, making sure that they were well overlapped and tucked under against the carpet too. Why should there not be a flicker? I asked myself. Someone with a candle visiting a privy. I wriggled back into bed.

I did not know what time it was and did not want to wake myself up again properly by striking a match and looking at my wristwatch, but if it had been midnight when I retired and I had drowsed for an hour before I saw the curtain moving, it was by now rather late for any of the cottagers to be up and about. And then, when I considered it fully, I could not think which precise cottager it would be. Surely that flicker came from the kirk, or the graveyard anyway; there was no cottage garden obliquely opposite the back of the manse.

Well, a very late stroll then, I told myself as at last I dared to stretch my feet down into the chilly reaches of sheet near the footboard, for I never can drop off if I am curled up in a ball. Slowly, delicious sleep began to steal over me, and I wafted down into a half-dream of walking barefoot in long, wet, tickling grass. It was pleasant enough, right up until the moment it ended, as those walking dreams so often do, with a sudden plummet and a startled awakening.

I lay still, waiting for my heart to cease hammering. The difficulty with the late stroll, I now realised, was that I had most definitely seen a candle, not a lantern, and no one would take a candle to go for a walk, even if anyone trying to train a puppy perhaps or barred from smoking their baccy in the house would be out walking on such a night as this. And young Mr Christie walked in the fields, not around the gardens of his neighbours and through the churchyard.

Go back to sleep, I told myself, for if I knew one thing about this case it was that the eventful evenings were a month apart and we were quite midway between the last and the next tonight.

Besides, it was ridiculous to imagine that, so soon after telling Mrs Hemingborough how I happened to look out of my window at the precise moment to witness a vital clue, I should do just that. I sank back against my pillows and invited sleep once more, dreamless for choice and lasting until morning.

Needless to say, some indeterminate time later, having jerked awake from an even more calamitous fall in a much more disquieting dream, I had my face pressed to the window again and this time the flickering, although no brighter, was scattered around, as though that first candle had been used to light some more.

CHAPTER FOURTEEN

Even with one cheek flattened against the glass I was never going to see any more than the flickering from here and, not wanting to appear foolish, I was loath to rouse Mr Tait before I knew more definitely what, if anything, was happening. So, casting my mind over the layout of the manse and deciding that the window at the far end of the passage must overlook the graveyard square on, I wrapped myself in my dressing gown and very softly crept to the door. I had to do without slippers for Grant's latest purchase in that department was a pair of not particularly well-fitting beaded Turkish mules with terribly clackety soles which made me sound as though I were tap-dancing whenever I moved. In a pair of thick bed socks I eased my bedroom door open and, taking my candle, padded along the dark passageway.

When I got there, however, I found that as well as having heavy curtains drawn across it, the end window was shuttered and the noise I should make opening a set of shutters was impracticable. I looked around at the closed doors on either side of me. Lorna's bedroom was to the front, in quite another wing, and I was sure I had heard Mr Tait harrumphing from a room near hers in the mornings, so . . . since there was no housekeeper, old governess or other favoured servant who might be given a room on the main floor I felt I was reasonably safe in turning the handle of the door nearest and stepping into the room.

What lay inside did, I will confess, give me a moment's pause. The good suite of heavy furniture, the immaculate but old-fashioned satins festooning the bed and window, the spray of silk flowers on the bedside table and, above all, the folded nightgown with white prayer book laid on top of it told me that I was in Lorna's mother's room and everything I had ever read, from Jane Eyre to the penny dreadfuls Nanny Palmer used to forbid me to look at although she left them lying around, told me to flee.

On the other hand, the curtains were drawn back and even from the door I could see that there was an excellent view of whatever it was flickering away down there in the graveyard. I scuttled over and peered out, snuffing my own candle as I did so.

There were at least four points of light, I thought, although the bare branches of the big trees in the manse driveway obscured the view somewhat. I was sure too that there was more than one person because every so often all the lights

241

would be hidden as though someone crossed in front of them and the crossings were surely too frequent to be just one individual, unless he were running laps.

I hesitated for a moment. I should tell Mr Tait straight away, but he might forbid me to go with him and find out what was going on. If I dressed first it would be harder for him to slip away without me, but I should not waste time dressing before I raised the alarm. There was, I have no shame in admitting it, no question of my striking out on my own; I should have died of fright to walk into a candlelit graveyard scene without someone there to protect me. At this—admittedly rather feeble—thought, at last I remembered. Alec! He was barely five mintues' walk away.

I threw some clothes on, padded downstairs and stole out onto the porch—Luckenlaw Manse was not the sort of place to lock its doors even at night and so I had no creaky key with which to wake the household. Once outside, I put on my shoes and then, with my lip caught between my teeth, I started down the drive, creeping along on the soft earth at its edge, trying to breathe as softly as I could and straining to see if I could hear anything.

I need not have strained: before I had cleared the gates of the manse, the sounds from beyond the graveyard wall were unmistakable. My scalp prickled and I almost turned back but, summoning reserves of courage from who knows where, I made my feet move again. Keeping to the shadows, shaking with fright, expecting every second to hear a voice raised in alarm or to feel a hand over my mouth, I moved as quickly as I stealthily could out of the gates and along the manse garden wall to

242

the first house in the village square then, with a deep breath, I stepped into the open and raced on tiptoe across the green to the schoolhouse lane and down to the ford. That sound! I began to whimper, unable to stop myself. Skidding on the patches of ice but somehow managing to stay upright, I ran onwards, trying to remember where the footbridge led across to the garden—it was as black as any coal mine down here tonight—until a sudden icy flood around my feet told me I had missed it. I splashed through the stream and sprinted over the grass, banging my leg hard against the stone balustrade at the side of the porch. That sound! It couldn't be true! I fumbled for the handle, found it, turned it and collapsed inside.

'Alec!' I shouted. The cottage was in darkness and I had no idea where anything was except the living room. 'Alec, wake up! There's someone in the graveyard.'

'Wha—' came a groggy voice to the left of me. 'Dandy, is that you?'

'There are people in the graveyard, Alec,' I said, feeling my way into the room from where his voice had come. 'Oh God, where are you? Where are your matches?' I heard the creak as he got out of bed and the rasp of a match being struck and at last his face, owlish with sleep above a striped nightshirt, appeared before me.

'People?'

'With candles set out,' I told him.

'What are they doing?' said Alec, reaching for his trousers. 'Who is it?'

'I've no idea who it is,' I said, 'but I know what they're doing. I heard the scrape of the shovels. Oh Alec, they're digging.'

He was only a moment dressing and we made
better time on the way back up the hill than I had
coming down, because Alec took an electric torch
and kept it trained on the path in front of us, only
switching it off when we reached the village green.
Again, feeling horribly exposed even in the
blackness we flitted across to the top corner, and
then slowly, without a sound, feeling for each
footstep before we made it, we crept along,
pressed into the hedge, to the corner of the
kirkyard wall. I do not know when I realised that
we were too late; it came upon me gradually. We
were nearly there and yet it was as dark as ever, no
flickering. We were at the gate of the kirkyard and
yet there was no sound to be heard.

'Are you sure?' Alec breathed.

'Of course I'm sure,' I said a little louder
although still whispering. 'But we've missed them.
Switch on your torch again.'

'Maybe they heard us,' said Alec. 'They could be
hiding in there.'

'No,' I said. 'They've gone.'

Alec turned the switch on his electric torch and I
could feel him bracing himself, but I was perfectly
at ease now. I knew they were nowhere near.

'But *where* have they gone?' said Alec. 'It can't
have been down through the village or we would
have passed them. Do you think they're in the
church?'

'No,' I said. 'I think the church is the very last
place they'll be.'

I sounded bleak with the aftermath of terror,

even to myself, and Alec, hearing it too, put an arm round me.

'Dandy,' he said. 'Are you absolutely sure you heard what you said you heard? Could it have been tree branches scraping in the wind?'

'What wind?' I retorted. 'And what about the candles?'

'Lovers?' said Alec, sounding doubtful. 'A poacher?' He heard me sigh and hastened to placate me. 'But let's look around by all means,' he said. 'Let's check thoroughly and see if anything's out of place. Where shall we start?'

'We don't need to look around,' I said. 'I know where the out-of-place thing is going to be. I know what they were doing.' And taking his torch, I led him to the spot, picking my way between the graves as though I was stepping through a flower meadow on a summer's day, all fear gone. When I got there, I played the torch briefly over the scene and then swung the beam backwards to light Alec's way.

'Well?' he said, when he drew up beside me. I shone the torch down at our feet once more. The grave was open and the coffin lid lay teetering on the heap of earth at its side. I played the torch around. There was one candle left there, forgotten, stuck with dripped wax to a jam pot lid.

'Sh-shine it inside,' said Alec, stuttering with cold or fear, I could not say which. I did as he asked and we both looked at the emptiness of it, the white folds of the linen covers flapped back, making it look grotesquely like a picnic basket down there.

'Now tell me I'm silly to think there could be witches,' I said.

'Wh-whose grave is it?' said Alec.

'Can't you guess?' I asked him. 'I knew she had something to do with all of this. I just *knew* it.' I moved the beam of the torch up to the headstone. It was partially obscured. I could make out *In my father's house are many mansions* but the rest of it, *Her sins, which are many, are forgiven*, was lost under the earth which had been thrown up out of the grave.

*　　　*　　　*

Alec took some persuading that he could not accompany me to fetch Mr Tait and I suppose it was gratifying that he did not wave me off into a night full of grave robbers without a care, but we wasted valuable time arguing before he finally gave way.

'Well, at least let me see you safely back to the manse,' he said. 'Then I'm going to come back here and hide behind a headstone to see what happens.'

'Darling, you can't,' I said. 'He'll probably call the police and if they come and find you lurking about they'll arrest you.'

'I could jump over the wall and run away if I hear them,' he said, sounding rather mulish for him, as though determined to be heroic in some way.

'If they come with klaxons blaring and wake up the village and then one of the awakened villagers sees you leaping over his garden wall, you're likely to be shot. On balance, I'd rather you were arrested.'

'Oh very well,' he said at last. 'But promise me you'll come down first thing and tell me what happened.' He switched his torch on again and held it aloft, training the beam up the manse drive. I squeezed his arm and squelched off in my sodden shoes, turning and waving before I opened the door.

It was easy to tell which was Mr Tait's room; a noise like someone trying to drink soup through a straw came rumbling from behind one of the doors, a noise Lorna could never have produced, even after an evening of neat gin and Woodbines. I knocked softly and immediately the rumble stopped.

'Come in, my dear,' said Mr Tait's voice. I hesitated and then opened the door and entered, blinking, into the darkness. 'I did not hear the telephone,' he said. 'I'm sorry you were disturbed, Lorna. Who is it who needs me?'

'It's me, Mr Tait,' I said. 'And it's not the telephone. Something dreadful has happened, I'm afraid.' I told him as succinctly as possible and trying as far as I was able to stick to what was true, although I got into an unforeseen little patch of difficulty trying to mesh the fact that I had heard the shovels with the fact that when I got there all was quiet and the players had left the stage. 'I fluffed it most dismally,' I said. 'I hadn't the courage to barge in, and so I dithered between lying in wait watching them and coming back here to get you and in the end I missed them.'

Mr Tait stretched out a hand and patted one of mine; I was sitting on the edge of his bed and he was propped up, apparently at his ease, listening and watching me over his spectacles.

'Do not berate yourself, my dear,' he told me. 'You were extremely courageous to go at all. And

247

now, if you will return to your rest, I'll get me up and see what's to do about it.'

'Shall I telephone to the police?' I said.

He patted my hand again and shushed me.

'Let me take care of all that,' he said.

'But who do you think it was?' I insisted. 'What do you think they're going to do with her?'

'Hush now,' said Mr Tait. 'Don't you worry. Just leave all that to me.'

He could not have sounded less ruffled if I had been telling him I had put out a pane in his greenhouse with my tennis ball. This was puzzling in the extreme and so, although I did leave him to dress in peace, I did not return to 'my rest', but waited until his feet had clumped downstairs and I heard the front door open and close again and then flitted back to the window of Mrs Tait's bedroom and knelt there, peeping over the sill to watch him. He took a long time to appear and I had begun to wonder if he had gone some other way when at last he came into view, holding a lantern in one hand and, I caught my breath when I saw it, a sturdy shovel in the other. I watched his progress all the way down the drive and then watched through the tree branches as the light bobbed along and came to rest where the candles had been before. I could see nothing more than the lantern light itself, but I did not need to: that shovel had told me as clearly as anything that there were to be no police klaxons or search of the village tonight, but instead a quiet tidying of the mess before anyone should wake at dawn and see it. What in heaven's name was going on? I leaned my head against the windowpane and watched the yellow glow grow shimmery as my breath misted the glass, wishing I could think of an excuse to go over and join him there. Could I perhaps take him a glass of brandy? I decided I could and settled down to wait until I thought he would be cold enough to welcome it.

I do not know what woke me, only that I lifted my head with a jerk and felt my neck go into a spasm. It was still pitch black outside, but now that I was awake I could hear faint sounds of movement from the bowels of the house and as I unfolded my stiff arms and hauled myself to my feet, shivering, I heard a door open and saw a slice of light grow upon the grass below, into which Bunty suddenly appeared, prancing and shaking her ears, greeting the dawn before the dawn had even arrived to be greeted. I looked over at the kirkyard but could see no lantern glow so, stumbling a little, my feet wooden with cold after their soaking and my legs thrumming as the feeling came slowly back into them, I hurried along the passage and crossed the landing to the front of the house. Knocking softly, I edged open Mr Tait's door, meaning to launch into the first of many questions while he was fuddled with sleep and at the psychological disadvantage of being in his nightshirt while I was dressed (albeit in last night's crumpled clothes and with my hair flattened on one side from resting on the windowsill). Mr Tait, though, was not there.

I slipped downstairs, hurrying, fearing that his night's work had proved too much for him—he was hardly a young man after all—and let myself out into the garden, to be given an ecstatic welcome by Bunty, who immediately stopped rolling in the piles of leaves and began wheeling around me on the drive, starting down it and then coming back to

249

my side, as though trying to whip me into embarking on a walk like a gird being made to roll by a cleek.

I took little persuasion, for once, and now that I was outside I could see that it was not really complete darkness after all, probably around six then and not too peculiar of me to be up and about should I happen upon a villager on my way.

There was no sign of Mr Tait in the kirkyard. In fact, I had to spend a moment convincing myself that the whole adventure had not been a dream. The grave was filled, the ground was flat and covered not only with grass but also with a quantity of fallen leaves. I stepped forward to peer at the writing on the headstone, suspecting that I had come to the wrong place somehow, and it was when I did this and felt my foot sink slightly into the ground that I knew I could trust my sense and my memory again. He had done a marvellous job; the turfs under the heap of leaves were fitted as close as tiles, and it was only the smears of earth on the grass all around, remnants of the heap that had been there the night before, and the fact that these leaves were rather sodden and mouldy, most unlike their crisp counterparts elsewhere, that hinted at the fakery of the thing at all. I walked around the church to the dark place under the far wall where, on my earlier visit, I had seen a leaf heap with a wheelbarrow propped against it. Right enough, here was a raw scar where turfs had been lifted and, on top of the heaped leaves, a pile of the earth which Mr Tait had been unable to fit tidily back into the hole. I wondered how he would explain these oddities to the beadle and wondered rather less idly, if his work were done and he had

250

not gone home to his warm bed, where this most vari-talented of ministers might be.

Bunty, always a tremendous mind-reader when one plans to take her home again before she feels a walk has really run its course, stopped dead in the lane with the manse gates ahead and the church gates behind and stood looking up at me with her tongue lolling and tail swinging. It was grey dawn by now and not having a lantern was no excuse for it, but I looked up the lane and down it and could summon no desire for either.

'I'm sorry, my darling,' I told her. 'I'm too tired. Promise a lovely long walk later.'

Bunty sat down and raised a paw to me, a display she can never be induced to wheel out on command but to which she resorts frequently in her own cause. I sighed, glanced up towards the start of the law rise again and jumped. It felt as though my feet had literally left the ground but I suppose it was only my heart which leapt really; there was Mr Tait, shovelless although still with the lantern, its glow diminshed now as the daylight crept up around it, coming down towards me at a harried but rather weary shuffle.

'Where did you spring from?' I said, blunt from the fright of him suddenly appearing that way.

'Where have you been?' he said, equally bluntly, drawing up beside me and absent-mindedly patting the head which Bunty shoved under his hand. He was white with exhaustion and his clothes, as might be expected, were filthy.

'I woke up and wondered where you were so I came to find you,' I told him.

'And did you meet anyone?' he said, looking wildly around him. 'Did you see anything?' He put his hands through his hair, leaving streaks of dirt upon his high, shining forehead.

'I—no,' I said. 'Mr Tait, has something happened? Something else, I mean?'

'Forgive me,' he muttered, and began to trot away. 'I must get back and get out of these things before anyone sees me.' And with another distracted scrub, at his face this time, which put a smear across his cheeks and knocked his spectacles crooked, he skipped and hobbled towards the front door of his house.

*   *   *

'As far removed from the man who sat up in bed and told me not to fret about it as a . . . as a . . . what sort of very harassed person is most unlike what sort of terribly calm one, Alec?' I said later that morning, when I had gone down to Ford Cottage to tell him the ending.

'As a grill chef is from a Buddhist monk,' supplied Alec, who was looking most satisfyingly engrossed and puzzled by what I had recounted to him.

'Thank you. Exactly. Only I'm too bone-tired from sleeping on a windowsill to think up similes of my own.'

'So, we have to ask ourselves, what happened in the interim?' I recognised in his tone the beginnings of one of our marathons of conjecture and I yawned, as I had been doing every five minutes since I had arrived.

'More coffee?' said Alec. I shook my head and shuddered.

'Sorry, darling, but it's perfectly vile. You must

252

ask someone to teach you how to make it if you ever try camping out again. And there's no use in me having a go. I've never made the stuff in my life and wouldn't know where to start.'

'Feeble old us,' said Alec. 'Compared with Mr Tait, anyway, turning his hand to landscape gardening at his age and running up and down the law at dawn.'

'I don't think he came down from the law,' I said. 'I should have seen him. I looked up there, towards the green, down at Bunty, up there again and bang! There he was as though he had popped out of a rabbit hole. And I don't think he came from any of the cottages either. I didn't hear a door and he had that rather set, dogged look that you only get when you've been on the go a while. Not at all the gait he would have had if he'd stepped out of a cottage and would be stepping in at his front door in a minute or two.'

'Hmm, rather nebulous,' said Alec, 'but I'll give you the door. You always hear everything in that hushed time in the very early morning. That's why the waking-up insomnia is so much worse than the can't-get-to-sleep kind. So . . . where was he?'

'I think,' I said slowly, 'that he must have emerged from the end of one of the little lanes that comes around the law.'

'Oh, super!' said Alec drily. 'That means he was at any of the five farms or one of their no doubt plentiful workers' cottages. Or even Luck House itself.'

'Not Luck House,' I said. 'The Howies are Lorna's friends, very much so, not his. He's never actually said anything but I can't see him feeling unperturbed because he thought he could rely on

253

them to get him out of trouble.'

'But what about if he thought that they were mixed up in it and then he found out they weren't, so he was stumped. We don't know, do we, whether it was confidants or culprits he went looking for.'

'Either way,' I said, 'he's rather too wary of the Howies to think he could take it in his stride if it was them behind it.'

'The mystery is how he could have thought that at all,' Alec said. 'I simply can't imagine what could make a minister, faced with the theft of a corpse from his own churchyard, say: "Ah well, not to worry. These things happen." It sounds absolutely mad.'

'It does rather, doesn't it,' I agreed. 'Nevertheless, that's exactly how it happened.'

'And anyway,' said Alec, 'it occurs to me now that he can't have thought he knew who it was. I've just realised: if he did, he would have gone round there and got the bones back to rebury them before he went to work, wouldn't he? He wouldn't have filled in the grave and made it unusable and *then* gone after the corpse.'

'Sorry,' I said. 'If only I weren't so tired I should have realised that.'

'So in some mysterious way that's not anything to do with recapturing the bones, he thought at first that all would be well and then having been somewhere around one of those five farms, he found it wouldn't be.'

'Yes,' I said. 'And that does make a bit of sense. He does tend to think of the farming contingent as the hub of his parish, I've noticed. More than once he has described the women of this place in general as "farmers' wives" and really hardly any of

254

them are. He said it the first time we met when he was telling me about the stranger: that it wasn't silly wee lassies any more. It was sensible farmers' wives whom he had known all his life.'

'But Mrs Fraser from August is a farmer's wife,' said Alec. 'And didn't you say that his own wife was from farming stock too?'

'True,' I said, frowning. 'Still, something about it bothered me. What did he say . . . ? Not silly girls, but sensible farmers' wives he'd known for years, grown wom— Aha! That's it. Grown women with children of their own. That's what's been niggling at me.'

'I don't follow,' said Alec.

'March, April and May were the three girls: Elspeth, Annie and Molly. Then came another three, none of whom has children since none of them has had time yet: Mrs Muirhead, whose first joyous confinement fast approaches, Mrs Torrance who only married that nice Drew Torrance from Ladybank way in the spring and was attacked in July—I heard that from a witness only yesterday, darling, although Mrs Torrance herself kept shtoom—and Mrs Fraser from Balniel who foiled Annette Martineau's hopes to be the lady of Balniel some time last year and has yet to be blessed. Then September—the only month in which a grown woman with children of her own who could have been attacked and then told Mr Tait about it had a chance to get into the busy programme.'

'Ergo: Mr Tait knew about her and did not tell you.'

'I think so,' I said. 'I really do think that might be true.'

'Why wouldn't he?' Alec asked.

I shrugged. 'Sworn to secrecy, perhaps, as I am with Mrs Muirhead?'

'And,' said Alec, 'do you think it might be this same someone in both cases? The woman who confided in Mr Tait and whoever he turned to last night who couldn't, in the end, help him?'

'It could be,' I answered slowly. 'Certainly whoever ousted that girl's bones from consecrated ground last night must believe the bad spirit has summoned the devil. Such a person might well turn to her minister if she thought the devil had come after her, and might very well beg him not to tell.'

'But even if that's right it doesn't help with who the stranger really is,' said Alec. 'I take it you don't believe that—'

'Of course not!' I said, glaring at him.

'Well, you seem to believe in witches these days,' said Alec, with a sly smile. 'Who's to say what else?'

'I don't "believe in witches",' I said hotly. 'I believe that some people do and that some of them are here at Luckenlaw.' One of his eyebrows lifted as though hooked on a fishing line. 'Alec, I *saw* it. The Rural badge is a witch's heart and quite a lot of the members wear one.'

'Presumably, though, the witches were not involved last night? I mean, candles and graveyards must be right up their street, but wouldn't they be pleased to have summoned the devil and be the last people to dig up bones and chuck them in efforts to get rid of him again?'

'I can't believe you're laughing at this. People have dug up a grave!'

256

'I know, I know, and it *is* nasty. But it's not as if it was someone's dear old mother. It was an ancient skeleton. It should probably have gone to a museum in the first place instead of getting a coffin and a headstone and what have you.'

I shook my head, speechless at his callousness.

'Anyway,' said Alec. 'To turn back to sense and sanity for a moment. I should be much happier if we could carve another path through all of this. If we could say that the stranger and the grave robber—one of the grave robbers, anyway—are the same person. Wouldn't you? Then we could forget all about witches completely.'

I groaned and put my head in my hands.

'Of course we couldn't,' I said. 'There are witches in the Rural and the villagers think the girl was a witch too. Witches are absolutely germane to both problems.' We stared at one another, surprised at how neat it sounded, put that way. When we spoke again, it was rather gingerly, as though we feared the idea might dissolve if we breathed too heavily on it.

'Someone is trying to sabotage the Rural because they suspect it's a coven,' said Alec slowly.

'And someone ousted the girl they thought was a witch from her grave,' I added.

'That could be the same person, couldn't it?'

'Easily.' We let our pent-up breath go and beamed at one another.

'Now,' said Alec, in a brisk voice. 'Who? Who do we know disapproves of the Rural? Let's start there.'

'Mr Black.'

'That's one.'

'And Miss Lindsay did say that a couple of the

menfolk had called out names in the street, remember. And she did wonder whether it was these same men who were behind the attacks. But it's all wrong,' I said. 'Their objection was political. She didn't say *what* names they called in the street, but it was finding out that Miss Lindsay and Miss McCallum had been on the Women's March that did it.' Alec opened his eyes very wide at that. 'Yes, exactly, darling,' I said. 'That's what I thought too.'

'Who was it anyway?' said Alec, and I fished my notebook out from my pocket and leafed back through it searching.

'Hmph, here we go,' I said at last, and I read through what I had written. 'My, my, I think we might be wrong. What I've got here suggests that it *wasn't* politics that was the problem at all. I said that Mr Tait had hinted at political concerns and Miss Lindsay replied: yes. *That too.* What do you think of that?'

'It suggests that Miss Lindsay being a Red under the bed was not the issue. Her politics were a problem, but not the problem.'

'Precisely. And as to who did the shouting: Mr McAdam and Mr Hemingborough.'

'In other words,' said Alec, 'two farmers who live on the lanes where Mr Tait might have been this morning.'

'Two farmers who were not at home on the night of the meeting when Mr Black went calling.'

'And one of whose wives had been very reluctant to admit the existence of the stranger.'

'Both of whose wives actually,' I said. 'Mrs McAdam is young Mrs Muirhead's Auntie Bessie and, when the poor girl related her ordeal, Auntie

Bessie—in very un-aunt-like fashion if you ask me—told her to keep quiet about it. Went as far, if you can believe it, as to tell her "not to be daft".'

'And didn't you say that your dairy maid's mistress, right back at the start, seemed reluctant to let her talk to you? What was her name, Dandy? Where was she from? And have you ever had the chance to view her husband's figure?'

'Steady on,' I said. 'Our suspects are multiplying most intemperately.'

'But you did say there were a few of them there at the graveside last night. And we already thought the husbands might have ganged up together.'

'Did we?'

'Well, I did. If half a dozen men are all out on the same night and keeping quiet about it, the simplest explanation is that they're all doing the same thing.'

'But their wives are members,' I pointed out.

'A bluff!' said Alec. 'The wives join up so that if anyone suspects their husbands someone will say, "But their wives are members." Don't you see?'

'And Mrs Hemingborough was attacked.'

'Another bluff! A corker of a bluff. This is it. I'm sure of it. Now, how many are there altogether? Who lives at the other farms? They do begin to swim in front of the eyes after a while, don't they?'

'Not if you have,' I said, fishing in my pocket again and drawing out the bundle of papers I had stuffed in there before leaving the manse, 'a handy pocket sketch map.' Alec leaned forward as I unfolded it.

'Working round from the village,' I said, 'there's Hinter Luck, where the wife denied the attack and the wiry husband shouted at Miss Lindsay; Easter

259

Luck, where Mrs Palmer put on a decent hundred yard dash to keep me away from Elspeth in the dairy and Mr Palmer remains to be seen. And then on the other side, Wester Luck where Mrs Torrance stood in the lane and denied to a woman who practically brought her up that the attack happened.'

'Mrs Torrance!' said Alec. 'What did you say about her home life, Dandy? She married a young man from a different village in the spring.'

'My goodness,' I said. 'Yes, perhaps young Drew Torrance from Ladybank way is not that nice after all. And in fact, Mrs Gow hinted that he had been giving his wife some kind of trouble although she wouldn't say what.'

'Any more?' said Alec. 'Not that we need any more.' He drew himself up and I recognised the superior look he gets when he is about to lecture me. 'It's just as well I didn't listen to you telling me there was nothing for me to do here, Dandy, because—'

I waved my hand to try to get him to shut up while I studied my map again.

'I've never been right round the top of the law,' I said, 'but up there somewhere are Over Luck where the pooh-poohing Mrs McAdam and her name-calling husband reside. He can't be the stranger because he's simply elephantine—I pity the dry stone dyke he clambers over—but he might be protecting the stranger, for he has relations everywhere, or at least his wife does. Mrs Muirhead is one, and Sergeant Doolan's wife and there might be others. And that leaves . . . Oh my goodness, Alec, Luckenlaw Mains.'

'The home of a young, snaky-figured man who

lives alone and is known to walk around at night for no good reason,' said Alec. I was nodding, marvelling at the way it had all fallen into place. Then the bubble popped.

'No, that's wrong,' I said. 'Remember Molly said it wasn't him.'

'But it's her word alone,' said Alec. 'And you did think she was less than certain.'

'True. What a pity Elspeth was too terrified to join us.'

'Terrified of what, though? Perhaps her mistress has that young dairy maid completely under her thumb and had warned her not to say Jock Christie was guilty.'

'That would explain why Mr McAdam was so concerned to get Jockie out of jail,' I said. 'If they were all in it together and Jock was doing the dirty work for them.'

'Jock or Drew Torrance or Mr Palmer or even Mr Hemingborough.'

'Maybe they take it in turns,' I said. 'Maybe the stranger is not the same man each time. Well! I knew they were pillars of the parish—Mr Tait and his farming families, you know—but if we're right, they've taken rather more on themselves than any church has a right to expect.'

'And does Mr Tait know, do you think?' Alec asked me.

'Of course not, goose,' I said. 'Mr Tait employed me to find out. I don't look forward to telling him, I must say. He's very fond of them all, and he wouldn't hear a word against young Christie before.'

'We need to do more than tell him,' said Alec. 'We need to prove it to him. I mean, there must be something. A man can't do what the stranger has done and not make at least one mistake along the way.'

'I don't know about that,' I said. 'He seems to have been extraordinarily lucky so far.'

'Catching him red-handed would be best of all,' Alec said. His eyes glittered at the prospect, as though it were some kind of adventure. All very well for Alec: the stranger was no threat to men.

'Hm,' I said. 'By all means, lie in wait for him, but we must stop him from doing any real harm— we could not loose the girls and ladies into the night like bait.'

'The girls are safe enough,' said Alec idly. 'And the young wives too, don't you think?'

'What do you mean?' I said.

'I'm not sure,' said Alec slowly. 'I spoke without thinking, only if you were making a bet who would you think he'd go for next? Three girls, three wives, two mothers and then what?' I swallowed hard, a sickly realisation spreading through me. This was the pattern I had almost seen for myself the evening before. 'Come Christmas time,' Alec went on, 'I'd say "Watch out, Grandma."'

'But that's ghastly,' I said. 'A deliberate pattern, all in threes, is not just wicked and nasty, it's . . . it's insane. It's as though he's playing them at their own game.'

'Yes,' said Alec. 'Ghastly and insane. Much like digging up a body and carting it off. Nothing about this case speaks much to the nobility of the human spirit really, does it, Dan?'

CHAPTER FIFTEEN

Alec was all business and bustle, planning his investigations of the wandering farmers, but I rather thought I should put in an appearance back at Gilverton, and I decided to break news of my departure to the Taits that very day. Mr Tait, however, foiled my plan.

'You seem in excellent spirits,' I said, when we assembled for tea. He had regained his colour and all of his buoyancy since the morning.

'I am,' he cried. 'I've had a tremendous idea, you see.'

Lorna and I waited expectantly.

'I'm going to organise a visit to the chamber in the Lucken Law.' This was declaimed with a triumphant flourish. 'I think I'm being overly squeamish in keeping it shut up this way,' he went on. 'In fact, I think we should set an example to the village—don't you, Lorna dear?—and start to treat it as the ancient curiosity it is. We should, we really should, put all the more unfortunate associations behind us.'

I was stumped for something to say. Right now, when what he called 'the more unfortunate associations' were being ripped from their resting place and spirited away, it seemed the very last moment to begin treating the chamber as a tourist attraction. On the other hand, I was agog to see it.

'I'm thinking of forming a little party,' Mr Tait said. 'Tomorrow afternoon perhaps for, if we don't go before the winter sets in, it will be cruelly cold and we shall have to wait until the spring.'

'A party?' I asked faintly.

'Yourself of course and the Howies—as the first family of the neighbourhood they are due the honour. Miss Lindsay and Miss McCallum perhaps, for they are keen scholars of local history although incomers both.'

'Captain Watson would surely be interested too,' said Lorna predictably.

'Indeed,' said Mr Tait. 'I have yet to meet this Captain Watson, but if he has an interest in the arts then he will certainly want to see the place. And if he is to be included perhaps we should make sure and ask the Miss Mortons too. I fear their noses are in a way to be out of joint over the warmth of the Captain's welcome, Lorna.'

Lorna looked uncomfortable at that.

'By all means, Father,' she said. 'The Miss Mortons must be asked along, but they won't come tomorrow.' She turned to me. 'They go to the Episcopal church, Mrs Gilver, and they're never home before tea on a Sunday, because it's three buses.'

'I keep telling them they're more than welcome to join my little flock,' said Mr Tait, 'but their uncle's a bishop, you know.'

'Father!' said Lorna.

'Och, I'm just teasing,' said Mr Tait. 'Of course it's their adherence to the Episcopalian principle that's worth the three buses and not the snob value of their uncle at all. Of course it is.' And winking at me, he took a hearty bite out of his scone. 'That's settled then. You could telephone around this evening, Lorna, if you like.'

'I will,' she said. 'Although of course Miss Lindsay and Captain Watson are not on the phone, so I'll just step over and tell them about it after tea.'

And from the moment that stepping over to Captain Watson's appeared on the agenda, Lorna seemed to put the whole of teatime into a higher and rather frantic gear, urging us to accept more tea before our cups were half finished and splitting scones to butter while we were still savouring the one before, until finally her father furnished her with an exit cue.

'I don't want to hurry you away from the fireside, Lorna dear,' he said, 'but if you're going to call at the schoolhouse and Ford Cottage, you had perhaps better do it sooner than later. Captain Watson I cannot answer for, but Miss Lindsay goes in for high tea, does she not, and this might be your only chance to catch her without disturbing a meal.'

He had hardly time to get all of this out before Lorna was up, patting vaguely at her hair and excusing herself to me.

'Dear Lorna,' said Mr Tait once she had gone. 'She seems very taken with this mysterious Captain. What did you make of him, Mrs Gilver?'

'I believe he is very "advanced" in his art,' I said carefully. I felt a bit of a heel, but someone had to arrange a few mattresses so that poor Lorna could fall onto something soft when the end came. 'So one does wonder whether he might not be equally "advanced" in his life.'

'But then he is a Captain,' said Mr Tait, reasonably enough. 'He cannot be quite lost to the "left bank" surely. And given the poet, it seems that Lorna has a yen for romantic types.' He roused himself—he had been staring into the fire—and smiled at me. 'Than which there are many worse things, don't you agree? I cannot set my face against every young man within ten miles.'

'I didn't know you had set your face against any,' I said, matching his jocular tone with my own.

'Well, it didn't come to that,' he said, more serious again. 'But we cannot help steering our children towards calm waters, no matter what our own lives may have given us to bear.' The only sense I could make of that mystifying statement was that some young clergyman had made faint advances towards Lorna and her father had headed him off, but it did not seem all that likely. One could imagine a coal miner or a circus acrobat wanting a different kind of life for his daughter than washing overalls or bringing up five children in a caravan but surely a minister's daughter could not be said to have fallen short of her father's hopes by becoming a minister's wife.

'You'll see soon enough,' said Mr Tait. 'When those boys of yours start to introduce young ladies to you at dances you'll find that not a one of them ever seems quite good enough in your eyes even if everyone you know is whispering at what a match it would be and urging you to give it your blessing. You'll see.'

I smiled, convinced that he was right. I am no soppy, clinging mother to my boys, far from it, but already at the few parties where I have seen them standing silent and awkward, surrounded by giggling little misses in ringlets, I have felt a strong urge to sweep one up under each arm and take them home.

'Your feelings do you great credit as a warm-hearted father,' I said, 'but if I might talk to the

266

meenister and no' the man for a moment: I haven't had a chance to ask you about last night.' Mr Tait stiffened visibly. 'I am here to help you, Mr Tait. You must let me help you with *this* or at the very least tell me why not, for I cannot understand why you won't take me into your confidence. Really, I cannot.'

'I have dealt with the matter,' said Mr Tait. 'I have no need of your help, although I thank you most sincerely for the offer.'

'Dealt with the matter?' I said. 'How?'

'She has been laid to rest in another parish, where none of the parishioners know and she won't be disturbed again.'

'And do you have any idea who it was who removed her? You must have or how did you know where to look to find her.'

Mr Tait sighed as though, with the sigh, he was trying to heave the sorrow of a lifetime out of him.

'My parishioners are good people,' he said, 'but they are old-fashioned and superstitious like people anywhere, and eager to lay the blame for their misfortunes anywhere but where it belongs.'

'I suppose,' I said. 'There is a marked reluctance to blame the attacks by the stranger on the stranger, for instance. But on the whole, I'd say laying blame is not a feature of the Luckenlaw folk at all. A remarkable stoicism seems very much more to the fore.'

'I'm not sure I follow you,' said Mr Tait.

'Oh, surely you've noticed,' I said. 'Mrs Hemingborough's quiet tidying up of her feathers was the least of it. Wells drying up, parasites in the earth, blight in the air, a house lost to fire and they take it all in their stride. "What's for you won't go by you," they say. If I've heard that once in the last weeks I've heard it a dozen times.' Mr Tait looked rather thunderstruck at this for some reason.

'You seem to have got to the heart of things in short order,' he said. 'But I suppose that's what you're here for, eh? And you're right, of course, there is a strain of that thinking running through my flock, but it's not in everyone.'

'Oh, I know,' I said. 'I've noticed that too.'

'Well, you'll have no trouble believing me, that some of the others, some of my parishioners less stocial, as you put it, more superstitious and—although I should not speak harshly of them for they are good souls really—more simple-minded, thought that if trouble came from taking the poor girl out of the law, then trouble would go if they undid what was done . . .'

'And put her back again?' I said.

'Of course,' said Mr Tait. 'It was wicked and wrong, that goes without saying, but it has a kind of sense to it.'

'It's even worse than I was imagining,' I said. 'Mr Tait, how can you say these are good people? How can you call this mere superstition? They sound as though they have given their souls to the devil. It sounds like . . . Well, I hesitate to say it in case you laugh or order me away from the house, but it sounds like witchcraft to me.' Mr Tait neither laughed nor took me by the collar and frogmarched me out of the manse, but just nodded as though what I had said was a mild notion that he could take or leave, but which caused him no upset.

'And if it is witchcraft, then I think I know who is behind it.' At that, he opened his eyes very wide

268

and stared at me, his face growing solemn.

'It's the Rural,' I said. 'The SWRI. And I can prove it too.' Mr Tait's mouth twitched and his eyes had started dancing again.

'I'm not joking,' I said. 'Their badge—the brooch they all wear—is called the witch's heart.'

At that, Mr Tait threw back his head and let out a peal of sustained laughter loud enough to set the pendulum in the mantel clock humming along with him.

'It is indeed,' he said. 'The witch's heart, quite so. But you have got the wrong end of the stick, I'm afraid. The witch's heart keeps witches *away*.'

'What?' I said, wondering how much of an improvement on my first suspicions that could really be.

'It was given as a love token by departing sweethearts, to keep the loved one safe from harm. Why, I gave one to my own wife when we were courting. Lorna wears it now.'

'I see,' I said, blushing furiously. 'But why was it chosen as the Lucken Law Rural badge?'

'No, the whole federation has this same one. There was a competition, you know, and our dear Miss Lindsay, who was a member of the Glamis branch back then, actually helped to draw the winning design.'

'Gosh, how exciting,' I said, and I hoped that my tone matched my words rather than the sickly flood of shame which was spreading through me. 'And tell me,' I went on for I have never sought to spare myself the pain of humiliation when it is deserved, 'what does it say on the blue banner across the heart shape? I couldn't decipher it.' I steeled myself to hear exactly how blameless and pure my so-called coded symbols might turn out to be.

'For Home and Country,' said Mr Tait, confirming my worst fears. 'And who could object to that? Witchcraft indeed!' I felt his enjoyment of my mistake was beginning to shade into rudeness, but I managed to keep smiling as though still enjoying the joke. 'So called by those who fear its power, Mrs Gilver,' he went on, and at last I understood that he was not harping on my blunder, but was mounting a little hobby-horse of his own. 'But I am a man of God and because of that I fear nothing. I find it better just to nod at "the old ways" if I pass them. That's what I call it—the old ways, for that's all it is. The midsummer bonfires and the honoured loaves of Lammas Day. Why, I'm sure your own lovely home is full of holly and mistletoe every Christmas time and that you rolled an egg every spring of your girlhood, didn't you?'

I nodded, conceding the point, but I was only half listening, my brain whirring round. If the bones of the girl were not removed by Mr Tait's devout busybodies after all, but were taken back to the law by villagers more in thrall to the 'old ways', and he did not know who exactly it was who moved them, then . . .

'Why have you organised this visit to the chamber?' I asked. Mr Tait laughed lustily again and leaned over from his chair to squeeze my knee and shake me in a friendly fashion.

'That's my girl!' he said. 'Nose back to the ground, eh? I thought it the best way to show the grave robbers that their plan has been foiled. And, to be honest, I meant what I said about starting to treat the place with a little more architectural and

270

historical interest and a little less reverence. It's one thing to nod but I don't want to be seen to honour the old ways. That wouldn't do at all.'

'To show the grave robbers . . .?' I echoed. 'Do you mean they're in the party?' I desperately tried to remember the names he and Lorna had suggested they invite. The Howies, the Miss Mortons, Miss Lindsay and her postmistress friend.

'Good Lord no,' said Mr Tait. 'That would look far too pointed even if I knew who they were. No, I'm just asking the proper people and trusting that village gossip will ensure it gets back to the ears of those who need to hear it. Miss McCallum talks to everyone over that post office counter, you know.'

It was a gem of a plan, subtle and yet bound to be effective, and I felt some admiration for Mr Tait for having thought of it, even while I felt a little pity for the unknowing guests being used to execute it for him. I was seeing him in a new light today, between this chamber visit and the quiet but effective finding of a new place to bury the bones. I wondered how much of the tale he had told the other minister who now sheltered the poor girl in his kirkyard, whether he had come clean or had acted as he had with me, while enticing me into taking the case; that is, told his colleague as much as he had to and as little as he could, planning to reveal the rest when it was too late to do anything but dig the wretched thing up again, which I imagined no man of the cloth would lightly do.

Just then an even more unwelcome and unsettling thought struck me. Was that the extent of Mr Tait's toying with me or was it even worse? Perhaps I was being fanciful, but it had seemed to

271

me more than once that Mr Tait's only surprise whenever I had told him of some little discovery, some little step forward in the case, was that I had got there, or got there so quickly and never, not once, surprise at where I had got. Was he using me to solve a mystery which had him stumped or did he feel he had better not know, that it would be much more suitable if I were the one who found it out?

I vowed that, from that moment on, I should keep a weather eye on Mr Tait. I would no longer trot along like a good little bloodhound and report my latest findings, the better to be shown the next bit of path towards where he was guiding me. Instead, I would plough my own furrow and find out, in the name of truth, just what the devil was going on.

*   *   *

We were six for luncheon the following day after church, Miss McCallum, Miss Lindsay, the Taits, 'Captain Watson' and me; making for a mood around the table which was somewhere between high spirits and hysteria, following as it did a terribly brimstone-ish sermon—surely designed to wag a finger at the culprits, should they be in the congregation, without alerting any of the innocent to what was going on—and preceding an outing which was a kind of Sunday School Trip imagined by Edgar Allan Poe. Added to that there was Lorna's solicitousness over her beloved Captain, which came out as relentless maternal clucking, Miss Lindsay and Miss McCallum's frosty disapproval of the clucking, Miss Lindsay's attempts to engage Alec in Arty Talk, Alec's mounting terror that this would uncover him for the sham he was, Miss McCallum's attempts to turn the talk to politics to find out if Captain Watson's captaincy or artistry was the determining factor *there*, Alec's mounting terror that she would uncover him for the *Tory* that he was and conclude that he could not be an artist too, Mr Tait's open appraisal of him, which was thankfully silent because if it had taken the form of words it would only too obviously have been a series of questions on his background, prospects and intentions, Alec's increasingly strained performance of upstanding chap (for Mr Tait), right-thinking, or rather left-thinking, modern young man (for Miss McCallum), talented and dedicated avant-garde artist (for Miss Lindsay) and friendly but unenthralled new acquaintance (for Lorna), and finally my dread that the rising bubbles of hilarity could not be contained inside my chest much longer and that any minute I was going to hiss like a steam kettle and have to slide off my chair to roll about under the table, screaming.

Mr Tait carved thin slices off the roast beef, and Lorna urged everyone—but especially Alec—to another and yet another of the Yorkshire puddings, little round ones as light and crisp as meringues and quite unlike the slab of flannel which usually masquerades as Yorkshire pudding north of the border. Even my own dear Mrs Tilling cannot quite shake off the ancestral influence when it comes to Yorkshire puddings: hundreds of years' worth of suet, after all, must eventually seep into the very soul.

'Mrs Wolstenthwaite's Yorkshire puddings are

Father's very favourite thing,' said Lorna. 'But he can get terribly caught up after church and end by sitting down to everything dried up and nasty at half-past three.'

'We are more fortunate today, my dear,' said Mr Tait.

'And I'm so happy to have you, Captain Watson,' she went on. 'I hate to think of you, down there all alone, frying sausages over a gas ring, while we sit down to such feasts. Would you be offended by an open invitation to luncheon any day you care to join us?'

Since I was sure that Alec could no more fry a sausage than make these little puffs of nothing with which I was at that moment mopping up gravy as though I had not eaten for a week, I thought that an open invitation to breakfast, luncheon, tea and supper would be a godsend.

Finally, when the large bowl of custard trifle had been finished, with Alec manfully spooning away the two helpings Lorna had insisted on serving him, and we were toying with our coffee cups, some of the pressure was relieved by the sound of the rather clanking manse doorbell.

'Aha,' said Mr Tait. 'I was beginning to worry that there had been some trouble on the road. Lorna?'

Lorna got up, giving me one of her most beaming smiles, and Mr Tait followed her. I saw him noticing Alec's unthinking rise as Lorna left the table and nodding in satisfaction at him for the properness of the little chivalry, just as Miss McCallum scowled at him for the same.

'Mrs Gilver,' said Mr Tait, 'would you step outside? We have a lovely surprise for you, Lorna and me.' Intrigued, I folded my napkin and went after them, noting Alec jerking upwards again and Miss McCallum's eyebrows jerking down. Outside in the hall, the housemaid was just turning the handle and hauling open the front door and there on the porch stood my lovely surprise.

'Hugh!' I exclaimed. Lorna clapped her hands in glee and then held them together under her chin, almost luminous with vicarious romance. Really, she was in for a dreadful let-down if she ever did manage to land a husband of her own.

'Sir, Miss Tait,' said Hugh, very properly, causing the beacon of Lorna's smile to dim just a little. 'Dandy,' he said at last.

'Hugh!' I said again even louder, loud enough to penetrate the dining-room door. 'Darling!' I rushed forward and threw my arms around him, almost knocking him over since he was—understandably—reeling from the shock of the greeting. Thankfully, we avoided toppling onto the porch floor and having to untangle ourselves. 'What a lovely treat to see you. Oh Mr Tait, you are a poppet, to remember how much Hugh wanted to come, isn't he, darling?' Hugh was stony with outrage; Mr Tait was one of his most revered boyhood heroes—poppet, indeed!

Then, unable to think of anything else, I compounded the insult by saying to Hugh in that flirtatious but bossy voice which we both hate to hear issuing from a wife to her husband and which I never use on him: 'Now, darling, you must come and say hello to Bunty. She always misses you so when I take her away. Come along, this way.' I threaded my arm through his and dragged him along the passage to the boot-room near the side door where Bunty had been quartered and, since he could hardly wrest himself from my grip in front of the Taits, he was forced to come with me.

'What's got into you?' he said, when the boot-room door was closed behind us and I was trying to stop Bunty from giving him too enthusiastic a welcome. She never does get the plain message which is fired in her direction every time her path crosses Hugh's. She still thinks he loves her.

'What?' I said, playing for time.

'Have you been drinking?' said Hugh. As an explanation this had its merits, but he could too easily find out that it was not true.

'I'm sorry,' I said. 'I just had to escape for a minute.'

'Escape?' said Hugh coldly.

'There's the most tremendous subterranean farce going on in the dining room,' I said. 'An artist, a suffragette and a socialist all squaring up to one another and poor Lorna Tait trying to keep things smooth. I've been fighting the giggles all through luncheon and when you gave me an excuse not to go back in, I couldn't resist it.'

It worked. Hugh, during my outburst in the hall, had been looking at me, really looking at me, but now he was back to normal again—viewing me—and, also as normal, viewing me with some disdain.

'I can't see what's funny about that,' he said. Artists, socialists and suffragettes were some of Hugh's least favourite characters in the world, and I am sure that the last time he had succumbed to a fit of helpless giggles was back in the days when he was in Mr Tait's catechism class at Kingoldrum. 'Now, before I'm made to look even more of a fool than I've been made to look already . . .' He gave

276

me a glare—again very much the norm, for being glared at is much more like being viewed than being looked at, really—and strode out of the room.

I hurried after him and caught up with him in the dining-room doorway. Beyond I could see Miss McCallum looking rather flushed, Miss Lindsay looking rather knowing, and Lorna with her mouth turned down at the corners and her shoulders in a slump.

'Artistic temperament, I daresay,' Mr Tait was saying. 'We've lost Captain Watson, Mrs Gilver. He rushed out while Hugh was saying hello to Bunty.'

'He suddenly went still when you were out of the room,' Miss Lindsay explained. 'Physically blanched, leapt up and said he had to get home immediately because he'd had a tremendous idea for a new work. I thought for a minute he was going to climb out of the window.'

*　　　*　　　*

After this inauspicious start to the proceedings, Hugh was at his stiffest and most quellingly polite to everyone in the party for the rest of the afternoon, and when the Howies arrived, dressed as outlandishly as ever, each in her own way, giggling like two schoolgirls on a spree, he became icy with disapproval for the whole bally lot of us and even rather short with Mr Tait for putting such a collection of individuals together and then inviting Hugh to make one of their number.

We set off for the burial chamber of the Lucken Law in three cars, making quite a procession as we swept out of the gates. Hugh was conveying

277

Mr Tait, naturally, and Miss McCallum and Miss Lindsay, showing a marked lack of sisterly respect, I thought, had plumped to be driven by him rather than me. Since Vashti Howie had a two-seater, that left Lorna and me to bring up the rear and me alone to try to raise Lorna's bruised spirits after the abrupt departure of the Captain.

'Perhaps you can show him the chamber another day,' I said. 'Just the two of you, I mean. I—um—I'd have thought that if he's interested in its . . . ambience, or its . . . ancient—um—aura, it would be far preferable for him to see it without the rest of us all galumphing around spoiling things.'

This worked rather too well, I thought, if my object was simply to cheer Lorna up and not to put Alec in danger of an inescapable tryst. She looked positively entranced by the notion and there was a long dreamy silence before she spoke again.

'They'll be turning off in a minute, Mrs Gilver,' she said. 'Get ready to slow down.' We had left the village and worked our way around the law beyond the gateposts of Luck House—really, the Howies had made a terribly inefficient journey down to the manse to meet us—when the two cars in front swung in at a road end and trundled down a drive to where a farmhouse sat, tucked under the slope of the hill above it. We passed straight through the farmyard and out the other side, ending up in a little cleft at the bottom of what was almost a cliff side, as though a portion of the hill itself had been carved away to make room for the farm. There was just space enough for the three motor cars side-by-side, although Mr Tait—the bulkiest of the party—had to squeeze out of Hugh's passenger door with a little shimmy.

278

Lorna, as I said, was her cheerful self again; the two spinster ladies were very serious and correct, with pencils and notebooks ready to sketch points of interest or copy down ancient runes; Hugh was unbending slightly at the prospect of such an utterly *Boy's Own Paper* adventure as was facing him. The surprise amongst our number came from the Howies. I had been expecting the usual valiant good cheer overlying the rather comical despondency, but they were as genuinely excited, keyed up almost, as I had ever seen them. Nicolette's face showed a hectic flush and she smoked intently, not waving the cigarette around in a long holder, but puffing on it with every breath, her eyes darting. Vashti, in contrast, was as pale as her muddy complexion could ever get and rather glittery about the eyes, which flared as she caught me looking at her.

'I've been dying to get a look at the place,' said Nicolette, 'but now that I'm here . . .'

'It's giving you the creeps?' I asked sympathetically.

'Absolutely the willies,' she said. 'One envies Miss Lindsay with her sketchbook. *She* obviously has no qualms.'

'We don't have to go,' muttered Vashti. 'I don't think I dare.'

'Dare what?' I said. 'You're surely not worried about a mummy's curse, are you? Haven't there been archaeologists and university scientists all over the place time and again?' If truth be told, I was feeling rather less hearty than this made me sound, for the last twenty-four hours had seen some terribly murky deeds unfold: this chamber was very far from being a mere historical site in

279

some people's reckoning.

'Scoff all you want to,' said Vashti. 'There are more things in heaven and earth . . .' But I was with Mr Tait on that one: firmly believing that there were rather fewer things in heaven and earth than one was wont to hear tales of, and that stout refusal to give the tales credence was perhaps best all round.

Standing just where the little cleft became almost a cave, overhung most disquietingly with jagged plates of fissured rock which looked as though they might slide out of place at any moment and plummet, spike first, to the earth, Mr Tait was gathering everyone's attention.

'Now then,' he said, 'it is perfectly safe inside, solid rock and all most carefully pinned and buttressed by our friends from the university not five years ago, so there is no danger. I have a lantern here, and Hugh has another. You don't mind coming at the back, Hugh, do you? The going is not arduous—I see you have all been sensible and worn stout shoes. So let us begin.'

He turned and walked into the cave and then, moving to one side, he disappeared, leaving the rest of us to give a collective gasp.

'Come along,' said Mr Tait's voice, sounding rather muffled. Miss McCallum strode after him and stopped at the point where he had vanished, standing with her hands on her hips, looking upwards, then she too walked as though into the solid face of the rock facing her. I followed.

Disappointingly, although I could understand how Mr Tait might have been unable to resist the little show he had given us, there was no mouth of a tunnel, tiny doorway with odd symbols carved above it, or any other fantastical portal to be found there, but just a set of rough steps which led between outcrops of rock, hidden from view and so lending themselves to theatricality, but otherwise, with their edging of brambles, and withered stinging nettle, looking very much like many another flight of steps hacked into a hillside up and down which I had been dragged during the country walks which punctuated the early years of my marriage. I started to climb, ignoring the brush of gorse and bracken against my skirt and hoping that we were not expected to go too far up the law on the outside before being admitted to its secret innards.

We went quite far enough, high above the hawthorn and elder which clothed the lower slopes and ending with a splendid view—almost worth it—of Wester and Over Luck Farms although the Mains was hidden by the trees below us. At last Mr Tait stopped, stepping off the path onto a flat place on the cropped grass, puffing like a bull walrus and with his spectacles slightly misted, and waited for everyone following to catch up with him.

'Round here,' he said. 'Here we are,' and he picked his way along a path as narrow as a sheep track which wound around and slightly downwards, veering out alarmingly to pass a rather twisted little rowan which was just about managing to cling to the rocky slope. On the other side of this, signs of interference by man could be seen. Earth had been shovelled out of place and was held back by restraining planks of rough wood, themselves buttressed by pegs driven deep into the ground. The resulting niche was floored with brick and there were four metal poles, rather rusted now, set in the corners which must have held up a canopy at one time. At the back of the niche was a plain wooden door, painted with creosote and shut with a sturdy padlock. Mr Tait fished in his trouser pocket and drew out a new-looking, very shiny key. He caught my eye.

'Yes, Mrs Gilver,' he said, loud enough for everyone to hear. 'We very often have to change the padlock on this place, I'm afraid. Boys will be boys, I suppose, and it's just too much of a temptation for some of the Luckenlaw rascals, this place sitting up here like the den of dens. Look, the staple and hasp are quite buckled with all the attempts over the years. And judging from these bright scratches, the scamps have been at it again not long since. Boys will be boys!'

While talking, he had undone the padlock, released the hasp and closed the padlock over the staple again, locking the door open, and now he grasped the handle and pulled. There was no spooky creaking as the door swung open, but beyond it was exactly what one might have hoped for—an older doorway, this one of stone and arched to a point at the top. Mr Tait took out a box of matches to light his lantern.

'Shall we?' he said. 'Better late than never, my dear Hugh. Now ladies, the first thing you will notice is the surprisingly modern-looking stonework of the entrance way, which suggests that this place was in use until perhaps Georgian times and was repaired using the builders' know-how of the day. Certainly these blocks you see in the lintel have been quarry-cut and dressed and could not be original, but as we go further you will be pleased to hear that the inner lintels are made of free surface slabs that . . .'

The history lesson had begun and it carried on the whole time we were in there, much to the evident delight of what I came to think of as the three scholars of the party, the schoolmistress, the postmistress and, of course, Hugh. The three sensation-seekers, if I might lump myself in with the Howies and describe us that way, would have been better served by a deathly hush or whispered legends, but it is perhaps just as well that Mr Tait did not indulge in such things, for Nicolette and Vashti looked quite mesmerised enough as it was, even while the description of hair-strengthened mortar and estimations of the weights of the stones and their provenance and the flint marks upon them and the significance of the whale-jaw shape to the entrance pillars droned on and on. Hugh, of course, was transported. The only one of us, in fact, who strolled down the passageway to the burial chamber, quite unruffled, neither enchanted nor intrigued, was Lorna.

Even when we reached the chamber itself, more of a cave really, she stood as calmly as though she were in a museum, looking at the exhibits in well-lit glass cases safely behind velvet ropes. I, in contrast, had icy prickles up the back of my neck and was concentrating on not noticing anything identifiable in the many prints on the dusty floor, dreading to see where the bones of the poor girl who had lain here all these years might have rested on their recent brief return.

'. . . can't have been *intended* for burial,' Mr Tait was saying. 'For as you know, a stone cist in the ground covered by a mound of earth is the normal thing in these parts, but it was probably used as a resting place for the king, or chieftain—hence the central sarcophagus—and for generations of his family too, judging by the number of cists which have been constructed over time.' He waved a hand at the tiers of little cubby-holes, half hewn out and half built on, all around the walls of the chamber, turning it into something resembling a giant honeycomb. 'The small size of these— smaller even than the usual short-cist—is thought to indicate ash burial or bone burial rather than the interment of recently deceased corpses.'

Beside me I could hear Vashti Howie's breath, fast and shallow.

'Are you all right?' I asked her.

'Perfectly,' she said, sounding anything but; sounding strangulated, her dry throat clicking as she swallowed. 'I've always hated little dark places, that's all,' she said, with an attempt at her usual drawl. 'Too many games of sardines with wicked old uncles in my youth, you know.' And she laughed, a sound ghastly enough to attract the attention of one or two others who turned towards her, frowning.

'And were all of the remains in place when the chamber was discovered?' said Hugh, turning away again.

'None of them,' said Mr Tait. 'Perfectly normal, so I believe. The place would have been cleared for use as a fortress in war or as a storage stronghold. The archaeologists told me they've found chicken droppings and old beer flagons and goodness only knows what in some of the places they've opened.'

'Had they ever found what they found here, though, Mr Tait?' said Nicolette. She was tracing a path around the perimeter of the chamber, trying to make it look desultory, I suppose, but appearing as though she feared with every step to put her foot upon an adder.

'Niccy,' said Lorna, mildly as ever—one could not imagine Lorna Tait ever sounding sharp—but clearly rather shocked at her friend for mentioning so plainly what everyone else was busy pretending to have forgotten.

'Good Lord,' said Nicolette, suddenly, peering into one of the honeycomb holes. 'Lorna darling, you have good eyes. What's that in there? I can't make it out.'

Lorna stared at her and made no move towards where she was pointing.

'What's this?' said Hugh. 'What have you found?' but he could not cross to where Nicolette stood, since Miss McCallum was peering intently down at the floor as Mr Tait described its construction and her broad beam was stuck immovably in his path.

'Oh Nic, don't tease,' said Vashti, pleadingly. 'Let's get out of here.'

'No, Vash,' said her sister. 'Look, there's something in there. Lorna?' Nicolette clasped Lorna's arm and wheeled her round so that they were both squinting into the darkness of the opening. Mr Tait had gone quiet and was watching them, and maybe it was just the upward shading from the lantern but he appeared to have a look almost of glee upon his usually kindly face.

Lorna stepped forward at last and stretched her arm into the dark place. We all heard the gritty scrape as she began to pull something out.

'Ugh,' she said, turning her head away as though

285

to save herself from breathing in an unpleasant smell.

'Please don't. Stop it,' said Vashti at my side, and I put an arm around her. Lorna Tait turned back to face the rest of us, cradling a white bundle in her hands, then a sudden look of horror flashed across her face and she dropped the bundle which unfurled like a sail, releasing a puff of dust.

'What—' said Nicolette.

Miss McCallum and Lorna both screamed and Miss McCallum lurched backwards, bumping into Hugh and setting his lantern swinging.

Vashti Howie crumpled in my arms and sank to the floor.

'A rat!' shrieked Miss McCallum. 'A rat!'

'Nonsense, only a mouse,' said Hugh.

'Father,' wailed Lorna, putting her hands over her head as the shadows skirled about and the screams echoed and echoed again.

'Where did it go?' said Miss Lindsay. 'I'll kill it, Hetty. I won't let a rat touch you.'

'It's a mouse!' said Hugh.

'Oh Hugh, for God's sake,' I said. 'Rat or mouse, can't you see this woman has fainted? And can't you steady that damned lantern before we all run mad?'

Hugh, stung at being addressed that way in public by his own wife, although I don't think anyone was listening, heaved into action at last, handing me the lantern and stooping to lift Vashti Howie into his arms.

'You go ahead with the light, Dandy,' he said. 'We need to get this lady some air.'

*   *   *

286

'It was just a dust sheet,' said Mr Tait, when the others had joined us on the little brick platform, where I was flapping my handkerchief rather uselessly in Vashti's face and wishing I had some water to splash on her. 'They must have left it behind when they were working here.'

'Here she comes,' said Hugh, looking at Vashti's fluttering lashes. She groaned and started a little as she opened her eyes and remembered where she was.

'Don't say anything, darling,' said Nicolette, kneeling at her side and shaking her head a little between her bejewelled hands. 'Who could blame you for fainting? I've never heard such a ghastly racket in my life.' She shot a poisonous glance at Miss McCallum, who was the colour of a vanilla custard and was being supported on one side by Miss Lindsay and on the other by Lorna Tait, who had either regained her colour or had never lost it despite the lusty shriek.

'If you hadn't gone poking about,' said Miss Lindsay to Nicolette.

'Now, now, ladies,' said Mr Tait. 'We've all had a nasty shock and I feel most remorseful about having put you in the way of it. Please, I beg you, forgive me. Now, if Mrs Howie is feeling quite recovered and Miss McCallum thinks her legs will stand it, I think we should make our way slowly back to base camp and go home for tea.'

It was a quite outstandingly mournful little procession which trailed back down through the gorse and bracken to the motor cars. When we got there, Nicolette helped her sister into the two-seater and left, hurtling backwards towards the farmyard without another word. Miss McCallum collapsed into the nearest seat, which happened to be in Hugh's Daimler, and Miss Lindsay inevitably hopped in beside her. Lorna, with a glance at her father, made a third and Hugh climbed in to chauffeur the three of them back to the village, reversing out very slowly, as though he thought the slightest bump under the wheels would start one of them off howling again.

That left Mr Tait and me. My legs were still feeling a little woolly from the alarums, but I managed to turn my motor car in the space and drive fairly smoothly down to the Mains farmyard and out onto the road. It was around about Wester Luck Cottage when I heard the first gulp from beside me and I looked round to see Mr Tait's lips twitch just once, before he drew his eyebrows down in a frown and cleared his throat. There was silence for a moment and then another gulp, this one with a slight whinny behind it. My lips twitched too, I let out a shriek to equal any of Miss McCallum's and then we both put our heads back and roared.

'A rat! A rat!' I said.

'Nonsense, only a mouse,' wept Mr Tait.

'I'll save you, Hetty,' I cried in a falsetto tremble.

'Good Lord,' said Mr Tait, wiping his eyes and forehead with his handkerchief. 'What a disaster.'

'Nonsense,' I told him. 'If you wanted the tale spread around, the more packed with incident it is the better.'

'Oh yes,' said Mr Tait, as though only just remembering. 'Yes, I suppose so.'

CHAPTER SIXTEEN

The next morning, Alec and I held a dawn meeting under cover of another early walk for Bunty. Hugh, still smarting at being ticked off so peremptorily in the chamber the day before, and in a considerable sulk about the way his long-awaited adventure had descended into hysterics, had taken himself off home straight after breakfast, not even pretending to care when—and possibly whether—I joined him there again. I had been all ready with a long list of dreary facts about household economy that I still needed to ascertain, but he had waved my explanation away with an imperious hand. If only he had known that my preparations for this wretched talk consisted of precisely one page of notes which read: *Insurance, daily/weekly marketing, pastry,* and that every time I imagined having to stand up and talk sense in front of all those women who thought I was either an expert or an idiot (and I knew not which was worse), I felt I should be lucky to faint dead away like Vashti Howie and be carried off in someone's manly arms.

'Well, that's a great pity,' said Alec, when I had brought him up to date. 'If the grave robbers are not in fact bent on preserving the honour of the church but are in thrall to the silliest kind of superstitious nonsense, and the SWRI is not, after all, a front for a band of witches, then our neat little picture looks rather dish-evelled again. I still believe that either Jock Christie or Drew Torrance could be the dark stranger, though. I took the

289

chance of going round to the Torrances' yesterday afternoon, after I ducked out of facing Hugh—what a narrow squeak that was, eh?—and had quite a long chat under cover of asking permission to paint on their land.'

'And?'

'Well, he's rather a poor specimen. Not quite rickety, but far from burly, so he fits the silhouette and he was not at all truthful about his moonlight meanderings.'

'How on earth did you get him onto that?'

'I bemoaned the fact that there's nothing to do in the evening in Luckenlaw—unless you were a female, I said, in which case you at least got a jaunt to the Rural once a month, but what were the men supposed to look to for entertainment?'

'Masterly,' I said. 'How did he answer?'

'He said that after a day of sweat and toil on the farm he was happy to kick his boots off and doze with his feet on the fender. As a matter of fact, once he was on the subject of agricultural toil, it was rather a job to get him off it again. It must be marvellous to be a policeman who can just rap on the door, ask ten questions, tip his hat and leave. I thought I was going to grow roots standing there.'

'So that just leaves Mr Palmer to be viewed,' I said. 'I suppose you'll do that, will you?' My enthusiasm for a wifely return to Perthshire had cooled, not to say chilled, after the short visit from Hugh, and I should be happy to find some excuse for remaining at Luckenlaw.

'Certainly,' said Alec. 'Perhaps the dairy at Easter Luck would lend itself to a study in white, but right now I'm off to Luckenlaw Mains where I hope to fall in with young Christie. And you should

290

keep on with your researches into the—'

'Oh, please don't say it,' I groaned. 'Every time I think of it, I could swoon.'

'Yes, but you could start with Mrs McAdam. You haven't spoken to her yet. You might even warn her—a married woman with children of her own—that she should be very careful at November's full moon. You might get some idea of just how well she knows that already.'

It was as cheerless as any day could be—grey, cold, never managing quite to rain or quite to stop, just near enough to frost to make one's feet cold but not near enough to freeze the mud and make the going easy. It was, in short, dreich and drumlie; two words which have always seemed to me to mean exactly the same thing but which, given the number of dreich and drumlie days to be described in Fife, are both absolutely essential. Bunty, nevertheless, managed to be in the same ebullient frame of mind as ever and watching her set off at a prancing trot with her head up and nose quivering hauled my spirits up just a shade too and I tried to enjoy the view of the distant sea and the great shrieking flocks of seagulls over the flat fields as they looped and wheeled, tying invisible knots and loosening them again.

*   *   *

Perhaps Monday morning was not the best time to catch and hold the attention of a busy farmer's wife since Monday was washday, in the farms of Luckenlaw the same as everywhere, and she had, I guessed from counting the petticoats and bodices she was shaking out and dipping into the bubbling

291

copper, at least three daughters as well as the husband whose overalls lay bundled on a sheet of newspaper on the floor awaiting the dregs of the wash-water once the daintier items had been seen to. On the other hand, it is always easier to talk to someone whose eyes and hands are occupied than to someone who is sitting across a table staring back at you, and the scented steam in the large kitchen-scullery was excellent camouflage, throwing both of us into what they call on the pictures 'soft focus', capable of making Mary Pickford look like a schoolgirl when she was thirty if a day and allowing me, I hoped, to appear as a kind of shimmering Fairy Godmother come to issue kindly advice, and not the gimlet-eyed nosy parker I was really.

It would be best, I had decided, to go fairly straight to the point and, thanks to my session with young Mrs Muirhead, I felt I had an opening.

'My brief, Mrs McAdam, as you know, is the household budget,' I began. 'But I have to say it's fading into the background the more I learn about what's going on here at Luckenlaw.' She did not look up—she was pounding energetically with her dolly—but I saw her stiffen slightly and I thought that the rhythm of the dolly became a little slower as though, instead of listening while she pounded, she was now pounding while she listened. Her dark head, the scraped-back hair just touched with grey but still strong and shining, inclined ever so slightly my way.

'I think I've just about got a handle on the thing now,' I went on, 'and so I've come to warn you.' A glance flicked my way, but she kept working. 'It was your—is she your niece or your goddaughter?

Young Mrs Muirhead, anyway—who got me interested in the problem. She had worked herself up into a dreadful state. Such a shame just when she should be keeping calm and thinking happy thoughts, don't you agree?'

'She'll be fine,' said Mrs McAdam. 'She's young and strong. But . . . can I trouble you to say just what it is you're getting at, madam? I'm not just quite following you.'

I pursed my lips at her words: I have always thought it monstrous to declare that a person is 'strong' simply to excuse oneself from being more kindly and careful than one feels like being. Indeed, the old saw which declares 'What does not kill you makes you stronger', no less than Luckenlaw's own 'Whatever's for you won't go by you', has always seemed to me to be the worst kind of heartless nonsense and the one time that a grand benefactor was heard to utter it, with oily condescension, in Moncrieffe House Convalescent Home, I was immensely gratified to witness him receiving a swift bop on the nose from a young lieutenant, with one arm blown off and a bad gas tummy. Mrs McAdam had just, unbeknownst to herself, got on my wrong side in rather a big way.

'I'm talking about these nasty attacks by the fellow they're calling the dark stranger,' I said. 'I've worked out the pattern, you see. I know what's going on, and I've come to warn you.' She let go of the handle of the dolly at last and it fell to the side of the copper with a dull clunk. Blowing a wisp of hair away from her eyes and putting her hands on her hips, she faced me.

'To warn me?' she said.

'Not to come in November,' I told her. 'To the

293

SWRI. It's like this you see: three young girls, three young women and two matrons attacked in that order, every month.'

'*Every* month?' said Mrs McAdam, frowning.

'Oh yes,' I told her airily. 'I've found them all. Every month since March it's been. And so married ladies with families, like yourself, need to be told to beware, because it's going to be one of you in two weeks' time if we're not careful.'

'This is what you've worked out, is it?' said Mrs McAdam, looking almost amused, which took some of the wind out of my sails. I thought I was due a bit of credit for having untangled it, surely. 'And what do you make of it, madam? What do you reckon it's all about?'

'Do you know,' I told her, 'I really don't care. Whether it's a saboteur, a mischief-maker, some poor fellow who should be in a sanatorium for his own sake as much as for others . . . I couldn't give a fig. All I know is that it's causing a great deal of silliness and nasty whispers about devils and demons, frightening women who should know better, and it's got to stop.'

'Och, it'll stop betimes,' said Mrs McAdam, 'when it's run its course.'

'But why should it?' I insisted, infuriated once again by the bovine insipidity, the sheer gormlessness of these women. If they were not colluding in it, how could they be so ready just to take this? 'Why should it get to run its course,' I demanded, 'any more than a burglar should get to burgle until he's set for life, or a murderer get to murder until he's removed everyone standing between him and his fortune? Why on earth should we take this lying down?'

294

'*We?*' said Mrs McAdam. 'Pardon me, but you've had to take nothing, and if those who have are not complaining I don't see why you should be.' As soon as she had said this, her eyes flared, her hand fluttered at her hair, and she turned to her copper again, in some confusion.

'Aha,' I said. 'My warning's too late then. You, Mrs McAdam, were September's victim. I wondered if you might be.'

'Aye well,' she said, sounding brusque with the annoyance she felt at her slip. 'Now you know and it's done me no harm, has it?'

'Now that we have things out in the open where they belong, then,' I said, 'perhaps you won't mind answering a question or two, because you can think what you like, but to my mind this stranger has to be stopped and if we can work out who he is, then we can stop him.'

'You'd best leave it alone,' said Mrs McAdam. 'Mark my words,'—and I knew exactly what words they were going to be—'what's for you won't go by you.'

'Humour me,' I insisted. 'I'm taking it as read that he came at you across the fields, flying over the ground, swooping over the dykes like a racehorse etc., etc., that he knocked you over, pinched you, ripped at your head and face and then was off again. How am I doing thus far?' Mrs McAdam shrugged reluctantly. 'And he was a wiry chap. Not very tall and rather snaky in his outline. Now,' I went on, drawing my little sketch map out of my pocket and spreading it on the kitchen table. 'My guess is that he came from . . . the direction of . . . Let me see now . . . Actually it's very hard to say. In the spring he was coming more

295

or less from the north, latterly from the south, almost as though he's always coming in towards the village from the outside.' Mrs McAdam had drifted over to my side and was peering over my shoulder at the arrows on my map.

'That's not right,' she said. I swung round on her.

'You know who it is, don't you?' I said.

'No!' she blurted. 'Only, he came at me from Luckenheart way.'

'Where's that?' I said.

'Next farm along,' said Mrs McAdam.

'In which direction?' I said.

'Och, that's right, I was forgetting,' she said, scowling. 'Thon Howies changed the name when they landed. Thought it made the place sound swankier, I daresay. Luck *Mains*. But Luckenheart Farm it always was and always will be.'

'He came at you from there?' I said. 'It is Jock Christie, isn't it? It must be. His name pops up over and over again.'

'He's nothing to do with it, poor lad,' said Mrs McAdam.

'Why poor?' I demanded. 'Why does everyone keep saying that? Is there something amiss there?'

'Amiss?' said Mrs McAdam, with a wry twist of her mouth. 'I'll say there is.'

'*Everyone* says there is.' Now that I knew that Luckenheart and the Mains were one and the same place, I was remembering. 'People shiver when they say the name.'

'Aye well,' said Mrs McAdam. 'You'd need to ask Mr Tait about that.'

I stared at her in puzzlement, but could not begin to imagine what she meant.

'And one more question,' I said presently, with my fingers crossed that her sudden mood of openness would not run out before I was finished. 'The dark stranger, when he attacked you that September night—what did he smell like?'

It was her turn to stare at me.

'What?'

'I agree it's an odd question,' I said. 'And, since you know who it is, it would make more sense for me to ask for his name, but if you won't tell me that, perhaps you'll at least give me a sporting chance to work it out for myself. Was there a smell?'

'What are you asking?' said Mrs McAdam. 'I don't just understand you.'

'Well,' I said, 'in March he smelled like eggs apparently, in April like flowers, in May like whisky, although that might not be as certain as some of the others, in June like bonfire smoke, in August like yeast, and I should like to know what he was dabbing behind his ears in September.'

Mrs McAdam looked thunderstruck and sank down at the table opposite me, her copper full of underclothes quite forgotten.

'I thought . . . I thought it was from coming through the fields,' she said softly. 'The smell of fresh cut corn on him.' She shook herself out of the reverie and looked at me piercingly. 'Say it again,' she commanded. 'Tell me again.' I ran through the peculiar little list a second time. She shook her head at the whisky but made no other response.

'What is it, Mrs McAdam?' I said. Her face was changing, her eyes darkening, her mouth turning to a grim line, two darts of white appearing on either side of her nose.

'Somebody's been making fools of all of us,' she said. 'Mr Tait was right all along.' She was rigid with fury now.

'So tell me who it is,' I said. 'Tell the police. I know it's hard if it's a neighbour, someone you've known all your life. I know ties run deep, but he's got to be stopped before he does someone a real injury.'

'A neighbour?' she cried. 'Someone I've known . . . I tell you this, madam, for nothing. If Luckenlaw had kept to folk born here, and meant to be here, we'd all be a sight better for it. I mind when Mr Tait come back, brought his wife home and that bonny baby girl, we were that happy to see them and we were managing Luckenheart just fine, until those flibbertigibbets changed the name and gave the place to a lad that's hardly more than a boy, as if a laddie alone could run Luckenheart, but they're Lorna's chums so what can we say?' The white darts were invisible now; her whole face was waxy, her eyes bulging. 'Even then, though, even then! But there's that Hetty McCallum at the post office down there and Morag Lindsay teaching our lassies glory knows what in that schoolroom. And Lorna Tait's as thick as thieves with the pair of them, getting her head turned and nobody saying a word against it. Through the fire and the dry wells and the air over our heads and the ground beneath us, we kept strong and kept believing it would all come right. And all these months, we went out into the night and endured whatever came to us. And now, you say, it was . . . she was . . . he's . . .' She ran out of steam at last and sat, panting.

In the silence that followed, I tried to make

298

sense of this, but in vain.

'I must be getting along, Mrs McAdam,' I said at last, the polite little formula sounding ridiculous after such histrionics. She nodded dumbly, still staring down at the table although her breathing was beginning to slow again. 'Can I make you a cup of tea before I go?' I said, hesitating to leave her in such distress even if I could not account for the cause of it. She shook her head. 'Can I just suggest, then,' I went on, 'that you don't leave the copper much longer?' The cauldron of little girls' underthings was almost at a rolling boil. She nodded again and put her hands to the table top to haul herself to her feet. With one last sympathetic look, I left. An interesting outcome from my point of view, I thought, striding away down the drive, but not a high point in Mrs McAdam's quiet life, me bringing shocks and horrors and leaving behind cold dismay and shrunken laundry. A lot of good I had done the McAdam household economy today.

One thing we had agreed on, however, was that there was something wrong at Luckenlaw Mains Farm, or Luckenheart to give it its traditional title, and so since I was almost there already I decided to go along and have a closer look.

Such was my brave plan when I was standing in Over Luck yard, untying Bunty; when I was out of sight of that dwelling my nerve began to fail me and when I passed into a little conifer wood and exchanged almost all of the feeble daylight for a dripping, dark green gloom, it was not only the cold which made me shiver.

Soon, however, I emerged again into the grey daylight, my sigh of released tension startling a crow, which gave a rasping croak and flapped off

299

wetly with Bunty chasing. I had arrived at Luckenlaw Mains. Motoring there with Lorna only the day before, I had noted no particular atmosphere about the place but, now, standing at the end of the drive, I felt a marked reluctance to go any closer to where the farmhouse and buildings lay in their little hollow. I did not think anyone was at home—there were no lights on in the house and no smoke curled from either range of chimney pots set into the gable ends—but the air of abandonment was more than just that. The garden was untended and the wall had been breached from the outside at some distant time in the past, flat stones now splaying out in heaps on either side of the gap and the rounded tops of the copestones showing amongst the long grass. A solitary cow stood ankle deep in mud in what should have been the drying green, and watched me speculatively.

I do not mind cows as a rule, but I decided not to take a chance on what this one was speculating about and so, when I finally summoned the resolve to approach the place, I went around into the farmyard ignoring the house and garden. The yard was somewhat tidier, byre doors neatly patched with odds bits of wood and gates held securely, if not decoratively, shut with twists of wire. I have seen it many times in Perthshire too: the farm shipshape and the house and garden a riot of neglect. As though to confirm my view, inside the wall which made a little inner yard around the kitchen door, red clay pots sat, mossy and abandoned, only a yellowed stalk here and there hinting at flowers from years ago. Indeed, a boot scraper with dark curls of fresh dirt clinging to it was the only indication that the house was inhabited at all.

'Not very jolly, is it, darling?' I said to Bunty. She was tucked in about my skirts, clearly no keener than me. I retreated thankfully back to the lane again.

Once there, though, I stopped and regarded the place, puzzled as to why I should have felt such disinclination to linger, for I am the very last person to be visited by 'the heebie-jeebies' as my sons call it since they learned the term in those American shockers which do the rounds of their dorms these days, and apart from the rather wild state of the garden and the dead flowers in their pots there was nothing to choose between this farm and many others: a perfectly ordinary grey stone steading, in a perfectly ordinary little hollow in the fields of Fife. True, it had that brute of a hill rearing up and glowering at it and so it was far from cheery, but no worse in that respect than Over Luck where I had just been. Still, I was glad to be off the place and I thought that even the cow looked glum to have to be staying.

Alec and I met up again practically at the gates of the manse. He was grappling with a canvas and easel, and had a fisherman's bag slung across his shoulder. He was rather red despite the cold and breathing heavily.

'I couldn't face tramping back round,' he said, 'so I came up and over. My word, it's steep, though.'

'Any luck?' I asked him.

'No sign of Christie anywhere, and the light was terrible. No point in staying any longer. It would look very suspicious if I sat there painting in the rain.'

I was puzzled for a moment by the torrent of explanation, but only for a moment.

'Ah,' I said. 'You felt it too?'

'Felt what?' said Alec, putting down his easel and busying himself with rearranging his bag. 'This thing weighs an absolute ton. I should have decanted the turpentine into a little flask, I suppose.'

'I stopped off at Luckenlaw Mains,' I said, 'and I've never felt such an atmosphere in my life. Not even in a graveyard.'

'Nor me,' said Alec. 'So take pity, Dan, and ask me back to the manse for sweet, strong tea. I'm sure Lorna won't mind.'

When we got inside, however, the sitting room was empty, although a fire had been laid and was burning cheerfully in expectation of someone's return, and I ushered Alec in and went to deliver Bunty to her quarters. She was rather muddy for the fireside, at least in someone else's house. Just then I heard a step descending from the landing and I put my head back round the boot-room door.

'Lorna?' I called. 'Captain Watson has come to see you, dear.'

It was not Lorna who appeared at the turn of the stairs, though, but Mrs Hemingborough, coming down with her coat buttoned up and her basket over her arm as though she had taken a short cut through the manse bedrooms on her way home from the village.

'She's not in, Mrs Gilver,' she told me. 'I was just looking for her too.'

'I'll tell her you called,' I said, reminding myself that she was the intimate and I the stranger here,

302

and that it was not so very unusual, in the country, for neighbours to walk freely in and out of one another's houses, although in my experience the ground floor was the normal limit.

'Wasn't that Mrs October?' said Alec, when the front door had closed behind her. He had taken a surreptitious peek when he heard me hailing someone. 'What is going on?'

'Oh, well as to that,' I said, 'I've no idea, but I'm not surprised to see Friend Hemingborough making free with the manse. From what I've been hearing at Over Luck this morning, relations between Mr Tait and his farmers' wives are a good deal closer and more complicated than meets the eye.'

'Meaning?' said Alec.

'Listen to what Mrs McAdam said,' I suggested, 'and if you can make sense of it, please tell me.'

At the end of my outpouring, Alec did not smile fondly and explain it all to me and perversely I would have welcomed it if he had. Instead, he crossed his eyes, puffed out his cheeks and made a long loud noise somewhere between a raspberry and an imitation of a horse.

'How very torrid,' he said. 'I haven't got a clue.'

'Well, at least try, darling,' I urged him.

'Mr Tait,' said Alec slowly, 'seems a good place to start. Mr Tait has always believed the dark stranger was just a man. That's why he got you to come and investigate.'

'To do the dirty work,' I said. 'To make the discovery—although I'm almost sure he knows who it is, Alec—and take the blame for what his parishioners would see as disloyalty.'

'Could a minister possibly be as twisty as all

that?' said Alec, screwing up his nose. 'And anyway, didn't his parishioners think the stranger was a demon?'

'And yet submitted to his attentions with the same kind of stoicism which saw them through all their farming troubles.'

'Until something you said to Mrs McAdam revealed that Mr Tait was right all along and set her off on the extended rant which still makes no sense at all.'

'Perhaps it wasn't actually related,' I said. 'Perhaps Mrs McAdam simply hated being proved wrong and resented Mr Tait for being right and so vented all her other resentments.'

'Those being?'

'That the Taits started the rot when they moved in, the postmistress and schoolmistress have undermined the heart of their village, the Howies are an abomination—poor Howies, although one can see almost what she means—and this slip of a lad who's been given a prime piece of farmland to ruin is the very last straw. But they were all Lorna's friends and out of respect for Mr Tait the neighbours didn't shun them as they would have liked to?'

'Goodness knows,' said Alec. 'I wonder what the vital clue was. What smell was it that struck her?'

'I have no idea,' I said. 'Nor why suddenly finding out that the stranger was human would make Mrs McAdam not just angry, but absolutely aghast. She turned as white as her laundry.'

We sat in silence, thinking, for a while.

'What about this?' said Alec at last. 'If, thinking the girl in the grave had unleashed a demon, you'd dug her up and got rid of her, then you found out

304

you were wrong and you'd dug the poor girl up for nothing, wouldn't that make you go pale? It would me.'

I was shaking my head.

'The "demon unleashed" contingent is quite separate from the . . . oh, what shall we call them? The fatalists. The stoics who think you can't dodge what's coming for you and if what's coming is a dark stranger then you take it, button your lip and endure. Mr Tait's farmers' wives can't have been the ones who were out digging.'

'Although maybe he thought they were,' said Alec, sitting up very straight all of a sudden. 'Maybe he went to Mrs Hemingborough or Mrs Palmer or someone that morning to say that they'd been seen, and they said "Seen doing what?" and that's why he was in a funk when you met him.'

'Yes!' I said. 'Only then he reasoned that whoever had taken her, he knew where they'd have put her so it was all one in the end anyway.'

'Precisely,' said Alec and sat back, looking satisfied. 'Now, where does that leave us?'

'Unless I'm mistaken, it leaves us not knowing who the stranger is or who the grave-diggers were,' I said, and we both sighed heftily.

'Right,' said Alec, slapping his hands on his thighs and looking ready to wrestle the thing to the ground. 'Fraser? No. His wife has left the Rural and he doesn't have the freedom to roam any more.'

'And he was roaming with Annette Martineau anyway,' I reminded him. 'Until she unaccountably took umbrage at his casual manners.'

'Hemingborough, McAdam, Torrance and Palmer have the same problem except at the other end. The stranger started his campaign long before their wives joined the Rural, so the menfolk couldn't have been slipping out from March onwards, even if they are slipping out now. I wish I could find out what they're up to. But back to our suspects. Black?'

'I can't see it,' I said. 'He's taking quite another tack—going around pounding on doors, clothed in righteousness. I don't think he would skulk about too. He's far too full of his own rectitude to think he would have to.'

'Jock Christie, then,' said Alec. 'It must be. *He* skulks about at night, and he's a single man of good prospect who has not managed to attract a wife—this in a village well served for spinsters. So there must be something off about him. And then there's the fact that two sensible people visiting his farm in broad daylight both came over all of a tremble.'

'But you haven't met him, darling,' I protested. 'I have and even through the bars of a jail cell he didn't seem the slightest bit evil or creepy. Whatever the nasty atmosphere is at the Mains or Luckenheart or whatever we should call it I don't think it's emanating from the farmer. And we *know* it wasn't him because Molly, even with an over-zealous police sergeant breathing down her neck, said so. I suppose he might have been one of those digging in the graveyard that night—although I can't see why—but there were at least three of them and probably more.'

'And you glimpsed them and hared off to get me,' said Alec. 'I wish you'd stopped to watch for a bit and worked out who they were, Dan.'

'I like that!' I said. 'It was pitch black.'

'It was a clear night, actually,' said Alec.

'At the dark of the moon,' I went on. 'Pitch black, there were tree branches in the way and it was all by candlelight.'

'Well, anyway,' said Alec, not very graciously. 'Returning to practicalities, I think our best plan remains to catch the stranger at it, as we said.'

'While making sure that no one else is attacked,' I said firmly. 'I will not send the good women of the Rural in like lambs to the slaughter and I'm not budging on that no matter what.' I folded my arms and shook my head as he started protesting. 'No. Give it up, darling. I'm adamant. Mrs Muirhead has been through mental torments since it happened to her and I'm not taking the chance that November's lucky winner will happen to be a sturdy unshakable soul and not someone with enough troubles already who'll be badly upset by it. With that proviso, though, by all means.'

'Agreed then,' said Alec. 'And I'm sure enough about Christie—no matter what you say—to make him my target. I shall lie in wait for him. But I'll have to move pretty smartly, Dan, because in the earlier part of the evening—wait for it!—I'm going to be at the Rural, just like you. I forgot to say earlier. I'm going to do a painting demonstration before your budget talk. What do you think of that?'

'Lorna finally twisted your arm?'

'With the Miss Mortons egging her on. They said they might even rejoin just to see me.'

'Did you ever find out why they left?' I asked him. 'It's been puzzling me what offended them, because none of the obvious reasons will do. They weathered the famous July meeting—and how I

307

wish I could get to the bottom of *that*!—and they escaped the attentions of you-know-who. So why did they suddenly take umbrage? They're as bad as Annette, suddenly giving up on her beau. There's a woeful streak of caprice running through the Luckenlaw spinsters, Alec, I tell you.'

'No, the Miss Mortons weren't being capricious,' said Alec. 'It was Miss McCallum that did it. They were quite happy, they told me, waiting patiently while the great and the good filled the programme in the first few months, but when it got to Miss McCallum and her crochet hook being put in front of them their pride was bruised black and blue.'

'Oh yes, I can see that,' I said laughing and then I stopped laughing as an idea began to take shape deep inside me. 'Alec, we've got it!' I cried. 'We've got something anyway. Listen. No one would suddenly be insulted by what she had formerly accepted unless it put her in the way of some new injury.'

'Hmm,' said Alec. 'Not as pithy a revelation as "Eureka!", Dan. What are you talking about?'

'Annette Martineau. She gave her fancy man— Fraser—his marching orders all of a sudden in May. Her mother came home to find her weeping buckets because Fraser once again had not seen her home. Now why would she suddenly be so upset?'

'May?' said Alec, trying to remember. 'May?'

'When the stranger, or so we thought, was unaccountably hiding in a coal shed instead of running across fields, and smelled of boring old whisky, and did much more than usual to his victim.'

'My God!' said Alec.

'You were right about Molly embellishing,' I said. 'Only you didn't go far enough. She made up the whole thing from start to finish. The dark stranger attacked Annette Martineau in May.'

'Yes!' said Alec, and then his shoulders slumped. 'But so what?'

'So *what*? Oh come on, darling, catch up.'

Alec stared back at me for a moment or two further and then gave a yelp and all but bounced out of his chair.

'The jail cell!' he yelled. 'Molly couldn't say who it was or who it wasn't if her life was at stake!'

'It's Jock Christie,' I said. 'At last we know.'

'And next full moon I'm going to nab him and give him two thick ears, two black eyes and a fat lip.'

We sat back and beamed at one another for a while, until presently Alec began to check his watch and rumble about making a move before Lorna Tait came home for luncheon and collared him.

'Poor Lorna,' I said. 'She's actually a very nice girl. Mrs McAdam didn't seem much of a fan, but I think it was just jealousy.'

'Of what?' said Alec, standing and stretching and arranging his lavender scarf as he caught sight of himself in the glass.

'Her father's indulgence of her, chiefly,' I said. We were in the hall now, and Alec, getting back into character as Captain Watson the artist, turned and took my hand, bowing over and brushing his lips against it.

'Eyes peeled, ears pricked, Dandy, and I shall see you anon.'

'For the last time,' I said. 'I don't need to be told

to keep my eyes peeled. It was dark. There were tree branch— Look.' I grasped his arm and dragged him across the hall, up the stairs and along to the end of the passageway. 'I couldn't see anything,' I said firmly, pointing down to the kirkyard.

'Oh, I don't know,' said Alec. 'There's quite a good gap if you ask me. I can see the headstone. It's that one between the Celtic cross and the angel with all the vines, isn't it?' I looked down at it and saw that he was right.

'Ah, but I wasn't at this window,' I said. 'It was shuttered. I was in here.' I turned the handle on the late Mrs Tait's bedroom door, but it wouldn't open. 'That's odd,' I said. 'It was open before.'

'I believe you,' said Alec, archly.

'It was!' I insisted. 'Why on earth would a bedroom be open at night and locked in the daytime?'

'I can't imagine,' said Alec, still very arch and most annoying.

'Oh, I can,' I said, wincing suddenly. 'I must have disturbed something. It's Lorna's mother's room, Alec, complete with prayer book on the pillow and a floral tribute. And now they know I was in there. I wonder if it was Mr Tait or Lorna who found out? Oh, I could just shrivel and die!'

'Hm,' said Alec. 'If you think that's embarrassing, how about this? Here comes Lorna.' He pointed out of the window and I saw Lorna Tait, cloth-covered shopping basket over one arm, almost all the way up the drive and heading for the front door.

'And if I'm not much mistaken,' said Alec, 'that's a basket full of sustaining treats for nice Captain

310

Watson. Only he wasn't there when she went to call on him because he's upstairs with Mrs Gilver who seemed like such a respectable soul. And in a minister's house too.'

I fled along the corridor to my bedroom and was safely inside when the front door opened. With my ear to the crack, I heard Lorna's voice raised in surprise as Alec's tread descended the stairs. '. . . must forgive me,' he said. '. . . saw from the ground that it would be a perfect composition if I could get high enough . . . looked up and saw a window at just the right place . . .' Lorna spoke again. 'Oh, that older lady who's staying with you?' said Alec. 'I forgot about her. No, I've no idea. I think she must be out.'

CHAPTER SEVENTEEN

And so all we had to do was wait. Alec had to wait at Luckenlaw, painting like fury in the few short hours of daylight whenever it was not raining, and trying to engage anyone who happened along upon the topic of folklore, moonlight, good and bad luck, ancient burial customs, and anything else that seemed at all likely to uncover the identity of the grave-diggers. I had to wait at Gilverton, drafting and redrafting my wretched talk, heaps of household manuals spread around me and so many spoiled sheets being thrown onto the fire that the housemaid began to clear the ash twice a day.

Mrs Tilling tried to help me, reaching back into her memories of a country childhood for hedgerow recipes and telling me about such esoteric matters as sealing the stalk of a stored pear with a blob of wax to stop it softening, feeling that the truth of the saying 'Waste not, want not' made all such hints perfectly relevant to the budget in the end.

'But really and truly, madam,' she concluded, 'when it comes to the hedgerow, the wild fruit is so tart you can use twice the sugar to get the jelly made, and you'd have been better with a nice basket of raspberries from the farm. And even if you did manage to get a squirrel pie over your back teeth, you'd want such a treat afterwards for pudding it's hardly worth it. I'd ask Miss Grant, madam, for it's always seemed to me that most of the extravagance downstairs at Gilverton goes on in that there laundry room. Did you know your lavender water comes from London? When the south wall is bursting with it all summer long? No, I thought not.'

When I asked Grant about economy she blanched, suspecting an end to the glorious spell of plenty she had been enjoying of late, and when I assured her that my interest was academic she only replied that she had lived in theatrical digs with insects the size of rats and rats the size of cats when her family was touring and once she had put that life behind her she had thought it best to remember nothing at all.

'Except for a Brillo in a mousehole,' she said. 'That works wonders—they don't like the taste.'

'I don't think my audience would be flattered if I weighed in with tips on seeing off vermin,' I replied, 'but thank you for trying.'

Alec kept me up to date, with daily postings from the kiosk on the green.

'I do like the old boy,' he said. 'Mr Tait, I mean.

He has a very dry wit for a parson. I only wish he had passed some of it on.'

'No one could call poor Lorna dry, right enough,' I said, laughing. 'Are you coping?'

'Oh, fairly well,' Alec said. 'There have been a couple of ticklish moments, chiefly when the Howies are on the scene. I'm sure Niccy Howie has seen through me, you know. She keeps giving these tremendous guffaws whenever I talk about Art, and she seems to find the Lorna angle highly diverting. But that's by the by. What I do need to tell you is that another one of those farmers' wives has been poking around the manse. Lorna told me.'

'Details?' I said, with a pencil at the ready to make notes.

'Very few,' said Alec. 'Lord, I wish those girls would shut up with their endless skipping and go home. Can you hear them?'

'Just,' I said. 'I thought they were charming, actually. Although the librettist tends to the macabre. And it's just as bad here with the twittering and squalling all day. Hugh might be convinced that his little bird tables are instrumental in turning the place into a botanical paradise, but I notice he hasn't plonked one right outside his window. Never mind that, though. What did Lorna tell you?'

'She asked my advice, actually. She thinks her father is having a dress made for her for her birthday. She says she found Mrs Torrance raking through her wardrobe and the woman wouldn't say what she was doing, which threw Lorna into a flutter, because the Howie ladies are organising her entire outfit and she thought her father knew that, and doesn't want to hurt his feelings.'

'And what are you supposed to do about it?' I said. 'She is a very peculiar girl in some ways.'

'I was supposed to have a view on it, as a man, you know. Mind you when she said that, Niccy Howie did another one of her snorts and Vashti joined her.'

'Hmm,' I said, shrinking from telling Alec that the Howies thought him much more able to debate the dressmaking than to give the man's-eye view. 'Now tell me, have you managed yet to track down Jockie Christie?'

Alec gave a mighty sigh, which caused a great deal of buzzing and fluffing on the line.

'I have,' he said. 'I've been up there painting that stairway thingummy for days—Cubist, don't you know, which I thought would lend itself to stairs but it's jolly difficult, actually—and by the end I was more depressed than I've been in my life, except for the trenches. But I don't think the gloom is coming from him. I like him.'

'He's still our first suspect, isn't he?' I asked.

'Oh yes,' said Alec. 'I haven't uncovered anything material. It's just that I like him. He's a miner's son from somewhere called Lochgelly, got a scholarship to grammar school, worked after school to buy his own books and uniform since his family were having none of it, decided he wanted to work on the land, got himself a scholarship to agricultural college, came out top of his class, and presented himself in answer to the Howies' advertisement. A really good sort. Knows no end of impressive stuff about soil improvement. I almost made a huge gaffe and asked him for advice, thinking about Dunelgar, you know, before

314

I remembered that Captain Watson doesn't have any soil to improve.'

'You're getting as bad as Hugh,' I told him. 'It's hardly a classic character reference, darling.'

In fact, the modern farming method angle was inclined to make me suspect him more. I had come across someone in the past who knew rather too much about flora and fauna than was normal and he had certainly been what my sons called, with great poetic economy, 'a stinker'. And did not some of these advanced types bury hollow horns full of sheep's wool in the corners of their crop fields, and pay a great deal of attention to the waxing and waning of the moon?

* * *

As the November moon waxed fatter and fatter in the tingling cold sky, I readied myself as best I could to face both my public and the showdown Alec and I had planned for afterwards. He was to open with his demonstration of painting and I was to follow up after tea, leaving him time to get to Luckenheart Farm and watch for the emergence of Jockie Christie before the ladies ventured home.

On the night, our plan—or my plan, rather, for Alec was keener on the interception than on the protection of the matrons—was all the better served by the fact that there were a few familiar faces missing from the schoolroom. Mrs Hemingborough was nowhere to be seen, clearly happy to risk missing any of the chicken feather poultices that her last month's audience might have brought along for her inspection. Mrs Palmer, Mrs Torrance and Mrs McAdam too were notable by their absence.

'Strange,' said Lorna. 'Mrs McAdam never said anything this afternoon.'

'You saw her today?' I asked and Lorna looked troubled.

'She was upstairs in the manse again,' said Lorna. 'Doing whatever it is they're doing. Oh, I hope it's not a frock, Mrs Gilver,' said Lorna. 'The one Nicolette and Vashti have got me is such a dream of a thing. It would crush me not to wear it.'

'What a write-up, my darling,' said a drawling voice from behind us and Nicolette Howie bent down and clashed her hot, painted cheek against Lorna's and then mine. 'I'm very glad you like it.'

'Rather thin on the ground tonight, aren't we?' said Vashti, looking around the room.

'We are,' said Nicolette, following her gaze. 'That's to say, the senior members have resisted the programme but there are plenty of girls. Looking rather well turned out too.' She winked at me.

'I'm sorry to tell you, Dandy,' said Vashti, 'that I rather suspect they are budding artists more than domestic economists in the making, don't you?' I smiled ruefully, for I agreed.

At that moment Alec arrived, carrying an enormous canvas that he only just managed to fit under his arm and hold onto with the very tips of his fingers. He was wearing the smock, which produced a terrific hoot from Niccy Howie (the first of many), and the cavalry boots, with bright red woollen stockings pulled up and folded over, and he had a few paintbrushes stuck behind each ear. Miss Lindsay fussed around getting him set up in a favourable spot and spreading waxed paper for

316

him to chuck his rags onto in between wiping his brushes. Miss McCallum sat lowering from under her sandy brows, obviously deploring the skittish air that the presence of a personable young man had brought to the proceedings.

I had been unable to speak to Alec alone since my arrival back at Luckenlaw that afternoon, and now he was trying to communicate something to me here in this crowded room. He rubbed ostentatiously at one eye, opening it and closing it repeatedly—or in other words, winking—and then he put a hand up to his head and quite deliberately pulled out one of his hairs and put it into his smock pocket.

'I think the poor lamb's nervous,' said Lorna, clearly itching to get up and go to comfort him. I thought he would be even more nervous to have heard himself called a poor lamb.

Then Miss Lindsay clapped her hands for order and the November meeting of the Luckenlaw SWRI was under way. First came a prayer for Armistice Day; the motto was: Punctuality is the politeness of princes—chosen rather pointedly after a pair of girls had come in at the last gasp, giggling; the competition was a moth-repeller in worked wool; and the social half-hour was to be filled with an entertainment chosen by . . .

'Our new face, tonight and for one night only,' said Miss Lindsay. 'Captain Watson, what's your pleasure? Singing, dancing, stories or parlour games?'

'Is anyone here familiar with Chinese ropes?' said Alec. There was a bemused silence and then a few murmurs of assent.

'Never heard of them,' said Vashti Howie. 'What

are they?'

'It's a kind of indoor skipping,' said Alec, 'done with rubber bands knotted together to make a frame. It's something that's easy to show and very hard to describe . . . a cross between hopscotch and cat's cradle, but with a rhythm to it. I have brought a quantity of bands along with me'—here he dug into a pocket and pulled out a spilling handful of what looked like very thin brown worms—'and if I can prevail upon someone with nimble fingers to tie them, I should like the social half-hour to be skipping tonight. Along with all the wonderful old skipping songs, of course.'

'Well,' said Miss Lindsay, 'I call that a grand idea. It's many a long year since any of us have had a good go of skipping and I look forward to the fun. Now Captain Watson, if you're ready.'

He was. 'Tonight,' he began in a thrillingly dramatic voice, quite different from the one he had used to suggest the skipping, 'I am going to attempt to show you yourselves *à l' art sauvage*, by painting in the barbarous style, the wild, the savage style, so eminently suited to the roiling skies of Fife, and the elemental phallic landscape of the Lucken Law.'

Had he really just said that word at the Rural? The Howies and I gaped at one another but either the rest of the meeting were so bowled over by the whole that the details escaped them or they did not know its meaning, for their faces remained as blankly uncomprehending and nervously polite as before.

He sloshed around a great many more long words and a lot of paint too, but I was unable to pay attention to anything outside me and sat

318

instead enveloped in a nauseous fog of foreboding over what was coming after tea. At last, Lorna shook my arm gently and I realised that Alec was in his seat and that Miss Lindsay was by the urn swilling hot water around in the enormous tin teapot.

The canvas Alec had been at work upon was dominated by a huge triangle in every shade of grey—the law—with a threatening dark red sky balanced on top of it like a boater on a bollard, leaving some naked canvas in between.

'It's ... um ...' said Lorna.

'It's twaddle,' said Nicolette Howie and Lorna's cheeks blossomed with two small pom-poms of bright pink.

'Oh Nic,' said Vashti. 'Niccy spent precisely six weeks living in a studio in London, while Johnny was working in his father's bank—just renting the studio, mind, not actually painting—and ever since she's thought she could be curator of the Louvre. Actually, I quite like it.'

I swallowed a mouthful of tea and felt it fall to the cold pit of my stomach and lie there. What had I decided? Rehearse the first sentence until it is word-perfect and you will have your audience with you. What was my first sentence? 'In these difficult times . . .' or was it 'Despite these peaceful times . . .' or had I decided to go with 'In times of peace and times of war . . .'? Oh God. Miss McCallum was collecting the cups. Miss Lindsay was smiling at me, but then . . .

'I wonder if I might trespass upon your patience just a little more,' said Alec's voice. He stood up and resumed his position by his canvas. 'I have painted the mighty law, and I have painted the

319

turbulent sky, but in between, around the hill, is the most important element of all . . . the beating heart of the land. The farms and cottages, the lanes and fields, the men and women who make this place sublime. If Mrs Gilver would be so gracious as to concede the floor a little longer, I could complete my expedition into the savage soul of Luckenlaw.'

Despite the scowls of Miss McCallum and the rolled eyes of some of the others there was no polite way to stop him. The Howies were entertained of course and Lorna was delighted, but even her heart could not have swelled with adoration like mine. On and on and on he droned, saving me.

He was still ladling on paint and blathering about inner space and the echo of the Lucken Law in the warm wombs of its daughters, when Miss Lindsay started to shift in her seat and consult her fob watch surreptitiously. Alec, spying her, immediately began to wind up.

'Art!' he declaimed. 'In the looking, in the seeing, and in the knowing. Here I will leave you. You will be here singing the old songs and dancing the ancient dances and I shall go out into the darkness and know that life pulses inside as we know the beating of our own blood in our bellies.'

There was a humming silence after this, as might well be expected. Lorna Tait broke it.

'Oh,' she said. 'Aren't you staying for the social?'

Vashti and Nicolette brayed like donkeys and a few of the others, fit to burst with pent-up hysteria from the long words and the sepulchral voice and the red socks over the tops of the bootlegs, gave up the fight and shook with laughter.

320

'I am not offended,' said Alec, his eyes dancing. 'Laughter is the chorus of our humanity. Laughter holds away the pressing darkness and welcomes the stranger. Laughter is the spirit dancing.' And he threw his scarf over one shoulder, picked up his bag of paints and all of his brushes and swept, magnificently, out.

The meeting was helpless for a good five minutes after he had gone; even Lorna Tait, feeling herself to have been given permission, indulged in a quiet chuckle or two.

'Aye, you can laugh,' said a young woman from across the room, 'but I've been sittin' here knottin' elastics for his blessed skippin' all night and he's no' even stayed to see it.' She held up a long, brown, kinked chain of rubber bands and the laughter grew louder again.

'Oh, let's do it anyway,' said Miss Lindsay. 'I hear those children at their skipping every day and I never get to join them.'

There were more titters at that, for who amongst us had not wondered when we were children whether the adults, especially the teachers, were really people like we were or whether they were just the boring grown-ups they appeared to be.

Willing hands cleared the chairs from the centre of the room and willing volunteers initiated the beginners into the mysteries of the Chinese ropes. When we had all gained a little proficiency, the singing began: the couple from the golden city, she of the black stockings with the wart on her nose, even (horribly) the thirteen grave robbers knocking at the door.

'Or how about this one?' said a plump young

woman. 'I mind of this one from when I was at the school.' She stepped onto the taut bands strung between the ankles of the two ladies who were taking their turn at providing the structure, and began to hop and jump, pinging the elastic and stepping into the spaces.

'Spring a lock o' bonny maidie,' she sang. Others picked it up and joined in.

> 'Summer lock o' wedded lady.
> Harvest lock o' baby's mammy.
> Who will be my true love?
> Three times twist me,
> All that I wish me.
> First time he kissed me
> He will be my true love.'

Before my eyes, the vision swam again of Alec plucking a hair from his head and putting it into his pocket, winking at me.

'I've never heard that one before,' I said, hoping my voice sounded steady. 'Is it a Fife speciality?'

'Heavens no,' said Nicolette Howie. 'That's a well-known little song.'

She might have been half right: it might have been well known but it was far more than a little song. It was what the stranger was doing. It was the answer. The locks of three girls, three wives and three matrons, in order, in season. It was the recipe for a . . . there was no other word for it . . . a spell. I remembered all the women telling me how he had plucked and pinched, ripped off their hats, nipped at their heads. He was pulling their hair out; some of them had even said as much. He was gathering hair, on the proper night and in the required order to make, if the song was to be believed, a love potion.

Jockie Christie. Sorely in need of a wife and unable to attract one. I shuddered. He had fooled me that night in the jail cell with his forlorn look and his ruddy cheeks—there was nothing fresh and ordinary about him at all. On the contrary, he was desperate, pathetic and rather ruthless. Even Molly Tweed, who had no idea who the stranger was, had hesitated before exonerating him; perhaps she had intuited some truth about him that I had missed. I felt a twinge of conscience about Molly. Certainly, she had made up the story of her attack but perhaps Christie had been laying siege to her instead of the other way around and perhaps if I had been subjected to his attentions for five years—I remembered the sickly feeling I had got at his farm and shivered—I should have ended up imagining things too.

And did Mr Tait know what Christie was up to? I had been sure he knew something. Had his patience finally run out when faced with this pitiful and furtive little scheme? I nodded to myself. Mr Tait had decided to stop smiling at the old ways for once, and had turned to me to help him. Accordingly, as the rubber bands were rolled into a ball and the chairs were rearranged, I piped up.

'Miss Lindsay, I hope you won't mind me butting in like this. I'd like to say something.'

'Oh, Mrs Gilver,' said Miss Lindsay. 'How can we refuse you anything now? Your wonderful talk that you've worked so hard on and you never got a chance to give it. We're going to have to ask you to wait another month, I'm afraid. What a bitter disappointment for us all!'

'Oh quite, quite,' I said, thinking that I could certainly summon the strength to bear it.

'But how can we help you?' Miss Lindsay continued. 'Ask anything.'

'How many of you here tonight are mothers?' I asked. A good few of them raised their hands uncertainly. 'I wonder then, if I might prevail upon you to stay behind, just a moment, and listen to something I have to say. And I do apologise. Miss Lindsay—I know it's your schoolroom, but I really must ask the others to step outside. What I have to say is not . . . for all ears, I hope you understand me.'

'Watch out, Niccy,' said Vashti, giggling. 'The "phallic element" could be outdone yet.'

'I shall make sure you all get home safely,' I said as the women who had raised their hands looked at one another in confusion. 'I won't take a minute of your time.'

It quite destroyed the mood of the meeting, although not as much as my household budget talk would have done, I daresay. Miss Lindsay and Miss McCallum, feeling slighted, carried the canvas away carefully to set it to dry in Miss Lindsay's private rooms. Niccy and Vashti mounted a spirited attempt to be allowed to stay, ridiculing the notion that there might be something I could say to the handful of matrons that I could not say to them, but I was adamant. The rest of the meeting melted away, although clearly beginning to feel as though what should be theirs had been comprehensively stolen from them by the outsiders tonight.

When everyone else had gone, I addressed the women remaining.

324

'It's about this dark stranger,' I said. There were a couple of groans and a couple of nervous giggles. 'He's going to strike again tonight,' I went on, ignoring all of it, 'and he's going to pick on someone who has children, a mother.' I waited to see if the penny would drop in any of the rest of them about the skipping rhyme we had heard only minutes ago, but it was just as Mr Tait had said right back on the first day: no one ever listens to the words. 'I am determined to get you all home safely, but there are too many for one trip in the motor car, so I propose we work out two sensible routes and in between times the second batch waits here.'

'I'm no' a believer in this dark stranger,' said one woman. 'I think it's just stories.'

'Luckenlaw's always had stories o' this and that, but it's nothin' to do wi' the likes o' us.' The speaker looked sharply around the room as she said this, then nodded. 'Naw, nothin' to do wi' us.'

'Aye,' said another. 'We dinna believe in a' they bad spirits and ghosties.'

'I assure you,' I said, 'if it were a spirit or a ghostie—if it were just a story, that is—no one would be more delighted than I, but he is real, he has attacked every month since March, although some have kept it quiet, and he will attack again tonight. He's not going to hurt you badly, but we do need to stop him. Now, how shall we get you home?'

'We both live on the green,' said one woman. 'And Cissie's just doon the road fae the post office.'

'Excellent,' I said. 'Three of you in the village itself. That's going to be very easy. Four can squash into the motor car with me somehow. Now, where

325

do you all live?'

Haltingly, and only too obviously still not believing, they told me. One was from a cottage in the Luckenlaw House grounds, one was from a road worker's house down towards Colinsburgh, the third was from Kilnconquhar but she always came to this Rural and stopped the night with her sister who was married to Mr Fraser's shepherd at Balniel, and the last was an ancient old lady who said she lived the back Largoward road and she couldna see any stranger making a beeline for her at her age, but mind if it was mothers he was after, who could say, for she'd had eleven of family all told.

'That's us off, Miss Lindsay,' I called into the sitting-room door as we hurried out to where my motor car was waiting. I bundled the four passengers in, which was rather a tight squeeze, but they were diverted enough by the prospect of the ride not to care, and once they were snugly packed, we crawled up the school lane at a juddering pace behind the three walkers and waited with headlamps shining as they scattered to their houses and shut their doors behind them. Then we set off down the road to Balniel to the shepherd's house, to the road worker's cottage beyond, around to the little place tucked amongst the trees on the estate at Luck House and eventually to the Largoward road, the old lady directing me, although with some difficulty because as she said it was that fast in a motor she nivver had time tae think where she was afore she was away past it. Our arrival brought to the door an ancient man in a patched jersey and with a scarf tied over his chest and a middle-aged son with a newspaper folded open and a pipe in his mouth. I left her to do whatever explaining she felt was needed and trundled off again.

After a little confusion amongst the unfamiliar lanes, I finally got back onto the road at Luck House and sat with the engine idling, tussling with myself. Our arrangement had been that I should go straight home to the manse, but I could not resist it. If Christie were our man, Alec would this very minute be creeping along behind him somewhere, in the moonlight. If we had been wrong, however, my gallant Watson would be crouched in a field, watching Christie's house and cursing, not a hundred yards from where I sat. I switched the engine off, stepped down and struck out along the lane. A cold, white light blanketed the empty fields, gave faces to all the stones in the dykes and turned every bush and gatepost into a silent, waiting stranger, but Luckenheart Farm was no more than a darker smudge against the greater hulking darkness of the law behind it. At the end of the drive I summoned all my courage and turned in.

'Alec?' I hissed. 'Alec, can you hear me? Are you there?'

There was not a sound, not a breath of wind, not so much as a snapping twig to say that any creature was abroad tonight except me. Slowly, the same feeling of crawling dread began to spread through me, but I scurried on.

'Alec?' I whispered more softly than ever.

I was almost at the farmyard when I heard something at last; a groan and the sound of feet stamping repeatedly as though some animal were pawing the ground. I stopped, held my breath, and peered ahead. I could just make out a figure standing in the shade of a hedge on the other side of the field dyke. It turned to face me; I could see the moonlight glinting off its hair. My heart leapt into my throat like a trapped frog, but my feet were rooted, my legs trembling. You fool, Dandy, I said to myself. You might be a sensible married woman with children of your own but you've been a fool tonight and you are just about to pay for it.

Then the figure spoke.

'Dandy? What the devil are you doing here? God, my back's killing me! And both my feet have gone to sleep.'

I willed my quivering legs to propel me forward and tried to keep my voice steady as I spoke.

'We were wrong then?' I said. 'Were we?'

'Thumpingly wrong,' said Alec. 'Staggeringly wrong. Either that or they're onto us.'

'What do you mean?' I had drawn up close to him now and was facing him across the top of the dyke, squinting to make out his features in the deep shadows. 'Who's "they"?'

'In there,' said Alec, gesturing towards the farmhouse. 'Where's the gate? I couldn't jump over a wall now if all the demons of hell were after me. I'm frozen solid. I swear, Dan, this damned field must lie in a direct draught straight from the Arctic.'

'Alec, please! Who is "they"? What's happening?'

'Well, as you could tell from the number of carts pulled up in Jock Christie's yard—if your eyes were attuned to the dark as mine are, having been crouched freezing to death in it for the last hour instead of tootling about in a cosy motor car—our sinister stranger has a houseful of visitors tonight. Drew Torrance, Logan McAdam, Bob Palmer and Tom Hemingborough are all in the kitchen with him. They've stabled their ponies across the yard there as though they're in for the night.'

'How do you know?'

'I crept up and looked in the window when I got here, just to check that I wasn't too late.'

'What are they doing?' I asked.

'No idea,' said Alec. 'They're bent over something or other at the table, looking pretty intent too but I didn't hang about long enough to see. It suddenly struck me that I—a stranger in these parts—was prowling around looking in windows and there were five large and rather handy-looking farmers whom I didn't want to catch me at it.'

'Are you sure they're all still there?' I asked. 'One of them couldn't have slipped out another way since you arrived?'

'There is no other way, unless it's a secret tunnel through the hillside. Not outside the bounds of possibility, I'll grant you. No, I've seen this place from up the hill when I've been painting and there's no side door. There's no way that anyone could have left tonight without crossing at least one patch of bright moonlight and being spotted.'

'But what else could they be doing,' I said, 'if not giving one another alibis?'

'No idea,' said Alec again. 'Cards, dice and the demon drink, perhaps, as Mr Black said all along?'

'And who is the stranger if not one of those five?'

'Mr Black himself?' said Alec. 'Could Mr Fraser be giving his wife the slip?'

'It could be someone else entirely,' I concluded. 'We could be right down at the tail of the snake again.'

We stood there for a moment or two longer, and I for one was feeling rather sheepish, then suddenly I became aware of the night cold creeping into me and shivered audibly.

'Yes, you run along, Dan,' said Alec. 'No point in both of us catching our deaths, is there?'

'Aren't you coming with me?' I said, surprised. 'What is there to wait here for? All the ladies are safely home now.'

'I'm not leaving until they do,' said Alec grimly. 'I might be able to work out what they're up to if they're still talking about it when they come out. Noise carries tremendously well on these icy cold nights, you know. Or maybe I'll throw caution to the wind—march up, bang on the door and join them. I could always say I was out painting and felt chilly.'

'I know you're joking,' I said. 'But promise me you won't do anything reckless.'

'I promise,' said Alec. 'I'm too precious to risk, I know. Now get home for heaven's sake before your chattering teeth bring them all out to see what the racket is.'

I gave him a quick squeeze for encouragement and warmth and then picked my way back up the drive and along the lane, stepping more cautiously than ever, now that I knew there was a gathering of our best—our only!—suspects just a stone's throw away. Before long, I could see the bulky outline of my motor car where I had left it at the junction and, clambering back in at last and closing the door softly but firmly behind me, I began my

330

journey, crawling along, scanning the fields as I went, loath still to leave the night and its adventures. After all, Alec had got the glory of working out the rhyme as well as the chills and cramp of waiting to nab the stranger. I could not help but smile when I thought of him standing in the kiosk one of the days after telephoning me, seething with irritation at the incessant chanting and then, all of a sudden, really hearing the words for the first time. I was nearly home now. Nothing stirring at Balniel tonight, just the empty fields, neatly ploughed and looking like candlewick in the moonlight.

Then it happened. Inching along, I saw on the road in front of me what I thought at first was a leaf flapping in the wind. I looked again. It wasn't a leaf: could it be a glove? I slowed down even further, peering at it in the beam of the headlamps, and it turned its head, showing me two dazzling eyes and a tiny mouth open in a soundless yell. It was a kitten. I was sure of it. And it was in considerable distress of some kind. I stopped the motor car, jumped out and hurried forward.

The kitten, a little tabby scrap, was mewing piteously and struggling in vain to run away, its claws scrabbling at the dirt of the lane. I crouched down beside it and tried to pick it up but I could not move it. I pulled at it and its mewing rose to a miniature squeak.

'What on earth . . . ?' I said, trying to sort out its paddling legs and still its writhing. And then I touched its tail, wet and sticky, finding something hard and flat which should not be there. Somehow it had got stuck under a piece of wood litter embedded in the ground. I picked at it, confused, and then took a closer look.

'No,' I breathed. 'No!'

At each end of the piece of wood, no more than a splinter really, there was something hard and shiny, like a button. This was no piece of wood litter caught under a stone; someone had nailed it to the road, with the kitten's tail trapped, bleeding, underneath it.

'But when?' I said. 'I can't have driven past you on the way down.' I was desperately trying to get my fingers under a nail head to prise it out. 'And why? Why in heaven's name would anyone do that?'

As soon as I asked the question I knew the answer and, as I rose, I felt no surprise to see the dark figure, rippling over the field towards me.

I could have run. I could have got into the motor car and locked the door, and yet I stood there. I should like to think it was courage. Hindsight might almost persuade me that it was clear thinking, the idea that the stranger must have emerged from Luckenheart Farm and Alec could not be far behind, that it would be better for the pair of us to catch the stranger in the very act. I am far from sure, though; it certainly did not feel like courage and common sense at the time. He was scaling the dyke now, up on one side and down on the other like a hound, like a panther. I took my hat off and bowed my head, walking away from the writhing kitten, waiting for it to happen, and I think this act of knowing submission must have fuddled him and distracted him from the fact that tonight, for the first time, he was running not into darkness where a tree, bush or building obscured the moon, but right into the glare of my headlamp light.

He was here, reaching out, breathing hotly on me, filling my nostrils with his stink, waxy and vegetative at the same time, familiar and yet strange. He took hold of a handful of hair and pulled. As though the pain had jerked me back to life again, I put my hands around his arms, gripping as hard as I could, and looked up from the black pumps on his feet to the close-fitting black suit of trousers and jersey into the black mask over his face, into the holes where his eyes were glittering. It was then, when I looked into his eyes, that he realised the mistake he had made. He snapped his head round to the lights and hissed with fury, a noise so dreadful that I stumbled back to get away from it and, free of my grasp, he was gone.

The eyes stayed burned into mine. They were not Jock Christie's eyes; I was sure of it. But I had seen them before. I had seen them tonight.

I crouched back down beside the kitten, which had quietened and was lying still now. My hat was on the road near me and I reached over, took the pin out and dug it under a nail head, slowly easing the shaft out of the ground, bending back the little wooden batten, ignoring the renewed cries.

'There, there,' I said, when it was free. 'There, there. Better now.' It was bleeding quite astonishingly freely for such a tiny thing and although I wound my handkerchief tightly around its tail it immediately seeped through. It protested when I lifted it, protested even louder when I cradled it close, and I looked around for a gentler way to bear it home. I had always hated that ludicrous Beefeater's hat, I thought, turning it up

333

and laying the kitten inside it then lifting it like a hammock.

'Let's see what the manse servants can do for you,' I said to it, carrying it back to the car and laying it gently on the seat beside me. 'What a night. I'm so sorry you had to get caught up in it at such a tender age. You've helped a lot—at great cost to your poor tail, of course—but you've helped a tremendous lot.'

And so he had. Or she had, for who can say with kittens? People, on the other hand, are easier to tell apart. Perhaps it was the black trousers that had done it—Luckenlaw was a backward kind of place, where the lounging pyjama was yet to make its mark—or perhaps it was the air of brutality and confidence combined, or a feeling, usually reliable enough, that frightening ladies in the night was a man's game, but they had all got it wrong. The dark stranger was a woman.

CHAPTER EIGHTEEN

Which woman, was a question for Alec and me to thrash out together, and no one could have been more surprised than we at where our thrashing led us.

'Nonsense!' Alec cried, when I said the name. 'Snaky, shimmering, gliding over walls and ditches? It can't be.' He was still a little disgruntled after his long sojourn in the field hedge at Luckenheart Farm. 'Ow! What are you planning to do with this thing, Dandy?' The kitten, its bandaged tail sticking straight out behind it like a

334

tiller, had launched itself at Alec's trouser leg and now hung there, its ears flat back and its eyes rolling with devilment.

'I'm taking her home,' I said. 'And if you were wearing proper suiting instead of striding about looking like Ali Baba her claws wouldn't have gone through to the skin. Besides, you're wrong about the snakiness, Alec dear. It's because everyone thought he was a man. He was wiry *for a man*, sinuous *for a man*. Think about pantomimes or fancy dress parties.'

'What about them?' said Alec.

'Simply how the leanest, lithest man you can imagine looks an absolute hulk when he puts a dress on. Believe me, Alec. We have our culprit.'

'Even if I can persuade myself about the silhouette,' he said, 'I still need convincing. So go on and convince me: Lorna Tait.'

'Ssh!' I said, glancing at the door. We were after all in Lorna Tait's own sitting room. I leaned forward and spoke softly. 'First of all, now we know it's a love charm, we have to ask ourselves who is the most lovelorn woman in Luckenlaw? There is a fair selection of spinsters, to be sure, but not many who seem desperate enough to cast spells. Secondly, we already suspected that Mr Tait knew who it was, but didn't want to make the official discovery. And he kept Lorna in the dark about what I was up to for no very convincing reason, when it comes right down to it. If Lorna is the stranger then all of that makes sense. Mr Tait has been masterminding the whole case like a puppeteer because he wanted his daughter stopped without it all getting out into the open. Consider the scandal—a minister's daughter dabbling in the occult. No matter what he says about the harmlessness of the old ways, it would be absolutely incendiary. And it explains why he might have tried to stop a romantic entanglement with a young minister, which he once hinted at to me.'

'I'm not so sure any of that makes sense,' said Alec. 'If he wanted Lorna frightened enough to chuck it in, why would he keep your investigation secret from her?'

'Well,' I said slowly, 'maybe that's not it after all. Maybe he knew what it was all about—the love charm—from the beginning, and knew it was going to run its course and then be over, but he wanted to be able to say he had tried to stop it in case it came out at a later date. He wanted to be able to show that he was not turning a blind eye or even in cahoots with her.'

'I suppose,' said Alec.

'And that's not all. Remember, dear Alec, how Mrs McAdam, who certainly knows more than she'll ever say, put Lorna Tait squarely in centre-stage when I spoke to her. She bemoaned the influence of the suffragettes, saying that it was only because they were Lorna's friends that they were irreproachable in Mr Tait's opinion. She said much the same about the Howies—that they were pestilential, but they were Lorna's friends, so they had to be borne.'

'I'm not sure I understand what that's got to do with it,' Alec said. The kitten, having scaled his legs and attained his lap, was now curled up sleeping, with Alec resolutely ignoring it, arms folded above the purring little mound.

'How you can gush so over a puppy and not be

336

even a bit enchanted by her, I'll never know,' I said.

'When did I gush over a puppy?' said Alec, shooting a look at my feet where Bunty had settled for a nap, forcing me to sit in a position which would give me cramp any minute.

'I forgot,' I said. 'It's *Barrow* who feeds Milly all the treats and titbits. Sorry. Anyway, returning to Mrs McAdam: she thinks Lorna is over-indulged by her father. Do you see?'

'Sort of,' said Alec. 'But how did the smells alert her? Speaking of which, has light dawned about last night's yet?' I had described as best I could the waxy, fetid smell of the stranger, but I could still not put my finger on it. 'It didn't actually remind you of Lorna in any way?'

'No,' I said. 'It reminded me of home.'

'Home?'

'Well . . . something very familiar and not particularly pleasant.'

Alec sat for a while, thinking.

'It was probably Annie Pellow that Mrs McAdam picked up on,' he said at last. 'She was the only one of the lot who said there was a smell she couldn't identify, wasn't she? Bluebells and cowslips and something else?'

'But her something else was spicy,' I reminded him. 'She thought it was a flower. No one could have believed that stink from last night was a flower. Of the vegetable kingdom perhaps, but not a flower.'

'Anyway,' said Alec.

'Anyway,' I agreed. 'Whatever it was that revealed the truth I am convinced that *this* was the example of Mr Tait indulging Lorna that made

337

Mrs McAdam blow her top. They had been putting it all down to Providence, stoically enduring the attacks—more than enduring, if you think about it, joining up just in time so that they would be the ones who suffered, Mrs Torrance in time for July, all the mothers come September—and then it turns out to have been a lot of silly nonsense that Mr Tait could have quashed if he had just put Lorna over his knee and slippered it out of her.'

'Very well,' said Alec, 'if that's what was really going on—and it does have some sense to it, I'll grant you—answer me this. What did they *think* was going on? Why did they join up in time to have their hair pulled out? Who are "they", anyway?'

I shook my head, stumped.

'Just Mr Tait's ladies,' I said at last. 'The first ranks of his parishioners, the inner circle of kirk elders, perhaps. I say, Alec, do you think it could be something as blameless as that that was going at Jock Christie's house last night? An elders' meeting? Parish Council?'

'The minister would be there and it would be at the church,' said Alec. 'Not under cover of darkness at the remotest possible farm and all in deepest secret. It can't be that. Why would you think so?'

'Well, I noticed that Mr Hemingborough passed the plate around at the Sunday service, that's all. So he must be the beadle. And remember the beadle has got to be in the know, because he must have seen the mess left behind by all the grave-digging that night.'

'I suppose so,' said Alec. 'And you reckon that the first ladies of the kirk might volunteer to be victims of the stranger just to keep it amongst themselves and avoid a scandal? It doesn't seem likely that they would go to the trouble when it's really nothing to do with them.'

'Oh Alec, in a place like this everything is to do with everyone. Remember how put out Mrs McAdam seemed about the Howies letting Luckenlaw Mains to an outsider? Almost as though she felt personally affected.'

'Hm,' said Alec. 'I have to disagree with her there. I can see that the other four farms belong to Luckenlaw but the Mains has always seemed supernumerary anyway.'

'Supernumerary?' I echoed.

'I've always felt it shouldn't be there.'

'What do you mean?'

'When I've been doing my endless painting,' he said. 'Think of the map. Over, Hinter, Easter and Wester. With the law in the middle and the manse and kirk at either side of the entrance way. I've been painting it as though from an aeroplane, you know—all very throbbing and significant—and that damned fifth farm just mucks the whole thing up.'

'Do you think a true artist would knock it down and turf it over just to make a tidy picture, then?' I said, laughing.

Alec laughed too.

'A true artist would be able to paint the picture so it didn't look like a lollipop,' he said.

'And anyway,' I told him, 'five is a far luckier number. It says so in a skipping song, so it must be true.' I could hear footsteps approaching and in a moment Lorna appeared in the sitting-room doorway. 'Lorna dear, I've just realised,' I said, 'we didn't hear the numbers song last night amongst the others.'

339

'I'm sorry?' said Lorna. She looked as serene as a lake on a still evening today, and I took that as proof. Yesterday she would have been put out to see Captain Watson ensconced with me, but this morning, knowing she had her three times three hairs to twist together and pull him to her, she was invincible.

'One and one make two and two makes true love,' I reminded her. She smiled again.

'I don't think that is a skipping song,' she said mildly. 'Now that I reflect on it, I'm sure it's something my mother used to sing to me. My father too, once she had passed away. Will you stay and eat with us, Captain Watson?' Alec nodded. 'Well, then I'll just step into the kitchen and make sure there's enough to go around.' She leaned over and looked at the sleeping kitten in his lap. 'Good to see her feeling better, isn't it, Mrs Gilver? I hope now you'll forgive yourself for the mishap.' And she glided out.

'What did you tell them?' said Alec, giving the kitten's head a reluctant nudge with the side of his finger, and setting off a noise like a swarm of angry bees. Even he could not be reminded that the little thing had been nailed to a road and not feel some tenderness.

'I said I had run over her in my motor car,' I told him. 'I don't suppose she'd have got away with a flattened tail if I really had, but no one has questioned it.'

'Not even Lorna?' said Alec. 'Who knows the truth?'

'She must imagine,' I said, 'that I'm hiding the nasty story from her out of politeness.'

'I don't know,' said Alec. 'Could she possibly be

340

so calm, if you're right, if it was her? She's acting, this morning, as though . . .'

'The harbour is in sight and the wind's behind?' I said. 'I think that backs my theory up, don't you? And if it weren't for the kitten's tail, I'd almost be inclined to say that it's run its course and we should just walk away from it.'

'A minister's daughter casting spells?' said Alec, looking rather shocked, for him. 'Causing such a rumpus that a girl gets dug up from her grave to quiet it down again? How could you walk away from that?'

Viewed that way, I was rather shocked at myself. Perhaps I had been so long at Luckenlaw among the demons and spirits and the talk of the devil, with Mr Tait nodding genially at it all and calling it harmless, that my instincts had deserted me.

'Well anyway,' I said, hoping I sounded less sulky than I felt at being chastised by him, 'there is also the fact of the kitten's tail. It can't be got away from.'

'And that's where I start to doubt again,' said Alec. 'I simply can't see Lorna Tait doing that.'

'She was desperate,' I reminded him. 'I had bundled away all the other ladies and I was going to park right outside the manse door and get into the hall in one mighty leap. She must have known that.'

'And where did she get the kitten? Did she have time to plan it all when she realised you were ferrying the others?'

'Plenty,' I said, 'and there are always kittens in the country, if you know where to look.'

'All right,' said Alec. 'I give in. It was Lorna. Now what? We're not going to the police, are we,

341

and she will know that we don't want a scandal for her father. So I don't see what just telling her she's undone will achieve. How are we going to convince her never to do such a thing again?'

'There's only one way I can think of,' I said. 'We have to show her that it hasn't worked. And there I think we are in luck. If she were to set her sights on some little curate or clerk and he happened to succumb to her advances, then she might well turn back to her spell book for the next thing her heart desired. But I think we can guess who her intended is, can't we?'

Alec nodded, looking as unenticed as a dog faced with bathwater.

'I feel dreadful about the poor Howies,' I said. 'They've put such toil into Lorna's party and we're going to knock the wind out of Lorna's sails and deliver a broken woman to them. They've spent your rent on it, you know.'

'I don't think we do have to,' said Alec. 'I would bet that the birthday party is probably exactly the night that Lorna plans to . . . How do you think it'll work? Oh God, don't tell me she's going to give me a little *bonne-bouche* full of hair to nibble on.'

'I don't expect so,' I said, shuddering. 'I rather think she'll fashion herself something and wear it. She'll be irresistible to all around, don't you know, but it'll be you she's aiming it at.'

'I think you're right,' said Alec, nodding slowly. 'I think that's why she's been so worried about her father getting a frock made for her. It never did seem all that likely, if you ask me, but because she dreaded it, it looked all the more certain.'

'Yes, I wondered at that assumption too,' I said. 'Although I suppose if the ladies she saw trooping

342

up and downstairs were known seamstresses, it could just about have been plausible. That's all done with, by the way. Mother's room is open again. I tried the handle this morning.'

'Right,' said Alec. 'Quick, here she comes, what have we decided? You tell Mr Tait all is well, go home and wait for the party. I think I'll take off too, in case she goes off at half-cock before the big night and I fluff it because I'm not ready. Then on Birthday Night I'll reel her in and drop her like a brick.' He said this with rather too much relish, and I had to concentrate very hard on the poor kitten not to feel a little sorry for Lorna again.

*   *   *

The Howies were the sort of people who throw parties simply by asking everyone they know and then standing back and laughing. Some raffish-looking chums were there, the Taits were there, the tenants were there—including the innocent Mr Christie—as well as a large contingent of SWRI ladies, resplendent in starched ruffles and witch-heart brooches and sipping uncertainly at their drinks as they stood around the room in little flocks. Captain Watson was there, naturally, and so was Hugh.

I had been thrown into a panic by Hugh's insistence that he come with me; Alec could hardly just leave by the window this time since our plan depended on him being there to soak up Lorna's affections, but I was reassured.

'I'm planning an outfit that will keep Hugh pinned against the opposite wall,' Alec said. 'I'll wear a hat with a big brim and . . . wait for it . . .

343

I've grown a goatee. Barrow's been topiarising me every morning. Wait till you see.'

He was right, both about Hugh and about the goatee being well worth seeing. Hugh stared coldly across the ballroom at the spectacle of Captain Watson and said in a hostile murmur without moving his lips:

'He's never from Fife.'

'No, indeed,' I said. 'That's the artist who ran off to be inspired instead of coming to the chamber with us all that day.'

'Good thing he did,' said Hugh. 'I shouldn't have been so ready to carry *him* out when he fainted, which I expect he would have. What a creature.' And he turned his back resolutely on Alec for the rest of the night, although facing the wall brought him little comfort, for the Howies' ideas on decoration combined Nicolette's penchant for excessive ornament with Vashti's rather slapdash theatricality and the ballroom was a perfect circus as a result.

The peeling painted walls were hidden behind towering stalks of dry hogweed hung with tinsel and what looked like stuffed hummingbirds. The bottoms of the stalks were poked into little heaps of wet sand to hold them steady so that, as the evening wore on and feet stepped into the sand heaps, the hogweed started to list and flop about and the dance floor under our feet began to feel gritty. The little supper tables—actually packing cases as one found out with a painful clunk if one tried to get one's feet under them—were covered with swathes of fuchsia-pink art silk, torn roughly from the bolt and fraying already, and the centrepieces were an odd collection of old bottles, slapped over with gilt paint and stuffed with feathers and beads on sticks in lieu of flowers, which would admittedly have been prohibitive in November. The room was lit by purple candles raging away smokily in wall sconces and in vast iron candelabra hung from the ceiling too, melting in great dollops all over anyone who happened to stand underneath and leaving permanent-looking wine-coloured stains on their shoulders. Through it all, Lorna Tait sailed like a great pink iceberg, looking as out of place in her setting and as pitifully unromantic in her over-trimmed frock as it was possible to be, but exuding confidence like a lighthouse.

I was lucky enough to witness her first full assault on the Captain.

'Are you a dancing man?' she asked, coming up to where Alec and the Howies were standing, after a turn around the floor with her father to a military two-step. (The Howies had had to take what they could get by way of a band.)

'Not as a general rule,' said Alec, bowing over the hand that she held out to him as elegantly as though she were trailing it off the back of a punt in summer. He looked up again and fixed Lorna with such a liquid gaze that I felt a sudden flash of worry. If the love charm actually had potency he would be on one knee promising undying devotion before she had cut the cake. 'I should be honoured to dance with you tonight,' he said.

Lorna's eyes, already dewy from tender feelings, or perhaps smarting from the kohl pencil into which one of the Howies had persuaded her, melted yet further at that.

'Only not to this, darlings,' said Vashti, glaring at

the band. 'Honestly, Niccy, I thought you had spoken to them.'

'I have,' Nicolette said wearily, 'but they're terribly set in their ways. Country dances now and slow ballroom after supper to aid the digestion.'

'How revolting,' said Vashti. 'I'm going over to put my foot down. It's one thing to have to do without the black bottom but this is only one step up from the Grand Old Duke of York. Come with me, Lorna darling. They wouldn't dare refuse you on your birthday.'

'Hurry back,' called Alec plaintively as Vashti swept Lorna off towards the stage where the troupe of elderly gentlemen were puffing away at their accordions and scraping their fiddles, with feet tapping. Nicolette made a strangled sound in her throat and rushed off after them.

'What's wrong with *her*?' said Alec. 'Was I too much?'

'Not at all,' I assured him. 'You almost had me convinced it was working.'

'So why the chortles?' he said. 'Why is it that Nicolette finds me so endlessly diverting, Dan?'

'Well,' I said, 'the thing is, she doesn't believe you're an artist. She thinks you're an . . . aesthete of a more general kind.'

He looked down at himself, the oyster-coloured trousers and the soft lemon-yellow shirt with the rolled collar.

'Ah,' he said, grinning. 'Is that what Lorna thinks too?'

'I doubt it's a subject which Lorna has ever pondered.'

'Good,' said Alec. 'We don't want Lorna declaring the experiment null and void. Have you spotted it, by the way?'

'What? The love charm?'

'Mm. It's in her hair, aptly enough. A tiny little waffle of plaited strands. I only noticed it because she keeps fingering it. Otherwise it's fairly unobtrusive.'

Lorna was returning, the Howies like a pair of handmaidens just behind her, and now that Alec mentioned it, she did keep putting her hand up to the back of her head as she sailed along.

Alec met her with his arm outstretched and ushered her reverently into the middle of the floor as the elderly gentlemen wheezed into a waltz.

'Dandy?' said Hugh, suddenly at my side. 'Care to dance?'

I managed not to let my mouth drop open in astonishment, and ignoring the Howies' titters—their husbands had shown their faces briefly and retired to a bridge table in another room with a pair of friends—I let Hugh lead me onto the floor.

'What did you find to say to *him*?' he asked me, nodding over at Alec, who was swishing around the floor as though he were a dancing instructor, with his chin in the air and his arms high and rigid in that silly pose that makes all men who adopt it look like broken umbrellas.

'This and that,' I answered airily. 'I was asking how his painting of the local landscape goes on.'

'Why?' said Hugh. 'Is he any good?

'Awful,' I told him. 'If there were one of his efforts hanging in one's house, one would never go outside again, for fear it had all come true.'

'Now look, Dandy,' said Hugh, confirming what I had suspected: this invitation to dance was just an excuse to boss me around about something or other without interruptions. 'We've come and done our duty. When can we go?'

'We haven't even had supper yet,' I said. 'We haven't sung Happy Birthday.'

'Well, conjure up a headache then,' said Hugh. 'If we left now we could get home tonight and I could be back at work in the morning. It so happens that I'm extremely busy just now and this dance has put me out considerably.'

'Well, you have the headache then,' I said. 'They're your friends and it was your idea that I got mixed up with them in the first place.'

'Nonsense,' said Hugh. 'What a fool I'd look, falling out over a headache at nine o'clock in the evening.'

'Yes, well. It's just the same for me,' I told him. 'So we'll be here until midnight, or until at least six others have left before us, whichever comes first.' It was our habitual agreement whenever Hugh wanted to get away from a party, which was often.

This one certainly was a challenge, though, and had I not needed to stick around to help with the bringing down of Lorna's little magic show, I should have been as eager as Hugh to get out of it. The Rural ladies enjoyed it well enough, once they had stopped trying to fit in and instead decided to treat it as an extended social half-hour. They paired up with their particular chums and got very hot and dishevelled, carrying out complicated patterns in the eightsome reel—the band, having made an exception for Alec and Lorna's first waltz, had since reverted.

After supper, rather heavy and tepid, and very far from the exquisite little salty nothings that help down the champagne at the parties of one's

348

imaginings, Hugh and I were sitting amidst the candle wax at one of the tea chests and eyeing the plates of birthday cake which lay before us when, at the other end of the room, I saw Alec slipping in through a door in the panelling and closing it behind him. He stepped over a toppled hogweed stalk and sauntered around the dance floor towards us. As he approached, Hugh turned away almost rudely and fixed his gaze upon the far horizon so Alec was unobserved by any but me as he flashed his eyes and jerked his head at the door by which he had entered.

'I give in,' I said to Hugh. 'I'm going to get my wrap.'

'Should think,' muttered Hugh, and he banged his legs audibly on the tea chest as he rose to bow me away.

Slipping out of the ballroom into the draughty corridor beyond, I paused and wondered where to begin seeking Lorna but, as soon as the noise of the band was cut off by the door shutting, I could hear her. An ugly, hacking, gulping noise as painful to listen to as it must have been to produce was coming from across the passageway. I stepped over and knocked softly.

'Is anyone there?' I said.

'Go away,' Lorna sobbed.

'Lorna?'

'Please go away,' she said, and no matter what she had done I felt a pulse of anger at Alec. Surely he could have let her down gently? How could he have done this to her and then sauntered back that way? I pushed the door open and crept inside. It was a kind of glorified cupboard, perhaps a linen store, and Lorna was perched on a little stool at the back of it, with her head on her knees and her arms wrapped around them.

'Mrs Gilver, please,' she implored me, raising her head and seeing who it was, 'leave me. Don't even look at me.' The kohl pencil was streaked down her cheeks like clown's paint and her elaborate party coiffure was unravelled over her shoulders. On the floor in front of her lay a little brown lump like a disembodied patch of darning.

'My dear Lorna,' I said, feeling an absolute heel. 'What has happened? Come now, you shouldn't cry on your birthday—it's the most fearful bad luck.' This was hardly the most opportune angle to take with her and the sobbing redoubled as soon as I had said it.

'Come, what's happened?' I asked again.

'I thought he liked me,' she said. 'He acted as if he liked me.'

'Who did, dear?' I said, kneeling in front of her and trying to do a bit of mopping.

'C-captain,' she managed to get out.

'Has he been nasty to you?' I said. 'Shall I fetch your father?'

'No!' wailed Lorna. 'And he hasn't been nasty. He's just . . . He asked if he could speak to me on my own and I thought . . . So we came in here, and then he said it was a most delicate matter and he hoped he wasn't going to shock me.'

Oh, Alec, I thought. What did you do?

'Then he said he had come to Luckenlaw to paint but almost immediately he had realised that Providence must have sent him here to meet his heart's desire, and if only he could be sure that his affections were returned he would be the happiest man alive.'

I waited, while a fresh bout of weeping swept over her. Time was I should have been thrown into confusion by watching people weep, but it is something of which a detective has to do a surprising amount, at least the way my cases seemed to unfold anyway. Presently she gulped, blew her nose and resumed.

'And then he asked me if he could be so bold as to press me into service for him. He asked if I would speak to the lady and see if she returned his affections. He said he could not bear to approach her and be turned down, because he thought it would kill him.'

'Who was it?' I said, genuinely keen to hear.

'Effie Morton,' shrieked Lorna.

'Miss Morton, the bishop's niece?' I blurted. 'I thought she was an old maid?'

'She is,' Lorna cried with an hysterical bleat in her voice. 'She's forty-three and he loves her.'

I brought all my self-command to bear to keep from laughing, for really it was not at all funny.

'Well, Lorna dear,' I said at last, when she seemed to be growing calm. 'I think Miss Morton is welcome to him. If he came badger-ing you for favours, on your birthday, if he was that full of his own concerns on what should have been your special night, then he is just the kind of selfish . . . nincompoop you can well do without.'

'You sound like Hetty McCallum,' Lorna said, smiling unsteadily, and she took a deep shuddering breath. 'There are worse people to sound like, I suppose.' She gave me a brave look. 'There are worse people to *be* like, I suppose.'

'Come, come,' I said. 'He is not the only, or even the best, young man in the world. And you are a

351

lovely girl with plenty of time left to meet a better one.' Right now, of course, she was quite freakish, with rivulets of kohl and ravaged hairdressing, but there were no mirrors in this linen cupboard.

'No,' she said. 'I believed and I tried and I failed and that's the end of it.'

I sat regarding her, wondering whether to leave it there since she had obviously learned her lesson or whether, for the kitten's sake, to make a point of it, birthday night or no. In the end, I decided to be thorough instead of kind, and so—if I were going to be as rigorous when I viewed my own actions as when I was viewing hers—one might say that everything that happened after that could be laid at my door.

'You believed?' I said, drawing myself away from her a little. 'You tried? My dear Lorna, you don't mean to tell me it's been you making this silly hair-piece, do you?' Her eyes darted to the floor and then fixed on my face. 'Oh yes, I know about it,' I said. 'I've been trying to get to the bottom of it for your father. Do you really mean to tell me it was you?'

Her chest was rising and falling at an alarming speed. She hesitated, rubbed her face with her hands and then, finally, nodded.

'I should never have believed it of you.'

'I know,' she groaned, dropping her head back to her knees again. 'I've been a fool.'

'That's putting it rather kindly, if you ask me. Nailing a kitten to the ground by its poor little tail is far beyond foolish.' She had gone quite still, shrinking into herself. 'As is digging up a soul that deserves her long-awaited rest.' I could hear that my voice was hard but I could not turn it gentle

352

again. Lorna looked up at me, white behind the clownish streaks.

'What?' she said.

'All right,' I assured her. 'I'll believe *that* wasn't you.'

'What are you talking about?' she said.

'Your father has been keeping rather a lot of horrid little secrets from you, Lorna,' I told her. 'But I think you should know. Someone in thrall to the old ways of spells and luck dug that poor girl's bones up out of her grave.'

'My father always said the old ways were harmless.'

'Well, they're not. This dabbling you've been doing, all in the name of love, has its ugly side, and if you dip a toe in it you can easily end up lost to goodness for ever.' She was nodding faster and faster.

'They dug up a grave?' she said. 'My father knows?'

'He has handled it all most sensitively,' I said. 'He is a lovely, kind, charming man and you should be glad that you have the chance to spend your years with him. Believe me. Marriage is not . . . the only way to a happy life, you know.'

'They dug her up out of her grave?' said Lorna, still unbelieving. 'Why?'

'To put her back where she belonged. In the chamber. To put things back as they should be.'

'But that's . . .' She stopped talking and simply shook her head very fast, as though trying to shake off the idea the way a dog shakes off water. I stood up to leave her. If she could be as horrified as all that then she was surely not lost to decent feeling. The kitten was an aberration, the desperate act of

353

a lonely, muddled girl, but she would come right in the end.

I hesitated at the door.

'Will you be all right?' I asked her. 'You're sure you don't want your father?'

'I'll be fine,' she said.

Her voice had an odd, strained note in it, but I told myself that anyone's voice would sound peculiar after such upsets and weeping, and so I walked away.

CHAPTER NINETEEN

I gave Mr Tait the briefest of reports the next morning, saying no more than that the trouble was over and no one knew or needed to know a thing about it.

'And you are sure there won't be a recurrence?' he said. I thought back to Lorna's broken bewilderment the evening before and shook my head firmly.

'You've done a splendid job, my dear Mrs Gilver,' he said. 'I couldn't have asked for more discretion.'

'I could have asked for quite a bit *less* discretion from you, Mr Tait,' I told him. 'You haven't been frank with me, exactly.'

'And what if I had been?' he said, smiling. 'Would you have come?'

'Certainly not!' It was out before I could stop it and he chuckled. 'If I'd heard all the lurid details before . . . well, before I got to know you, I might even have tried to stop the luncheons at Gilverton.'

'Well, well,' he concluded, nodding benignly with his hands folded across his middle. 'All shall be well and all shall be well and all manner of things shall be well.'

Than which one cannot really hope for a better epitaph to one's labours. I rose, picking up my gloves and Bunty's lead, and took my leave of him.

*　　*　　*

Alec had decided to stay on for a bit at Ford Cottage. He said it was because his disguise could not just be folded up and put away if the good he had done Lorna was to last, and I suppose there was something to that, but I suspected too that he felt remorseful for having let her down with such a thump and wanted to see what he could do by way of a belated cushioning. Personally I thought her bruised pride, if not her heart, would heal more quickly if she never saw him again but he was determined and so I left him there when Bunty and I accompanied Hugh back to Gilverton the day after the party.

'Only watch out for Effie Morton,' I warned him when he telephoned. 'If Lorna tells her how inflamed you are, she might just throw her watercolours and sketching pad over her shoulder in a knotted hanky and move in.'

'She's a bishop's niece, Dandy,' said Alec. 'Even if she did get wind of how I feel about her—God, though, you should see the creature—I could put her off me with a few well-judged anecdotes about my Montmartre days.'

'You certainly do have a callous streak,' I said.

'Not compared with Lorna,' he said. 'Or, as you

355

still insist on calling her, "poor" Lorna. How is the kitten?'

I looked over to the combined slumbering heap of large spotted dog and tiny tabby cat, and smiled.

'She's fine,' I said. 'Her tail has the most darling little kink in it, like a piglet's. Hugh, of course, hates her with a passion already and has the cheek to suggest that the reaction of his pack of mutts— which was to chase her all over the house, licking their chops and baying—is more properly dog-like than Bunty's welcome.'

'Well, I'd better go,' said Alec. 'That Mrs Martineau on the corner is watching me from behind her curtains again.'

'She'll be after you for Annette if she hears you're on the market,' I told him.

I hung up the receiver, gazed fondly at Bunty and the kitten for another moment, and sat down at my desk to open my morning's letters and pick up the reins, once again, of my between-thrills, non-detecting life.

The very next morning I found out how wrong I had been to imagine that it was over.

I woke early and lay for a moment wondering what had disturbed me, then sighed with irritation as I realised I could hear the first breakfast sitting at the bird table outside. If Hugh could not be persuaded to move the thing away from the house, then I should at least tell the kitchen maids to restrain themselves a little.

I rose, bathed, dressed and let Bunty out of the side door, then I went to fetch the kitten from her overnight quarters, but kittens are notoriously early risers and, when I saw that she was up and off already, I made my way to my sitting room to wait for breakfast, nudging the french window open just an inch or two in spite of the chill so that Bunty and her little friend could get in when they had finished their morning's ablutions in the garden.

The noise from the bird table was really quite extraordinary today; crows and magpies quarrelling over the feast, all the robins and sparrows driven off to chatter their annoyance from the terrace balustrades. What on earth had the silly girl put out there, I wondered, hoping that if it was a knuckle of ham—for that is what it looked like from the window—crows were the worst of it and I was not about to see a rat climb the solitary leg and haul itself onto the platform.

Even as I watched, I saw the second kitchen maid trooping round the corner of the house with her apron tented up in front of her, scattering crumbs on the grass as she went along. I rapped on the window and pointed fiercely to the bird table but she misunderstood and nodded cheerfully down at her bellied apron skirt as though reassuring me that yes, she was just on her way with some more. I sighed, fastened the window against the racket and was just turning away when a new, shriller cry was added to the birds' squabble. I turned back. She was standing, apron hem fallen and breadcrumbs tumbled about her feet, her hands over her mouth and her eyes wide with horror.

I rushed outside and over the frosty grass towards the bird table. Bunty, seeing me from across the lawn, came forward at a gambol and we reached the maid together, as she flapped at the crows, weeping, trying to drive them away.

I took just one look, just enough to see a scrap

of tabby fur and a dull eye, before I reeled away, shrieking.

Hugh arrived as the kitchen maid and I were comforting one another, Bunty howling with her head back—she cannot bear to see me cry.

'What in the name of the devil—' said Hugh, unknowingly apt for once.

I pointed behind me, but could not look at it.

'Good God,' he said, and I could hear in his voice that his lip had curled with revulsion.

'Please take it away,' I said.

'I'll fetch a gardener,' said Hugh. As he was leaving, he paused, and said: 'This is what happens, you see. Cats will hunt birds, Dandy, and this one has got its comeuppance.'

The look I gave him felt from my side like a dart of pure cold hatred and, from the way he started, it must have seemed much the same from his end too. He cleared his throat and strode away towards the kitchen gardens. The maid, with wonderful if belated presence of mind, took off her apron and threw it over the little platform, winding the strings around the pole and tying them tightly. At this, the crows lost interest in the scene and flapped off blackly.

'I'm sorry, madam,' the girl said. 'But that there wee kitty never climbed that pole, and she never could have got caught by a crow because she would have jumped off again, wouldn't she not? I don't think Master is right.'

I am afraid that, at that moment, I said I thought Hugh was a thing which the kitchen maid clearly never expected she would hear a lady such as myself say of anyone, much less my own husband, much less in front of the very lowliest of

358

my own servants, and she knew that I meant it.

White with rage, I stalked back in through the french windows, lifted the telephone and asked to be put through to the number for the Luckenlaw manse. The gardener had arrived outside and I put down the receiver to draw the curtains closed, so by the time I picked it up again Mr Tait's voice was saying:

'Hello? Hello? I'm sorry, my dear, I think the call has gone astray somewhere.'

'It's me, Mr Tait,' I said, and I heard the click of the operator leaving us. 'Might I speak to Lorna, please?'

'I'm afraid you can't,' he said. 'I can't find her this morning. She appears to have had an early breakfast before anyone else was up and now she's disappeared off somewhere. My old car has gone from the coach-house.'

'How odd,' I said, thinking of course that it was anything but. 'I shall try again later then.'

Next, I asked to be put through to Miss McCallum at the post office and when she answered, I tried my best to sound light and cheerful, as befitted a harmless errand.

'I know you can't desert your post, dear,' I said, 'but I wonder, if anyone happens in, could you ask for a message to be given to Captain Watson down at the cottage? Could he ring Mrs Gilver, please? I've found him a commission, for a painting, you know.'

'Never!' said Miss McCallum. 'Well, what a funny world it would be if we were all the same. Aye right, Mrs Gilver, here's Mrs Kinnaird coming now, I'll get her to step down the lane and tell him.'

After that I waited, trying to ignore the sounds from outside as the gardener dealt with the mess and trying to ignore Bunty, who had followed me in and was snuffling round the rugs and cushions and looking enquiringly up at me, unable to understand that her little companion was gone again.

Less than ten minutes later, Alec rang me.

'But what was the point of it?' he said when I had told him. 'All the way up to Gilverton in a bone-shaker to kill a kitten?'

'It might just be spite,' I replied, 'to pay me back for being the one who found her out, but I fear it's a threat . . . of what exactly, I cannot say.'

'She's a remarkable actress, isn't she?' said Alec. 'All this going on and she swans around looking like an angel.'

'What should we do?'

'I think it's time to go to the police,' said Alec. 'As you say, this still might not be the worst of it. She must be stopped now.'

'Yes,' I said. 'All right then. But don't say a word to her father. He's so well wrapped around her finger that he might try to smooth over even this.'

'Agreed,' said Alec. 'And Dandy, this is horrid, I know, but you should keep the kitten, darling. They might be able to tell what happened to it.'

'It's going to be very unpleasant for Mr Tait,' I said. 'And for Luckenlaw.'

'I'll do my best,' said Alec. 'I'll try to persuade Lorna, when she gets back, to come with me to the police station and hand herself in. It would save blaring sirens and constables rushing in and dragging her off from the manse in handcuffs, and if we could keep it out of the papers somehow . . .'

'Yes, I suppose so,' I said. 'I'm not feeling very charitable right now, I have to say, and a bit of dragging in handcuffs seems quite fitting. But I suppose it's hospital she needs, really. And I daresay that will feel enough like punishment—I know I shouldn't care to be in one.'

'I'll ring you when it's done,' Alec said.

After hanging up, I steeled myself to go back outside. The gardener had placed the bundled apron aside and was digging the leg of the bird table out of the lawn, with Hugh looking on.

'I thought you wouldn't want it there as a reminder,' Hugh said gruffly. 'I'll stick it somewhere more out of the way.' Then, having been caught out in such sentimental extravagance, he was forced to leave and I had a chance to ask the gardener:

'Please don't throw the poor thing in the boiler, Timpson. If you could find a stout box and put her in the flower room on the stone floor, I'll bury her later.'

'Just you give me a shout, madam, and I'll dig the hole,' said Timpson, and the kindness in his voice made my eyes fill again. 'I'm fond o' a cat myself,' he went on. 'Verra clean wee creatures and they keep the finches out o' the fruit garden like nothin' else can.' Timpson and Hugh did not see eye to eye on the question of birds, it seemed.

For the rest of the day I sat in my own room, moping a little, waiting for Alec to ring back, eventually trying the manse again, in case he had missed her return.

'I'm beginning to feel quite worried, Mrs Gilver,' Mr Tait told me. 'I haven't seen her all day, and even if she had happened upon some

361

poor soul in need of succour and she was busy making broth in a cottage somewhere she would have got word to me, I'm sure of it.'

'Have you tried her friends?' I said.

'I can't seem to find anyone,' he answered. 'Miss Lindsay's house is in darkness and Miss McCallum isn't in the post house—they must have gone off somewhere together, I suppose. No answer from the Howies all day, either. And Captain Watson hasn't seen her, for I went down and asked him.'

'I shouldn't worry,' I told him. 'She's a big girl and she can look after herself. Only, you will tell her I rang, won't you?'

He had surprised me when he said that Miss Lindsay's house was in darkness—I had not realised how the day was passing—but looking out of my window now I saw that night had indeed fallen and I went over to close the shutters. I sighed heavily, looking out, but I could not even see the little break in the turf of the lawn which showed where the scene of the morning's horrors had been. It was a perfectly black, moonless night. That was right, I realised, calculating it, exactly a month since that other perfectly black moonless night when I looked out and saw the grave robbers at Luckenlaw. Well, at least I knew that was nothing to do with Lorna. Her surprise, the night of her party when she heard of it, was quite genuine. 'They robbed a grave?' she had said. 'But that's . . .' what had she called it? No, I remembered, she had been incapable of words at the thought.

And yet, how could it be so? How could someone be responsible for what happened at the

362

full moon and for what had happened to my poor kitten at the dark moon last night, and yet be so shocked by the dark deeds of the moon before? It was just as the little girls sang: dark night, moonlight . . . and then how did it go? Haunt me something, something white. Moonlight, dark night, shut the coffin lid tight, like any other little rhyme carving up the days and weeks into tidy parcels. Sneeze on a Monday, kiss a stranger, sneeze on a Tuesday, sneeze for danger. The days of the week with their meanings and the phases of the moon, each with their allotted tasks. Surely, it would make more sense to think that the same person was responsible for it all.

But she could not have been; she was speechless with horror at the very idea of it. 'They dug up a grave?' she had said, again and again. 'But that's . . .' All of a sudden, my memory seemed to sharpen and an idea took hold of me. 'But that's . . .' she had said, and I had imagined she was going to go on and call it evil or insane. But what if she had been going to say something quite different? What if she had been going to say it was no good, that it would never work, that it was not old dug-up bones that needed to be put there. And was it not true that when we visited the chamber that awful, hilarious day Lorna had been perfectly unperturbed even when she had reached into the little hollow and pulled out the dust sheet? She only screamed when she saw that it was empty.

Was I making something out of nothing? Rattled by the horridness of the kitten that morning, was I sitting here telling myself ghost stories like any ghoul?

It was the dark of the moon again. Miss Lindsay

was missing, Miss McCallum was missing, and Lorna had not gone home after her trip to my garden last night. She believed in charms and spells and yet her love charm had been powerless. Would she blame that on the grave robbers—whoever they were—putting tired old bones into the law? Was it possible that this time she would replace them with something fresher? Miss Lindsay, Miss McCallum and the Howies were all missing from home.

I started to pace up and down my sitting room. The Howies were safe, I was sure. They were married women and was it not most likely that the sacrifice of a young girl was less to do with her youth than with her virginity? So Miss McCallum and Miss Lindsay could be in danger. Who could I turn to? Who could I tell?

I imagined ringing the manse again and saying this to Mr Tait, imagined myself being wrong and him telling Hugh and Hugh making me go and speak to the kind of doctor I thought Lorna needed. Alec could not be reached except by telegram. I could ask to be put through to the kiosk on the green and let it ring and ring, hoping for someone to answer, but time was wasting.

I looked at the clock above the fire. It was half-past seven now. I had wasted hours here.

'Stay, stay,' I said to Bunty as I rushed to the door. I could say I was upset about the kitten and that I had driven away to have a good cry where no one could hear me. I could say the motor car broke down and I had to walk miles to find help. I would worry about all of that later. Right now, I simply had to go.

There was no one in at Ford Cottage, two hours later, when I pounded on the door—where was he?—so I drove through the ford, praying that the full, midwinter stream would not be too much for my motor car. There was a moment when I could have sworn I was afloat and the engine spluttered alarmingly, but I made it up the other side and was soon bucketing along the winding back lane which would eventually bring me around the west side of the law to Luckenheart Farm and the steps leading to the chamber. I had a crowbar beside me on the seat, taken from the old stable we used as a garage now, but I was sure I should not need it. I was sure that the padlock would be open when I got to the little wooden door. At last, I spied in the light of my headlamps the rather crumbling gateposts and sagging rusted gates of Luck House and I knew I was almost there.

A door opened and a light appeared as I shot through the farmyard on my way to the rocky cleft at the foot of the hill, so I slowed and allowed the motor car to roll backwards until I was beside Jock Christie, who was holding up his lantern and staring at me.

'Mrs Gilver?' he said. 'Is something wrong?'

'Are you alone tonight?' I asked him, looking wildly around for carts, hoping against hope that his kitchen was full of large, competent farmers who could help.

'Of course,' said Jock Christie. 'Mrs Gilver, what's wrong?'

Part of me—most of me, if I am brutally honest—wanted to beg him to come with me, but

365

he looked such a child standing there in the lantern light and I had no idea what was waiting up the hill.

'Nothing,' I told him then I put the engine back into gear and roared off, leaving him blinking. At the stopping place, I climbed out, switched on my electric torch and began to play the beam around, looking for the opening where the stairs were cut into the rock. My mind was all stern resolve and courage, but already, as so many times before, I could feel my body, my blood, my heart, my trembling legs, begin to warn me that dreadful things were coming.

Oh, Alec, where *are* you? I thought again. And then I stopped. It might not be one of the Misses Lindsay or McCallum that she would set her sights upon tonight. After all, they were her friends. Suddenly I was sure I knew who was in danger, for if she had wanted simply to warn me off and cause me grief this morning she would have gone for Bunty, but she must have felt that she needed to pay the kitten back for being the creature which showed me what an evil woman she really was. Well, would she not do the same tonight? If she needed a victim, would she not choose the one who had hurt and humiliated her so badly at that terrible party?

Could she overpower Alec? If she surprised him, could she throttle him or hit him so hard that he fainted? I stumbled up the rocky steps on shaking legs, praying that I was not already too late.

As I rounded the rowan bush and came upon the platform, my torchlight picked out the glitter of the key in the open padlock and the bright, unweathered wood on the inside of the little door. The mouth of the tunnel disappeared into thick, brownish darkness. I stopped to try to quiet my panting breaths, carefully lifting the padlock off the hasp and dropping it into my coat pocket, key and all, for the thought of someone coming after me and turning the lock, the thought of being trapped in there, was enough to run a trickle of cold terror down my spine. I shook myself, put out my torch and stole inside. Along the chill, dank passageway I crept, towards the faint glow of a light at the end. I could smell cigarette smoke, acrid and unpleasant in this closed-in place before I got to the arched stone doorway, the tiny glow of light went out and I could hear someone grinding the cigarette stub on the stone floor, the dust grating.

'That was quick,' said Nicolette Howie's voice out of the darkness. 'Put your torch on, darling, and let's get on with it. It's far too cold to hang around in here.'

I clicked the switch on my torch, too dumbfounded at her air of ease to think whether or not I should. She spoke as though we had met on a street while out shopping.

'Where is she, then?' said Nicolette, rising from her perch on the stone slab in the middle of the room. Then she turned and saw me.

'What?' she breathed. 'What are you doing here? Where are they? What have you done?'

I could not answer her. I did not know. But I began to babble feverishly, unable to stop myself.

'Where's Lorna?' I said. 'Niccy, you must come with me. All these games you've been playing—if you've been playing them too—they must stop.

She's dangerous. Where's Vashti? Do you know where Miss McCallum and Miss Lindsay are? Are they safe?'

Nicolette's face broke into a smile.

'Oh dear,' she said. 'You have got in a muddle, haven't you? I have no idea where Miss Lindsay and her little pink gnome of a friend are. Gone on another Women's March probably. And no, my dear Dandy. Lorna is not dangerous. She's just silly and getting extremely tiresome. I, on the other hand . . .' She looked just as calm and amused as ever, rearranging the strings of beads across the lapels of her little suit and smirking up at me from under her lashes.

'I don't understand,' I said. 'I thought it was . . . What are you doing here? How did you get the key?'

'Lorna brought it,' said Nicolette. 'She's such a sweet girl. She'd do anything for her dear friends, you know.'

She was so calm, so very unperturbed, that I feared for a moment I had imagined everything.

'Did you . . .' I began. 'Don't laugh at me for asking this, but did you rob the grave?' I waited to see if her eyes would widen, if she would shriek with laughter and tell me I was a scream, but there was not so much as a flicker.

'Yes, well that didn't work terribly well, did it?' she said.

'I can't believe it,' I said. 'You dug someone out of her grave?'

'Well, Irvine and Johnny helped with the actual spadework,' said Nicolette, deliberately misunderstanding me, 'once we had finally talked them into it. But they absolutely refused to enter

368

into the spirit, which can't have helped. No matter—we're going to make a proper job of it tonight, just Vash and me.'

'But why?' I said. 'For God's sake, why?'

'Well, not for God's sake,' said Nicolette, with an ugly laugh. 'For our sake. Vash's and mine. Do you know, Dandy, it was six weeks after we bought that God-awful pile that they found the entrance to this place. Six pathetic weeks and then the very thing that gave Luckenlaw its power was stripped away and we were left there with nothing.'

'You moved here for that? How did you know?'

'Oh, it's very well known about in certain circles,' said Nicolette. She had lit another cigarette now and the smell of it in the dank air of the chamber was sickening. 'But since the day those wretched archaeologists took her out everything's gone wrong. Everything we've touched has failed.'

'Do you mean money? That's happening to everyone.'

'But it wasn't supposed to happen to me,' she said, so grimly she was almost croaking. 'We come from an illustrious line, Vash and I.'

'An illustrious line of what?' I asked, although I was sure I knew.

'Enchantresses,' said Nicolette, rolling the ludicrous word around her mouth like brandy. 'We always knew it—our mother taught us our history from when we were tiny and she made us swot it all up and practise like anything. She was determined that no matter what degradations my useless father made us suffer—rented rooms, Dandy, with the landlady looking down her nose as though we were nobodies—we would find our rightful place in the world one day. And we did, although she didn't live to see it.' Here Nicolette gave a small sigh. Her face had grown gentle as she spoke and she gazed at a spot above my head, remembering. Then suddenly her attention snapped back to me and her voice hardened again. 'We married into Balnagowan just in time for that loathsome Ross cousin to sell it out from under us. And of course we found out that Irvine and Johnny couldn't care less about it, hardly knew about the family much less tried to keep up the traditions. Vash and I had to nag them to death to make them move here. And no sooner had we arrived than Mr holier-than-thou Tait put those precious bones into the filthy soil of a churchyard and we were stuck here, for nothing, with two useless boobs of husbands and no hope of getting out. We tried all sorts of things over the next few years, everything our mother had taught us, but nothing worked. And so, eventually, we realised that we had to take matters into our own hands and put right what was wrong.

'Only we needed another one. Three is the powerful number, you know. And there were only two of us, which is where dear Lorna came in. Of course, she didn't know what was happening. Such a very bovine trusting creature, isn't she? Only, just recently we began to think it would be better all round if she was . . . How can I put it? . . . a full board member? So we thought we would convince her, show her what riches, what power, what ecstasies were in store.'

Her high-flown language, like something from a cheap adventure, made the tide of terror which had been rising in me begin to subside again. I felt sickened and angry, but no longer scared.

'So you made her the love charm,' I said. 'As an advertisement of attractions to come.'

'And to earn her gratitude, of course,' Nicolette went on. 'Except it didn't, did it?' She almost spat the words. 'Not only—thanks to you, I might add—did she find out about the "poor darling little kitty-witty" and decide that Vash and I were beyond the pale, she heard about the stupid skeleton too—you again, I assume—and that shocked our Lorna to her milk-and-water little core. But worst of all—and this will make you laugh—she sent him packing. Our beautiful charm, nine months in the making, worked so well that it brought that maggot Watson to his knees, and Lorna turned him down.'

'That's what she told you?' I said.

'That's what happened,' said Nicolette. 'We found her in a broom cupboard at her party all upset because he'd forced himself on her. And so, you see . . .' Her voice trailed off and she was silent for a moment. 'Anyway,' she went on, 'what brings you here tonight?'

'What do you think?' I said. 'If you hoped to get away with it, why did you kill the cat?'

'What?' barked Nicolette, her ease gone in an instant.

'This morning,' I said. 'Someone killed the little cat that I saved on the road.'

'Oh Lord,' said Nicolette. '*That's* where she was then. My sister! I don't know what to do with her. She was very angry with you—we both were, actually—but Vashti takes it so seriously. I mean, look how she dresses, darling. She was most mysterious at supper last night, saying that unpropitious elements had to be swept away to allow the power to flow. So, she came and slaughtered the cat, did she? How theatrical. How very typical of Vashti. Still, she did volunteer for the messy end of tonight's work, so I'm not complaining.'

'The messy . . . ?' I said. 'What are you talking about?'

'She's killing two birds with one stone tonight,' said Nicolette. 'She's restoring the fortunes of Luckenlaw and shaking that irritating creature off our backs for good. I do admire neatness, don't you?'

'What do you mean?' I asked. 'Where is Vashti? What's she doing?'

'She's preparing Lorna.' I held onto the rough stone of the wall behind me as my head clouded and cleared again. 'We've been at it all day, actually,' Nicolette went on. 'We asked Lorna to come round for breakfast and bring her father's car. Wasn't that a clever touch? My idea, if you'll forgive me bragging. I thought even if she was missed no one would think she was anywhere nearby so long as the car was gone too.'

'But how can it work?' I said, thinking furiously. 'There are only two of you. I thought you needed three.'

'Impressive, isn't it?' said Nicolette. 'I expect when the two are as talented as Vash and me the third is immaterial. Look at the love charm after all. That was two of us. Vash in her cat-burglar suit and me doing the incantations. And if Lorna hadn't spoiled it by turning him down it would have worked . . . well, like a charm.' She threw her head back and cackled, smoke billowing out of her nose and mouth, making her look diabolical in the torchlight.

'Where are they?' I said.

'Oh, surely you don't think I'm going to tell you?' she said, still cackling. 'You'll only spoil it all. Although, actually, I'm surprised you can't guess.' I frowned at her. What did she mean by that?

'I suppose you *would* spoil it, wouldn't you?' she said, half into herself. 'I don't suppose you'd help out instead?'

Where could they be? I was so sure this place would be the scene of the nightmare if it was going to happen.

'I mean to say, I really do think Vash and I could do anything we set our minds to, but three is more traditional.'

Would they be in the graveyard? At the kirk? I tried to think of the whole of Luckenlaw, laid out in those sketch maps I had drawn, and in Alec's terrible pictures where he said it looked like a lollipop.

'It's the most tremendous fun,' Niccy was saying, 'except for some of the really grisly bits, and Vash does all that.'

The road, leading up, the village in a cluster, the kirk and manse like gateposts, the five farms all around and . . . the law. Of course, the Lucken Law.

'And there is a way to make it even more fun. I've got some tonight to give me courage if it's nasty.'

I began to sidle along to the doorway now, feeling for where the passageway led away to the outside.

'Oh, don't go,' said Nicolette. 'Aren't you listening to me? It's marvellous fun. A scream.' She was stalking towards me. 'Look, try some of

373

this if you need to.' She rummaged in the pocket of her tight little suit, bearing down on me. 'You're going to love it, truly.'

At the same time as I sprang away from her into the passageway, she lunged for me and knocked me to the ground. I fell on my side and felt a sharp crack as I came down onto the unyielding lump of the padlock. The pain shot through me, needle-sharp and sickening, but still I struggled and rolled, ignoring it, trying to get away from her, to get out from under her as she lay across me, using her weight to pin me down, while she wrestled with something she held in her hand. At last I heard a popping sound and Nicolette giggled.

'Welcome to Wonderland,' she said, and before I knew what was happening she had poured a stream of thick, bitter liquid into my mouth. I choked on it and tried to spit it out but I could feel some of it trickling down my throat, burning. With all of my strength I heaved her off me and got to my knees, gagging.

'Ow!' said Nicolette, sounding amused. 'Careful now. You could have hurt me.'

Whimpering with pain and trying to scrub out my mouth with my coat-sleeve I hauled myself up. The torch lay on its side a little way from us. Nicolette was still on the floor of the cave, with her legs tucked demurely to one side, ankles together, as we had been taught to sit on picnics, but when she had finished tidying her necklaces and turning her many rings around to the front of her hands again, all of a sudden she changed. She leapt up to her feet and stood, braced in a half-crouch with her arms wide, her hands flexed like little claws and a new look of excited concentration on her

374

painted face.

'Now, Dandy,' she said. 'You've had your fun, but you surely didn't think I was going to let you walk away, did you?'

With that, she sprang towards me. I dropped to the floor and kicked out with all my strength. Nicolette's feet shot away from under her, her high heels screeching against the stone, and I heard a dull, wet clunk as her head hit the wall above. She rolled down, groaning, but she was starting to scrabble her way up again before I had even got to my feet and so, hugging my ribs with both arms and biting down hard on my lip to bear the pain, I groped my way along the passage to the open door.

I could hear her dragging herself after me and did I only imagine that, as I scraped the door round on its gritty hinges and forced the hasp closed, I could feel her weight slump against the other side? I snapped the padlock shut and stood against the door, trying to breathe without moving.

I was out. And if she had poisoned me then it was poison that might leave me time to get Lorna before I fell. I started first one way along the little sheep track and then the other, but I needed to get to the top, so I put my hands down on the steep grass slope stretching upwards and started to climb. I could see nothing, but Nicolette's face still hung in front of me, swinging like a pendulum and cackling, and the cackling was the grating of my bones and the pendulum swing was the new booming pain that swelled up around it.

On and on I scrambled, slipping back almost as much as I pressed upwards, clutching at tussocks to stop myself from sliding all the way. My hands were scratched and I felt my nails bend back and break as the earth pitted in behind them. My knees were raw, scraped bare through my stockings. Still I climbed, and time began to slow down, to roll past, falling away behind me in heavy folds; each time I lifted a hand and hauled myself upwards it was like a tree uprooting itself; each time my foot struck the ground a tide rushed up through me and shattered behind my eyes.

Was that a light? Was I imagining it? Up ahead of me I thought I could see a thick glow smeared across the darkness and I could hear a noise that was not a hum and was not a howl but was both of them and neither and then I was up on top of the law standing immensely tall, with all the darkness splintered and streaming away from me, my ears rushing with the howling humming sound and there was the dark stranger, all in black, but his legs had stuck together and turned into a bell and the bell swung around as he moved. It was Vashti, it must be, in a black robe like a bell and there were the bones, white and shimmering, too big to be a kitten's bones. And they were clothed with flesh again and it was Lorna's body, lying white and still.

I moaned and the humming howl broke off, whispering and rustling like a thousand crows' wings all around me. I staggered forward and fell as the black bell turned, clanging.

There were five of them, stone angels, their carved robes grey-white like bones, and they were coming from all sides. And they were past me, closing in on her now, walking slowly in their grey stone robes, chanting. Four of them closing over the black bell, making it stop, and one of them, huge, monstrous, bigger than the hill, bigger than the sky, bowing over the bones that were clothed in flesh, that was Lorna, and lifting her. The black bell clanged.

I closed my eyes. It was over.

CHAPTER TWENTY

The moon, looking as tremulous and iridescent as a soap bubble balanced on the branch tips of the bare dark trees, shone down through the windows of the schoolroom onto the heads of the Rural ladies. Miss Lindsay, standing on a set of steps with a taper in her hand, began touching its glowing tip to the candles and as the dots of light steadily grew into pointed, flickering flames and the flames spread all around the tree with each touch, the ladies began to murmur.

'Oh, did you ever see so bonny!'

'My, those bottle tops fair catch the light when they're strung together.'

'Away. It's your bobbles you made that are twinkling.'

'And what a fair heat comes off it. You've got the fire bucket there, eh no, Miss McCallum?'

Miss Lindsay stepped down and blew out the taper and we stood in silence for a while, admiring.

'Let's not put the lamps on again,' she said. 'Let's have our tea in the candlelight.'

'Are those mincemeat pies warmed through yet, Moyra?'

'Aye, they're rare and hot.' And then, sotto voce. 'I'd be as happy with a scone myself, mind.'

'No! Fruit only lies heavy if you've put too much

377

peel through it. You'd better have one of my ones, Mrs Martineau—with the wee stars on the top—and you'll be fine.'

When we had collected our cups from the tea table and sat back down in the ring of chairs around the tree we looked, in the soft light, like children gathered around a manger, or rather like children pretending to be wise men gathered around a manger, half the air of wonderment acting and half of it real.

Miss McCallum settled down next to me.

'I'm sorry about your talk, Mrs Gilver,' she said. 'You're fated never to give it, it seems.'

'If I'd insisted on the Household Budget instead of a Christmas party with a tree, there might have been a riot,' I said and there was some soft chuckling from the ladies nearest us, who were listening in.

'Well, you're always welcome to come back and join us,' said Mrs Hemingborough, from across the way. 'You've been a good friend to Luckenlaw.'

'Aye, some folk can fit in anywhere,' said another voice, sounding rather grim for the setting. 'And some folk just fit in nowhere, try as they will.'

There was a slight silence after that, and a few throats were cleared. I had seen the board as I drove past the gateposts of Luck House on my way down that afternoon. *Fine small estate, historic mansion house, tenanted farm, cottages, trout stream, stocked shoot. Enquiries and viewing strictly through agents.*

'I hear that Vashti one is still in the hospital,' said Annette Martineau. 'What is it that's wrong with her again?'

'They've never said,' said Molly.

378

'I heard the pair of them had been dabbling . . .' said a timid voice. I stiffened. 'In . . . drugs.'

'Now, ladies,' said Miss Lindsay. 'The Rural is no place for gossip.' There was a rumble of assent, with just a hint of amusement too. 'There but for the grace of God . . .'

'I cannot agree with you there,' said Mrs Palmer. 'I think you make your own luck in this world.'

'You're right,' said Mary Torrance. 'The good you do and the harm you do: both come back to you threefold.'

'And what's for you won't go by you,' said Mrs McAdam, of course, because someone had to.

'Let's not dwell on it,' said Miss Lindsay. 'It's Christmas time. Let's be happy that we've got this first year behind us and the Rural is going strong.'

'And we've a lot to look forward to next year,' said a voice from the other side of the tree, sounding slightly knowing. 'I hear we've a wedding coming.'

Lorna Tait looked down and said nothing, but she was smiling. Jock Christie from Luckenheart Farm had been there at the manse for tea before the meeting tonight, very well-scrubbed and uncomfortable in his good shirt and squeaky shoes, looking younger than ever but not much younger than Lorna with her rosy cheeks and dancing eyes, and while I was changing I heard from Grant who had heard from Mrs Wolstenthwaite in the kitchen that he was there two and three times a week, and they had been seen out walking together with no chaperone, and last Sunday young Christie had sat in the manse pew at the kirk and Mr Tait had looked mightily pleased and said nothing.

It could not have been the ideal way to meet

one's future mate, being carried down a hillside in a dead faint and laid on his kitchen table wearing nothing but a blanket, but Alec told me that Christie had taken it all in his stride and had attended to Lorna as he would attend to any sick calf or heifer struck with milk fever.

He had had time to gather himself, right enough. He had, of course, not believed me that nothing was wrong and had run to the manse at a sprint as soon as I had left him. He met Alec coming out of the gates.

'I need to see Mr Tait,' Christie panted.

'He's not in,' said Alec, whose sides were also heaving. 'I'm trying to find him too. I've just been up the law and there are lights, candles. I saw them and went to investigate but there's no one to be found.'

'I think they're in that cave-thing at my place,' said John Christie. 'That dark-haired lady went in after them.'

'A dark-haired lady?' said Alec, starting to run. 'Didn't you try to stop her?'

By the time they had reached the cleft in the rock and Alec had seen my motor car sitting there, Mr Tait was almost all the way down the hill with Lorna in his arms, his knees threatening to give out at the strain.

'Help!' he shouted. 'Captain Watson? Jockie? Someone help me.'

'I've got her, sir. You can let go now,' said Christie.

'Where is she?' demanded Alec.

'I saw the lights,' said Mr Tait. 'I should have gone for help, but I was so worried about Lorna I just hared off up there alone and—'

380

'Where is she?' Alec almost shouted.

'I'm sorry,' said Mr Tait, sounding enfeebled by his fright and exhaustion. 'I couldn't manage them both. She's still up there.'

So she was, but she was quite safe. I had one of the stone angels kneeling at my side, smoothing back my hair and murmuring softly until, hearing Alec gallop up the stony steps and scramble to the top of the law, his breath ragged, she melted away. Alec returned to the rest of the party with me over his shoulder, like a fireman, and we all staggered and stumbled into Luckenheart Farm kitchen and collapsed there.

I did not remember any of this, of course. I remembered nothing after the black bell that was Vashti and the five stone angels who had disappeared except perhaps for that one who sat with me, but when Alec told me about the kitchen and, afterwards, the journey to the manse laid out across the back seat of my motor car beside Lorna, it was as though he was reminding me about a dream someone had told me a long time ago, or describing a picture I had seen once in a book in my nursery, but only once and never again.

The first thing I remember clearly was coming round in the spare bedroom, feeling sick and weak, and turning my head to find Hugh at my bedside, staring at me.

'Mr Tait has told me everything,' he said.

'Lucky you,' I croaked back. Hugh held out an invalid's cup of water to me and I sucked thirstily on the spout before speaking again. 'He's hardly told me anything,' I said.

'A private detective?' said Hugh, but I could not tell what he might be thinking from his voice,

381

which was as blank as his face. 'Why didn't you tell me?'

I thought about it for a moment.

'We're not given to confidences,' I pointed out. 'I have no idea what you're doing most days.' Hugh looked at me as though he were my school matron and he had caught me inking my legs instead of darning my stockings like a good girl. 'All right,' I said at last. 'I thought you would stop me.'

'And how did you think I should do that?' said Hugh, sounding resigned. 'What have I ever managed to stop you doing?'

'What else have I ever done?' I said.

Hugh regarded me for a long time before he spoke again.

'I saw "Captain Watson" this morning.'

'Ah,' I said. 'Well, the thing is, Hugh, that Alec is my . . . assistant. Actually my Watson, you know.'

'Really?'

'And truly.'

'I thought,' Hugh began, but then cleared his throat and started again. 'I'm glad to hear that. I'm glad to hear you're not foolish enough to be harbouring ideas, Dandy.'

'What do you mean?' I said, lifting my head a little but letting it fall back to the pillow as my head swirled and a sharp stab of pain reminded me that my rib was broken. 'Ugh, I feel so sick. I could never be a bohemian.'

'What do you think I meant?' said Hugh. 'You'd be making a fool of yourself, that's all. You are very unworldly, my dear, which is a pleasant trait for any woman to exhibit, so don't think I'm complaining, but what you don't realise is that Osborne is no threat to another man's wife.'

'It was a disguise,' I said, gaping at him. 'You know it was. He was pretending to be an artist.'

'Well, he looked very at home in it,' said Hugh, sounding so comfortable and superior that I wished I felt well enough to kick him. 'One man can tell these things about another.'

I forbore from pointing out that Hugh had been as thick as thieves with Alec over their two estates, their walls and drains and spaniel puppies and bird tables for the last two years, and had not been able to 'tell' anything.

'Besides,' he went on, 'you must admit that you haven't been a good judge of character recently.'

'I admit no such thing,' I retorted. 'Which characters? The Howies were perfectly respectable people as far as anyone could tell.'

'Mr Tait tells me they were connections of the Balnagowan Rosses,' said Hugh.

'Exactly!' I said. 'Those women never shut up about the Balnagowan Rosses and their illustrious ancestress.' Hugh stared at me, his mouth pursing in that way that makes his moustache bristle.

'The illustrious Ross ancestress,' he said, 'poisoned half her family and killed the other half with darts driven into wax dolls. And then her son, if memory serves me, buried his brother alive and sold him to the devil in exchange for his own life.'

I stared at him.

'When was this?' I asked, boggling at the matter-of-fact way he spoke.

'Oh, a while back,' said Hugh. 'But still.'

'That explains a great deal,' I said. 'They married into a lineage and found out their husbands couldn't care less about it.'

'Best thing I've heard about them,' said Hugh.

'And I'm glad I could clear it up for you, Dandy. I only wish you had asked me before.'

This, it pained me to reflect, was a good point. In fact, if I had ever listened to Hugh on the subject of ancient Scots history I might have been able to see the Howies for what they were at the outset. I closed my eyes, not feeling up to admitting it out loud.

'That's right, you rest,' said Hugh. 'I'll go and tell Mr and Miss Tait that you are quite recovered and there's no need to fuss you. They've had a dreadful shock, finding out about those two . . . women. And I have to say, Dandy, you didn't really handle this case with a light touch. Surely it would have been better to get to the bottom of things without a lot of rushing about in the night and fainting. In fact . . .'

With great thankfulness, I felt myself beginning to fall into a doze again and when I reawakened, he was gone.

*   *   *

He had barely referred to any of it since then, but he had looked askance at me when I said I was coming back to Luckenlaw for the Christmas Social.

'Very well, then,' he had replied at last. 'But let that be the end of it. I am putting my foot down.'

Poor Hugh, I suppose he had to be allowed to put his foot down about something; now that I had told him a bit more about a detective's rates of pay he certainly was not going to stamp on *that*. So, I concluded, I should just have to find it in myself to let the chance of addressing the Rural on the topic of the Household Budget pass me by.

I was glad to have the chance to see them all one last time, though, and to have a quiet word with Mr Tait the next day too, once Lorna had excused herself. She was off to Luckenheart Farm with a basket over her arm.

'Taking a picnic luncheon?' I asked her.

'No,' she said. 'I'm going to plant some crocuses in all those clay pots at the back door. They look a fair disgrace sitting there empty.'

'And I'm sure they'll be very happy,' I said to her father as we watched her stroll off down the drive from his study window. 'I'm glad the young curate didn't work out in the end, aren't you?'

'Curate?' said Mr Tait.

'Wasn't there a minister in the offing at one time, whom you dissuaded?'

'No,' said Mr Tait. 'It was John Christie I was trying to keep her away from. I could tell he took to her from the first time he clapped eyes on her five years ago.'

'And you disapproved?'

'We all want the best for our children, don't we?' said Mr Tait. 'We all want better for our children than we've had ourselves. It's the one thing that we can do to change things.'

'Well, it's a hard life, I suppose, being a farmer's wife,' I said, slightly puzzled. 'But he seems an excellent young man. Lettered and cultured, not at all a . . . well, a peasant, although it makes me sound a fearful snob to say so. And your wife was a farmer's daughter after all.'

Mr Tait smiled at me for a while before he spoke again.

'What can't be cured must be endured, or even

embraced—which makes for a happier life in the end, don't you think, Mrs Gilver?'

I nodded, absently. I was still puzzled by his reluctance about Jock Christie, but there were many more puzzles besides.

'What of the Howies?' I asked him. 'Are you adamant about not going to the police?'

'No good would come of it,' said Mr Tait. 'And a great deal of harm.'

'They kidnapped Lorna when you get right down to it,' I reminded him, although he surely could not need reminding. 'And they killed the kitten. They should be punished.'

'Oh, they will be, I'm sure,' said Mr Tait.

'Where will they go now? What will they do?'

'I neither know nor care,' said Mr Tait. 'Mischievous, muddle-headed women the pair of them and those husbands no more use than . . . Ah, but I suppose I should find some charity in myself even for the likes of the Howies.'

'They really believed it, you know,' I said to him. This was still a struggle for me to comprehend. 'They thought that putting a girl back in the chamber—whether the same girl or another one—would bring back the good times to Luckenlaw.'

'Fools the pair of them,' said Mr Tait. 'I don't know where they got their ideas, for they didn't understand the first thing about it.'

I was eyeing him, speculatively.

'And what if they did?' I said. 'What would they think then?'

He eyed me just as thoughtfully before he spoke.

'I suppose I owe you an explanation,' he said at last. 'And doesn't our contract bind you to silence

386

on whatever I tell you?'

'It does, as would yours with me if you were that kind of minister.' We both smiled.

'Well,' he said, 'there *are* those who think the Howies brought all the trouble with them. They were the ones who gave Luckenheart Farm to a boy on his own and changed its name. There are those who think none of it was anything to do with the girl in the chamber at all.'

'I rather got the impression,' I said, 'that those people who seemed most concerned about Luckenheart—the farmers' wives, you know—did believe in that girl.'

'Oh, they did, they did, they do,' said Mr Tait. 'They thought she was causing the bother with the dark stranger. I'm talking about the other trouble. Are you familiar with the five elements, Mrs Gilver?'

'Earth, air, fire, water and . . . I can never remember the other one.'

'Ether,' said Mr Tait. 'Spirit. Well, there are those who looked at the blight and the fluke, the dry wells and the burned-out house and saw it as a punishment for what had happened at Luckenheart Farm.'

'And Luckenheart Farm itself?' I said. 'Do you mean there was bad . . . ether there? That the place had a bad spirit?' I spoke rather tentatively, unable to believe that I could be having this conversation, with a minister of the kirk, in *Fife*.

'No spirit at all,' said Mr Tait. 'The place was dead with just that young boy who didn't belong here. Although there was no harm in him, none whatsover. So that was the trouble—for those who believe it.'

'But they thought the girl who had been buried in the law was the cause of the dark stranger?'

'Until you found out about all the bread and bonfires and eggs and flowers and all that nonsense.'

'I worked out the last smell in the end,' I told him. 'The first day I ventured out for a walk at Gilverton, it hit me. Stubble turnips.'

'Wonderful winter fodder,' said Mr Tait. 'I'm quite with Hugh there.'

I shuddered. It has always been one of the least pleasant features of country life in the depths of winter as far as I am concerned—the smell of half-frozen turnips strewn in the bare fields for the sheep to nibble, rotting slowly there until spring.

'It was a jack o' lantern I could smell,' I said. 'For Hallowe'en. Candle wax and smouldering turnip. Eggs in March, flowers in April, bonfire smoke in June.'

'Easter, Beltane and the Solstice,' said Mr Tait. 'Yeast in August and corn in September.'

'Corn for the Autumnal Equinox,' I said. 'But what was the yeast in August for?'

'Lammas bread,' said Mr Tait, but he sounded very scathing. 'That was just like those Howies, making a pantomime of what they didn't understand.'

'What do you imagine they did exactly?' I asked him.

'Oh, they probably just cobbled together some little ceremony out of their books, some blessing or what have you.'

'In their motor car?' I said, but actually it did make some kind of sense; I had always thought the timing was odd on that first night when Vashti

Howie had reported seeing the stranger. If they had drawn into a hedgerow to sprinkle seasonal foodstuffs around, it would have used up a good while. This thought immediately sparked another.

'The change of direction,' I said, smacking my hand against my forehead. 'At first the stranger was coming from the north and then from July he suddenly started coming from the south. The only thing that changed in July was that the Howies joined the Rural. Vashti Howie always drove on the main road, never round the lanes. There was a solid, physical clue there all along, that was nothing to do with strangers or devils or any of it.'

'I was sure there would be,' said Mr Tait. 'That's why I needed you, my dear, to unearth the solid clues.'

'I was so distracted by all those men,' I said, 'out of their houses and refusing to say where they'd been. Do you know what they were doing at Jock Christie's all those nights their wives were at the Rural?'

'I do,' said Mr Tait, and a rich chuckle burbled up from deep inside him. 'You were right enough, my dear. Their wives wouldn't have turned a hair at cards or drinking, but this . . . !'

'What?' I said, leaning forward in my seat.

'It started when Jock Christie came,' said Mr Tait. His tone was sepulchral, but I could tell he was teasing me. 'He's lured them all in one by one and now they're planning something big. Utterly in thrall to it, they are.'

' "It" being?' I asked, smiling back at him.

'The "new ways",' said Mr Tait. 'They're clubbing together to buy a tractor. And a potato sorter and a steam thresher. That young Christie

389

and his college ways have turned their heads completely.'

'The more I hear, the less I can believe it,' I said. 'Mr Hemingborough and Mr McAdam embracing science? I thought they were such stick-in-the-muds.'

'Now, wherever did you get that impression?' said Mr Tait, his eyes very wide. For once, he did not seem to be teasing.

'I don't really know,' I said, casting my mind back over the case trying to remember. 'Aha! That's it. It was because they taunted Miss Lindsay about setting up the Rural. It seems odd, somehow, that they should be so down on new ideas for women if they're so keen on new ideas for men. But they shouted names at her in the street, you know.'

'I wouldn't go that far,' said Mr Tait. 'There was an altercation, certainly. And names were used. But you've got the thing entirely about face, my dear. They were berating Miss Lindsay for the wasted opportunity, you see. They thought the Rural could achieve great things, wanted their wives to join and learn some modern ways. Bessie McAdam has a cousin whose Rural has had talks on "incubators for poultry farmers" and "the Education Bill".'

'So what were the names?' I asked.

'Well, I believe it was the night of the home-made hair tonics and egg-cosies from four continents that made Tom Hemingborough see red in the end. He called Miss Lindsay a feather-brain and a coquette.'

'A coquette? Morag Lindsay?' I was laughing again now.

'Och, he'll have heard it on the pictures,' said Mr Tait. 'He probably doesn't know what it means. So you see, it's all of a piece, really. The wind of change must sweep through every farm and through the Rural too, if those five men have anything to say about it.'

'And you think they really feared to tell their wives about their plans?' I said.

'For sure!' exclaimed Mr Tait. 'My own dear wife was the same. Nothing altered, nothing new, nothing different, everything as it always was. Mrs McAdam, for one, will be much more disturbed by the tractor than she was by the Howies' goings-on. And if Mary Torrance knew that Drew was planning to sort his tattie crop with a machine, instead of having the tinkers down from Tayside as her father always did, she would be shocked to her core.'

'Speaking of shocking to the core,' I said, 'here's something I always wanted to ask, but never could. What on earth happened at the Rural in July, Mr Tait? You invited that Wisconsin preacher into the place, so it should by rights be you who has to tell me.'

Mr Tait always did a lot of laughing, but at this he clutched his ample frontage and shook all over.

'Oh my, oh my,' he gasped. 'I wasn't there, of course, but I got caught up in the aftermath. Pastor Ammon showed me everything, appealing for my support. Oh my, oh my.'

'But what was it?' I said.

'His wife,' said Mr Tait, sighing and catching his breath, 'was supposed to talk on the subject of "The Modern Family". And so she did. It turned out, though, that what makes a family truly modern

391

in Wisconsin is well-spaced children and not too many of them.'

'No!'

'It was a cataclysm, my dear Mrs Gilver. Not only a lecture, but enormous diagrams and . . .' Here Mr Tait lost the power of speech again briefly. '. . . sample appliances! Marie *Stopes* would have blushed. And then it came out afterwards that Mrs Ammon had gone to tea with the Howies the day before, and realising—rather late in the day—that she had better make sure her material was suitable, she had asked Vashti and Nicolette for their opinion.'

'And they egged her on then came along to watch the explosion?' I was giggling a little, but my overwhelming feeling was relief that I had not been there to see it. I was surprised at Mr Tait too. He seemed, not only for a minister but taken against the population at large, to be absolutely unshockable.

'I can imagine what the devotees of the old ways made of that!' I concluded at last. 'Not to mention your even more staid parishioners.' Then I went back to attacking another little corner of what was still a mystery to me. 'Speaking of how people take what befalls them,' I said, 'the villagers in general had what we might call a normal reaction to the dark stranger—they were scared stiff and made sure they never got in his way again—but if the farmers' wives believed it was an angry spirit, as you say, why were they so willing to put themselves in harm's way?'

'They thought it was their due just to let her do what she would, for she had clearly been wronged.' Mr Tait's chuckles had evaporated and he spoke sombrely again.

'Ah.' I understood at last. 'What's for you won't go by you.'

'They believe so,' he said. 'The good you do and the harm you do: both will come back on you threefold. Or on your daughter or your daughter's daughter or whoever it is that's there to be paid back when the time comes.' He drew a hefty sigh. 'Those farms have always passed down from mother to daughter, always.'

'All the daughters of Luckenlaw.'

'Quite so,' said Mr Tait. 'I daresay that's where the belief began. The belief that for all to be well there must be five daughters around the law, that harm followed because there were only four.'

'What's wrong with four?' I said.

'Nothing,' said Mr Tait. 'But five is a good number, so they say, those who follow the old ways. Another thing those silly Howies got wrong. Three might be powerful, but five is best. All the years that Luckenheart stood empty, after my wife's mother died, the other four women tended the place and kept it in good heart, but they always felt the strain of it, with someone missing.'

'And now they're back up to strength with Lorna anyway,' I said, and then I seemed to hear what I was saying and I stopped to stare at him. Mr Tait's sombre frown deepened and his eyes glistened as though with sudden, unshed tears.

'I've tried so hard for so long,' he said. 'Tried to keep a balance, tried to keep everyone in this place happy enough so that no one rocks the boat and we can all muddle on together somehow. Tried, more than anything, to keep Lorna away from it all.'

'Does she know?' I said.

Mr Tait shook his head.

'I never told her. But she's young and strong and she'll learn. And besides, I've always asked myself about my wife, you know.'

'What about her?'

'If maybe she would be here today if she hadn't left her home. She never thrived up there at Kingoldrum, and when I brought her back, I think it was already too late.'

There was such a weight of sadness in his voice that I could not bring myself to jolly him out of these strange things he was saying.

'And when you get right down it,' he concluded, 'it isn't for me to choose Lorna's life, is it? That's another thing they believe. They do not approve of casting spells and trying to influence others, but they do believe this: if it harms no one, do what you will.'

'In other words,' I said, 'play bonny.'

'It's time for me to let Lorna make her own life.'

I nodded, rather uncertainly.

'You've done a remarkable job of bringing her up alone,' I said.

'I've had a lot of help,' said Mr Tait. 'And would have had more, if I hadn't been so set on some of my ways getting a look in too.'

'She has not gone short of love, even for a motherless girl,' I assured him. 'Why, last month she even thought you were organising a secret party frock for her.' Again I stopped, thunderstruck by a new idea. Mr Tait waited, smiling. 'You never took that girl to another minister to be buried, did you?' I said. He shook his head. 'She was in your wife's bedroom and they all came to pay their respects.' He nodded. 'Then

394

what?' I said. 'After she was in the bedroom. She's not there now.'

'You tell me,' he said. 'You're nearly there. I'll give you a clue. When was it? Ask yourself when and you'll know what.'

I thought hard for a moment and then smiled.

'The full moon,' I said. 'The dark of the moon is a time for dark deeds, but they were doing good by her. That's why none of your farmers' wives were at the Rural meeting last month when the stranger came for me. They were busy putting things right on the perfect night to do so.'

'And where is she?' said Mr Tait. He was teasing me again, but so gently I did not mind it.

'She's where she belongs,' I said. 'On top of the law? In a good place?' He was nodding. 'Would she have been a witch?' I hazarded. He nodded again.

'That's the common name for it, although hardly a kind one,' he said. 'Killed by the mob and left like an animal,' he added softly, sounding sorrowful. 'And even the five daughters of the Lucken Law, whoever they were all those years ago when it happened, couldn't save her.'

'And so their descendants believed that when she was let out of the chamber she hit out?'

'She visited threefold harm upon them—girls, brides and women—and they had to grin and bear it.'

'Except she didn't. It was Vashti and Nicolette mucking about with flower garlands and lucky loaves of bread, playing at spells. I should have guessed really, because they were quite open about their interest in folklore and their seasonally themed parties and it all makes sense in its own terms if you try hard enough to look at it that way.

395

Almost all, that is. Except this. It's what you keep saying about five, Mr Tait. I was sure there were five of them on the law the night that Vashti had Lorna there. Five figures in grey.'

'There are only four daughters just now,' said Mr Tait.

'I know. Mrs Hemingborough, Mrs Palmer, Mrs McAdam, Mrs Torrance. But I'm sure someone else was there too. Who was it?'

'Jock Christie was there and Captain Watson.'

'I don't mean them,' I said. 'There were five stone angels. Five . . . witches, shall we call them.'

'You were not yourself that night,' Mr Tait told me. 'You could never have known if it was four or five.'

'But could good have come from four?' I insisted. 'Would the same people who thought that having four around the farms instead of five had brought all their troubles have even tried with four? And that other night—would *four* have laid her to rest on top of the law and expected peace to follow?'

'Don't worry about it,' said Mr Tait.

'I'm not worried,' I assured him. '*I* don't believe it.'

'None of it?' said Mr Tait, giving me one of his amused looks.

'Of course not!' I exclaimed. He nodded slowly.

'I see,' he said. 'You never felt anything . . . odd . . . up at Luckenheart Farm, for instance?' I hesitated, remembering. He swept on. 'No, of course you didn't. It's just harmless old stories and sayings, nothing in it at all.'

'Well, whether I believe it or not,' I said, colouring slightly, 'I'm puzzled at the behaviour of those who do. And besides, I'm sure there were five. Four swooped down on Vashti and one—the biggest one—tended to Lorna. I know I was confused, but I remember that clearly.'

'My advice is not to fret about it,' said Mr Tait, and then he said what he had said before: 'All shall be well and all shall be well and all manner of things shall be well. *All* manner of things, Mrs Gilver.'

'Where in the Bible is that?' I asked him. 'It's lovely but I can't place it.'

'It's not from the Bible,' said Mr Tait. 'It was Julian of Norwich who said it.'

'Who was he?'

'She,' he told me. 'She. A woman of God.' He sighed. 'I always think she'd have finished up as the Pope if she'd been a man.' He shook his head, but not sorrowfully this time. 'Wouldn't the world be a simpler place, Mrs Gilver, if a woman could be a priest and a man could be . . .'

'A what?' I asked him. He only looked back at me, with those kindly dancing eyes.

'Oh Mr Tait!' I said at last as, finally, I got it. He chuckled. 'Please can I ask an enormous favour?' I begged him. 'Please can I be there if you ever tell Hugh?'

TOPOGRAPHICAL NOTE

Kellie Law and Largo Law are real, but the Lucken Law and the village of Luckenlaw are entirely from my imagination. Fife is a real place but none of this could ever have happened there.

I would like to thank:

My mother, Jean McPherson, who gave me *Jam and Jerusalem: a pictorial history of the WI* by Simon Goodenough and Wendy Bellars, who gave me *The Wee Book of Calvin* by Bill Duncan. These two together lit the spark.

Nan, (the spirit of) Jack, Grandad Hugh, Colin, Brian, Andrew, Ian, Elaine, Douglas, Aly, Mig, John, Gail and George for their Fifishness, the cadence of their voices and the gallows humour (I don't think you even know you're doing it). Thanks too to Ann and Elaine for the flavour of Aberdeen, which, of course, is even more so.

More thanks than usual to Lisa Moylett for steering everything through a difficult year and making it look easy and to Nathalie Sfakianos for the incisive comments on the first draft.

I am enormously grateful to Alex Bonham for her editing. This is a far better book than the one she first saw. Thanks too to Imogen Olsen, who has once again licked her hanky and wiped the face of the manuscript until it shines.

Finally, and most of all, I would like to thank my husband, Neil McRoberts, my favourite Fifer.

spers of murder.